Graham Hurley is a writer and television producer. Many of his documentary films have won awards. His six part ITV series, *In Time of War*, marked the tenth anniversary of the Falklands Campaign. He is co-director of *Project Icarus*, a charity active in health education. His novels, *Rules of Engagement* (1990), *Reaper* (1991), *The Devil's Breath* (1993) and *Thunder in the Blood* (1994) are all available in Pan paperback.

Also by Graham Hurley in Pan Books

Rules of Engagement

GRAHAM HURLEY

REAPER

PAN BOOKS

'One bomb on the mainland is worth a hundred in Belfast'
– Richard O'Sullivan Burke, 13th December 1987

First published 1991 by Macmillan London Limited
This edition published 1992 by Pan Books Ltd
Cavaye Place, London SW10 9PG

5 7 9 8 6 4

© Graham Hurley 1991

ISBN 0 330 32544 2

Printed and bound in Great Britain by
BPC Paperbacks Ltd

for Linnie with love
and sunshine

PRELUDE

Tuesday, 5th May, 1981

In the end, as the priests and the doctors had predicted, it was painless. Already, his face had caved in, an empty mask. The eyes were colourless and without focus, and whatever was left behind the pale, blank expression registered only in tiny movements of the fingertips or one corner of the mouth. During the final week, the terrible dry retching that had so angered him suddenly ceased. At first, the nurses were baffled. Was it possible that this remorseless descent into coma might somehow be reversible? The doctors, tight-lipped as ever, said no. Sixty days of starvation had begun to destroy the man's most primitive responses. He no longer tried to throw up because his body had forgotten how to. The nurses nodded, faintly disappointed. In a land of miracles, they felt somehow robbed.

Two days before he died, there was a final attempt to revive negotiations with London. Perhaps the prisoners' demands might be reframed. Perhaps a minor concession or two might be worth the price of a man's life. Telephone calls were made. The old invitations renewed. Nothing happened. Thirty-six hours later, during a sudden icy squall that rattled the windows in the prison hospital, the man died.

That evening, in a room over a timberyard in a small seaside town eighty miles to the west, five men sat down around a table. One of them poured tea into an assortment of china mugs. The single plastic spoon passed from hand to hand. No one said a word. The announcement from the prison authorities had dominated every broadcast since dawn. The news had been utterly predictable, another life hazarded and spent, but the sense of shock, of personal injury, had come as a surprise. Making sense of it all was a complex proposition. Retribution was far simpler.

The man with the teapot, the man they called the Chief, sat down and wiped his hands on a dishcloth. Then he looked up.

"Something special," he said finally. "Has to be."

Next morning, in Belfast, she finally remembered the diplomat's name.

"Leeson," she said carefully. "His name is Leeson."

The man across the room, the counsellor, nodded. He never wrote anything down. She'd noticed that. He simply listened, and looked at the end of his roll-up, and murmured encouragement from time to time, and when they were fifty minutes in, towards the end of the hour she always booked, he'd go back over it, and rearrange it all a little, and offer it back to her in a shape she could cope with. That was his trick. That was what she came here for.

"Leeson," he repeated.

"He's a friend of Derek's. He talks about him sometimes. They were at school together."

"Is he a serving diplomat?" The counsellor paused. "Is he at work at the moment?"

"I . . ." she hesitated, not really knowing, "I think so."

"Is he based in London?"

"Yes. He tries to phone sometimes."

"To your friend?"

"Yes. For Derek."

"Doesn't your friend want to talk to him?"

"No."

"Why not?"

"I don't know."

The counsellor nodded again, and folded one long leg over the other. They always sat on the floor in this room he hired over the laundrette, backs against the wall. They smoked together sometimes, stuff he brought in from God knows where. He said it helped. He said it was a relaxant. He was prompting her again. He could, just occasionally, be very persistent.

"These friends of your husband's. Danny's friends. The ones we talk about . . ."

4

"Yes?"

"Would they be interested in this man?"

"Yes," she nodded, "that's the point. Oh, yes. I'm sure they would."

"Why?"

She shrugged.

"That's the kind of thing they want to know, Danny's friends . . ." She nodded out of the window. The rain. The traffic. Belfast. There was a long silence. The counsellor toppled ash into his empty mug. She'd been surprised how young he was. Just out of college, the doctor had told her, cutting his teeth.

"So . . ." she looked at him, "what's your advice? What should I do?"

"About what?"

"About yer man. Leeson. Should I tell them? Will that make it any easier? Will that make them go away? Leave me alone?" She hesitated a moment. "Or not?"

The counsellor studied a crack in the wall opposite. She looked at it. It was quite a big crack.

"You're here for therapy,' he said, "not political advice."

"It's the same thing, isn't it?" she said. "In this city?"

"I don't know." He frowned. "Would it make you feel better? If you told them?"

"God knows,' she said, "but it might make them go away."

He smiled at her. He had a nice smile.

"OK," he said, "go ahead. Tell them."

Miller took the name with him, scribbled in a spare page of his diary, back to the bare single room on the fourth floor of the officers' accommodation block, back to' the billet he called home. He threw his briefcase onto the bed and stood by the window, gazing down at the big white "H" stencilled on the tarmac landing zone, watching the last of the afternoon choppers lifting off, the helmeted crewman at the open door, yet another four-man patrol inside, outward bound, tasked for South Armagh.

The helicopter dipped its nose and banked sharply,

chattering away into the gathering darkness. Miller glanced down at the diary, thinking again of the diplomat, Leeson, wondering whether – at last – they'd found the key they needed. Downing Street, he understood, was open to offers. Put the right way, with patience and a little luck, he might even get the freedoms he needed. Either way, whatever happened, the Hunger Strike was bound to make a difference. One man dead. More to follow. The geology of the place shifting. Aftershocks going on and on. Nothing quite the same again.

He slipped the diary back into his jacket pocket and stared down at the landing zone for a full minute, the black puddles dimpled with rain, thinking again about the one they called The Reaper, the one they had to find, and wondering whether there might, after all, be a way.

BOOK ONE

December, 1981

ONE

Buddy Little had been in the Persian Gulf just six days
when his wife, back in England, broke her neck.

She'd been riding, out in the forest, first light, bitterly
cold, the grass still stiff with frost. She'd mucked out the
stables early, all six horses, saddling the big bay gelding,
Duke, and cantering away through the icy mist, up towards
the top of the forest, tracks new to both of them. They'd
ridden for an hour, longer than usual, the sweat chill on her
face, the trees tearing past, one long brown blur, and now
they were on the road again, deep in the country, heading
back to the stables, and she wanted nothing more than a
hot shower, and toast, and at least two mugs of Buddy's
strong Dutch coffee. She missed the man more than she
liked to admit. He'd been gone barely a week, and she
thought about him constantly.

She glanced at her watch, and eased the big horse into a
trot. In an hour, the first of the morning's bookings would
arrive, an estate car full of kids who'd started the course
only the previous month. The hour's lesson was probably
the high point of their week. They deserved the very best
that she could give them.

She taught well, and she knew it. She'd earned the school
the best reputation in the area, and while the work was
sometimes repetitive, she never tired of it. Horse-riding, she
often thought, was like real life. If you confronted it – if you
were brave, if you trusted the horse, if you never lost your
nerve – then it gave you a bucket of thrills, and it was the
promise of that experience that she held out to her pupils.
She grinned, remembering the morning's ride again, the big
horse panting and snorting beneath her, the excitement raw

9

enough to taste. Buddy, she thought again, the smile widening.

They rounded a bend, and she kept the horse tight against the hedge, her view obscured by the high bank. On the other side of the hedge, she knew, was a small bungalow. A gypsy family had lived there for generations. The garden was littered with old cars, and discarded washing machines, and prams with no wheels. There were rumours of fights there, and most of the villagers kept well clear. There were half a dozen or so kids in the family, and a couple of the kids had dogs.

They trotted past the bungalow. The front gate was hanging open, one of the hinges torn away in some nameless accident. She caught a movement in the corner of her eye, something small and dark, something bounding through the tall grass in the front garden. The horse saw it too, and then there was a bark, and she felt Duke sidestepping quickly across the road, and her hand went down at once, patting him, comforting him, trying to steady him. "Hey," she whispered, "hey, there."

The dog burst onto the road, yapping and snarling, a small dog, black and white. Duke began to rear, and as he did so, one of his hind legs skidded on a patch of ice in the road. He began to go down, sideways, and she felt herself toppling forward, the horse no longer there, the reins snatching at her hands. She heard the big horse neighing, the fear in him, the legs everywhere, and then she hit the road with a bang, her body twisted, the back of her head against the cold tarmac.

The force of the impact drove the breath from her body, and when she opened her eyes there was nothing, just blackness and a far-away whistling in her ears. Mentally, she tried to take stock, to work out whether or not she still had the reins, to check what hurt and where and how badly, but in the darkness it was hard to come to conclusions. All that mattered was the horse. She could hear the horse but she couldn't see it. She told herself she had to find the horse.

Slowly, sensation returned, and with it a sharp pain where her right hand had scraped along the road. Still in total darkness, she flexed it. Where the nail on her little finger had punctured the flesh on the next finger, it hurt even more. She tried blinking, but nothing happened. Whatever she did with her eyes, the darkness wouldn't go away. Confusion gave way to fear. For the first time, she tasted blood. She realized that her left hip hurt like hell. She began to panic. Then she passed out.

Some time later, seconds perhaps or minutes or even longer, there were voices, the sound of a car door, footsteps, people running. She lifted her arms to her head, thinking of the horse again, Duke, how bad he must be, but she found her riding hat wedged immovably over her face. "Get it off . . ." she pleaded. "Get it off me! I can't breathe . . ."

Someone knelt beside her, asking if she was OK, and she said yes, please get the goddam hat off, the words muffled by the warm blood in her mouth. Then there were hands at her head, pulling back the riding hat, pulling hard, letting in the daylight and the fresh air, and as she began to focus, looking up, seeing the faces, searching for the horse, everything suddenly went away, the pain in her finger, the throb of her hip. Instinctively, hearing Duke, she tried to move.

Nothing happened.

Buddy Little got the news about his wife on the radio telephone from the diving office in Jubail.

It was late afternoon. He'd already dived twice, air dives, sixty feet, and now he was out of time. He lay on a mattress on the foredeck, enjoying the last of the sunshine, reading an old *Newsweek* magazine. The Captain, an ex-trawlerman from Hull, appeared on the bridge wing.

"Bloke on the beach,' he said, "for you."

Buddy got up and padded quickly across the deck. The plating was hot beneath his bare feet. He ducked inside the companionway, and mounted the ladder to the tiny, airless radio room. The line was still open, the telephone lying on the desk. He picked it up. A voice at the other end, an American, asked him his name, then told him to get hold of a pencil. Buddy did so, scribbling a fourteen-digit number.

"Get through as soon as you can," the voice said, "sounds bad."

11

The line went dead and Buddy stared at the pad. The middle group of digits in the phone number he recognized. 703. The Southampton code. The Captain appeared at the door. He'd obviously been listening in.

"Go ahead,' he said. "Dial out."

Buddy did so. First time, the on-shore operator was too busy to help. Ten minutes later, he rang back, patching Buddy through a maze of connections to a voice somewhere in Southampton. The line was appalling, and Buddy had to shout his name several times before someone else came to the phone, a cultured voice, someone talking about an accident, Judith, his wife, Intensive Care. As the phrases slipped through the static, it began to dawn on Buddy that the man at the other end was a doctor, and that something had happened, something involving Jude, something not just bad but bloody awful.

"How is she?" he kept shouting. "What's happened?"

The line went dead again, and Buddy turned to find the Captain examining the end of his cigarette. The man was a born pessimist, and loved nothing better than other people's bad news.

"Trouble?" he queried.

Buddy shook his head, a gesture of hopelessness. He felt physically ill. "Dunno," he said.

The Captain pulled a face. "Must be," he said, "them bothering to phone."

Buddy looked at him blankly. "When's the supply boat due?" he said.

The Captain glanced at his watch. The supply boat came out from Jubail every three days with mail and fresh food, touring the dive ships in the area. The latest consignment was due in an hour's time.

"Six o'clock," the Captain said glumly. "If they manage to find us."

Buddy returned to his cabin. He packed both his bags, clearing his clothes from the locker, his books from the shelves, the photos of Jude taped on the wall by his bunk, knowing in his heart that he'd never be back. By the time the supply boat arrived, nudging alongside, the Arab crew filling the lifting net with boxes of bread and fresh vegetables, Buddy was at the rail, the Jacob's ladder rolled ready at his feet, his bags labelled for whichever flight would get him back fastest. He said goodbye to the rest of the diving team, mentioning nothing about the call. He didn't even bother to acknowledge the Captain's limp departing wave from the bridge.

Back in Jubail, nine in the evening, he went to the diving office. The diving office was closed. There was an emergency number on the door. He phoned from the lobby of a hotel across the street, recognizing the American he'd spoken to earlier. He told the man he was going home, and asked him for details of flights. His voice was flat, expressionless. He announced his plans as a matter of fact. There was no prospect of asking for formal leave. The question of permission didn't arise. He was going home. It was as simple as that.

The American was sympathetic, booking him onto a late feeder flight to Dubai, and an onward connection with British Airways to Heathrow. The flight would touch down at 09.10, and the ticket – pre-paid – would be waiting for him at the airport. The fare, the company would subtract from money already owed to him. The details completed, the American wished him good luck and hung up.

Buddy took a cab to the airport at Dhahran. From there, he flew to Dubai. At Dubai, the big BA jumbo was already on the tarmac, slightly ahead of schedule, and lifted off for the long leg to London ten minutes early. By half past eleven the next morning, Buddy was sitting on a coach on the M3, his bags beside him, barely an hour's drive away from Southampton.

By now, he knew that Jude was in trouble. He'd phoned from the airport, the first phone he could find, one of a cluster by the baggage carousel. He fed in a pile of coins he'd acquired from the stewardess, stacking up time on the meter, while the nurse at the other end found the doctor he needed to talk to. Finally, he came, a quiet, tired-sounding voice, already sympathetic. Buddy asked what had happened, how she was, whether she was badly injured, and the doctor told him that she'd had an accident, a fall, and that she'd sustained a serious injury. More than that he

13

couldn't say, telling Buddy that it was best that he make
his way to the hospital, and that they meet face to face, and
talk the thing through. Buddy didn't like the sound of that,
and said so, but the doctor was adamant. She's in no danger,
he kept saying. She won't die. Buddy wanted to take the
conversation further, to insist on his rights, but he was tired
now, and a little confused, and when the doctor brought the
conversation to a close he simply accepted it. I'm on my
way, he said, I'll be there as soon as I can.

On the coach journey down, he brooded, going back over
the conversation time and again. He tried to find the key
phrase, the clue that would open it all up for him, that
would tell him what had really happened to Jude, what
they'd done to her, what she'd look like, how she'd be, but
his knowledge of medical science was limited to the demands
that diving made on his own body, and the rest of it was a
mystery. He'd never been in hospital in his life. He hated
the places.

The coach plunged into the heart of Southampton, down
the tree-lined avenue that Buddy had last driven only a
week before, Jude beside him, after a farewell blow-out at
a favourite Italian restaurant. At the coach station, he took
a cab to the hospital. The cab dropped him outside the
main entrance. At the reception desk, he gave Jude's name,
and his own, and waited while the receptionist rang a series
of numbers. Then she looked across at him.

"She's in Intensive Care," she told him, "you'll find it on
the fifth floor."

Buddy gazed at her. Intensive Care. Fifth floor. He turned
on his heel, and walked to the lifts. He felt sick again, and
slightly dizzy. The lift stopped at the fifth floor. Facing him
was a long corridor. At the end of the corridor was a large,
four-bedded bay. A sign suspended from the roof said:
INTENSIVE CARE UNIT. QUIET PLEASE. He stood in the entrance
to the Unit, a small, stocky man, lightly tanned, combative,
two large holdalls, one in each hand. He looked at the beds.
All the beds were occupied. Bandaged faces. Bodies barely
breathing. Endless loops of tubing.

He edged slowly into the Unit, leaving his bags outside.
A nurse looked up and came across. He gave her his name.

She looked at him a moment longer than she needed to, a look of mute sympathy, and then she nodded and led him over to a bed by the window. He stood by the bedside and looked down. He couldn't believe it. Jude, his Jude, her face on the pillow, hideous metal tongs, like a pair of headphones, bracketing her head, the points of the tongs embedded in her temples, a wire stretched taut from the crest of the tongs, over a pulley, and down towards the floor. On the end of the wire, was a set of weights. Buddy swallowed hard.

"What's that?" he said.

The nurse glanced up at him. "We call it traction," she said, "it takes the pressure off her spine."

"*Spine?*"

Jude's eyes flickered open. She saw Buddy standing there. She smiled up at him and then her eyes closed again. He looked at her, the graze on the end of the snub nose, the long body under the blanket, the swell of the cage protecting her broken thigh, her arms lying on the crisp white sheets. He bent to her, and kissed her, and the eyes opened again.

"Buddy," she said.

"Yeah."

He reached for her hand and held it. It felt strangely flabby, no reaction, no grip. She licked her lips, as if she wanted to say a word or two, something else, then her face was shadowed as the nurse bent over her, moistening her lips with a bag full of ice cubes. Buddy stared at it.

"Give her a drink," he muttered, "she's thirsty."

The nurse said nothing for a moment, then shook her head.

"Can't," she said.

"Can't?"

"No," she withdrew the ice cubes, "she might choke."

Buddy turned again to Jude, frightened now, wondering what else the sheets might hide, what other terrible injury Jude might have sustained. The nurse turned to go. Buddy caught her arm.

"What's the matter with her?" he said, his voice low and urgent. "What's she done?"

The nurse smiled again. "The doctor will be down in a minute," she said. "You'd better ask him."

"You tell me."

"I can't."

The nurse disappeared into a side room. Buddy heard a fridge door open and close. He looked down at Jude again. She was very pale, her chest barely moving as she breathed, and Buddy dimly began to understand that something truly terrible had happened to her, something beyond his comprehension, that something had gone from her, been taken from her, and the knowledge was all the worse because he didn't know what it was. He turned away, feeling the hot tears running down his face, ashamed of himself, the betrayal of her, his strength quite gone. A figure appeared at the door, a youngish man, with a thin, kindly, pale face and a long white coat. The nurse intercepted him at the door. They had a whispered conversation. The man in the white coat looked over at Buddy and nodded.

"Mr Little?"

"Yeah."

"My name is Cassidy. I'm the doctor in charge here."

Buddy followed him into a side office. There was a desk and a calendar. The doctor shut the door and offered him a seat. Buddy didn't move.

"What's the matter with her?" he said. "What's wrong?"

The doctor looked out, through the windows of the office, across the Unit. The nurse was back beside Jude's bed, making some adjustment to the weights.

"She's broken her neck," he said slowly. "We're doing all we can but . . ." he trailed off.

Buddy stared at him. The words made no sense. It wasn't real. It didn't happen to real people. Certainly not to Jude.

"She's done what?" he said.

The doctor looked up. He told Buddy about the accident, the dog, the horse. He said she'd been lucky. It might, he said, have been worse. Buddy gazed across at her. The nurse had gone again.

"How?" he said. "How could it have been worse?"

"She might have died."

"But?"

"But . . ." he shrugged, "she didn't. She's survived. After a fashion."

16

He looked up at Buddy again, trying to gauge how best to put it, what to say and what not to say, how much detail to risk. He told him about the injury to her neck, the fifth cervical, bone number five, the spinal cord damaged, probably for ever.

"So . . . ?"

"So . . ." He dipped his head, not finding it easy, looking for some formula that might soften the next few seconds. Buddy was still staring across the ward.

"So?" he said again, looking back at the doctor.

"So . . ." the doctor drew a line across the desk top with his fingertip, an almost unconscious movement, "so . . . she may never walk again. Or move her arms. Or feel anything below here . . ." The finger left the desk and drew a line across his own body, one shoulder to the other.

Buddy's hand felt for the wall. "You mean paralysed? She'll be paralysed? Rest of her life?"

The doctor nodded. "I'm sorry," he said, "I'm truly sorry."

Buddy opened his mouth. Nothing happened. Then he tried again.

"No," he said.

The doctor nodded again, the worst of it over.

"Yes," he said, "I'm afraid so."

"No," Buddy said for the second time.

The doctor closed his eyes a moment, wanting the exchange to end, knowing there was nothing left to say, not now, not at this precise moment. Later, there'd be plenty of time, all too much of it, for the fine print, the care she'd need, the nursing, the limitless patience, the endless days, the years ahead, half a lifetime still to come. For now, though, it was enough to simply absorb the worst of it. His wife in a wheelchair. Probably for ever.

The doctor opened his eyes again. Buddy had left the office. He was walking back across the ward. He was returning to her bedside. The doctor went after him, fearing the worst, a scene of some kind, the inevitable torrent of anger and grief. But something in Buddy's manner held him back. The man was in complete possession of himself. He paused by the bedside. He bent to the pillow. The doctor stepped

17

a little closer, curious now. Jude's eyes were still closed. Her breathing was as shallow as ever. A tiny vein was pulsing slowly in her temple. Buddy's lips began to move, some private message, and the doctor strained to catch the words, but it was impossible. Buddy's fingertips brushed his wife's face. He kissed her. Then he turned, and left.

TWO

Derek Connolly sat in the perpetual twilight of the Oxford and Cambridge Club, waiting for Leeson. He'd arrived forty minutes early, an over-cautious estimate on the bus transfer from Heathrow, and already he felt wrong-footed. He hadn't seen the man for nearly two years. He'd avoided every phone call, left every letter unanswered, and now he'd have to account for it. The prospect had been haunting him all week. Now, he felt slightly nauseous, searching desperately in his wardrobe of personas for something that might see him through the next couple of hours.

He stirred the lukewarm tea the waiter had brought him. The obvious ploy was the line he'd taken on the phone. Just passing through. Thought it might be nice to meet, catch up on mutual friends, swap gossip, compare notes, but he knew Leeson wouldn't be fooled. Opaque and imperturbable as ever, he'd want to know why the sudden interest, why the voice from the past. On the phone, before Connolly had hung up, he'd suggested dinner. A new Thai place in Gerrard Street. Coffee afterwards at home. Connolly shuddered at the implications, trying to dam the images that flooded back at the sound of the man's voice. Better, he decided, to think about Mairead. If it was a cause he needed, and he did, she was better than most. More to the point, the phone call had been her suggestion.

She'd first mentioned it a couple of weeks back. He'd talked about Leeson three or four times, part of the past he'd left behind him, back on the mainland, before he'd made the firm decision for Belfast. He'd told her about the years at Glennister, the scholarship boy with the world at his feet, the obligatory membership of the Old Boys' Association that went with his elevation to Head of School.

He described the meetings he'd attended, the formal dinners, the clatter of spoons banging on the long refectory tables, the accents and the attitudes that went with this curious freemasonry of public school glitterati. Deep down, he'd hated it, but for three terms, at the very top of the school, it went with the job, and he lacked the courage to decline the endless invitations.

Leeson's had been the most insistent. He was half a decade older than Connolly, a diplomat of ten years' standing, already a high flyer at the Foreign Office. He spoke fluent French and Spanish, adequate German. He knew his way around the capitals of South America, and had served with distinction in the embassy at Buenos Aires. On the diplomatic circuit, he was tipped as an early prospect for First Secretary at one of the blue riband embassies, Paris or Washington. He was a credit to his housemaster, and to the old school tie he often wore in preference to the dozens of others in his ample wardrobe. With his slow smile, and his almost insolent charm, everyone agreed he was a bit of a star.

That he was also gay, Connolly had been slow to understand. At first, he'd been flattered at the older man's attentions. He'd enjoyed his guided tour of the Foreign Office, and the meal afterwards had been exquisite. He'd never tasted Rioja before, and after six years of school food, it smacked of something infinitely rich and infinitely promising. For the first time, over the crisp pink tablecloth, he'd realized that there might be something more to life than three good A-levels and a place at Cambridge, and the modest excitements of this discovery blinded him to the likelihood of what was to follow.

In the taxi, that first time, it had been subtle, a glance from Leeson, the lightest pressure on his thigh, one eye raised in mock salute behind the thick pebble glasses as Connolly said his goodbyes and made his way across the pavement towards Victoria Station.

Mairead, the product of a keener education, marvelled at his innocence.

"Six years locked up with them?" she queried. "And you *still* didn't guess?"

20

"It was different. It wasn't school. It was outside. You don't understand."

She hadn't, either. And neither had he. The invitations had continued. Theatre tickets. A Bartok concert at the Royal Festival Hall. A couple of casual excursions around Cambridge once he'd left Glennister and found his feet in the small college room with the sunless view of the Department of Anatomy morgue. It had been a tender, infinitely considerate courtship, each fresh advance undertaken in such a way that it brooked a thousand interpretations. In a curious sense, as Connolly had begun to realize, getting him into bed had itself been a masterpiece of diplomacy. Charming, funny, enormously well-informed, Leeson had deftly shepherded him towards that chill November day when there suddenly seemed no other option.

They'd drunk, between them, three bottles of wine. They'd picked at a bad Bengali curry. Back in college, the rain had been falling on the black cobblestones, and Leeson had propped his umbrella in the raffia wastepaper basket by the door before undressing at the tiny sink and carefully soaping himself all over. There was, in that simple action, an abrupt resolution of all the games playing, all the ambiguity. It meant they were going to bed. It meant they'd make love. There was no prospect of anything else. And so they'd pulled the curtains, left the light on, and afterwards Connolly had been sick. Leeson, watching him from the bed, had lit a small cigar, an act of modest celebration.

"For a beginner," he said, "you were outstanding."

Now, there was a movement by the door. Connolly glanced up. Leeson stood there, folding his camel-hair coat carefully over his arm. He was silhouetted in the light from the street outside, but Connolly sensed instinctively that something didn't fit. He was swaying slightly on his feet, and when he stepped across and paused beside the big leather armchair, Connolly knew at once what was wrong. Leeson was blind drunk.

Connolly got up, held out his hand. The same light kiss of palm on palm. The same warm squeeze.

"Good evening."

"Hello."

Connolly looked at him, trying to mask the sense of physical shock. F. G. L. Leeson. The hero who'd stalked his adolescent dreams. Gold copperplate letters on the Glennister Honours Board. Twice winner of the Victor Ludorum. The best Hamlet since the war. Balliol Exhibitioner. Pissed out of his brain.

Instinctively, Connolly gestured him into the empty chair, doctor and patient, elementary first aid. Leeson watched him, amused as ever, the old ironic spark not quite extinguished. He shook his head, reaching out and touching Connolly lightly on the shoulder.

"Come . . ." he said, "with me."

They took a cab to the Thai restaurant in Gerrard Street. Connolly guided Leeson to a table by the window. They ordered by numbers. Fourteen. Thirty-three. Heavenly Chicken. Singapore Noodles. Leeson sat slumped in the bentwood chair, his head tipped back against the pale, weathered timber boards. He had both hands on the table cloth and made no attempt to lift the glass of wine Connolly had decanted from the flask of house Soave.

"So," he said softly, "how's life in the front line?"

Connolly blinked, recognizing the old dig, Belfast, the war-wracked city, everyone's favourite nightmare.

"Fine," he said, "it's hardly Beirut. As you know."

Leeson narrowed his eyes, and then smiled. "I meant the University," he said, "that job of yours."

Connolly felt himself blushing. Despite appearances, despite everything, the man had boxed him in yet again. His control, as ever, was quite effortless. Connolly began to stammer. A relic from his Lower School days.

"Sorry," he said, "I thought . . ."

Leeson kept looking at him. One finger began to circle the rim of his wine glass.

"Well," he said, "still at it?"

"Yes. Of course."

"Not bored?"

"No."

"Getting on with the natives?"

"Yes."

"Anyone special?"

22

Connolly hesitated a moment, then shook his head.

"No."

"Sure?"

"Yes."

Leeson nodded, a new directness in his manner, something infinitely cruder than Connolly had ever known in the man before.

"Well . . ." he said, reaching for the chopsticks, "mustn't get lonely, must we?"

In the taxi, afterwards, Connolly thought again about Mairead. Anything, she'd told him. Anything the wee man might have to offer. What she'd meant was maddeningly imprecise, unspoken, and when Connolly had pushed her, she'd refused to elaborate. Enough, she'd said, to get close to the man, to find out what he might be worth. She knew nothing about the physical side to it. If she ever did, Connolly knew the relationship would be over.

He glanced across at Leeson, wedged into the corner of the cab. His eyes were closed. He didn't appear to be breathing. Connolly touched him gently on the cheek. A day's growth. At least.

"How about you?" he said. "How's life in the Camel Corps?"

The phrase was a souvenir from the first time they'd met, when Leeson was fending off the threat of a posting to the Middle East. It had always been worth a smile, but now he didn't react. The cab stopped at a set of traffic lights in Notting Hill. Connolly glanced out. A young West Indian was sandwiched between two policemen. He was struggling. Connolly watched, fascinated. Leeson stirred beside him.

"You really want to know?"

"Yes."

"Bloody awful."

Connolly looked at him in surprise. Here it was, then. The drink. The eyes. The sense of utter detachment.

"*Bloody* awful?"

"Yes."

"You want to talk about it?"

"I don't know. Do you want to listen?"

"Yes."

"Truly?"

Leeson looked at him. Connolly smiled, genuinely touched. The man might, after all, be human. Beached and helpless, just like the rest of us. Leeson's hand found his in the half-darkness. Connolly squeezed it. Simple friendship. The traffic lights changed and the cabbie engaged gear. Connolly glanced out again. The larger of the two policemen had pushed the West Indian up against a wall. The other was talking urgently into a radio. There was blood on the West Indian's face. Leeson followed Connolly's gaze, craning his head backwards as the cab accelerated away.

"Bastards," Connolly said softly, "Fascist bastards."

Leeson smiled. "Sweet," he said.

Connolly frowned, still watching the street. "Them?"

"You."

The cab turned left, towards Holland Park.

"Where are we going?" Leeson said.

"Your place."

"Hmm . . ." Leeson lay back and closed his eyes again. "Good oh . . ."

Leeson's neighbourhood, a street of red-brick terrace houses in the no man's land between Chiswick and Hammersmith, had visibly improved since Connolly had last visited. Neatly trimmed privet hedges. Hardwood double glazing. A couple of brand-new "X" reg. BMWs, one with an in-car phone.

Connolly sat in the tiny downstairs living room, watching the street outside, waiting for the kettle to boil in the kitchen next door. He could hear Leeson moving around in the bedroom overhead. Twice he stumbled. Once there was a squeal of bedsprings. Then the slow clump-clump of footsteps downstairs, and the fumble of fingertips on the lock of the door of the ground-floor bathroom. Already, he sounded like an old man.

Connolly glanced round. The place looked shabby and forlorn, smelling faintly of stale cheese. There were newspapers strewn haphazardly on the floor, circling the armchair where Leeson evidently spent most of his time. Connolly picked one up. It was in Spanish. Entitled *La Prensa*, it was datelined Buenos Aires, octubre 13, barely a month

24

old. Two articles on the front page were ringed in heavy red Pentel. There was a picture of a naval admiral, and an advert for Marlboro cigarettes. Connolly replaced the paper on the floor. Beside the fireplace were a pair of slippers and a saucer of milk. The milk had pooled in lumps in the middle of the saucer and there were yellowing tide marks around the edge.

Next door, in the kitchen, the kettle began to boil. Connolly stepped through. The draining board was littered with unwashed plates. Looking for sugar, Connolly found nothing but tins of cheap cat food and empty boxes of Anadin. Giving up on the sugar, he tore open two tiny catering sachets of instant coffee, loot from some distant hotel bedroom, and tipped the thin brown powder into two mugs. He was still stirring the boiling water when Leeson appeared at the door. He had a cheroot in one hand and a bottle of brandy in the other. He was wearing a red dressing-gown. Connolly recognized the stitch patterns on the quilted lapels, and the swirl of dragons as Leeson dismissed the coffee with a wave and led Connolly back into the living room.

There were two glasses on the table, a crystal tumbler and a toothmug. Leeson waved the bottle wordlessly at Connolly. Connolly nodded. Leeson tipped the brandy into the crystal tumbler and nudged it towards Connolly with his elbow. Connolly caught the tumbler before it fell onto the floor. He licked the splash of brandy off the back of his hand. Leeson filled the toothmug with brandy, holding it up to the light, examining the pale Armagnac through the smeared glass. Connolly could smell soap, something expensive, doubtless another souvenir from the same hotel bedroom. The man must have washed all over. Old habits die hard.

"Well?" he said softly, tipping his own glass in salute.

Leeson caught the invitation in his voice. He lifted his head a moment, narrowing his eyes, the gourmet diner contemplating the meal of his dreams.

"Well?" he countered.

Connolly swallowed a mouthful of Armagnac. The stuff hurt.

"You were going to tell me," he said, "about that lousy job you've got."

Leeson nodded. There was a long silence. Connolly pulled at the brandy again. The glass was already half empty. His eyes began to water. Leeson watched him carefully, and then smiled. The old routine. The long surrender. Connolly pulled the glass towards him. Mairead, he thought. Her smile. Her smell. The secrets that lay beyond her. Leeson reached for the bottle and tipped it carefully over Connolly's glass. Connolly watched the glass fill, remembering the first time with Mairead, the only time with Mairead, how young her body was, how old the rest of her. Leeson corked the bottle, and pushed it to one side. After the third glass, as they both knew, nothing much would matter.

"I'm flattered," he said, "that you're still interested."

"I am."

"Why?"

"Because . . ." Connolly shrugged. "Does it matter?"

"Yes," Leeson nodded, "it does."

Connolly swallowed hard. He knew what Leeson wanted, some small intimation that he cared, a scrap of affection to garnish the next few hours. Always, between them, it had seemed a simple courtesy, the verbal equivalent of a good wash. Now, though, it clearly mattered. Connolly looked at him, saying nothing. In two years, the man had aged a decade. The hair was thinning. The eyes had sunk. He looked old, disappointed, worn out. His hands trembled slightly as he toyed with the toothmug. He'd cut his chin shaving, the blood still fresh. Connolly reached for his hand, hearing his own voice, surprised at the way words came out.

"I care about you," he said, "if that matters."

Leeson sat absolutely motionless. No physical response whatsoever.

"It does," he said, "a great deal."

Connolly nodded. "Then tell me what you want to tell me. I'm here to listen."

Connolly stayed for two days with Leeson, phoning Mairead

from a call box on the first morning and asking her to contact the University.

"Tell them I'm ill," he said, "say I'll be back next week."

"Are you ill?"

"Yes. Sort of."

"What's the matter?"

"Nothing much. I get it from time to time. It's nothing serious."

He said goodbye and put the phone down, savouring the small truth of his excuse.

Back at Leeson's house, he stored the quart carton of milk in the fridge and made a fresh pot of tea. Then he took the tea, and the copy of *The Times* he'd bought with the milk, up to Leeson's bedroom. Leeson was lying on his side with his back to the door. Naked, the man was diminished even more, physically somehow slighter. Connolly had noticed it the previous evening. He'd lost the small folds of flesh around his midriff. His rib cage had begun to show, and his chest was purpled with a curious rash. His legs, once well muscled, were thinner. His libido had gone, too, the old appetites so easily sated that they'd both been asleep by midnight.

Now, Connolly put the tea tray carefully onto the bed. Leeson grunted, reaching automatically for his glasses and rolling over onto one elbow. Connolly decanted tea into two mugs and gestured at the bag of sugar. Leeson nodded.

"Please," he said, yawning.

Connolly spooned the sugar into Leeson's tea. Then he uncapped the bottle of Anadin he'd found in the kitchen, and shook two onto the tray. Leeson swallowed them without a word, closing his eyes as he did so. The previous evening, before coming to bed, he'd talked at length about the Falkland Islands, a colonial relic off the coast of Argentina. Much of it was incoherent, and from time to time he'd lapsed into Spanish, scrabbling amongst the piles of *La Prensa*, indicating this article or that. Connolly had done his best to follow the argument, understanding at the very least that Leeson believed that trouble lay in store. Quite what shape this trouble would take was far from clear, but what became very evident was the gap between Leeson, his

27

colleagues in the South American Department, and their political masters. Time and again, Leeson would break off a sentence, and shake his head, and nod at the newspapers scattered at his feet, a small gesture of despair. They don't understand, he'd say. They have the facts, and they will not act.

Later, in the darkened hall, one foot on the stairs, he'd paused. The real trouble, he said, was the political process. Whichever party, whatever government, the politicians will not act. He'd said it twice, inviting a response. Connolly had obliged.

"Why not?" he'd said.

Leeson had turned to him in the darkness, the expression on his face invisible. Then he'd laughed, a brisk, derisive bark of laughter, before resuming his way upstairs. None the wiser, Connolly had followed him. Before they'd put the light out, he'd heard Leeson's cat, padding around on the newspapers in the living room, circling the bowl of rancid milk.

The teapot empty, Leeson got carefully out of bed, shrugged his way into the red silk dressing-gown, and walked across to the window. He pulled back the curtains and gazed down at the street. Connolly watched him from the bed.

"It's Wednesday," he pointed out. "Aren't you going to work?"

Leeson shook his head. "No."

"Why not? Are you on leave?"

"No."

"Sick?"

There was a long silence, then Leeson turned back into the room, letting the dressing-gown part as he did so. Connolly looked, at once understanding Leeson's lack of verbal response. Sick or otherwise, the next few minutes were spoken for. For a moment, he wondered about saying no, about offering some excuse or other, about pleading some pressing appointment of his own, and then he remembered again about Mairead, about the neat little council house up in Andersonstown, and about the long slow years when nothing much seemed to matter, and how different it was now, now that he had something to believe in.

He looked up and managed the beginnings of a smile, lying back in the bed as Leeson stepped out of the dressing-gown and pulled back the sheet. The last thing Connolly registered before he closed his eyes was the rash on Leeson's chest. There was more of it than he'd thought. It had begun to cover his upper arms, too.

They began to talk seriously that afternoon, on a bench in Battersea Park, Leeson clad in his thick camel-hair coat against a chill wind off the river. Connolly beside him, freezing.

"You'll know what 'PV' means," Leeson said, "with that nice degree of yours."

Connolly shook his head.

"No," he said.

"It means Positive Vetting. They ask you lots of questions. You tell them everything. It's a Civil Service speciality." He glanced across at Connolly. "It's called Security. It's meant to make you a very safe person to have around."

"And does it work?"

"No. But that's not the point." He patted Connolly on the thigh and smiled. "There are various things, character traits, they don't much like. One of them is this . . ." he nodded down at his hand, still circling Connolly's thigh.

Connolly nodded. "Why's that?"

Leeson shrugged. "They think it makes you a liability overseas. They worry about blackmail. Buggery's strictly for the boys back home. We play it straight."

"So what happens if . . ."

"They find out?"

"Exactly."

Leeson smiled, and drew a gloved finger across his throat.

"Out," he said. "Finis. Terminé. Kaput."

"Really? Bit radical, isn't it?"

"Very."

"So what have you told them? So far?"

"Nothing."

"But they have asked you?"

"Of course."

29

"And you've lied?"

"Every time."

"Is that wise?"

Leeson smiled again. "It's second nature," he said, "you lie for your country. You lie for yourself." He shrugged. "It becomes a habit."

Connolly frowned, trying to keep pace with Leeson's logic. Leeson gazed at him, almost sympathetic.

"For a history don, you're remarkably naïve," he said at last. "Diplomacy, my friend, relies on the selective suppression of the truth. We are, at bottom, deeply subversive. We smile a lot. We bend arms. And, on occasions, we lie. That's what we're paid for. That's why we're so good at it. And that's why Positive Vetting is a joke."

"But they'll know already, surely?"

"About what? Precisely?"

"You. Me." Connolly shrugged. "Whoever else."

Leeson looked at him for a moment, the old opacity back in his eyes.

"No," he said at last, "they'll know nothing." He paused. "I've girlfriends, too, in case you're wondering." He glanced across at Connolly. "Does that disappoint you?"

Connolly said nothing. There was a barge on the river, pushing upstream against the ebb tide, shoulders of brown water folding back from the stubby bow. What Leeson was saying made perfect sense. He'd never felt able to enquire before, always taking his cue from the older man, his curiosity constrained by the years between them, but he'd always supposed that Leeson's problem was sheer appetite. The man was simply greedy for it. Life was a game. Victor Ludorum conquers all, regardless of gender. He glanced across at the older man.

"How often do they do this . . . PV?"

"Every year or so. Routinely before the offer of an overseas posting."

"And?"

Leeson was silent for a moment. The front half of the barge had disappeared beneath Battersea Bridge.

"Next week," he said at last. "They want to send me to Washington."

"Good move?"

"Excellent move." He paused. "The best."

Connolly nodded. "So what's the problem?"

Leeson pursed his lips, pondering the proposition. His face, pinched by the cold, had sagged even further. Abruptly, Connolly realized they'd reached the heart of it. The man wanted to go to Washington. His career had taken off. Yet something, by the look on his face, had gone terribly wrong. So here it was. The missing piece. The answer to Mairead's prayers. He reached across and put his hand on Leeson's. Instinctively, Leeson withdrew. Connolly mumbled an apology. Leeson shook his head, a gesture of mute irritation. There was a long silence. Finally he cleared his throat.

"A year ago, I had a . . . little fling," he began, "nothing serious. Lots of action. Very pleasant, in fact."

"And?"

Leeson glanced across. "He was American. It lasted a couple of months. Sometimes here. Sometimes his place. New York." He paused. "He phoned me last week."

"And?"

"He's had a mystery disease. Nothing the medics can identify. Nothing specific. But he thought it best I know."

Connolly frowned, thinking of the blotches again, the dry, persistent cough, the rheumy eyes.

"Is it serious?" he said.

"Yes."

"How is he?"

"He's dying."

"Ah . . ."

Connolly looked away, not knowing quite what to say. Leeson was silent for a moment. Then he smiled, a thin cold smile.

"This disease . . ." He glanced across at Connolly.

"Yes?"

"I understand it may be infectious." He paused. "They're calling it 'gay plague'. Rather picturesque, don't you think?"

Connolly looked at him for a moment, feeling the chill steal towards his own heart. Then he looked away. The barge had quite gone.

31

THREE

Scullen met the Chief at the edge of Ballyliffin Strand, the
tide half a mile out, not a soul on the long, lonely stretch of
beach. The Chief had come down from Derry, slipping
across the border on an unadopted road, accompanied by
two bodyguards. He limped over the sand, and shook the
older man by the hand.

"Padraig," he murmured.

He'd known Scullen for a decade, the shadowed bony
face, the carefully parted hair, the stiff, slightly awkward
walk, the affection for dark suits and well-polished shoes,
the grim – slightly morbid – sense of humour. Others in the
movement said he was eccentric, a washed-up relic from an
older Republicanism, but the Chief had immense respect for
him, the brain on the man, his ideas, his originality, his
uncanny knack of finding new answers to old problems. The
Chief knew that the decision to offer him command of the
England Department had been – in its way – a stroke of
genius, and in two busy years Scullen had produced some
remarkable results, the only currency that ever mattered.

Now, the Chief pulled the thin anorak around him, stamp-
ing the chill from his feet. The weather in Donegal was
rarely warm, but this morning was especially bleak. The
wind blew in from the Atlantic, driving the sand ankle high
across the beach. Even the seagulls looked miserable.

Scullen blew into his cupped hands. An expensive Hom-
burg, pulled low, hid most of his long pale face. He eyed
the Chief.

"You're well?"

"Fine." The Chief nodded up at the cliffs, steep, black,
dotted with birds' nests. "We're safe here?"

32

Scullen nodded, a faint impatience. "Half a dozen men," he said.

The Chief peered round. The place looked as empty as ever.

"Grand," he said. "So why am I here? Fireworks, is it?"

Scullen smiled at him, a rare event. The invitation to Ballyliffin had come a week back. There'd been talk of a device, a demonstration. Scullen had recently gone hi-tech, encouraging a small circle of volunteers in Dundalk to adapt bits and pieces of domestic hardware – programming chips from video recorders, timers from washing machines – in the interests of a new kind of war. Scullen's term for it was pre-emption. It depended on wit, and a certain technical virtuosity, and – above all – surprise. Surprise, he said, was the key to victory. Without surprise, the Brits would – in the end – stiff them all.

Now, he pointed to a distant rock, standing alone, half a mile down the beach.

"That," he said to the Chief, "is her car."

The Chief nodded. He liked Scullen. The man had imagination.

"Sure," he said, "big fat Daimler."

Scullen smiled again, twice in one day. He produced a small black box, plastic, with a dial on the front. He peered closely at the figures on the dial, adjusted it slightly, and gave it to the Chief.

"This," he said, "is the fuse."

"Fuse?"

"Blows up the Daimler."

"It does?"

Scullen nodded, indicating a small yellow button below the dial.

"You press that," he said. "Bit of a treat."

The Chief looked at him a moment, then shrugged. He gazed out, along the beach, towards the rock. His gloved finger found the button. He pressed it. There was an explosion somewhere above and behind them, a serious bang, high on the cliff face. The Chief, no stranger to explosions, instinctively flinched. He looked up. There were seagulls everywhere, flying in high, wide circles. A large

33

wedge of rock, ten, twenty tons, was detaching itself from the cliff face immediately above them, and toppling slowly down. The rock landed in a cloud of dust on the sand, about fifty yards away. Seconds later, he could still feel the ground shaking beneath them. Neither of the two men had moved.

"Close," the Chief remarked. "What happened to the Daimler?"

Scullen nodded vigorously.

"Surprise," he said, peering out at the distant lump of rock, still intact on the beach. "Expect one thing to happen. Get the shock of your life when it doesn't." He glanced across at the Chief. "No?"

The Chief frowned. He looked far from amused.

"But you broke the rules," he pointed out. "You told me the Daimler was along the beach there. Not half-way up the fucking cliff."

Scullen nodded. "Exactly," he said.

On the third day, Jude Little was transferred from Southampton to the Regional Spinal Unit, fifty miles north.

Buddy went along with her in the ambulance, 25 mph, the driver flattening every bump in the road, slowing to a crawl for every corner, behind a succession of police motorcycle escorts. Jude lay in the back in her hospital bed, the traction weights still hanging from the tongs embedded in her skull. Buddy rode beside her, squatting on the tiny bench seat, holding her hand, not saying much.

Since the Gulf, he'd barely slept at all, returning to the cottage in the New Forest for a wash and a change of clothes, circling the empty bedroom, the sheets still rumpled. Jude's clothes everywhere, a paperback half open on the small bedside table. Exhausted, that first time, he'd collapsed onto the bed and tried to trick his body into sleep, but her scent lay on the pillow, musty, slightly sweet, and every time he closed his eyes, images from the hospital swarmed up. They were like a blanket, suffocating him, and after a minute or so he gave up, swinging his legs off the bed and clattering down the narrow wooden staircase, back to the safety of the living room, already cold and damp.

There were photographs of the wedding, framed, on the mantelpiece, a small private affair, the pair of them outside the Register Office, blinking in the afternoon sunshine, Jude slightly taller, scarlet dress, long black hair, high leather boots, Buddy beside her, grinning madly, still not quite believing the big fat peach that life had been saving up for him. Twenty-odd years of bachelordom, vigorous, self-contained, content. And then this extraordinary woman, a chance encounter they'd both turned into real life.

Gus had been there too, at the wedding. Gus was his mucker from the rigs. They'd shared the best years on the North Sea, and he'd been Buddy's automatic choice for best man. He knew Buddy like a brother, and he'd watched the relationship grow over the five brief months they'd been together.

Gus was a married man. He had a fat wife called Marge, and two appalling kids, and when the letters started arriving on the daily chopper out of Aberdeen, Jude's distinctive handwriting on the long brown envelopes, the big confident loops on her gs and her fs, Buddy had shared the odd phrase, the odd promise, whetting Gus's appetite, a subtle assurance that this was no ordinary affair, that life wasn't baiting a trap for him, a mortgage, and slippers, and a brace of squalling infants.

The letters. Buddy shook his head. He'd never read anything quite as frank, quite as direct. Jude wrote the way she talked, staccato, little punctuation, not a shred of grammar to mask the sound of her voice, and she put it all on paper, the smallest, most intimate details, charting the relationship as it developed, word perfect. He'd kept the letters in his locker in the tiny two-man cabin. Most nights he retired early from the cribbage school to read and reread them. He still had them now, clothespegged together on the kitchen shelf, certain phrases filed permanently in his brain.

One letter, in particular, had taken his breath away. He'd known her for less than three months. They'd shared just two weekends. Yet here she was, putting it all down on paper, committing herself. Don't get uptight, she'd written, but it's true. I loved you the moment I saw you. You're very funny, and you're a beautiful man, and if all this bothers you chuck it in the ocean and think of me as bare-assed. Think of me the way you like it best. Think of me sitting on your face and count the days till they let you off again. I love you, Buddy. Tough shit. Buddy had folded this particular letter into his wallet and locked it away. If Gus ever read it, he'd have a stroke. If Marge ever sat on *his* face, he'd be fucking lucky to survive.

Buddy paused in the gloom, gazing at the photos. He wanted to reach out and touch them. He wanted to carry them with him, a talisman against the terrible words these doctors kept using. Paralysis. Wheelchairs. Rehabilitation. What did any of that have to do with this woman of his? With her spirit? Her gutsiness? The way she laughed, throwing back her head? The mornings she woke him up? Curled in his crutch? Lapping and lapping? Straddling him? Opening their private set of curtains on the world?

She'd been married before. Her husband had been a personnel manager with an investment house in the City, and they'd been man and wife for nine years when he fell in love with a girl on the train. She wore glasses and worked for a television company. Evidently, she produced prize-winning films about the tropical rain forest, and fretted about the end of the world. She was doubtless great in the sack, but she was soulful too, and after he'd confessed it all, he even wanted to bring her home. Nice little supper. In-depth debate afterwards on the ethics of American multinationals. Jude had attacked him physically with a cast-iron skillet and changed the locks the next day. Since then, she'd seen him only once, the morning her lawyer escorted her to court. He looked thinner, and older, and had grown his hair long. Word was he was thinking of emigrating to Canada to work with the Eskimos. He'd waited at the end to talk to her, but she'd turned her back and walked out to the street. "Strictly no prisoners," she often told Buddy, "camp rules."

Now, in the living room, he backed away again, retreating into the kitchen, with its rows and rows of carefully labelled jars, aduki beans, and kidney beans, and chick peas, and heavy brown rice, Jude's chosen diet, the one favour she always said she owed her body. They drank famously, the pair of them, pints in the evening, and they ate well, this stuff of hers, herbed and spiced. Another door she'd opened for him. Another cupboard they'd shared.

He reached up and touched them, glass jars for Chrissakes, and then withdrew again, scorched by the memories, determined to keep going, a moving target. He knew there were endless things to see to – lessons to cancel, help to arrange for the horses, bills to pay – and he'd done what he could on the telephone, keeping grief at bay with a kind of manic energy, part fury, part desperation, that baffled friends who offered to help. By the second night, he was dead on his feet, but he still drove back to the hospital believing somehow that faith alone, his sheer presence at the bedside, might restore a flicker of movement – the old Jude – to the long pale body beneath the sheets.

By agreement with the doctors, she had yet to learn the full implications of what had happened. He'd told them that it would be a private conversation, just the two of them, and that he'd break the news in his own way, when he thought it was right. Jude was the strongest woman he'd ever met, but he dreaded what the word "paralysis" might do to her. She'd never had any time for illness or complaint. She'd always confronted life head-on, something he'd occasionally associated with her nationality. Americans, he told himself, knew nothing about defeat. That's why they'd always got on so well. That's why he loved her so much.

Now, fifteen miles north of Winchester, he looked down at her. In three long days, she seemed to have physically diminished. She looked thinner. The flesh on her arms had somehow loosened. Her face, normally so mobile, was the colour of chalk. Only her eyes were the same, a deep hazel, flicking left and right, patrolling the edges of this new world of hers.

He tried to grin at her and she tried to grin back.

"Lotta fuss," she said, "all this."

He nodded. Her voice was still weak, barely audible above the purr of the engine.

"Only the best," he said, "for little you."

She looked at him for a moment, then her eyes went to the window.

"So tell me," she whispered, "what's it like out there?"

He didn't bother to look but bent to the pillow and kissed her gently on the forehead.

"That feels good," she said, "do it again."

He kissed her again, his lips moving softly across her face. Two days' growth of beard left a faint redness on her skin. He reached her lips, and his tongue met hers, the old greeting, the old hors-d'oeuvre. He began to explore her mouth, her teeth nibbling his tongue, teasing it. Then he withdrew, looking down at her, smiling. He nodded at the window.

"Go to sleep," he said. "You're not missing much."

She blinked a couple of times, her eyes suddenly wet with tears.

"Neither are you," she whispered.

They arrived at the Regional Unit at dusk. The hospital lay on the outskirts of the town, a collection of single-storey brick-built wards. There were lights on at the windows, a glimpse of beds inside. The place had a faint air of impermanence.

The ambulancemen unbolted the bed from the floor, and carried Jude carefully into the hospital. Buddy walked beside her for a yard or two, but a woman in a uniform intercepted him, asking for a minute or two of his time, and before he could think of a reason for saying no, Jude had gone.

The woman took him to one side and sat down in a chair by the wall. She had a clipboard and a biro. She was very businesslike.

"Just some personal details," she said, not bothering to look up.

Buddy sank into the chair beside her, and told her what she wanted to know. Jude's full name. Their address. Her date of birth. Her nationality. The woman scribbled busily on the form. Then she looked up.

"You're married?"

"Yes."

"Children?"

"No."

She nodded, making no comment, but her expression was enough. Just as well, it said. Lucky you. Buddy looked at her, too tired to pursue the point, to enquire why she'd asked. He hated the hospital already, the long central corridor disappearing into the middle distance, the wheelchairs rolling past, the smell. Jude didn't belong here. And neither did he.

"Where is she?" he said.

"Who?"

"My wife."

"She'll be on the ward by now. There's an assessment procedure. It'll be an hour or so yet." The pen paused. "There's a canteen for visitors. They do cakes and things." She stood up. "Look for the signs off the main corridor."

She smiled at him, a vague rearrangement of the bottom half of her face, and bustled away.

Buddy watched her go, feeling suddenly exhausted. He found the canteen, a cheerless collection of tables and chairs, and had two cups of tea. After half an hour, he set off in search of his wife. He found her in one of the women's wards, a long white room, shiny lino, beds down each side. Jude was at the far end. The weights were still attached to her head, and her eyes were closed. Buddy paused at the foot of the bed. There was a medical chart already clipped to the bed, figures in black biro, lines on a graph. Buddy stared at them. They made no sense. A nurse appeared and began to pull the curtains on the long, metal-framed windows. Buddy caught her eye.

"My wife," he said, nodding at Jude.

The nurse smiled at him. She was young and pretty, short curly hair. She came over and glanced at the chart at the foot of the bed. Buddy could tell from her face that the news wasn't good. The nurse looked up.

"Mr Little?" she said.

"That's right."

"I'm afraid she's asleep. You're welcome to stay."

Buddy thanked her, seeing Jude's eyes flick open, the sound of his voice. He walked across to her, bending low over the bed. She looked up at him.

Something was wrong. She was frowning.

"Tell me . . ." she whispered.

"Tell you what?"

39

"Tell me . . ." she paused and took a shallow breath. "Tell me why the place is full of goddam dwarfs."

"Goddam what?"

"Dwarfs."

Buddy stared at her. Dwarfs? He looked round the ward, trying to make some sense of the question. Then he brought his eyeline down to hers, tried to imagine himself flat on his back, his head clamped tight, unable to move, and he realized at last what she meant. Jude had seen only the heads of patients rolling past. What she hadn't seen were the wheelchairs in which they sat, propelling themselves endlessly along the corridors, nosing in and out of wards, fellow cripples, wheels instead of legs. He swallowed hard, resisting the truth. Then he grinned down at her. And kissed her again.

"Dwarfs," he agreed, "thousands of 'em."

Buddy left the hospital at nine, Jude asleep again. He walked the mile and a half into the town and booked into a small guest house. He lay on the bed for a moment, still fully clothed, and was asleep in seconds. He awoke, briefly, at three, pulling off his jeans and getting under the covers. Next day, he was back at the hospital by mid-morning, strong again, cheerful, determined. Sleep had worked the usual miracle. Jude, he knew, would recover. There had to be a way.

He found her in the bed at the end of the ward. She looked even more pale than yesterday, and he knew at once that she'd been crying. He glanced across at the nurse. The nurse turned away. He sat down on the bed. He looked at her. Her eyes didn't leave the ceiling.

"You didn't tell me," she said.

"Tell you what?"

"What the matter was. All this . . ." she paused, and Buddy could see the tears welling up again. He reached across for a box of tissues at the bedside. She followed the movement of his hands.

"Don't," she said.

"Why not?"

"I don't want you to."

Buddy looked at her, saying nothing. Two beds away, he

could hear a middle-aged woman telling a girl about a holiday she'd booked. A week on a specially adapted canal barge. It would be marvellous, she said. They had special lifts. She'd even be allowed a turn at the wheel. He looked at Jude again.

"Who told you?"

"The doctor."

"Doctor who?"

"I don't know."

"What did he say?"

"He said I was tetraplegic."

"What?"

"It means I'll never use my arms again. Or my legs." She paused. "He said he'd seen the X-rays."

She stared at the ceiling, her voice a whisper. Buddy closed his eyes. The anger began at his toes, in his fingertips, at the furthest ends of his body. It gathered force, and it surged through him. He bent towards her.

"He's wrong," he said.

"He's a doctor. He must know."

"He's wrong," he said again.

"Yeah?"

She looked at him for the first time. Her voice was so low, he couldn't be sure of the inflection. It might have been hope. Or it might have been despair.

Abruptly, Buddy got up. The nurse he'd seen the previous evening was standing at the other end of the ward, checking the contents of a trolley. He stopped beside her.

"My wife," he said thickly. "What's the name of her doctor?"

"Bishop," she said, not looking up, "Dr Bishop."

"Where do I find him?"

"Down the corridor. Third door on the right."

Buddy turned and left the ward. The door of Bishop's office was closed. He knocked once and went in. A man of about forty sat behind a desk. He wore a white coat. He was on the telephone. Buddy closed the door and sat down in front of the desk. The doctor watched him, expressionless, carrying on with the conversation. The conversation came

41

to an end. He put the phone down. He made a note on a pad, then looked up at Buddy.

"Yes?" he said.

Buddy took a deep breath, controlling himself, damming the anger.

"My wife," he said, "is in your hospital. You've just seen her. You told her— "

The doctor interrupted him, leaning back in the chair, his hands clasped behind his head. He was older than Buddy had first thought, perhaps fifty. He had longish curly hair and wore a green bow tie. There was a large Mickey Mouse watch on his wrist. The man was a joke. Some kind of comedian. Certainly not what Buddy had expected. He studied Buddy for a moment or two, taking his time.

"Mrs . . .?" he said at last.

"Little."

"Ah . . ." he let the chair tip slowly forward, "C5."

"What?"

"Fifth cervical. This bone here . . ." he indicated a bone in his own neck, midway between his shoulder blades, "nasty break."

Buddy stared at him, determined not to lose the initiative, determined to make his point.

"You told her she'd never walk again," he said.

"She won't."

"How do you know? Without looking? Getting inside? Operating?"

"We never operate," he said mildly. "It doesn't do the patients any good."

Buddy frowned, out of his depth, confused. "But how will she ever get better?"

"She won't," he said again, "she'll adapt. Like you will. Like people always do." He smiled. "You'll be amazed. You think it's the end of the world. But it isn't."

Buddy blinked at him. "Adapt?" he said.

"Yes."

"You mean *accept* it?"

"Yes." He smiled again. "I'm afraid you'll have to. You have no other choice."

Buddy gazed at him, hating the man, his complacency,

42

his tone of voice, his utter lack of passion. Cripples were meat and drink to him. His world would fall apart without them.

"There must be other places," Buddy said. "Somewhere else."

The doctor shrugged.

"There are," he said, "and you're welcome to try them. But I tell you this, my friend. Your wife has a very severe injury, and a very poor prognosis. One day, medical science may be able to help her, but not yet. Getting better means coping. It means learning to cope. That's what we do here. We teach people to cope. I happen to think there's no other way. If you know better, prove me wrong."

The doctor glanced at his watch, the exchange evidently over, and for a moment Buddy was tempted to hit him. It was something he'd occasionally done in his life when words wouldn't work any more, and he'd always regretted it afterwards. But there was an arrogance about this man that touched a nerve in him, and he wanted to express exactly what he felt, driving a fist into his face, battering him senseless against the wall, trusting that one day, when he'd had a chance to think about it, the poor fool would have the wit to associate his job with something useful. Like a cure. Buddy sat motionless for several moments, enjoying the thought, his hands clenched in his lap. Then he stood up.

"I'm sorry to have barged in,' he said stiffly, "it was out of order."

The doctor shrugged. "You're angry," he said, "like everyone gets angry."

Buddy stepped towards the door. Then he turned on him again, provoked by his tone of voice, the smugness of the man, the utter conviction that he was right. He put his hands flat on the desk, his face very close, staring him out.

"One day," he said softly, "we'll be back. Both of us. Standing here. We'll do a little dance for you. Then you'll *know* you're fucking wrong."

FOUR

The meeting in the small sunny office in Downing Street, second floor, was scheduled for three o'clock but began a quarter of an hour early.

There were three people present. No minutes were taken. The older of the two men, a civil servant with responsibility for the Joint Intelligence Committee, glanced at his watch and opened a thin buff folder. Inside the folder was a two-page typed report. In all, there were three copies, individually numbered. He scanned the report quickly, then distributed the other copies around the table. The other man was gazing out of the window. He was wearing a suit, grey, with the faintest stripe. It looked out of place on him, as if he'd borrowed it.

"Colonel Miller . . . ?"

The other man turned his head. He had a strong, wide face, dusted with freckles. "Yes?"

The civil servant lifted the report. "Are you sure about this?"

"As sure as I can be."

"You're aware of the . . . ah . . ." He glanced across the table. The Prime Minister was watching him carefully. "The implications?"

"Of course."

"But you stand by what you've written?"

"Yes."

The civil servant nodded, glancing down at the report again, one finger on the text. "What makes you think this man is so important?" he said.

"He fits the Intelligence picture. His movements tally. All our intercepts confirm it."

"And you want to take him out?"

44

"I want to bring him in."

"Same thing, isn't it?"

"No. Taking him out means killing him. Bringing him in means having a chat."

"And afterwards?"

Miller looked at him, the faintest smile, but said nothing. There was a long silence. The civil servant frowned.

"So why don't you pick him up?" he said. "I don't understand." There were the beginnings of another silence. Miller glanced at the Prime Minister. The Prime Minister smiled back. Good question, her expression suggested.

"Because we can't find him," Miller said at last, "not at the moment. He's in the Republic. He's always on the move. What we need is . . ." He shrugged, not finishing the sentence. The civil servant smiled.

"A clear run?" he suggested.

"Exactly."

The civil servant nodded, but said nothing. Miller leaned forward. He'd been rehearsing this speech for nearly a week, trying to work out how best to put it. In the end, there seemed no point in dressing it up. Time was precious. Especially at this address. He glanced at the Prime Minister again. He noticed that the smile had gone.

"The Hunger Strikes killed ten of them," he said. "They hold you responsible. This man of theirs has been tasked to kill you. He's not at the sharp end. He's a planner. But he's exceptionally gifted. By far the best they've got . . ." He paused, fingering his copy of the report, his own phrases on the pale cream paper. Then he looked up again. "The way I see it, you have a choice. Either you leave it to normal channels. With all that implies . . ."

"Or?"

"You leave it to us."

The Prime Minister nodded. She glanced briefly at the civil servant. "Why should I do that?" she said.

"Because our sources are better than anyone else's."

"Can you prove that?"

"Yes."

"How?"

Miller hesitated a moment. He'd spent a great deal of

time – weeks – anticipating this very question. The kind of freedoms he wanted, the licence he'd come for, would only be available at a price. If he got the price wrong, he'd go away empty handed. If he got the price right, if he could truly open their eyes, then the gloves, at last, would be off. He bent forward.

"You're opening a new factory soon," he said, "in Basingstoke."

"Am I?"

The civil servant nodded. "Qualitech," he said, "January 18th."

Miller glanced at him, then looked at the Prime Minister again. "There's a device planned for the eighteenth," he said. "At the factory."

"You mean a bomb?"

"Yes. I gather it's a big bomb. Enough to kill you." He paused. "They're generous that way."

The Prime Minister nodded, absorbing the news. Then she looked up.

"So when do they plan to plant this . . . ah . . . device?"

"They don't."

"Don't?"

She frowned and Miller leaned forward, the opening he'd been waiting for. "No," he said, "it's already in place. At the factory. I have the details here. That's why I came."

There was another, long silence. The civil servant cleared his throat. He looked slightly shocked, and Miller wondered for a moment whether he'd gone too far. Finally, the Prime Minister stood up and extended a hand.

"Thank you for coming, Colonel Miller," she said, "I think you'll find I'm grateful."

Connolly spent Christmas with Mairead in Belfast.

He took the bus from the Ferryport, up through the City Centre, up past the towering grey concrete of the Divis flats, up the Falls Road, and finally into Andersonstown, a vast Catholic housing estate that sprawled over the lower slopes of Belfast's Divis Mountain. He walked the quarter-mile from the bus stop to the council house where Mairead lived.

Mid-evening, the streets were empty, and there was a cold keen wind blowing flurries of snow in from the north.

Connolly walked briskly, the single holdall looped over his shoulder, savouring the silence, and the sour tangy smell from dozens of peat fires. It was a bleak estate, with its treeless roads, and abandoned shopping trolleys, and rusting cars skewed by the kerbside, but there was life here too, an indefinable resilience, something that Connolly rather loftily put down to a triumph of the spirit. He'd seen it in the women, and on the faces of the kids. It bonded them against the weather, and the Brits, and the harsher dictates of a sixty per cent unemployment rate. They laughed a lot, these people, and cursed a lot, and two-fingered the old enemies, and if life boiled down to yet another plateful of potatoes and cabbage, then so be it.

At the corner of Mairead's road, Connolly paused. There was a lamppost here, taller than the rest, out of keeping with the scale of the houses around it. Connolly was hopeless at estimating height, but it must have been thirty feet at least. After dark, it cast a hostile, sickly, slightly orange glare over the scrawny hedges and threadbare front gardens, and the locals talked meaningfully of surveillance and hidden cameras. It was, they said, part of the security apparatus, another brick in the wall that the Brits had built around them. Connolly didn't know whether this was true or not, but circling the lamppost at its base was an old bicycle tyre. Nobody knew who'd done it, who'd shinned up the impossibly smooth metal and slipped the tyre over the light at the top, but it had been there for months and no one had ever touched it. Connolly loved the gesture. It was derisive. It registered a small, anonymous, yet very public victory. It did, he thought, say it all.

Outside Mairead's house, Connolly paused again and eased the holdall from his shoulder. He'd brought presents for the kids, something special for Mairead, and a large bottle of Johnny Walker from the ferry. The curtains at the front were tightly drawn, but he could see the glow of the television set through the thin cotton.

He rang the doorbell. He heard the dog bark. The door opened. Mairead stood there. She was wearing an old nylon housecoat, open at the front. The slogan on her T-shirt read "Queen's University, Belfast". She was barefoot, her toes curling on the cold lino.

"Where've you been?" she said at once.

Connolly shrugged, recognizing the smell of the place, the kids, and the dog, and the peat fire, and the remains of tea on the stove in the small kitchen at the back.

"Away," he said simply.

"You're not after phoning, then?"

"I did. Twice."

"Please God you did." She smiled at him. "Twice."

There was a movement in the hall behind. Laughter. An uptilted face at the door. Connolly bent and kissed the face.

"Bronagh," he said, "Happy Christmas!"

The child giggled, and wriggled away from him, running back down the hall. He could hear her chanting his name in the lounge – Uncle Derek, Uncle Derek – and a sudden roar of laughter from a studio audience as one of the other kids turned up the television in response. Liam, probably. His father's son. Connolly glanced up.

"Snowing," he said.

Mairead nodded, stepping back into the hall and holding the door open. She was shorter than Connolly, twenty-eight years old, curly black hair, and a wide, open, cheerful face. Her skin was flawless, and her eyes were green, and she habitually wore a pair of large gold ear-rings, a trophy from her one visit abroad, a two-week holiday in Magaluf, ten years back. Connolly had never quite got the measure of her, knowing only that she was irresistibly the centre of everything, her own world, and his as well. She shut the door behind him and reached for his coat. He shrugged off the anorak, the snowflakes darkening already in the warmth.

"So why didn't you phone?" she said.

"No time."

"You've no time to lift the phone? And all those things you were telling me before you went? Should I believe you . . . ?" She paused. "Or is it a half decent Christmas you're back for?"

She didn't wait for an answer but folded his anorak over the banisters, and indicated the door to the front room.

48

Connolly grinned at her, absurdly pleased to be back, and went in.

The room looked smaller than ever. There were loops of tinsel hanging from the picture rail, and a lattice of crêpe streamers overhead, criss-crossing the room. By the window, there was a small mountain of presents heaped around the base of a Christmas tree, and there were dozens of cards propped carefully amongst the branches. Connolly gazed round, looking for signs of the room he'd left only weeks before. The dim glow of the turf fire in the grate. The damp clothes drying on the backs of chairs. The wooden harp on the mantelpiece and the framed colour photo of the Pope hanging on the wall overhead. He unzipped the holdall, and took out all the presents, one by one. Instinctively, the kids turned away from the television, sprawled on the floor, looking up at him. There were three of them: Bronagh, Declan, and Liam. Liam, at eleven, was the oldest, blond, freckled, watchful, quiet. Declan was a year younger, a louder child, long-legged, slightly awkward, kind. The two boys shared a tiny bedroom at the top of the stairs, while Bronagh still slept with her mother. Bronagh, at seven, was the baby of the family, perceptibly spoiled, a perpetual escapee from the discipline which Mairead dished out to the boys.

Connolly held out the largest of the presents. It was wrapped in green paper. The card attached to one corner showed a footballer scoring a goal. Liam eyed it. Connolly glanced across at Mairead. "OK?" he queried.

Mairead shook her head, and nodded at the tree. "Tomorrow," she said.

Liam groaned and turned over on his stomach, back to the television. Declan gazed at the other two presents. Bronagh giggled and lunged at the dog, an ancient long-haired mongrel with soft brown eyes and appalling halitosis. Mairead opened the door again. "You'll be having tea?"

Connolly shook his head, added his presents to the pile under the tree, and produced the bottle of whisky. Mairead hesitated a moment, then left the room. Connolly joined her in the kitchen, unscrewing the bottle as he went. The kitchen smelled of burned fat. On the half-scraped plates beside the sink were the remains of an Ulster fry: smears of egg yolk, curls of bacon rind, discarded triangles of soda bread, and a small puddle of baked beans, the sauce already congealing. Mairead cleared a space on the dresser and produced two glasses. Connolly poured the whisky, tipping his glass in salute.

"Happy Christmas," he said, "Tiocfaidh Ar La."

He wound his tongue around the unfamiliar syllables, savouring the sound of the phrase, the strange, opening guttural, the sing-song end. In fifteen months in Belfast, it was the one piece of Gaelic he'd managed to master. Tiocfaidh Ar La. Our Day Will Come. The traditional, age-old Republican salute.

Mairead bent her head, refusing to even acknowledge the phrase. Connolly said nothing for a moment, then swallowed another mouthful of the Scotch, letting the tiny kitchen close itself around him. He'd always felt instantly at home here, the one room in the house that Mairead preserved for herself, her own modest price for a domestic life that was otherwise totally devoted to her kids. Most of their relationship, such as it was, had been nurtured here. Hours of talking, Connolly to begin with, later – when she trusted him – Mairead.

He'd first kissed her here, first brought her closely into himself, trying to imagine what it would be like, done properly, with space and time and no prospect of interruptions from the kids. It had never happened that way, ever, and the one time he'd slept with Mairead was Bronagh's first and only night away, staying three houses down the street with Kath, her best friend. Mairead had made him get up at dawn and return downstairs before Liam appeared on the landing. From his sleeping bag on the floor of the lounge, Connolly had listened to the boy's footsteps on the bare lino overhead, the unoiled hinge on Mairead's bedroom door, the mumble of conversation, recognizing the noises for what they were: the sound of the eldest son, patrolling the family's space, seeking the reassurance of his mother's otherwise empty bed. It had never been easy here, never simple, but the more he got to know Mairead, the more he belonged to her, a form of surrender in which he knew he had no say whatsoever.

He'd gone to London because she'd asked him to. He'd met Leeson, and he'd well and truly renewed the friendship, and now he was back, the faithful messenger, full of talk of the Falkland Islands. He reached for the bottle and poured himself another generous measure.

"You'll want to know about my friend," he said. "Leeson."

"I will?"

Connolly looked at her. Her voice had hardened. She looked tense, even angry. Quite why she'd asked him to go to London, to see Leeson, to pick up the threads again, he didn't know. He'd never told her about the physical relationship between them, and he didn't propose to start now. But that, in any case, was irrelevant. All that mattered was the request itself, her need for whatever he could find out. Normally, she asked very little of him, apart from time. She never wanted money. She never yearned for nights out in the city, or the pub. And so this strange suggestion had been quite unexpected, out of character. Go see yer man, she'd said. Find out about him. What he does. Who he knows. Then come back and tell me all about him. And so here he was, Christmas Eve, back home with her, two glasses down, full of news.

"He's wrecked," he said. "Alcoholic."

"Really?"

She looked pointedly at the bottle of Scotch on the table, and Connolly began to wonder about the wisdom of not phoning more often, of what it might have done to their relationship. More than anything else, he wanted to spend Christmas with her. The thought of returning to the small, bleak flat off the Ormeau Road was more than he could face.

"What is it?" he said. "What's the matter?"

She looked at him a moment, and then shook her head, turning away, her own glass untouched. Connolly glanced up the hall. The hall was empty, the sound of the television audible through the closed door of the lounge. Peals of canned laughter. Christmas Eve with Des O'Connor.

51

Connolly reached out and touched Mairead lightly on the cheek. She shook her head again, then turned into him.

"You'll not want to be a part of this," she said.

"Part of what?"

"All this."

She gestured hopelessly around her, the kitchen, the sink, the pile of neatly folded washing on the stool under the window.

"This?" Connolly frowned. "This life of yours?"

She looked up at him, very close now, wide green eyes.

"No," she said softly, "The Rah."

Connolly blinked. The Rah was the Republican Army, the Provisional IRA, street slang for the ever-younger gunmen who slipped in and out of the headlines, hooded figures in combat jackets and old jeans and cheap trainers, terrorists in Whitehall, facts of life in Andersonstown.

"The Rah?" Connolly prompted.

Mairead nodded, swallowing hard. "You'll have seen your man. Leeson."

"Yes," Connolly smiled, "like you asked."

She shook her head, an abrupt, emphatic movement. "I was wrong."

"Why?"

She looked at him for a long moment, her eyes moist. "So help me God, please . . ."

She turned away and began to cry. Connolly stepped forward, holding her against himself, comforting her. The smell of her body. Her hair soft against his cheek. Leeson had opened up a new path to her. She'd asked, and he'd complied, and now he was back, ready to deliver. Except something had gone horribly wrong.

"What is it?" he whispered. "Tell me."

She shook her head again, and began to sob. Connolly pushed the door shut with his foot.

"I saw him," he said, "truly."

"I'm sure you did."

"And it's fine. I can tell you everything. It's OK."

Abruptly, she stopped crying.

"No," she said, "it's not OK. I'm wrong. Wrong to have mentioned it. Wrong to have asked you. Just wrong."

"Why?"

She looked at him again, drying her eyes with the corner of a dish cloth.

"Because I shouldn't have listened to them."

"Who?"

"Danny's friends."

Connolly gazed at her. Danny had been her husband, a thick-set, broad-shouldered youth with a mop of blond hair and a permanent smile. There were photographs of him around the house, two of them beside Liam's bed. Mairead had met him at a dance, seventeen years old, and they were married six months later. From what little else she'd said, it had been the happiest of marriages – fond, loyal, perpetually broke – until Danny had been picked up in an Army sweep and interrogated for a week in Castlereagh. He'd emerged with broken ribs and a permanently damaged kidney, his innocence protested until the last, every shred of tolerance gone for ever. As a result, in secret, he'd joined the Provisional IRA.

Four years later, on a wet night in March 1976, he'd been cornered by a patrol of squaddies in an unlit cul-de-sac in Ballymurphy. They'd shot him four times through the head and left his body on the pavement for the ambulance to collect. There was so little left of his face that afterwards, in the hospital mortuary, Mairead had been denied the chance to say goodbye.

She'd protested, of course. She'd phoned the Army PR people at Lisburn and demanded an official inquiry, but the tired, over-polite major on the other end of the line had simply said he was sorry. Her husband had been transporting a weapon. Other lives had been at stake. It was all very regrettable. She hadn't believed him, knowing it was the usual Brit flannel, and two days later, at his funeral in Milltown Cemetery, she'd watched in disbelief as men in black balaclavas emerged from the crowd of mourners, fired a volley of shots over the coffin, and disappeared again. They gave the lie to her outrage and her anger. They told the world, and the watching Brits in the helicopter overhead, that her husband was indeed a Volunteer. Riding back to Andersonstown in the big black car, and for weeks afterwards, she'd tried to reconcile herself to the life that Danny had led, and to its loss. Her Danny. Her man. The father of her children. Gone.

Now, in the kitchen, she began to sip at the whisky. Connolly watched her carefully.

"These friends of Danny's . . ." he said.

She nodded, gazing down at the whisky. "They came round for a wee while. A month back. I hadn't seen them for years."

"And what did they say?"

She glanced up at him. "They wanted to know about you."

"What about me?"

"What you did. Who you are." She paused. "What it is between us."

Connolly looked at her. "And what did you tell them?"

"I said you were a teacher. At the University. I said you taught history. I said you were very clever."

"And?"

She glanced up, blushing. "I said we were good friends." She hesitated. "That OK with you?"

"Yeah."

She sniffed, and sipped again at the whisky, closing her eyes as the neat spirit burned her throat.

"They wanted to know about your connections. How well connected you are. Who you know. Back in England." She paused. "They also told me about Danny. Things he'd said to them. Things I didn't know."

"Like what?"

She was silent a moment, tipping the glass slowly sideways until the whisky touched the rim. Her hand began to tremble. "They said that the cause meant more to him than anything else. Come the finish of it."

"They were lying."

"Maybe." She looked up. "They said if I loved him, I'd help the cause too." She shrugged, hopelessly. "So I did . . ."

Connolly nodded, understanding at last. He looked at the ceiling, remembering the afternoon on the bench in Battersea Park, Leeson thin and cold beside him, and his own visit three days later to a VD Clinic in the Middlesex Hospital. When he'd described Leeson's symptoms, and the nature of their relationship, they'd looked bemused. They'd blood-tested him for syphilis, and inspected him for herpes, and gonorrhoea, and NSU, and on all four counts they'd drawn a blank. Finally, when he'd mentioned "gay plague", one of the younger male nurses had nodded wisely and said he'd seen the phrase in *Time* magazine. Evidently, there was a mystery disease puzzling physicians in San Francisco and New York. Some said a new virus was attacking the immune system. Others said it was a more routine infection. Either way, it appeared to be limited to the gay community. Maybe Connolly should try celibacy for a while. Maybe he should see how things developed.

Now, looking at Mairead, he smiled.

"I love you," he said softly, marvelling at how easy it was to say, after nine long months. He reached out for her, turning her in towards him. She kept the glass between their bodies, self-defence. He looked down at her.

"So what do they say? These friends of Danny's?"

She closed her eyes for a moment. She took a deep breath.

"They want to see you," she said at last.

"When?"

"Soon," she sniffed again, "Tuesday night. They told me to tell you."

"Ask me?"

"Tell you." She looked at him, and began to sob again, shaking her head, hands cupping the glass, tears running down her face.

"What's the matter?" Connolly said softly. "What can't you say?" She gazed up at him, suddenly limp.

"Losing one was bad enough . . ." she said, "I don't want it to happen again."

Leeson called the mini-cab company midmorning. The cab arrived within minutes, driving him the six miles to Whitehall. In Great George Street, beneath the imposing Palladian façade of the Foreign Office, Leeson paid the £4 fare, added a large festive tip, and paused for a moment as the cab disappeared in a cloud of blue exhaust.

For Christmas Day, the weather was unseasonably mild. Only yesterday, the Met Office had been warning of snow falls in the north, and rain elsewhere, but now it was sunny and almost warm, tiny bubbles of white cloud in an otherwise perfect sky. Across Parliament Square, worshippers were streaming out of Westminster Abbey, the men sombre in black or grey, the women splashed with brighter colours. Even at a distance, Leeson could recognize the odd face, top politicians, a couple of Law Lords, a senior Treasury figure, men who counted the Abbey as their parish church, and Westminster as their personal fiefdom.

Leeson hesitated a moment longer, then rounded the corner to King Charles Street, and pushed into the Foreign Office through the big double doors. He hadn't been in the office for nearly two weeks, phoning in to the Personnel Department to offer his regrets and the assurance of a doctor's note on his return. The response, as ever, had been politely guarded. Expressions of concern that he'd been under the weather. Hopes that he'd be back in harness this side of Christmas. And a gentle reminder that his PV was pending, and shouldn't be unduly postponed.

Leeson stood for a moment in the marbled silence of the Foreign Office lobby, pulling his coat around him. The place felt cold. He began to cough again, his hand to his mouth, thinking vaguely about his American friend. The news from the States had been more than a little alarming, but Leeson was an optimist by nature and saw no point in getting unduly worried. His GP, he vaguely supposed, had it about right. A passing virus. One of life's little hazards. He walked across the lobby and took the lift to the third floor. His office was at the south-eastern corner of the building, behind a large panelled door marked "South American Department, F3". He shared it with three colleagues and an assortment of filing cabinets, but today it was empty. He took off his coat and folded it over the back of a chair. The tray beside his blotter was full, nearly two weeks' work, but he gave it only a cursory glance before unlocking his desk and removing a blue manila file.

Much of the conversations with Connolly, the last two days before he'd left, had returned to the subject of Argentina. It was a country that had preoccupied Leeson for years, ever since he'd cut his diplomatic teeth in the large, tree-fronted embassy off the Plaza Augusta. It was a fascinating place, awash with traditional money, fine sportsmen, beautiful women, and a dark appetite for military dictatorship, and the more he got to know it, the more subtle and addictive the experience became. With his fluent Spanish, and a growing series of excellent contacts, he'd begun to understand the way the place ticked, what mattered and what didn't. It was a country, above all, where face and machismo counted for a great deal, and from eight and a half thousand miles, he knew that was imperfectly understood.

He switched on the small desktop photocopier in the corner of the office, and returned to the file. Before Connolly had returned to Belfast, he'd promised him a look at some of the key documents that underpinned their interminable discussions, memorandums and letters and intelligence digests that – in Leeson's view – flagged the path to disaster. What the politicians – and soon the world – couldn't grasp was the potential of the crisis that would shortly overtake them. Something so abrupt, so sudden, and yet so predictable, that the Government would have no choice but to react in kind.

It was a scenario that had so far formed the merest footnote to the deliberations of various Whitehall committees. The Argies might want the islands back, went the accepted wisdom, but they'd never invade. And even if they did, there'd be weeks and weeks of warning. And even if that was somehow circumvented, then world opinion, or the UN, or President Reagan, or a couple of nuclear submarines, would rapidly restore the status quo.

Knowing a lot about Argentina, and a little about geography, Leeson – in common with a handful of colleagues – had other ideas. The Argentinians would take the islands because the British left them no other option. And they left them no other option because – as ever – they refused to see the smoke in the wind.

Leeson pulled his in-tray towards him, sifting quickly

through the waiting pile of memorandums and letters, looking for the latest digest from Buenos Aires. Beside the telephone, a fresh delivery from the Registry messenger, he found it. He opened the buff envelope and shook two sheets of cream paper onto the desk. He scanned them quickly and then read them again. In essence, the overnights from Buenos Aires added very little to the reports he'd already picked up in Thursday's *Times*.

Power had changed hands in Argentina. President Viola had been succeeded by the Commander-in-Chief of the Army. The new President was to retain his Army command, and the incoming Junta had been considerably strengthened by the support of Admiral Anaya, the most extreme of the hard-liners on the Falklands issue.

Leeson read the digest a third time, interpreting the new power structure for what it was: macho, super-patriotic, intensely proud of the recent *rapprochement* with the big players in Washington. With the backing of the Reagan administration, fellow crusaders against communism, the new boys in the Casa Rosada would soon be bold enough to embark on a few adventures of their own. He reached for the blue file, extracting a number of documents, the new President's name on his lips. He and Connolly had been discussing him only the previous evening: tall, handsome, vain, hard-drinking, with a larger-than-life helping of South American machismo. General Leopold Galtieri.

There was a footfall in the corridor outside. The door opened. One of the security staff peered inside. He looked surprised.

"Sir?"

Leeson glanced up at him. "Merry Christmas," he said, heading for the photocopier, "and a happy New Year."

FIVE

Buddy Little's search for a cure began at the public library.

By now, Jude had been at the Regional Unit for over a week. It was Christmas, the ward festooned with streamers, bottles of sherry for the nurses, gifts from grateful patients. Buddy had spent Christmas Day itself at Jude's bedside, a glum time, both of them preoccupied behind the brittle smiles and Buddy's faltering attempts at festive small talk.

Jude was still on a special diet while her digestive system recovered from the trauma of the accident. That meant bowls of powdered eggs and potatoes, spoon fed. The stuff tasted like cotton wool, she said, and it was all the worse because she could smell the turkey and the bacon and the steaming Christmas pudding on the catering trolley. She'd asked the doctor for a special dispensation, just the odd forkful or two, but Bishop had shaken his head, and given her a brisk lecture on the risks of irritating the membranes of the lower gut. She'd thought about it afterwards, what he'd said, and when Buddy arrived with his paper hats, and his box of crackers, she told him she'd reached rock bottom.

"Pathetic," she'd said, her eyes flicking down at her body. "It won't even fart any more."

Now, bent over a pile of textbooks, Buddy tried to understand the biology of it all. With some kind of map, some kind of reference, perhaps he could find a path out of this hideous jungle, back to a place of safety.

In essence, it seemed simple enough. The spinal cord carried messages from the brain to the rest of the body. Without these messages, the muscles under conscious control wouldn't work. Buddy poured over the pages of illustration. Wiring diagrams, he thought, the nerves radiating out from the big transformer in the brain, out down the spinal cord, out to the farthest reaches of the body.

The spinal cord itself ran through a canal in the middle of the backbone. The backbone was composed of a column of small vertebrae. Buddy had seen them in Jude's X-rays. The doctor had shown him, off-hand as ever, dark irregular shapes, interlocking, one on top of another. Jude's fifth bone down was clearly displaced, pushed forwards and upwards by the accident. The bone had pressed in on the spinal cord, damaging it. The cord had swollen, not able to work any more, blocking the messages from the brain.

Traction, the books told Buddy, released the pressure on the spinal cord. In time, the displaced bone would re-align itself. But the damage to the bundles of nervous tissue was permanent. Because the brain and the spinal cord, unlike the nerves of the rest of the body, can't repair themselves. Thus the diagnosis. Thus the paralysis. Thus Jude, lying on her back, washed, fed, and emptied, twice a day.

Buddy paused, looking up from the books. Already, at the hospital, they were telling him about the care she'd need back home, constant nursing, her body turned in the bed every two hours, the perpetual watch for bedsores, the need for nappies, and laxatives, and suppositories, another pair of hands taking over from a body which simply wouldn't work any more. Buddy made sure that these conversations were conducted away from the bed, out of Jude's earshot. Once she found out the degree of her helplessness, how long it would last, she'd simply quit. He knew it. Which was why he was here, in the library, looking for another answer.

He closed his eyes a moment, fighting off the tiredness, knowing he could do it. He'd spent his working life in appalling conditions, hundreds of feet below the surface, zero visibility. He'd built an entire career on never giving up, on finding underwater solutions to problems the guys on the beach had despaired about. Part navvy, part engineer, he'd pioneered new techniques for patching up derelict structures, freeing corroded valves, remaking dodgy welds. The impossible was his stock-in-trade. He knew there was always a better way.

And so he read on, day after day, an hour or so every

morning, a table of his own in the reference department of the town's public library. And as the pile of textbooks slowly diminished, he began to borrow magazines from a friendly social worker at the hospital, publications for the handicapped, each with its monthly digest of news – new feeding aids, new makes of wheelchair, discounts on special creams for nappy rash, the latest adjustments in disability benefit. One of the publications, an import from America, had a regular section on medical research, and it was these precious pages that began to preoccupy Buddy.

He understood now that the problems were enormous. The stuff in the backbone wouldn't regenerate. Once it was dead, it was dead. Therefore you had to take risks.

One answer was to operate. In America, it seemed, there were surgeons prepared to do just that, to open up the backbone and insert metal rods to realign the broken vertebra. Done quickly enough, within hours of the injury, it sometimes worked. The spinal cord was allowed to swell. It wasn't caged by the broken bone. Damage was minimal. Movement was restored.

But Jude's injury was already ten days old. The damage had been done. It was far too late to operate. And so, once again, there had to be another way.

He read on. In New York, they were using steroids to reduce swelling. In the American Mid-West, they were trying ice. In Australia, they locked injured patients in a diving compression chamber and kept them there for hours, feeding hyberbaric oxygen to the injured tissues.

But again, it was all acute care. Treatments to be administered at once, in the accident room, the injury still young. What Buddy needed was something more fundamental. Not treatment. Not first aid. But a cure.

On the last day of the year, he found it. He'd been reading about a research programme at a university in Ohio. The programme involved encasing cripples in metal calipers – arms and legs for a C5 break – and then motorizing the joints. An elaborate computer program would control the calipers, acting as a brain, effectively duplicating the movements of the body. There was a photo alongside the article. It showed a young girl, festooned with wires, her arms and legs braced. She looked like Frankenstein. She looked monstrous.

Buddy was about to close the magazine when another article, much shorter, caught his eye. A South American neurosurgeon, working in Massachusetts, was pioneering a brand-new technique. He was grafting nerve cells from unborn rats onto the injury site, bridging the dead tissue. The preliminary results were encouraging. Messages from the brain were evidently getting through. A little sensation, a little control, had been restored. It was described as a nerve by-pass. It sounded immensely hopeful.

Buddy read the article a second time, and then a third. He made a note of the neurosurgeon's name. Dr Pascale. Evidently he worked at a small private hospital in Cambridge, Massachusetts. Buddy crossed the library to a shelf by the door. There were phone directories for every major city in the world. He found the surgeon's name. He made a note of his phone number and returned the book to the shelf.

Half an hour later, slightly out of breath, he was back in the ward at the hospital. Jude was reading, a Steinbeck novel, *The Grapes of Wrath*, the book clipped to a metal frame above her bed. Buddy settled on the chair beside her. Her eyes blinked a welcome. He bent and kissed her. She smiled at him.

"You smell of fresh air," she said. "Nice."

Buddy grinned at her. Then he reached in his pocket, and produced a small square of paper, the fruits of his labours, their future together. He held it up, above her head, so she could see. She peered at it.

"Fancy the States?" he said. "For the New Year?"

Connolly sat in the PD, nursing a glass of lager. The PD was a club off the Falls Road, originally set up for Prisoners' Dependants, a couple of echoing, barn-like rooms, given over most nights to bingo, drinking and live music. Tuesdays featured a group called Crazy Paving, four anonymous white T-shirts, moving slowly in the smoky gloom, curiously detached from the howling guitars in the bank of second-hand speakers framing the tiny stage.

Connolly sat by himself at a table near the door. Mairead had brought him here half an hour earlier, refusing the offer of a drink, insisting she had to get back for the kids. Christmas had come and gone, a litter of discarded wrapping paper, and a new rubber bone for the dog, and a tidy bill at the off-licence down by the Broo. It had been pleasant enough, anarchic games of Ludo on the floor with the kids, quieter times with Mairead in front of the late-night movie, the kids away in bed, but they both knew that something had happened between them, some strange discord. Mairead, when he'd challenged her, had blamed the Rah. "See wee Dermot," she'd told him, "get it over and done."

Connolly sipped at the lager, resisting the temptation to stiffen it with a chaser of Jameson's. Around him, tables of women bent inwards over ashtrays, heads down, shoulders in, scrums of conversation. He listened idly to their chatter. Most of them, he knew, had husbands away in the Kesh or Maghaberry, men behind the wire, ten, twelve years at a stretch. They paid weekly visits, gathering outside the Public Baths in the Falls Road, waiting for the battered Ford Transit with the steamy windows and the leaking roof, complimentary transport out to the prison. There, they'd queue for a while in the rain, waiting for the first of the endless doors to open, the ritual warnings about forbidden objects, the searches, then the precious hour with their men, some meagre compensation for the prospect of half a lifetime spent alone.

In the Kesh, in the early days, the regime had been relatively lax, Republicans treated like prisoners of war, maintaining the upper hand, refusing to wear prisoners' dress, insisting on establishing some modest control of their lives in open defiance of prison rules. This incessant battle against an authority they refused to recognize was deeply personal, reinforced at odd corners of the day by whispered threats against individual screws. "We know you, so we do," went the line. "We know you, and we know your wee home, and that's a nice family you have, so you do."

The intimidation, the constant war of nerves, had worked.

Rules were relaxed, education classes permitted, discipline handed over to IRA commanders within the prison itself. There were even rumours that at least one child had been conceived during one of the weekly visits, furniture stacked against the open back of the interview booth, the warder dismissed with an oath.

These, Connolly knew, had been small local victories, the stuff of street ballads and the huge end-of-terrace murals that decorated the maze of streets off the Falls Road. In the mid-seventies, though, the special category status had been withdrawn for all new prisoners. Henceforth, said Whitehall, all Republican prisoners were to be treated in exactly the same way as any other criminal. They were to do menial prison work. They were to wear regulation prison uniform. Many of the men had refused, lying naked under a single blanket in the H-blocks, rejecting the system, preserving their precious identity.

Over the next two years, the situation had worsened. Warders beat the prisoners. The prisoners, in response, wrecked their cells. The cells were emptied of everything but a blanket and a mattress, the prisoners refusing to step out to wash or defecate, smearing the walls with their own excreta, providing the world outside with a series of lank-haired, Christ-like images, the ultimate symbols of Republic suffering.

It hadn't worked. Whitehall refused to concede a return to special category status. And so plans were laid for a hunger strike. A first strike was called off after apparent concessions by the authorities. The concessions proved illusory. Then, in March 1981, a second hunger strike had begun, a two-week interval separating each fresh striker.

Two months later, the first hunger striker, Bobby Sands, had died. A hundred thousand mourners attended his burial. The world was appalled. The IRA waited for the expected concessions. Nothing happened. By October, ten men were dead, the victims of a test of political will, not the small bitter encounters between the screws and their grim-faced charges, but a grand, set-piece battle conducted on the front pages of newspapers all over the world. It was a battle the Republicans had to win, fought on territory of their own choosing, against a British Prime Minister whose beliefs and language were no less absolute than their own.

The demands of the hunger strikers were clearly spelled out and well understood, but the battle itself became quickly more important than any specific list of grievances. To stand back, to refuse negotiations, to do absolutely nothing while ten men starved to death showed a certain chill courage. And although each death continued to produce world-wide condemnation, propaganda coups of considerable proportions, Republican leaders were uncomfortably aware that ten more graves in Milltown Cemetery was a very curious kind of victory. The hunger strikers had wagered their lives against a Brit capitulation over their precious demands. They will, went the rationale, they must, give in. But the handful of concessions they'd finally wrung from Whitehall were hardly worth the lives of the strikers who'd died. It was, the leadership quietly agreed, a defeat.

The group on stage paused for a moment and Connolly heard a throat clearing in the tannoy.

"Mr Connolly," a voice boomed, "a taxi for Mr Connolly."

Connolly looked round, surprised. Mairead had said nothing about leaving the club. He stayed put for a moment or two, fingering his glass, dry-mouthed. Then a figure appeared at the door, a boy of about seventeen, jeans and a T-shirt, short black hair. He peered into the gloom and saw Connolly at once. He beckoned him towards the door. Connolly felt himself getting up. He left his glass on the table, most of the lager untouched. He stepped outside, through the wire mesh cage, out into the night.

There was a car on a patch of wasteland across the road, an old Cortina. There was a man at the wheel. Someone else beside him. The back door hinged open. Connolly crossed the road and got in, the youth beside him. The car smelled of roll-ups, and someone's dog. The door closed.

The man beside the driver turned round. It was difficult to be sure under the street lamps, but he looked about thirty. He had a thin moustache and wore dark glasses. He held out his hand.

"You'll have a driving licence?"

Connolly, off guard, nodded. "Yes. Of course."

The man said nothing, his hand still outstretched. A big hand. Deep calluses and bitten nails. Connolly fumbled in his pocket, produced a wallet, and extracted his driving licence. The man in the front scrutinized it under the light in the glove compartment.

"29 Mons Crescent? Carshalton?" he queried.

Connolly nodded. It was his mother's address. He hadn't bothered to have it changed since moving to Belfast. The man in the front pocketed the driving licence. Connolly looked at the back of his head.

"Why do you want it?"

The man didn't turn round. "Be nice to know where to find you," he said, "if you ever leave that other place of yours."

"What place of mine?"

The man turned round. The smile didn't suit him. "Up by the University," he said, "number seventeen."

They drove for an hour or so, out west, along the motorway. Connolly, whose knowledge of Northern Ireland was mainly confined to Belfast, was soon lost. They travelled in near silence, no conversation, the merest whisper of music from the radio. Deep in the country, the car slowed, and turned left. A minor road, no traffic, a farmhouse or cottage every mile or so. Finally, the car drew to a halt. The driver flashed his headlights twice, peering ahead into the darkness. Connolly saw no response, no answering blink of light, but the driver grunted just the same, engaged gear, drove another quarter of a mile, then pulled sharply right, bumping along a narrow track, flanked by dry stone walls. It was raining now. Only one of the wipers worked. The car stopped outside a low, single-storey building. There was a light on inside. Connolly exchanged glances with the youth beside him. The youth nodded, a gesture that seemed to suggest they'd arrived.

Outside the car, the darkness smelled of manure, and tractor oil, and warm hay. The rain had thinned to a fine drizzle. The ground was soft underfoot. Connolly was escorted to the door of the cottage. Away to the left, he could see the dim outline of a barn, modern, corrugated iron walls and roof. There was a leak somewhere from a gutter, the steady drip-drip of rain onto wet mud. The front door of the cottage opened, and he heard voices. Someone's name. Padraig. He walked towards the oblong of light, and stepped inside. Only the passenger in the front of the car, the man with his licence, entered with him, pausing briefly before stepping back outside, into the darkness.

The room was small, low ceilinged, bare plastered walls, deep set windows, stone floor, and a one-bar electric fire in the open hearth. Sitting at a long, wooden table was a man in his forties, open white shirt, dark trousers. He had a spare, pale face, grey — almost colourless — eyes, and a slightly clerical manner. His hair was dark, parted carefully on one side. He held himself curiously erect, the posture of a teacher or a bank manager, a man with responsibilities and a certain self-esteem. He was a stranger in the room, wholly alien, a man from elsewhere. He didn't look remotely agricultural.

He glanced up at Connolly. No warmth. No welcome.

"Dermot?" Connolly ventured.

The man smiled thinly and shook his head. "No."

Connolly nodded and said nothing. The man told him to sit down. He did so. Someone else appeared from the room next door. Jeans and an old leather jacket. About twenty-five. A soft voice. Somewhere west.

"You'll be taking tea with us?"

"Please."

"Milk? Sugar?"

"Both, please."

The man at the table extended his hands, intertwining his long, thin, white fingers. His voice was as cold as his manner.

"There's reasons why we asked you here,' he said briskly. "We thank you for coming."

"Pleasure," Connolly said drily.

"You'll return afterwards. You'll be taken back."

"Thank you."

"But you'll be saying nothing."

"No."

67

There was a brief pause, the point underlined with the sharpest of glances.

"You understand?"

"Perfectly."

The man behind the table nodded. He fingered a small mole beneath his left ear, saying nothing, and Connolly began to think seriously about where he came from, what he really wanted. The man was clearly highly placed. His whole manner, the way he sat, his tone of voice, brooked no argument.

"Well?" he said at last.

Connolly, nonplussed, gazed at him.

"Well what?"

"What do you have for us?" He paused. "Danny's girl talks of a man called Leeson. You know a man called Leeson?"

Connolly studied him carefully, trying to decide exactly where to begin, what to say, what not to say. He'd been anticipating this conversation since Christmas Eve, not quite this setting, not quite this man, but the same opening query. Who's Leeson? In one sense, without much prompting, he could explain it all: the man's position, his access to the Foreign Office, his contacts in the diplomatic world, his seat in the Establishment's Upper Circle. He could talk about his own relationship with Leeson, his foibles, his weaknesses, his fondness for good conversation, and fine wine, and unlimited helpings of interesting sex. He could even throw open the whole of it, his contempt for his political masters, his alcoholism, and the fact that he was ill. In the event, though, he did none of these things.

"You should meet him," he said carefully.

"Why?"

"Because you might find him interesting."

"Why?"

Connolly shrugged. "I can't imagine," he said, "except that I'm here."

The other man nodded, accepting the logic of the conversation. The tea arrived, two mugs. They sat steaming on the table between them. The other man ignored them, not taking his eyes off Connolly.

"Your name," he said, "it's an Irish name."

"It is."

"Are you Irish?"

"Third generation. My great-grandfather was a butcher. In Clonmel."

"But you follow events?"

"It's my job."

"You're a teacher."

"I lecture," Connolly smiled, trying to warm the atmosphere, trying to melt the ice around this man. "Events are my speciality. What they meant then. What they mean now. What they've done to us all in between." He paused. "We Brits call it history."

"A loose term."

"I agree."

The other man smiled for the first time, a slight inclination of his head, point made, *touché*. Connolly reached for one of the mugs of tea. The other man's hand closed over his, an almost apologetic gesture, warmer than Connolly might have anticipated, taking the mug for himself, an act of restoration. Connolly looked at it. It was block-stencilled with the figure of a man with a long-handled scythe, green against the white china. It was the kind of mug you might pick up in a craft shop. Connolly looked up again, smiling an apology, sipping sweet tea from the other mug, glad of the warmth, happy to let the other man make the running again.

"This friend of yours . . ." he began.

Connolly nodded. "Leeson," he said.

"How well do you know him?"

"Quite well."

"Well enough to . . . arrange a meeting?"

"Certainly."

The other man nodded. "And would that be in our interests?"

"I've no idea."

The other man nodded. A plate of biscuits had appeared. Connolly tried one. Rich tea. Very stale. He glanced at his watch. Mairead had promised he'd be back by ten. It was nearly quarter to nine. He looked at the other man, and extended his hand.

"You haven't told me your name," he said.

The other man reached for his mug and drained it slowly, putting it down between them, winding the conversation backwards, ignoring Connolly's question.

"If you teach history . . ." he mused, "you'll know what we're about."

Connolly nodded. "I do," he said.

"And you'll know why we do what we do."

"Yes."

"Is that the same as saying you sympathize?" He looked up. "Or am I going too fast for you?"

Connolly hesitated a moment. The question had preoccupied him for several years. Meeting Mairead, getting to know her, had sharpened but not resolved it. Soon, he knew, he'd have to form a view. He frowned.

"You think it can work?" he said. "All this?"

"All what?"

"The gun. The bullet. The bomb."

The other man shrugged. "Of course."

"You're that sure?"

"Yes."

"Why?"

The other man looked at him a moment. His elbows were on the table. His fingertips were pressed lightly together. His forehead puckered with the beginnings of a frown. A teacher, Connolly thought. Definitely a teacher. The man glanced away a moment, a gesture of slight irritation.

"It wasn't our idea," he said at last. "As you know, Carson reintroduced the gun. Not us."

Connolly nodded, conceding the point. In 1912, the British had been close to granting a measure of self-government to the Irish. Lord Carson, a Protestant, had threatened a revolt in the north. A hundred thousand men marched and drilled. Twenty-five thousand guns were smuggled in. Only the First World War had averted a blood bath. Connolly leaned forward, engaged.

"But now?" he said. "What about now?"

The other man shrugged again. "We're well armed," he said. "Well funded. We fight because we have no choice. We're an army. They'll never defeat us."

"Is that the same as winning?"

"Yes."

The word hung in the air between them. Total conviction. Connolly leaned back in the chair. "So what do you need from me?" he said. "Why am I here?"

The other man pondered the question. "Access," he said at last. "Leeson probably has it. If so, we need it."

"But what do I have?"

"You?" He paused. "You have access too."

"To what? To whom?"

The other man looked at him a moment. "Leeson," he said at last.

"Is he that important to you?"

"He might be."

"And what if I say no?"

Connolly leaned forward, across the table, searching for the heart of the conversation, the answer that might shape the days to come. The man said nothing. His eyes looked beyond Connolly.

There was a movement behind him. Connolly glanced round. The man with the leather jacket had reappeared from the other room. He stood by the electric fire, hands in his pockets, resting lightly on the balls of his feet. He had a quiet attentiveness Connolly recognized from a piece he'd once done for the University newspaper in Cambridge, after a crop of street assaults from the local heavies. He'd spent several evenings at a variety of unarmed combat courses, preparing a student's guide to DIY survival. He'd watched, as ever, from the sidelines, making mental notes, taking it all in. The best of the instructors had been quiet, like this man, the lowest of profiles, the steadiest of expressions, experts in the disciplined application of extreme violence.

Connolly looked across the table again, at the man with no name. Then he began to get up, knowing at once that it was an act of impertinence, and a mistake. The man in the leather jacket slid into the seat beside him. He took an automatic from the back of his waistband and placed it carefully on the table in front of him. He smelled faintly of aftershave. The letters L-O-V-E were tattooed across the knuckles of his right hand. All three men gazed at the automatic. Connolly noted the cross-hatching on the butt, the well-oiled click as the man in the leather jacket slid the mechanism back and forth, easing a bullet into the breech. He swallowed hard, but his voice gave him away, higher than usual, slightly querulous.

"Is that the answer?" he said. "To my question?"

The man across the table motioned him to sit down again. He was looking thoughtfully at the gun.

"It's an insurance," he said at last. "An incentive. A gesture of intent. Ambiguity's a terrible thing. Far better to be frank . . ." he offered Connolly a thin smile, "from the outset."

There was a long silence. The man across the table was studying the remains of his tea.

"They know us all," he said quietly. "Every one of us. They have us on file. They have our photographs. They follow us around. Here. In the Republic. Everywhere. They know the size of our shoes, the way we like our tea, the names of our loved ones. They know what we eat, whether we drink or not, everything . . ." He paused. "So what we need, what we always need, are new people . . . friends . . . comrades . . ." He paused again. "That's what they fear the most. People with no record. No past. No file. Faces totally unknown to them. Someone to take them by surprise . . ."

He cupped his hands around the mug, warming them, letting the silence descend.

Connolly stared at him. "Me?" he said at last.

The man across the table nodded.

"You."

"You want me to join the movement?"

"I want you to help us with Leeson." He looked up. "And I want you to think about Mairead."

"Isn't that the same thing?"

The man hesitated for a moment. Then he smiled. "Yes," he said, "I think it is."

Connolly said nothing for a moment, looking at the gun. Then he shrugged and glanced up, amazed at how quickly this small moment of choice had come and gone.

"How do I stay in touch?" he said.

"You don't."

72

"I don't?"

"No," the other man paused, "we do."

"I see."

There was another silence. The gun disappeared. Then the man across the table leaned towards him.

"You'll have heard of Robert Mugabe . . .?" he began.

Connolly nodded assent, back on safe ground. The negotiations on Rhodesian independence were barely a year old, but he was already thinking of incorporating the salient points in one of his second-year lectures.

"Of course," he said.

"Then think of us as fellow travellers," he said. "Same tactics. Same prize."

Connolly looked at him for a moment, wondering about the comparison, whether it was legitimate or not. Finally he concluded that it didn't really matter. Whether there was any real parallel between the new President of Zimbabwe, and this forbidding figure across the table, was – in the strictest sense of the word – academic. What mattered now was getting out. Back to West Belfast. Back to Mairead.

"Tiocfaidh Ar La," Connolly said, his voice hollow.

The other man inclined his head, accepting it like a benediction.

"Tiocfaidh Ar La," he said.

SIX

Leeson's postponed PV took place a week later.

He dressed for it with care, not too formal, not too smart, nothing to indicate that he found the occasion special in any way whatsoever. No concessions, in short, to the man he knew he'd find behind the desk, the jowly, heavy-set, permanently tired Intelligence professional he'd so far met on four previous occasions, the man from MI5 who held his file.

He took the tube from Hammersmith to Hyde Park Corner, then the underpass to the north exit, and emerged, blinking, into the daylight. In the lee of the hotels along Park Lane, there was a hint of warmth in the sun, and he slowed, glancing at his watch, taking his time, enjoying himself. Since Christmas, he'd felt much, much better. The old zest, the old confidence, had returned. The strange purple rash was still there, chest and upper arms, but he was eating well, and the cough had gone completely. He was ready, he felt, for anything.

Past the Dorchester, he turned into Mayfair. He'd been given the usual address in South Audley Street, the handsome, four-storeyed house with the black-glossed railings, and the matching front door. He knocked twice. The door opened. A man in a dark suit smiled a welcome and addressed him by name. He stepped inside, accepting the invitation to wait in a small side room, the low reproduction table beside his chair amply stocked with copies of *Country Life*.

They kept him waiting for ten minutes or so, a cup of coffee at his elbow. Then the man in the suit appeared again, ever friendly, taking him into the heart of the building, up the broad staircase, past the pale watercolours, along a wood-panelled hall, to a door at the end. The man in the suit knocked once, didn't wait for an answer, opened the door. Leeson stepped inside, his coat over his arm. He half-turned to say thank you, but he was too late. The door was already closing. The man had gone.

Leeson turned back into the room. Something was different already. Usually he attended his vettings in a room with two tall windows and a view across the street to the terrace opposite, a handsome room, well-proportioned, with a beautifully restored Adam fireplace and a couple of decent oils on the wall. This room was small, shadowed, a single window, barred on the outside, with a glimpse of a fire escape. The walls were bare. There was a desk, and two chairs, and not very much else. Leeson paused for a moment, taking stock, smiling his careful smile at the man behind the desk, a stranger, someone new, someone different, like the room in which he sat.

The man glanced up. He was shorter than Leeson, and a little older, perhaps fifty, but broad, strongly made, with wide shoulders, and big hands, and a shock of sandy hair, receding slightly at the temples. His face was open, and weathered, freckles everywhere, and there were laughter lines, deeply etched at the corners of his eyes. He wore a plaid shirt, fraying slightly at the collar, open at the neck. An old black leather jacket hung on the back of the chair. He reminded Leeson of a rugby coach, someone used to physical violence and the company of large men, someone who'd been around a bit, someone it might be all too easy to underestimate. Not at all the sallow, watchful, cipher-like spooks he'd previously encountered from the world of Intelligence.

The man behind the desk got to his feet and held out his hand.

"My name's Miller," he said, "we've never met before."

Leeson stepped towards the desk, returning the smile of welcome. The man had a rural accent, possibly Bristol, possibly somewhere further west, the vowels rounded, soft. The voice went well with the look of the man. His own person, untouched by the Establishment's tribal markings. They shook hands. Miller had a light, dry handshake. He nodded at Leeson's coat.

"There's a hook on the back of the door," he said. "Use that." Leeson did what he was told. He could feel Miller watching him. It wasn't an unpleasant feeling, no sense of threat, none of the usual MI5 heebie-jeebies. Leeson returned to the desk and sat down, making himself comfortable, easing one leg over the other, careful to preserve the creases in his trousers, wondering quite what had happened to his usual inquisitor. A palace coup, perhaps, or a transfer to some distant out-station or other. Recently, life in the Intelligence Services had become something of a standing joke in Whitehall. The Irish situation had sharpened the old inter-service rivalries, MI5 battling for turf against MI6, the pair of them plotting against the other agencies in the field: Military Intelligence, RUC, Special Branch, and the dozens of other tiny empires spawned by the twelve-year conflict. Lately, the shadowy world of Intelligence had acquired an almost Central American feel, fuelled by gossip and rumour, heads rolling, reputations in shreds. Safer, said some, to take a job in El Salvador. At least you might last the month.

Leeson masked a smile, and glanced across at Miller. Miller was deep in a file, one thick finger tracing a path down a page of dense print. Leeson gazed round, noticing for the first time a holdall on the floor beside the desk. It was beige, standard Army issue, as battered as the leather jacket on the back of Miller's chair. Somehow it reinforced the overwhelming impression the man had already made. That he didn't, somehow, belong here. That he'd come in from somewhere else, and borrowed this bare, musty room, and paused a while to ask a question or two, and that soon he'd disappear again. Quite where Leeson fitted into all this was beyond him, but Miller looked a good deal more engaging than his oaflike predecessor, and for that Leeson was grateful. Life, after all, still owed him a surprise or two. Perhaps he'd even enjoy it.

Miller looked up and smiled at him, a gesture of apology, and then began to run briskly through the facts of Leeson's life. He began at the beginning, birthplace, parents, siblings, early days at prep school, the move to Glennister, the first taste of the glittering prizes, then the step onward to Oxford, and the First in Modern Greats, and then the real meat of it, the ten years in the Service, the effortless moves upward from Grade Eight to Grade Five, First Secretary, the overseas postings along the way, and now the imminent move to Washington.

Leeson listened, impressed. Miller made his life sound more than a collection of jobs, dates, promotions. There was a hint of admiration there, even applause. It sounded like a grand adventure.

"So . . ." Miller eased slowly back in the chair, "how did I do?"

Leeson smiled. "Word perfect," he said, 'alpha plus."

"Happy with it all?"

"Your version," Leeson was still smiling, "or mine?"

"Yours. This life of yours." Miller tapped the thick file, still open on the desk. "This career."

Leeson looked at him a moment, resisting the easy answer. His previous inquisitor he'd treated like a tradesman: with patience, good humour, and the faintest disdain. There'd never been any kind of relationship on offer, any kind of rapport, and so this attitude of his had seemed – at the time – about right. The man had been entirely witless. He'd asked the wrong questions, in the wrong way, and in consequence his annual grillings had been about as psychologically revealing as a dental inspection. But this man, Miller, was different. He seemed genuinely interested. He touched a deeper nerve. His whole manner invited an indiscretion or two, and Leeson – ever game – was willing to risk it. He gazed down at his own file, still pondering Miller's last question.

"It's been fun," he said at last, "so far."

"Frustrating? Ever?"

"Yes. Oh . . . certainly."

"Bosses? Policy?" He paused. "Politicians?"

Leeson smiled. "All three. One time or another." He paused. "How much do you know about the set-up?"

Miller shrugged. "Bits and pieces," he said, "the bare essentials. Enough to listen."

He slowly closed the file, a curiously intimate gesture: trust me, go off the record, bare what's left of your soul.

Leeson realized where they were heading, and began, imperceptibly, to slow down.

"I'm not here to complain," he said.

"I'm not asking you to."

"I'm sure you're not."

There was the beginnings of a silence. Miller smiled, and ran a big hand backwards through his hair. The backs of his hands were freckled, like his face.

"You're off to the States," he suggested.

"Yes."

"Nervous?"

"Excited." He paused. "It's another step forward. Like they've all been."

Miller nodded, changing tack. "That planning staff set-up you've got over there. Ever been tempted?"

Leeson blinked at him, surprised at the depth of the man's knowledge. The Planning Staff was an autonomous unit, much maligned by working diplomats, a tiny coterie of civil servants, young, bright, paid by the ship of state to scale the rigging, and search the horizon, and spot the oncoming icebergs before they became a problem. They operated from an imposing ground-floor room next to the Head of the Diplomatic Corps' suite. They had ready access to the Permanent Secretary and the Joint Intelligence Committee and they had the right to see all incoming telegrams. They had a licence to think the unthinkable, to play make-believe games with the big divisions, and recently Leeson had wondered whether his own doubts about the Falklands policy shouldn't be their concern too. He'd toyed with approaching them directly, but somehow it had smacked, however faintly, of treason, a betrayal of working colleagues, of men and women at the sharp end. They saw as much of the staff from Buenos Aires as he did. They should, by now, have reached the same conclusions. The fact that they hadn't had simply reinforced his cynicism.

"They're academic," he murmured, 'I'm a humble diplomat."

"Doesn't policy matter to you?"

"Policy?" Leeson looked up. "We don't have a policy any more. We have rhetoric. There's a difference."

There was a brief silence, long enough for Leeson to mask the beginnings of a smile. Then Miller leaned back in his chair.

"So how do you see your job? What do they pay you for?"

Leeson looked him in the eye, bringing himself to a full stop, acknowledging the man's professionalism, the rapport he'd established, the ten brief minutes it had taken him to coax a little of the truth from Leeson.

"I represent my country's interests," he said carefully.

"And where do you think those interests lie?"

Leeson pondered the question, aware of Miller watching him, alert, friendly, a passing stranger enjoying half an hour's good conversation.

"In finding a new role," he said finally. 'In matching means to ends."

Miller nodded, toying with a pencil. "Are you some kind of salesman?" he wondered aloud. "Is that it?"

"Sometimes."

"Peddling the national line?"

"Helping define it."

"And where none exists?"

Leeson looked at him for a moment, then shrugged. "We make it up," he said, "as you well know."

Miller nodded, and smiled, evidently happy with the answer, then he returned to the file, riffling through it, checking a detail here, a date there, covering the obvious squares, Leeson's political leanings, his religious beliefs, his connections in the City, and the media, and the countless other worlds beyond the doors of the Foreign Office. None of it added to what Leeson knew was already in the file, and he was beginning to feel slightly bored, even disappointed, when Miller turned a page in the file and glanced up.

"You've been ill," he said casually. "Sick."

"I have."

"What was the matter?"

Leeson shrugged. "Chest infection. Something I picked up. The doctor gave me some antibiotics. I'm fine now." He smiled. "Thanks very much."

"A cold, was it? To begin with?"

"I don't think so."

"Did you get chilled at all? Wet?"

"Not that I remember."

Miller nodded, all sympathy. "Lots of it about," he said, "this time of year." He glanced down at the file. "This doctor of yours . . . good man?"

"Good doctor."

"Known him long?"

"Ten years or so. Since I've lived there."

"Anything else been the matter?"

Leeson hesitated for a moment. "I don't think so," he said.

"Sure?"

"Yes."

Leeson looked at him, wondering how far the man would push, how much he could possibly know. After a long conversation with Connolly on the phone, he'd paid a visit to a private clinic off the Holloway Road. He'd given them a candid account of his affair with the American, and he'd shown them the rash on his chest. A cheque for £400 had bought a series of exhaustive tests. The results of the tests were due soon, and they came with the assurance of total anonymity. For that price, he suspected they probably meant it. Miller was up a blind alley. Had to be. Leeson smiled at him.

"I'm fine," he said. "Fit as a butcher's dog."

Miller returned the smile, glanced at his watch, and then – abruptly – closed the file. "Good," he said, standing up and extending his hand. "Good to hear it."

Leeson blinked up at him. Vettings normally lasted most of the morning, sometimes longer. He'd been here barely forty minutes.

"Is that it?" he said.

Miller nodded, putting on his leather jacket and extracting a crumpled tie from a side pocket. "That's it," he said. "Time is money." He grinned. "That's the new line, isn't it?"

He grinned again, an almost conspiratorial gesture that took Leeson by surprise, two civil servants confronting the same keen wind blowing through the corridors of Whitehall.

Cost effectiveness. Value for money. A fitter, leaner bureaucracy. Leeson shrugged.

"*Plus ça change*," he murmured.

Miller stepped out from behind the desk, knotting his tie.

"What's that mean?" he said cheerfully.

"It means nothing ever changes. *Plus ça change*. All talk. No do."

Miller nodded, checking his tie in the reflection in the window.

"Nice theory," he said, "but wrong."

Leeson looked at him a moment, wondering quite where the man's connections began and ended.

"You think she means it," he said, "the PM?"

Miller shepherded him towards the door. The tie was dark red. No patterns. No motif.

"I know she does," he said.

Leeson began to answer, to parry the assertion, to enquire a little further, but then changed his mind. Instead, he retrieved his coat and extended a hand.

"Goodbye . . ." he said. "If you're ever in Washington . . ."

Miller looked at him.

"Yes?"

"Drop in. South American section. Fourth floor."

Miller nodded, barely touching Leeson's hand.

"I will," he said. "You bet."

He opened the door, and watched Leeson walk slowly away down the hall. Then he returned to the desk. Unzipping the holdall, he took out another file, mustard colour, and laid it carefully beside Leeson's. On the cover of the mustard file, top left hand cover, was a stamp in black ink. It said "19th Intelligence. Eyes only." He opened Leeson's file, and removed two photographs, recent shots of Leeson, head and shoulders, specially commissioned by the security people in the Washington Embassy. He opened the other file. Paper-clipped inside the front cover was another photo. It showed a man in his forties, long, pale face, carefully parted hair, open-necked white shirt. The photo was slightly blurred, as if it had been taken through glass, or at speed. The man had his head back against some sort of rest. His face was quarter profile. He might have been travelling in a car. He eased the photo away from the file, and turned it over, looking for a detail, a date or a name. Across the back, in steady capitals, was the man's name. Padraig Antony Scullen. B. Kiltyclogher, 13th January, 1934.

Miller murmured the name to himself, took a final glance at the face on the other side, then sandwiched the print between the shots of Leeson, replacing all three photos in the mustard file. The phone on the desk began to trill. He picked it up. A voice on the other end said the cab was waiting. He glanced at his watch. Downing Street was ten minutes away. He smiled.

"Terrific," he said. "Spot on."

Scullen sipped tea from a white china mug, standing by the window, gazing out at the stone-grey waters of Lough Swilly. It was a cold day, windy, a single fishing boat butting in against the ebb tide, a cloud of seagulls at its stern. Directly beneath him, on the tiny forecourt, two men were unloading sawn timber from the back of a flatbed lorry, piling the planks, one on top of another, carrying them into the yard. Across the road, at the wheel of an old Mercedes, sat his bodyguard, McParland. He was sitting back, relaxed, one arm stretched across the top of the front seats, the other hand on the dashboard, fingers drumming along to the rhythm of some song or other on the car radio.

Scullen watched him for a moment, taking another pull at the mug of tea. The steam clouded the cold glass. He moved back across the tiny cluttered office, looking down again at the desk. The scribbled message in his own handwriting on the pad by the phone was as puzzling as ever. "Qualitech not ours," it read. "Beware."

He sat down, putting the mug carefully on a folded envelope, sparing what little was left of the varnish on the desk. He'd picked up the first clues from yesterday's national papers, brought over the border from Derry. There'd been headlines about a bomb found in a new factory due to be opened by the Prime Minister, wafers of Semtex wrapped around a detonator and a timing device. The bomb had been hidden in a cavity behind a single layer of bricks. The cavity was next to the foundation stone. Had the Prime Minister opened the factory at 3 p.m., the time listed in the local paper, she'd have been killed. He'd read the report with a mixture of emotions. Admiration for the ASU that had dreamed the stunt up. Disappointment that the Brits had got there first.

Now, though, it didn't seem that way at all. He looked again at the message on the pad. The voice had been quite explicit, a thirty-second conversation, open line, direct contravention of Standing Orders, real emergency. "No way," the voice had said, "not us." Scullen had asked for more details, but the voice refused, simply repeating that the thing was black propaganda, or the work of some other group. Meanwhile, they needed more paint brushes, and more emulsion. Paint brushes meant mercury tilt detonators for the car bombs. Emulsion was code for money. Scullen had promised more of both, and the voice had hung up.

Now, he thought through the conversation again, its implications. He'd recognized the voice at once. It belonged to O'Mahoney. The man had been with him now for a year, a difficult character, independent, mulish, deeply unforgiving, but a man with a great deal of mainland experience, a man he knew he could trust. O'Mahoney, like all his Commanders, had total freedom of action. He could select his own targets. He could choose when and how to attack. The Qualitech hit had the man's fingerprints all over it. A brilliant concept, the boldest stroke. Yet here he was. Flatly denying it.

Scullen leaned back in his chair, his fingertips circling the mole beneath his left ear. Since the effective transfer of command from Dublin to the North, he'd been charged with running the Provo Away Teams, the handful of men and women whose job it was to re-export the iniquities of British rule back to the mainland. One good bomb in Britain, went the argument, was worth a hundred in Belfast, and he knew it was true.

Over the past three months, there'd been dozens of incidents over the border, in Derry, in Enniskillen, in Lurgan, in Belfast, many of them worth no more than a line or two in the British national press, barely penetrating the thick callus of indifference that separated Northern Ireland from the mainland. Yet four times, over there, his cells had struck – once outside Chelsea Barracks, once in Oxford Street, twice against key Establishment figures – and each of these incidents had sent the media into orbit. He kept the cuttings in a scrap book in the locked steel cabinet in the corner, modest battle honours in a war he knew would go on for decades. The headlines spoke of "outrage" and "carnage". Leader writers wrung their hands at the hopelessness of it all. Backbenchers in Parliament bellowed for the return of the death penalty. Yet all the time, he knew, the man in the street was beginning to wonder not just if it was worth it, whether withdrawal from Northern Ireland wasn't better than yet more deaths, but what strange colonial logic had put the border there in the first place. One day, without doubt, the penny would drop. One day, the obvious truth of it all would dawn. That Ireland, all Ireland, was Irish. And that the natives, left to their own devices, would sort the thing out.

He reached for the last of the tea. He'd been running the Away Teams now for two years. At once, on the basis of his own experience, he'd abandoned the use of Irish communities on the mainland, the recruiting of second and third generation families to provide safe houses, and food, and shelter, and logistical support. The goodwill was there, for sure, and the willingness to run risks, but the Brits had quickly penetrated every corner of the Irish communities, using all the old tricks to turn Irishman against Irishman, throwing money at a man with gambling debts, drink at the alcoholics, threats at the easily frightened, anything to recruit a small army of touts, the eyes and ears of the security forces.

The policy had worked. Nothing put a man away quicker, he knew, than sending him to the Irish quarter of a big English city. They'd be lifted in weeks, if not days, the victims of the man who knew the man who knew the wee quare fella that filled his glass and bellowed the old rebel songs while our friend here, the newcomer, the man from over the water, looked on. No, if the thing was to be done at all, then it had to be done properly. Tiny cells, ASUs, Active Service Units, four or five strong, each cell insulated from above and below, taking its orders from Belfast, or here in Buncrana, supplied by courier, living a life of quiet moderation behind the grey anonymity of rented flats and curtained windows.

These men and women he'd sent out had learned their trade the hard way, the way he'd had to learn. They learned to lie low, and draw the minimum of attention to themselves. They looked ordinary. They never got drunk in public. They never fought, or sang, or spent maudlin afternoons at the bookie's. Every time they went out, which was rarely, they gave the lie to their Irishness. They were simply another couple, or another threesome, or even a single fella on his own, having a quiet drink, or a meal, his nose in the paper, his table near the door.

To date, it had worked well. It depended, of course, on money, and on a steady supply of material, but neither had been in short supply. In recent years, Belfast had become a cash till for the Republicans. Levies had been imposed on the drinking clubs, and the black taxis. Millions had been creamed from the huge re-housing programme. Scarcely a brick was laid, or a pint consumed, without the tinkle of a fresh coin into the movement's coffers. Better still, the Hunger Strike had opened American wallets. Every time another man had died, there'd been a fresh flood of money into the Noraid offices in Boston, and New York, and the Midwest. The strike had been tragic, sure, but Brit intransigence – the refusal to even talk about concessions – had funded the armed struggle for years to come. For Scullen, it was a sweet irony, all the sweeter for his own sure knowledge that some of that money – enough to do the job – would be used to exact a personal revenge, a debt of blood. Qualitech, he had to admit, was a mystery, and there was something about the incident that bothered him, but the away teams were still out there, a fact of life, and sooner or later they'd get to her. The woman was responsible. The woman must be killed. And surprise was still the key.

Scullen smiled. He had no personal taste for killing. As a religious man, he abhorred the waste of life. But his job was to make the occupation of the Six Counties intolerable for the Brits, to break the national will to stay, and that meant exporting violence on as grand and unexpected a scale as high technology and clever targeting would permit. It was a war they were fighting, a just war, and there'd be no true peace without due sacrifice.

To date, he'd done well. But his particular brand of Republicanism – his reverence for the past, his respect for the old heroes, his rectitude, his insistence on strict discipline – was fast going out of fashion. The new breed of Volunteer, men like O'Mahoney, owed nothing to this world of his, and did little to hide their derision. In Belfast's phrase, his shelf life was strictly limited, and he knew it. But before the tide of history swept on, leaving him finally beached, he wanted to make one last mark on the movement, a contribution so unique that his name would never be forgotten. This yearning for a kind of immortality was, he accepted, a weakness. It smacked of vanity, of showmanship, but that didn't matter. History, after all, was his subject, and no one knew better than he did that history was written by the men who took the biggest risks.

He gazed out of the window. When it was all over he'd retire. The place down in Kerry was nearly ready. The purchase had gone through, and the builders had the alterations well in hand, and by early summer the farmhouse should be ready for habitation. The upstairs room at the back, his favourite, was already designated as a study. It had a fine view of the valley, and plenty of space for his books. There, in years to come, he could finally turn his full attention to the project he'd been hatching for so long. Daniel O'Connell. The Great Liberator. The definitive biography.

He smiled. O'Connell had been one of his earliest Republican heroes, a giant figure from the nineteenth century, a man of the law who'd taken the battle for Catholic Emancipation to Westminster, and won. Scullen had first read about him as a child at home in the tiny village of Kiltyclogher, and later – when he'd graduated from college and begun to teach at the little schools in County Leitrim – he'd devoted lesson after lesson to the man. Now, he shook his head, thinking about it. O'Connell had come from Kerry. His family home, at Derrynane, was only ten miles or so from the farmhouse he'd bought, yet another reason for choosing the place.

He bent to the desk again. He kept a photograph of the farmhouse in his top drawer, and he looked at it now. He'd found it by chance. It was miles from anywhere. It would give him everything he'd ever wanted, the silence and the peace he'd grown up with. It would bring his life full circle, the perfect coda to the busy, dangerous years in the front line.

There were three hoots from the Mercedes across the road, two short, one long, the agreed signal for a visitor. He heard voices outside, a brief conversation on the garage forecourt, then footsteps up the stairs. There was a knock at the door, a precautionary tap-tap, before the door opened. A man stepped in, blowing warmth into his cupped hands. He was in his thirties, small, dark, with a heavy sweater against the weather, and an almost permanent frown. He'd been the Organization's Acting Quartermaster for more than a year, and had – said some – aged a decade.

The two men nodded to each other. Scullen gestured at the message by the telephone. The Quartermaster read it.

"Yeah," he said, "I heard already. McParland told me. It's a puzzle."

"Could have been worse. They could have done it. And been caught."

"Oh sure, sure. Are we bringing them back now? Is that the way it's to be? Only— "

Scullen shook his head, cutting him off.

"No," he said shortly. "They need more tilts. And money."

The Quartermaster's frown deepened. One of the reasons he'd got the job was a legendary meanness. A night out was a packet of crisps and a soda bread sandwich. Marge, not butter.

"How much?" he said.

"He didn't say." Scullen paused. "When's Maura across?"

"Next week. Out of Rosslare."

"Give her five. And tell her to tell them to ease up. Christmas is over. Times are hard."

"Sure."

The Quartermaster hesitated. He had the air of a man who always badly wanted to be elsewhere, regardless of the weather.

"That'll be all?" he enquired.

Scullen fell silent for a moment, leaning back in his chair, just far enough to look down the street, out towards the quay. The fishing boat had berthed alongside. The men were stacking blue plastic boxes on the wet cobbles. He watched them for a moment, thinking about the morning's news. Every new operation was a gambler's throw, a bid against the odds, but the Qualitech hit, had it worked, would have been the perfect counter-stroke, an eye for an eye after the obscenities of the hunger strike. But it hadn't happened that way. Instead, he was looking at a man offloading boxes of cod, and a scribbled note on a pad by the phone, and the struggle advanced not a single inch. Somehow, somewhere, there had to be an answer, the operation of his dreams, an operation so simple, so bold, so unexpected, that the world would hold its breath, and put its hands together, prayer and applause and an end – at last – to the old indifference. He sniffed. He had a cold coming on. He turned into the room.

"There's a fella called Leeson," he said, "I think we need to talk."

SEVEN

Buddy Little sat in the back of the big 747, buckling his seat belt, thinking, yet again, of Jude.

Lately, the last week or so, he'd taken to carrying a photo of her in his wallet, a single print. It went everywhere with him. He'd selected it from the dozens he had of her. It showed her sitting on a diving board in a hotel pool in Morocco. It had been their first holiday together. She was wearing a tiny white bikini. She was very brown. She was smiling. She was in great shape. He'd chosen it because he remembered the dive she'd done for him seconds later. It was perfect, flawless, a tiny circle of ripples, her body still underwater, swimming the length of the pool. He looked at the photo now. It had been a brilliant holiday. One day, he told himself, they'd go back. Do it all again. The whole length. Underwater.

Jude. He gazed out of the window. He'd said goodbye to her less than a day ago. She'd smiled up at him, whispering good luck, and he'd squeezed her dead hand, and said he'd phone as soon as he had some news. Pascale, he told her for the umpteenth time, had been more than helpful. He'd talked to the man on the phone and given him the relevant details, and the man had said there was every chance of a positive outcome. That was the phrase he'd used. Positive outcome.

On the phone, ever impatient, Buddy had pumped him. Could he guarantee a cure? Would his wife get better? Could they go back to square one? Start all over? Pascale had laughed, sympathy not derision, and said they had to discuss it. Not now, not on a telephone line, constant interruptions from his secretary, but face to face. Buddy, he'd said, should fly over. He'd show him the clinic. He could meet the team.

They'd talk. The plane ticket, he'd said, would be the best investment he'd ever have the chance to make.

Buddy liked the sound of that, optimism at last, and now – gazing down at the long curl of Cape Cod – he mused on the conversation. He'd been to Massachusetts before, an awkward demolitions job on a wreck near the main shipping lanes off Martha's Vineyard, his first real break after leaving the Navy. He'd stayed three months, living aboard the dive ship, spending weekends on the Cape. He'd liked the place, the scale of it, the way everything worked, the attitudes of the men he'd worked with, their easy can-do enthusiasm. There was nothing they ever bitched about. Whenever they hit a problem, they sat down, and figured it all out, and spent whatever was necessary, and solved it. For a Brit, used to tight budgets and the usual weary resignation, it was a profound culture shock, proof that there was always another way. Buddy smiled. That an American-based neurosurgeon should have cracked paralysis – American know-how, American money – was, on reflection, no sur-prise.

The plane banked steeply, and settled on its final descent. The brown waters of Boston Harbor flashed by beneath the wing. Then grass, and tarmac, and the rumble of the undercarriage as the big plane touched down. They taxied across to the terminal buildings, and the jumbo crawled to a halt. Buddy, travelling light, cabin baggage only, was through Immigration and looking for a cab within the hour.

The cab took him through the downtown area, and out across the Charles River, into Cambridge. Buddy knew enough by now to recognize the kind of area Pascale had selected for his private clinic. It was a class address. He had Harvard University and MIT for neighbours. These were blue-chip institutions, world leaders in their field. For Buddy, tired but exultant, it was the very best collateral.

The cab dropped him at a Holiday Inn. He registered at reception and spent an hour or so lying on the huge king-size bed, watching television, not thinking very much. Pascale had agreed to meet him at seven. He was to take a cab to the clinic and bring the X-rays with him. He had the X-rays in his bag. Jude's doctor had refused to part with his own, and in the end he'd had to commission a new set, at twenty pounds a throw. Bishop, learning of his plans, had told him he was a fool. It was, he'd said, a waste of money. More importantly, he was raising Jude's hopes at precisely the time when he and Jude should be getting down to the sterner realities of rehabilitation. The sooner they both confronted reality, the better. Pascale, he'd implied, was a fraud.

Buddy had shrugged the little speech aside. For the first time, standing there in the big main corridor, an island in a stream of wheelchairs, he felt he'd regained the initiative. He'd smiled at Bishop, and said goodbye.

"I'll be back," he'd said, "for my wife."

The journey out to the Clinic took Buddy along the river again. The river was wide and black. The wind was blowing down from the north, occasional flurries of snow, and there were wavelets lapping against the further bank. Buddy could see them under the street lights, little explosions of white. He blinked, thinking of Jude.

The Clinic lay in a wide, tree-lined avenue off Memorial Drive. There was a high wall and a substantial garden and a security phone beside the tall wrought-iron gates. Buddy bent to the speaker, pressed a button, gave his name. The gate hinged open, totally silent, no sound of a motor. Buddy walked in, impressed. Good sign, he thought. Nice piece of engineering.

He made his way up the drive. The Clinic was modern, two storeys, shallow pitched roof, white venetian blinds at the windows. The front door opened as he approached. A man stood on the top step, sniffing the night air, his hand already outstretched. Backlit, he was tall, slim. He wore a white coat, unbuttoned.

Buddy stepped in, out of the light. The man smiled, perfect teeth in a wide mouth. He looked about forty, well-made, jet black hair swept back from his face. His face was dark, Mediterranean blood. Buddy shook his hand, introduced himself. The other man nodded.

"My name's Pascale," he said. "Call me Alvar."

Buddy followed him down the hall. The place smelled of lemons. There were doors off the hall, all of them white.

Pascale opened a door at the end, and led Buddy into a small study. He shut the door behind him and sat down behind a large desk. The desk was piled with papers. He waved Buddy into another chair, offering him a jelly bean from a large glass jar by his elbow. Buddy smiled at him, shaking his head, sensing at once that Pascale was a lady's man. Something to do with the way he held his body, the expressive movements of his hands. The hands were long and slender, perfect nails. He used them constantly. They went with the voice, low, confidential, with a hint of faint amusement.

"You took the morning flight over?"

"Yes."

"That's fine. No problems. West–east's different. That's a killer. Especially at night."

Buddy agreed, not caring which direction he flew, wanting only an answer, some kind of decision. He picked up the big buff envelope, opening it and passing over the X-rays. Pascale switched on a small desk lamp, and held up the first of the films. He studied it a moment, and Buddy watched his face, a blur through the dense grey negative. He knew what he wanted, confirmation that the job could be done, that his journey might end here, in this small room, three thousand miles from the wheelchairs and the bowel evacuations and the endless stream of well-intentioned chatter.

Pascale made a note on a pad, and glanced quickly through the rest of the X-rays. There were six in all. He tidied them into a pile and put them back in the envelope. Buddy was still watching his face. He looked up.

"Well?" Buddy said.

Pascale picked up the envelope. "I'll need to keep these," he said, "that OK with you?"

Buddy nodded. "Of course," he said. "Does that mean . . . ?"

Pascale smiled at him, holding up a cautionary hand, stopping him in mid-sentence.

"It means . . ." he said gently, "that I'll be taking another look. I need to go over them carefully. I need to talk to your wife's physician. I need more information."

"She's paralysed. She can't move. Can't eat properly. Can't shit. Nothing."

"I know that."

"Her doctor won't talk. I've already asked him."

"Won't?" Pascale echoed the word, the softest inflection, an air of pained bemusement. "Won't?"

Buddy shook his head, vigorous, sure of himself. "No," he said, "he's very anti. He thinks you shouldn't . . . you know . . ." he shrugged, "mess around."

Pascale laughed at the phrase, nodding, enjoying it. Plainly, he'd heard it before.

"You bet," he said. There was a brief silence. He tapped Buddy's envelope. "What do *you* want?" he said.

"I want my wife back."

"And you're prepared to have her undergo major surgery?" He paused. "After all that stuff your physician has told you?"

"If it'll work, yes . . ." Buddy hesitated, the old question back again, impossible to defer. "So . . ." he said, "*will* it work?"

Pascale got up and stepped across to a cupboard. Inside, there were racks of hanging files. His hand moved quickly from file to file, extracting documents. Watching him, Buddy realized that it was something he'd done before, probably often, the hand scarcely hesitating between each file. Finally, he returned to the desk, patting the documents into a neat pile and passing them over to Buddy.

"These are reprints," he said, "articles of mine. Respectable medical journals. If you think I'm covering my butt, you'd be right. But I'm no charlatan. Neither am I rich. Neither am I mad." He paused. "What I'm doing isn't popular. Especially with people like your physician."

Buddy glanced down at the pile of papers in his lap. The first article was from the *New England Journal of Medicine*. It was entitled "Transplant Techniques for Foetal Rat Tissue". He looked up again.

"How many of these operations have you done?" he said. "To date?"

"Yes."

"Seven."

93

"Have they worked?"

Pascale composed his fingers into a bridge, studying Buddy for a moment before he answered.

"Worked isn't a word I'd use," he said. "In the majority of cases, we have established significant sensory gains."

"What does that mean?"

"It means we've achieved measurable improvement."

"So it *has* worked."

Pascale nodded slowly.

"Yes," he said, "as long as we agree on definitions."

There was a long silence. Then Buddy stirred in the chair.

"So what happens next?" he said.

Pascale leaned forward, suddenly businesslike.

"Next, I talk to your physician. There won't be a problem. I establish a prognosis. I assess your wife's case. And if it's appropriate, I shall suggest she undergoes surgery. That process won't happen unless I feel there's a substantial chance of success."

Buddy nodded. "How long . . ." he said, "will all that take?"

Pascale glanced at his watch. It was a slender watch, gold, plain leather strap. "Three weeks," he said. "Possibly a day or two longer."

Buddy nodded again. Pascale's eyes had gone back to the envelope. He slid out the first of the X-rays, and peered at it for the second time.

"It's a tough break," he said. "How old is your wife?"

"Thirty-four."

"Is she fit?"

"Very."

"Is she cheerful?"

"No."

He nodded slowly, sliding the X-ray back into the envelope.

"I'm sorry," he said, "it's a horrible injury. Which is why guys like your physician should be a little more . . . ah . . . adventurous."

"Yeah?"

"You bet."

There was another long silence. Miles away, Buddy could

94

hear the wail of a siren. He thought of the river, the flurries of snow, the black water.

"One thing . . ." he began.

Pascale looked up. "Yes?"

"How much will it cost? All this?"

Pascale fingered the envelope. He sat back in his chair.

"Assuming your wife is a suitable candidate, I'll need her here at least a week before we operate. She'll need to recover from the flight. I'll need more X-rays. Plus we do various other diagnostic procedures. The operation itself takes ten hours. We have full convalescent facilities here, on the premises. She'll be on her back, post-operative, at least three weeks. So . . ." he frowned, "including medications, surgery, after-care . . ." He paused. "About eighty thousand."

Buddy blinked. "*How* much?" he said.

"Eighty thousand." Pascale smiled. "Dollars, of course."

Connolly met Mairead in the Botanical Gardens, in Belfast, two days later. He'd come straight from a morning lecture at the University, barely a quarter of a mile away. Mairead was sitting on a bench by the Palm House. There was a baby on her lap and an empty buggy by her side. She looked cold.

Connolly sat down beside her. She squinted at him in the weak sunshine.

"Hi," she said, "stranger."

Connolly looked at the baby. He'd not seen Mairead now for nearly a week, not since the Cortina had driven him back into the city, back from the exchange across the table in the cold empty cottage out west. The experience had overwhelmed him, a mix of disbelief, and confusion, and a kind of surreal detachment, and he'd spent the next forty-eight hours trying to sort out what he really felt. It was fear.

"Hi," he said. "Nice baby."

"His name's Kieron. He's mine for the morning."

Connolly reached across and tickled the baby under the chin. The baby started to cry. Mairead rocked it softly, backwards and forwards. She'd phoned Connolly first thing in the morning, at his flat off the Ormeau Road. The meeting had been her idea. She bent low over the baby's face, warming the cold flesh with her own breath.

"Why haven't you been round?" she said. "What did they do to you?"

"Nothing."

"Are you sure?"

She looked up at him, and he knew at once that she didn't believe him. He nodded.

"Certain," he said, trying to sound as matter-of-fact as possible. "They took me off for a while. Little chat."

"Where?"

"I don't know. Somewhere out west. Or maybe south. I don't know. A long way. It was very dark."

"Who were they?"

"I've no idea."

"No names?"

"No."

"They hurt you?"

"They didn't touch me." He paused. "Why should they?"

Mairead ducked her head again, catching the inflection in the last question, the way it lifted his voice. There was anger under there, and she knew it.

"They're gangsters," she said. "They're bad people. I've been worried sick. No word from you."

Connolly said nothing. The night they'd brought him back, they'd dropped him in the city centre. It was too late for the buses up to Andersonstown, and he didn't have enough money for a cab, and he suspected that the walk would have exhausted what little courage he had left. Two years lecturing about the perils of colonial disengagement should have prepared him for the real thing, but somehow it hadn't. He'd never seen a gun before, not so close. He'd never thought seriously about the possibility of his own death, what it might feel like.

He looked across at her. He wanted to touch her. Hug her. Kiss her. Be part of her again. Get back to the person he'd once been. A week ago. A month ago. She knew nothing of what had happened between Leeson and himself, of how far he'd let the relationship develop, how he'd contributed his own sexuality to the cause. Not the Provos. Not the pale-faced man across the table in the cottage. But her. Mairead. If she ever found out about this small truth of his, about lying in bed with Leeson, about the possibility of "gay plague", he knew she'd be gone and away. He could plead necessity, means and ends, battle damage, but none of it would make any difference. She'd think him mad, and sick, and dangerous to know, despite the fact that he'd done it, after all, for her. Another blind alley on the map of his life that he was no longer able to recognize. And now this, the men in the Cortina, who knew all about him, what he looked like, where he lived.

"Tell me who you talked to," he said, hearing his own voice, cold.

"I told you."

"Tell me again."

"They were Danny's friends."

"Tell me their names."

She looked up at him. The baby was asleep.

"I don't know their names," she said, "it's God's truth."

"I thought you said they were Danny's friends?"

"They were. They said they were."

"But you'd never seen them before?"

"No." She paused. "I never knew that Danny was up to it all. I've told you that."

"But afterwards, after he died, after the funeral, you'd have met them then. They'd have come round, given you money, help, clothes, whatever. They'd have made contact. I'm sure they would."

She nodded. "Yes," she said. "They did."

"But not these men?"

"No."

"So how . . ." Connolly frowned, "how did you know they *were* Danny's friends?"

There was a long silence. Mairead looked away, over the park.

"I didn't," she said softly. "And I still don't. Danny had lots of friends. They say they knew him . . ." She shrugged hopelessly. "So I suppose they did."

"So you told them about me?"

"They asked."

"And you told them?"

She nodded, saying nothing. Then she turned back. She was crying.

"I had to," she said.

Connolly gazed at her, unmoved.

"Why?"

"Because otherwise they'd see to Liam," she sniffed. "You have to live here to know what that means. It means they'll take him away and break his legs. They do it with concrete blocks. From the building sites. It happens all the time. That's the kind of men they are."

"These friends of Danny's?"

"Yes."

"Doing that to Danny's child?"

"Yes."

There was a long silence, Mairead leaning into him, her head on his shoulder, and Connolly realized with a shock why she'd phoned. Not because she missed him. Not because she was worried sick. But something far more businesslike.

"They've been round again," he said.

She nodded, not looking up.

"Yes."

"And you've a message."

"Yes."

"What is it?"

"They want to meet you. This weekend."

"Where?"

Mairead lifted her head and nodded at the buggy. Hanging on the back of the buggy was a plastic bag.

"In there," she said, "a brown envelope."

Connolly got up and retrieved the bag. Inside the envelope, there was a sheaf of twenty-pound notes. He counted them quickly. £500. He stared at the money.

"What's that for?"

"God knows."

Connolly looked in the envelope again. There was a single sheet of carefully folded paper. He took it out and opened it up. It was a photocopy of a street plan. He looked at it, uncomprehending, aware of Mairead beside him.

"Ranelagh?" he said. "Rathmines?"

Mairead was looking carefully at the map.

"Dublin," she said after a while.

Connolly gazed down at the map. There was a blue cross on a street off the Rathgar Road, and a number, one hundred and twelve. He turned the map over. The address was repeated on the other side, 112 Garville Street, and a time, Saturday, 2.30 p.m. Mairead was at his shoulder again, looking down. He laid the map carefully on the seat between them, the envelope with the money on top.

"Is this why you phoned me?" he asked her. "This morning?"

She said nothing for a moment. The baby was awake now, gazing up, light blue eyes and the beginnings of a frown. Mairead nodded.

"Yes," she said, "it is."

"To tell me to go to Dublin?"

"Yes."

"Nothing else?"

She looked at him, her eyes dry now, her skin pinched by the cold. For the first time, Connolly realized how much weight she'd lost, how thin she'd got. The old optimism, the sparkle and the wit, had quite gone.

"What do you think?" she said.

"I don't know."

She tried to smile but it didn't work. Then she leaned across and kissed him. Her lips were cold on his cheek.

"Then I'll tell you," she said. "I once thought I'd nothing left to lose. Not as far as men were concerned. I thought it was all over for me. But it's not . . ." She hesitated for a moment. "I love you. You should know that. And when this madness is over, I'll think of ways of showing you."

Connolly nodded, saying nothing. The contract between them, the deal, was quite explicit. Go to it, get it over with, and get yourself back in one piece. Until then, it was a question of Liam's legs, and probably the rest of him, and the other kids too, and what was left of her own peace of mind. Connolly looked at her for a moment. She was back with the baby, nuzzling it with her cheek.

"Is that why you've not phoned before?" he said.

She nodded, not looking up. "Yes."

He hesitated a moment, then folded the map, checked the envelope, and slid both into his pocket. He leaned towards her, meaning to kiss her, then changed his mind and stood up. The wind had stiffened from the north. It was colder. He gazed down at her for a moment.

"Bye," he said, turning on his heel, and walking away.

An unmarked civilian car, a dark red Maxi with Northern Irish plates, picked up Miller from RAF Aldergrove, Belfast's principal airport. He arrived after dark, stepping off the evening BA shuttle, carrying the single holdall as cabin luggage, walking straight past the queue at the reclaim carousel, out onto the concourse. The waiting driver also wore civvies. Miller, who knew him by name, greeted him with a smile and a nod of the head.

They drove south, skirting the shores of Lough Neagh, down past Lurgan, avoiding Belfast. At Newry, they turned right, the driver checking and rechecking his mirror, watching the pattern of cars behind, looking for the tell-tale signs of a shadow. At the barracks at Bessbrook, he slowed, turning in past the sandbagged entrance, showing his pass at the gate. The younger of the two sentries, a newcomer to Northern Ireland, squinted after the departing Maxi. Normally, every civvie had to submit to a search. On this occasion, a quick visual and a nod had seemed enough.

"What's that all about then?" he queried.

The other man, a corporal, didn't take his eyes off the road outside.

"Nineteenth," he said simply.

The Maxi drove to a remote corner of the barracks and stopped outside a two-storey block. Lights were on in the rooms downstairs, curtains tightly drawn against the darkness outside. There were TV surveillance cameras mounted high on the brickwork. The brackets looked new. Miller retrieved his holdall, thanked the driver, and walked the twenty yards across the grass to the building's main entrance.

Inside, past the armed guard at the door, it looked like a school: green walls, red fire extinguishers, a single long corridor, and a musty, slightly sour, institutional smell. Miller walked down the corridor, pausing at a door near the end. He glanced briefly at his watch, then went in. The room was small, and warm, and fuggy. There was a grey filing cabinet in one corner, and a battered old sofa, and a couple of chairs, and a single desk. Standing over the desk was a youth in his early twenties. He wore jeans and a heavy, knitted sweater. His hair was long, tied in a neat pony tail, and there was half a roll-up smouldering in the ashtray beside an open map. The map was spread the length of the desk. Miller looked at it, recognizing the familiar contours of South Armagh, the browns shading into yellows across the border, the tiny villages dotted black. The youth behind the desk glanced up, and stiffened.

"Sir."

Miller smiled, dropping the holdall onto the sofa. "Charlie," he said briefly.

"Good trip?"

"Excellent."

"Tea, sir?"

"Please."

Charlie stepped across to the window, checked an electric kettle on the floor, and plugged it in. He had a soft, Irish accent, but a military training had settled perceptibly upon him. He reacted quickly. He showed respect. The two men obviously knew each other well. The kettle began to hum. Charlie glanced back over his shoulder. Miller had sat down on the sofa, and was loosening his shoes. He kicked one off after the other, stretching the length of the sofa.

"I liberated some Scotch," he said, "compliments of Curzon Street. Here."

He unzipped the holdall and took out a bottle of Johnny Walker. He tossed it across the room. Charlie caught it deftly, surprised. He'd never put Miller down as a drinker.

"Now?" he said.

"Please."

"Tea as well?"

"Why not?"

Charlie shrugged, unscrewing the Scotch and decanting two glassfuls.

"Dunno," he said, "just thought I'd ask." He paused and looked up. "Not celebrating, are we?"

There was a brief silence, then a chuckle as Miller's head went back, and his eyes closed.

"You tell me," he said, "you bloody found the man."

Two hours later, in one of the briefing rooms upstairs, Miller addressed the small squad of men he'd already hand-picked for the operation. Including Charlie, there were four of them, a tight, flexible unit, ASU-size, ideal for what he had in mind. They sat in a loose semi-circle, jeans and T-shirts, and curls of smoke from another of Charlie's roll-ups. They listened intently, occasionally making notes on the Army-issue tear-pads, following his careful exposition, step by step.

He began by sketching in background, the recent main-land bombing campaign, the casualties they'd taken in Chelsea and Oxford Street, the car bomb that had so nearly robbed the Royal Marines of their commanding officer, all of it evidence of careful planning, and decent fieldwork. Over December, he told them, there'd been a lull. Scotland Yard had talked cautiously of a withdrawal, or some kind of home goal. Then, only days ago, the Qualitech bomb, a straightforward assassination attempt, the clearest possible warning that the boys from Belfast were back in business. The mood in Downing Street was, he remarked drily, a little tense. The Anti-Terrorist mob were pursuing certain leads, and with luck they might come up with something before the end of the decade, but now – in the real world – there were calls for a counter-stroke. It was no longer enough to wait. It was time to seize the initiative.

He paused and looked round. All of these men had been part of Nineteenth Intelligence for at least a year. They'd come from the regular SAS battalions at Hereford, and they had no illusions about the glamour of the job. They knew it was nasty, and they knew it was dangerous, but they knew as well that they had a real insulation from the normal chains of command. They had unprecedented freedom of action, and access to whatever firepower they required. They roamed selected areas of the Province, sometimes Belfast, sometimes the smaller towns, sometimes the wild border country down in Fermanagh and South Armagh. Occasionally, they strayed a mile or so into the Republic. Always working undercover, they developed contacts, acquired information, analysed it, and – when the time was right – drew the appropriate operational conclusions. Executing the latter – a burst of gunfire in the hills, a stake-out in Belfast – had rapidly become the Nineteenth's speciality. They fought a war without uniforms, a war without rules, and more often than not, they won.

Miller reached for his mustard-yellow file and took out a sheaf of photocopied maps. Charlie distributed them, one to each man. Miller began to outline the operation, carefully rationing the information, telling these men no more than they needed to know. It was to be a snatch, he said. A man of forty-eight. A top Provo staff officer believed to be in charge of the current England Department. He was to be taken on Saturday afternoon, at a known address, and transported in the boot of a car. He was to be handed over to a special interrogation unit, flown over from London. They would empty him of every particle of information, and afterwards – if there was an afterwards – he'd be put away. If what he heard was true, he said, then yer man was the real thing. The once-in-a-decade breakthrough. The mother lode.

He paused, then directed their attention to the maps. Heads bent. One man, quicker than the rest, whistled softly.

"Dublin?" He sounded incredulous. "Do the locals know?"

Miller grinned at him. "Good question."

Another man looked up, his finger on the black chinagraphed cross on the Dublin street map. "Well?" he said. "Do they?"

Miller shook his head. "No," he said. "The locals know nothing. We're in and out. The money's on not getting caught."

"But what if . . ." he shrugged, "we do?"

"We won't. We can't. The Garda won't wear a joint operation. Not in the middle of Dublin. And higher up it's politically impossible to even ask. So we're on our own. As ever."

There was a long silence while the men absorbed the implications of Miller's cheerful optimism. A couple of hours staking out a farmhouse three or four miles the other side of the border was one thing. A run into Dublin was quite another. They were hardly Bomber Command.

Charlie plugged in a small projector, and loaded it with two slides, while Miller filled in more details. They'd be working in three teams, three separate cars. They'd be leaving Bessbrook at first light, Saturday morning for the two-hour run to Dublin. The cars would have Republican number plates. They'd rendezvous north of the airport in a car-park in Swords. Unit One would drive into Dublin and establish surveillance on the property in question. In all likelihood, the target would already be inside the house. Unit Two would go to the airport and await an inbound London flight. A second target would arrive on the flight and travel to the house under surveillance. Unit Two would follow him. Unit Three, meanwhile, would be in reserve. Miller himself would be part of Unit One. He'd make the decision to snatch the target. The target would be taken in, or near, the house at gunpoint. He'd be drugged, taped, and driven north in the boot of the Unit One car. They'd cross the border on an unadopted road between Castleblayney and Cullyhanna. With luck, they'd be back in Bessbrook in time for supper. He detailed the radio frequencies they'd be using, both primary and secondary, and then he closed the file.

One man looked up. "This address," he said. "How do we know it's kosher?"

Miller looked at him. "Can't say."

"But is it?"

"Yes."

"We're sure?"

Miller hesitated a moment, knowing where a truthful answer might lead. No other Intelligence agencies were yet involved, not even MI5, so there were no cross-checks, no correlation. He simply had to trust his source. He glanced across at Charlie. Charlie was studying his fingernails.

"Yes," Miller said, "we're sure."

There was another silence, the men still looking at him,

the most obvious question of all still unanswered. Miller nodded at Charlie. Charlie switched on the projector, focusing the image on the fading yellow paint of the wall opposite. Heads turned. Eyes narrowed. The first slide showed a man in his thirties, head and shoulders, collar and tie, a large, bony face with a hint of amusement in the eyes behind the thick rimless glasses. The shot was well-lit, and looked official. Miller stood between the men and the wall, inspecting it.

"Name's Leeson," he said briefly, "he's the one on the plane."

He nodded again at Charlie. Charlie changed the slide. Another head swam into focus, quarter profile, a man in his forties, long solemn face, carefully parted hair, possibly in a car, obviously a snatched shot, the detail grainy, the subject – or the camera – moving at speed. Miller let the image register for a full ten seconds. Then he eased into the pool of reflected light, gazing up at the face on the wall.

"This one's the target," he said. "He's the star prize. His name's Scullen . . ." He turned back into the room. "He has a nickname, too. We'll use it to code the operation."

Miller glanced up at the wall again. For a moment, there was silence. Then a voice from the back, the obvious question.

"Well, boss? What is it? What do they call him?"

Miller looked back at them, his eyes narrowed against the beam of light from the projector, his head casting a harsh black shadow against the image on the wall. He began to smile.

"Reaper," he said softly.

BOOK TWO

BOOK TWO

EIGHT

The big four-engined C–130, grey, fat-bellied, Argentinian roundels stencilling the bulge of the fuselage, lifted off from the air base at Comodoro Rivadavia. Wheeling left over the Gulf of San Jorge, it began to climb towards the thin layer of high, wispy cloud feathering the sky above. The Met. Officer at the pre-breakfast briefing had waxed lyrical about the forecast weather. *En route*, he'd said, they could expect light beam winds from the south, and negligible turbulence. Over the target, for once, he could guarantee no cloud cover, and near-perfect visibility. They could run in low, or select a higher altitude, as they wished. As luck would have it, a perfect summer's day.

The C–130 thundered south-east. The engineer served hot, sweet coffee from a Thermos, and distributed small, iced tea-cakes his wife had made specially. Up in the cockpit, the captain donned Air Force issue wraparounds against the glare of the sun, while the co-pilot plotted satellite co-ordinates against the chinagraphed line on the map on his lap. Thirty thousand feet beneath them, the South Atlantic shimmered, deep blue, for once undisturbed by the long swells that normally rolled in from the Southern Ocean.

Two and a half hours later, at a prompt from the co-pilot, the captain eased back the throttles. The black nose of the C–130 began to dip. He eased the aircraft into a gentle left-hand turn. Already, ahead on the horizon, he could make out the low blur of the islands, West Falkland and East Falkland, with a ribbon of silvery water between them.

The engine note changed again, as he began to arrest the descent. At two thousand feet he levelled out, cutting the airspeed to 220 knots, a compromise he'd already agreed with the boys from Buenos Aires, busy adjusting their equipment, way back in the belly of the plane. At 220 knots, they'd have the steadiest of platforms with wide fields of view; while if he had trouble, there was at least seventy knots in hand before the big aircraft was in any danger of stalling. Not that trouble was expected. He'd been tasked for this same operation on four previous occasions. Each time, even at low level, the reconnaissance runs had been child's play. Of the two thousand islanders, *campesinos ingleses*, there'd been very little sign, and the few figures he'd spotted – the odd sheep farmer out on the hills, a handful of shoppers in Port Stanley – had offered nothing more menacing than simple curiosity, their faces tilted up, their hands shading their eyes, arms and fingers stretched upwards, pointing. If it ever came to bullets, the most they could manage would be twelve-bore shot-guns and high-velocity hunting rifles. And that, in a sense, said it all. The Malvinas belonged to Argentina. Restoration, when it happened, would be the merest formality.

The big aircraft dipped a wing, and banked to the right, the four turboprops whining, the compass steadying onto a new heading. The first pass, at two thousand feet, was perfect. The photographers bent to their viewfinders, the greens and the browns of the endless tussocks unspooling beneath them, then the rocky outcrops around Mount Kent and Two Sisters, the long swell of Tumbledown, then the red-roofed bungalows dotting the outskirts of Port Stanley, and the ribbon of tarmac that served as the main street, the ancient Land-Rovers parked untidily outside the West Store, the supply boat from the mainland moored out in the bay. Wheeling left, the Captain took the C–130 north, leaving Port Stanley behind, covering the six miles to the airport in a fraction over two minutes. The airport's single runway was empty. An Aerolineas Fokker Friendship stood on the tarmac in front of the cluster of prefabs that served as the terminal buildings. There was a fuel bowser near by, and further away, a ragged line of single-engined, private aircraft parked beside the airport's only hangar.

Out beyond the airport, the Captain began to climb. He fingered the button on the control column that accessed the aircraft's intercom. They'd want, he knew, a second run, higher, offering a wider view. The planners in the Ministry of National Defence off the Plaza de Mayo liked to work off a single photographic image, high resolution, Port Stanley and the surrounding area, two hundred square miles at least.

He peered down at the islands below. His own taste was for Buenos Aires: people, and restaurants, and the constant buzz of big-city life. There was a potent symbolism about the Malvinas, a catch in the national throat, and he shared it, but he'd need a great deal of persuading to actually set foot on the islands. They were bare, and windswept, and entirely without charm. The weather was awful, and the food worse, and even the sheep were rumoured to be half-crazy. Quite why people lived there at all was beyond him. You had to be British to be that anti-social.

There was a crackle of static in his headphones. Then one of the photographers began to come through. He sounded pleased with himself.

"*Perfecto*," he said. "*Perfecto*. Give us one more run, then we're through. Ten thousand, if you can manage it."

The captain murmured an acknowledgement on the intercom, pushing the throttles forward, easing the control column back, watching the altimeter wind ever upwards. The sun was on his face again. There was, to his certain knowledge, at least another cupful of coffee in the Thermos.

"Ten thousand feet," he confirmed with a smile. "*Perfecto*."

Jude Little was out of traction by the time Buddy returned to the hospital.

He'd come straight from Heathrow on the overnight flight from Boston. He'd slept for an hour or so on the plane, but had spent the rest of the time reading and rereading the articles Pascale had given him. They were difficult going, sure, but the hours he'd put in at the public library had given him the basics, and he could more or less guess the rest.

The theory seemed simple enough. Central nervous tissue from unborn rats had a certain growth capacity that researchers were investigating. It could conduct tiny – but measurable – quantities of electricity. Grafted across dead human tissue in the spinal cord, there was – in theory – no reason why it shouldn't reopen a pathway for messages from the brain. The academic debate had been raging in the States for more than a year. Would it work for human tetraplegics? Or would the body simply reject the grafts? The scientific establishment said it was dangerous nonsense. A handful of researchers said they were wrong. Pascale's contribution was to take the shortest cut of all, and try it out. For real.

The articles Buddy had read were convincing enough. They spoke of real sensory gains, and functioning neural pathways. His tour of the Clinic, too, had impressed him: half a dozen airy, spacious bedrooms, beautifully appointed, for patients under treatment, full physiotherapy facilities, a small heated indoor pool, and an operating suite that looked – to Buddy – the equal of any facility he'd ever seen. The tour over, Pascale had accompanied him to the waiting cab. He'd been scrupulously even-handed throughout, careful not to overstate the prospects, but far from defensive. The three patients currently awaiting treatment, he'd pointed out, had all had similar injuries to Jude's. Their prognosis was awful. They faced the certainty of the rest of their lives in a wheelchair. All Pascale was doing was offering them a second chance. It might work. They might regain a little feeling, a little movement. It was a risk, he considered, worth taking.

Buddy had listened to him, nodding, absorbing it all, standing by the cab, the snow beginning to fleck his denim jacket. Pascale had come to an end, extending a hand, wishing him a good flight back. Buddy had shaken his hand briefly, his brain slightly fuddled.

"But tell me again . . ." he'd said, "what happens if it *doesn't* work?"

Pascale had looked at him for a moment. Then he'd shrugged. "Nothing," he'd said, "which is why you're here in the first place."

Now, sitting on Jude's bed again, Buddy told her every-thing, bending in towards her, trying to share his

112

excitement. Jude listened without comment, and as he developed the story, telling her about Pascale, what he looked like, the way he talked, the sheer confidence of the man, he began to detect a certain disbelief, as if he might not have gone there at all, as if it were some fairy-tale to keep her spirits up. When he started to talk about sensory gain, and the chance of real improvement, she nodded, and abruptly changed the subject.

"Feel my hair," she said.

Buddy did so, reaching forward and running his fingers through her hair. It was clean and light. There were two tiny scabs, dried blood, where the points of the tongs had been embedded in her temples. She looked up at him, smiling, and told him about her first shampoo.

The traction had been off now for two days, and one of the nurses had washed her hair. Her face and neck and scalp were the only bits of her she could feel any more, and this first shampoo in two weeks had, she said, been brilliant. The nurse had taken her time, kneading her scalp, working the lather in, and Jude had watched her hands, smelling the scent of the shampoo, something really expensive. It had smelled of some herb, she'd said, probably rosemary. The nurse had stopped by a chemist on the way in, and bought it specially, a treat. She'd used bowls and bowls of water, deliciously hot, sluicing it all away, and she'd been able to feel the water at the back of her, dribbling down, wetting the sheet, until it got to the nape of her neck, and the feeling stopped. Afterwards, the nurse had used a new towel, lots of nap, rubbing and rubbing, drying her hair, and at the end of it her head had been tingling all over, an almost sexual glow. She looked up at him, smiling.

"So party nights . . .' she said wistfully, "you'll know what to do."

Buddy stroked her hair again, returning to Massachusetts, the Clinic, Pascale. He knew what had happened while he'd been away. Bishop had been at her, at her bedside, telling her what a waste of time it all was, how science had no answers, what a fraud Pascale would turn out to be. But he no longer cared about any of that. He, Buddy, had been there. He'd seen the place, met the man, and as soon as they could raise the money, they'd be on the next plane out. It was worth a shot. It was better than lying there, simply taking it all. They owed it to each other to at least try.

"How much?" she said quietly.

"Eighty thousand." He paused. "Dollars."

She smiled. "We don't have eighty thousand dollars," she said. "Eighty thousand dollars is a fortune."

"We'll sell the house."

"I don't want to sell the house."

"We'll raise a loan."

"On what kind of security? Me?"

"I'll talk to your father."

"I have already."

"And what did he say?"

"He was devastated." She paused. "He says I'll need various aids. Lifts. Special arrangements. He knows about all this stuff. His best friend's son came back in a wheelchair from 'Nam."

"Oh . . ."

Buddy nodded. Jude's father was an executive with a big company in Atlanta, a cautious, practical man with none of Jude's zest. Buddy had met him once. They'd talked about the economics of peanut farming.

"You told him? About Pascale? Me going across?"

Jude nodded. "Yes," she said.

"And what did he say?"

"He said it was fantasy."

Buddy looked at her for a moment. "Shit," he said softly. "He's wrong."

Jude smiled up at him.

"Maybe," she said, "maybe not."

They said nothing for a moment, and Buddy realized that she'd taken charge of the conversation, not wanting to hurt him, not wanting to douse his enthusiasm. If she had arms, he thought, she'd put them round me. He stood up, confused, a little angry, hating this place, every exit blocked. She was still smiling.

"You must be tired," she said.

He shook his head. "No."

114

There was another silence. A nurse walked past and nodded at Buddy. Jude watched her.

"She's the one," she said softly. "Did the shampoo."

Buddy looked down at her, noticing the little scabs of blood again, where the tongs had been. He touched one of them.

"That hurt?"

She moved her head on the pillow.

"No."

"Good to have the thing off?"

"Great."

"What good did it do? They tell you?"

She nodded. "Yes," she said.

Buddy smiled at her. "Well?"

Jude didn't answer for a moment. The nurse came back. She was carrying a flask of urine. Jude coughed, a thin dry noise in her throat. Then she turned her head away.

"Nothing," she said, "it's made no difference."

Leeson was still reading the reports of the latest Argentinian overflight when they told him he wouldn't be going to Washington.

The news arrived with his midday post. It came in a long, white envelope marked "Confidential, Addressee Only". He put the envelope to one side for nearly half an hour while the office emptied for lunch, thinking that it contained news of a different sort about the posting, confirmation of his overseas allowances, information he'd requested about DC accommodation bureaux, more guff on exactly how much he'd be permitted to ship over before he'd have to start paying commercial freight charges. Only when he'd finished drafting the note on the overflight, with its attached photocopy of a long article from the latest edition of *Siete Días*, did he reach over the desk, his mind still elsewhere, and slit open the envelope.

Inside, there was a single sheet of paper. He smoothed it on the desk, one eye still scanning the photocopied article. *Siete Días* was an influential Buenos Aires publication, offering a weekly analysis of political events. It had impeccable sources and was often used to float various government lines, testing them out on an informed readership. The latest article reviewed the negotiations between Argentina and the UK on the Falklands issue. The negotiations, it said, had been effectively stalled by the British. 1982 would be the key year for the recovery of the islands. If the British weren't prepared to talk, then force would have to be used. It would be wholly justified, and entirely the consequence of British intransigence. The military occupation of the Malvinas was a last resort, but the time had come for the issue to be finally resolved.

Leeson reached for a Pentel and highlighted the key phrases. In conjunction with his note on the latest overflight – the subject of the morning's alarmed telex from Government House in Port Stanley – it might, at last, concentrate the appropriate minds. Short of sending a letter of intent, or declaring war, the new administration in Buenos Aires was making the clearest possible noises. The Falklands, they were saying, belong to us. And sooner or later, you'll have to acknowledge it.

He leaned back from the desk, picking up the note from the Confidential envelope, wondering just what difference an American perspective might make to his analysis. Galtieri, he knew, had been in Washington only months ago. He'd had dinner with the Secretary of State for Defense, a comfortable, friendly occasion warmed by a common view of what was best for South America. Galtieri, according to the telegrams from the embassy on Pennsylvania Avenue, had gone down a storm. His particular brand of macho, right-wing nationalism had an obvious appeal to the Reagan honchos, and they'd clearly gone out of their way to make him feel at home. The President's National Security Adviser, no less, had called him "a majestic personality". With endorsements like that, Galtieri would feel immune from international criticism. With the Americans in the bag, nothing could come between Argentina and her precious Malvinas. That, at least, was Leeson's view.

He picked up the Confidential note and read it for the first time. He blinked, glanced round, then read it again, more slowly, letting each phrase settle in his mind. "Contrary to previous indications," it went, "a decision has been taken to withdraw the offer to you of a Grade Four post in the Washington Embassy. Until further notice, you will continue your work in the South American Department at the Foreign and Commonwealth Office. There will be no upward adjustment of your grading or your salary commensurate with the promotion discussed with you at the minuted meeting of 16th September, 1981. Should you now decide to review your position in the Diplomatic Service, you will, of course, be aware of the appropriate procedures. This letter will be placed on your file, and supersedes all other correspondence on the matter."

Leeson read the letter for the third time. It was brutally short. No mention of a reason. No reference to a cut-back in Establishment numbers, or plans for an alternative promotion. No hint of an apology, nor even a note of regret. Just the bare facts, plus a thin-lipped suggestion that he might choose to consider resignation. Washington's off. Take it or leave it. Your call.

He got to his feet and walked to the window. The office was empty, still lunchtime. He gazed out, down King Charles Street, out to St James's Park beyond. It looked bleak and bare, the trees still leafless, a single middle-aged figure, clad in a long black coat, bent against the wind, feeding bread to the ducks. He let his head fall against the window. He felt physically sick, recognizing the letter for what it was, a declaration of war, a long thin finger pointing him towards the door, an invitation for him to do the decent thing and resign before the papers got hold of it, and turned a lifetime's indiscretions into a nasty little scandal.

He thought about his vetting, Miller, how foolish he'd been to underestimate the man, to trust him. Of course they'd known about his social life, his proclivities, his taste for sexual danger and a little pain. Of course they knew about the consequences, the possibility of blackmail, the likelihood of some hideous disease. For all he knew, they might even have acquired the results of the tests he'd undergone, getting the information before he did. God knows, they might even be running the clinic, a modest little investment, even profitable, an early warning radar to spot the

117

unguided missile before it did them – in their estimation – untold harm.

He returned to the desk and gazed down at the note, wondering whether he might, after all, be a little hasty in his conclusions. On the face of it, in terms of strict textual analysis, his career had simply been stalled, parked for a while in this dull, empty office, while someone else was chosen to fill the Washington post, or – just as likely – the post itself fell victim to some cost-cutting directive or other. That was the way it might have gone, forces beyond his control, an individual's chances of promotion counting for nothing against the over-riding need to trim, cut back, save money. If so, he had the right to find out. He could ask for a formal interview, his Head of Department, the Personnel Director in the Establishment Section, whoever else might be able to offer him a little official consolation. That, he had to admit, sounded reasonable enough. There might be a post going somewhere else. They might get him to Washington later in the year. They might even express a little mild regret.

He took off his glasses and sank into his chair at the desk, knowing in his heart that it was fantasy. The gun was loaded, pointing his way. Act the injured innocent, seek clarification, and they'd simply pull the trigger. They knew about him. They knew what he was like, where he'd been, what he'd been up to. He could tell, just by reading the letter, picturing the man who'd drafted it, the curl of the lip, the distaste, the contempt. The phrases he'd used came straight from the deep-freeze, that special pot of formal English they used when the time for communication, for dialogue, for answering back, was over. If nothing else, the last ten years had taught him to read properly, to accept nothing on paper at face value, to hunt for the hidden, undeclared subtext, to understand what the words were *not* saying. He gazed down again. This letter was a small masterpiece of its kind. It informed him of one decision and invited him to take another. As he'd first suspected, he'd no other choice but to tidy his desk, and find out about the pension arrangements, and return his security pass, and go.

He leaned back in the chair again and closed his eyes,

thinking – quite suddenly – of Connolly. The boy, after all, had been right. By the river, that bitter day, he'd simply pointed out the follies of excess. While Leeson had been sword-dancing in the minefield, his had been the voice of gentle moderation. For moderation, of course, Leeson had never had any time. It smacked of compromise, and caution, and that fitful series of false starts most people called their working lives. None of that had ever been for him. He'd been a player, famous for it, devious and charming and full of irresistible mischief. He could drink all evening and still make sense at midnight. He could lay his colleague's wife, with discretion and some skill, and still be godfather to the kids. He could fuck some perfect stranger most of the night, and still not know his name when he left next day. He'd wanted it all, all the time, and now it was nearly over. He folded the letter, slowly, and slid it into his pocket, still thinking of Connolly. He realized he felt unaccountably lonely. He realized he missed the boy.

He got up and reached for his coat. Any minute now, his colleagues would be back from lunch. He wanted, very much, not to be there when they returned. He paused by the door, more clear-headed, more decisive, than he could remember. First, he'd go to the clinic. His results were due, and they owed him a verdict. Then he'd have a drink, and a think, and decide what to do. He buttoned the coat, opened the door, then – as an afterthought – returned to the desk. He picked up his report on the Falklands, with its attached photocopy, and folded that, too, into his pocket. Then he left.

Miller's request for increased London surveillance on Leeson landed on a desk in Paddington Green police station. The desk, and the small office, belonged to a thirty-two-year-old Special Branch officer called Ingle. Ingle, who was easily bored and had a pathological hatred of surveillance work, read the accompanying brief twice and lifted the phone. He dialled a number from memory, straightening a paper clip and picking his teeth while the number went burr-burr in his ear. Finally, the number answered.

"Ingle," he said briefly, "sir."

"Yes?"

"Who's Miller?"

There was a brief pause while the man at the other end, the Inspector in charge of assignments, tuned himself in to Ingle's frequency. The two men had never got on. It was a working relationship that could have been eased with a little tolerance on both sides, but Ingle never believed in taking prisoners. The man was a prat. Always had been. Ingle yawned.

"Miller," he repeated, "he wants the evil eye on a bloke called Leeson."

"Yes, I know."

"Well? Who is he?"

There was another silence, and Ingle leaned back in the chair, his feet on the desk. A promising Christmas had been wrecked by the abrupt return of his estranged wife. For a week now, he'd been thinking about emigration. There was a crackle on the line.

"He's in the military," the Inspector said, "Northern Ireland."

Ingle nodded, his eyes rolling up to the ceiling. He'd got that far himself.

"Which part of the military?"

"Can't say."

"Nineteenth?"

"Yes."

Ingle nodded again, fingering Miller's request form. He'd done a couple of months himself in Belfast, staying long enough to glimpse the kind of jungle that a decade of counter-terrorism had produced. Everyone battling for turf. Everyone at each other's throats. RUC. Military Intelligence. MI5. MI6. Even his own lot, mainland Special Branch, yet another bunch of spooks from over the water. To Ingle, it had been a wonder that any of the Provos ever got nicked at all. Most Brits he'd known were too busy trying to screw each other.

"Nineteenth are cowboys . . ." he mused aloud, "should we be working for them?"

"Not our decision."

"Good question, though." He paused. "Don't you think?"

He waited for an answer, picturing the scene in the busy open-plan office two floors above him, the Inspector at his neat little desk, safe behind a picket of secretaries and photocopiers, the man whose biggest operational thrill was filling in another square on his wall chart.

"Well?" he said.

"Well what?"

"Why should we be running errands for Nineteenth?"

"God knows."

"This bloke Miller know someone? Got pull, has he?"

"Pass."

"Hmm . . ."

Ingle picked up the request form. There were categories of surveillance. The scale ran from one to five. Five was the works: blokes on the ground, complex set-ups at key points, multiple vehicles, fancy radio procedures, the lot. Ingle squinted at the form.

"He wants Cat Two." He paused. "Bit modest, isn't it? For them?"

"Not really."

"No?"

"No. They wanted Cat Four. I said Cat Two was our limit. Bearing in mind the overtime."

Ingle smiled. Recently, budgets had been slashed. The bosses said that it was a purely temporary measure, but Ingle knew different. The economy was shot to ribbons. The country was going to the dogs. He shut his eyes a moment, leaning back in the chair again. New Zealand, he thought. Or maybe Western Australia. Somewhere hot. Somewhere a man could spread his wings.

"Cat Two . . ." he said.

"Yeah. You and Kee." The Inspector paused. "You read the bit about trips abroad?"

"Yeah. If he goes to the airport, we stay on the ground."

"But phone."

"Yeah. Phone."

"With the flight number and the destination." He paused again. "You've got their number?"

Ingle peered at the form again. There was a contact

121

number in the box beneath the carefully typed name. He recognized the Newry STD code. Bessbrook, he thought. Definitely Nineteenth.

"Yeah," he said briefly, "I have the number." He hesitated a moment. "What are we in for?" he said at last. "Only I'm due some leave."

There was a pause at the other end. The board, Ingle thought. He's turning round and looking at the fucking board. The Inspector came back, the ever-patient voice in his ear.

"A week?" he said. "A fortnight? You tell me."

"Thanks." Ingle frowned. "I hate these bastards. You know I do. They think they're in the movies. They're totally out of order."

"You're jealous."

In spite of himself, Ingle grinned. It was the first time in a year he'd heard the Inspector say anything remotely perceptive.

"You're right," he said, "I am."

"Don't be. It's a doddle. The bloke stays in most of the time. He's bent, by the way."

"Oh?" Ingle eyed the form again. "Been there before, have we?"

There was a moment's silence. Then the Inspector was back again, yet another chuckle in his voice.

"Had the haircut yet?" he said. "This month's bath?"

Ingle grinned again. "No," he said, checking his appearance in the window, "gays love a bit of rough."

He put the phone down and stood up. Category Two surveillance was the grimmest news, himself and the new boy, Kee, hours in freezing cars, nothing to read but the paper, nothing to listen to but Radio One. He walked across to the window and stared down the street, wondering about the recent flurry of activity over the water. On the grapevine, he'd heard of other surveillance requests, other agonized conversations about overtime allocations and budgetary constraints. Somewhere along the line, in some way or other, he assumed it was to do with the latest bomb they'd found, down in Basingstoke, the one they'd dug out of the brickwork in the factory she was due to open. He'd read some of the reports. It had been a real stroke, though quite what it might have to do with Miller's lot he didn't know.

He paused, thinking about Nineteenth again. The freedoms they'd acquired were legendary. Ditto, their arrogance. One day, he thought, they'll hit the wall. One day, they'll push it too far. He hesitated a moment longer, thinking about the factory again, how neat it had been, then he shook his head and returned to the desk, lifting the phone and dialling Kee's home number. The number took a full minute to answer. When Ingle asked why, Kee said he'd been asleep.

"I'm on nights," he said drily, "as you know."

"Oh, yeah," Ingle yawned, "I forgot." He paused, reaching for Miller's request form, looking for the target's name again. "We copped the big one," he said at last. "Faggot called Leeson."

Buddy made the call from the pay phone in the hospital lobby. He'd found the number from Directory Enquiries, and worked out more or less what he wanted to say. The number rang a couple of times. Then a woman's voice, on a switchboard.

"Features Department, please," Buddy said briskly. "The people who write the longer pieces."

There was a crackle on the line, more ringing. Then another woman, younger, a little impatient. Buddy introduced himself and explained the situation. His wife was paralysed. Local girl. Ran a riding stables. The medics said she'd never walk again. He'd found a way of proving them wrong. To get her back on her feet, he needed publicity. The right article, in the right hands, might sort out all his problems. Time was short. He needed to get her across pretty soon. Would someone be willing, at least, to listen?

There was a silence at the other end. Buddy had kept it brief, but there was passion in his voice, and anger, and he knew it. He closed his eyes a moment, trying to picture the scene at the other end. He'd never been in a newspaper office in his life. He supposed they got calls like this all the time. Nutters, mostly. Or blokes on the make. The woman came back. She asked him to repeat his name. He did so.

"Buddy?" she said. "As in B-U-D . . . ?"

"Yeah."

Another silence. The whisper of conversation in the background. Then the voice again, the woman.

"Maybe we should meet," she said. "Can you make it into the office?"

Buddy grinned into the middle distance. A man in a passing wheelchair grinned back.

"You bet," Buddy said. "Whenever you like."

NINE

Miller met Charlie, late afternoon, in a car-park in Newry.

Miller had spent the day at Army HQ in Lisburn, attending a debrief on another E4A incident the previous evening. E4A was a specialized RUC unit, current jewel in the Unionist crown, tasked to confront terrorism on its own terms. The RUC guarded its secrets with a passionate jealousy, and the potential for conflicts with outfits like Nineteenth Intelligence were obvious. All too frequently, they found themselves competing for the same touts, running the same agents, and the opposition was becoming ever more skilful at setting the various Intelligence agencies at each other's throats.

The previous evening, a hurried E4A operation had gunned down a youth in the Markets area of Belfast. There was some concern that the youth may well have been on a job for MI5. Miller, with a current operation to protect, had been obliged to attend a council of war. Four hours of argument round a table in a hot, stuffy room at Lisburn had done nothing but confirm his own conviction that the best hits were the ones you kept good and tight, that the real danger lay in inviting other people to your party, that you'd best keep your mouth shut, and your fingers crossed, and your powder dry.

Charlie was waiting by the ticket machine in the car-park. In ten minutes or so he was off down to Dublin to recce the target house, take a quiet selection of surveillance shots, and weigh the chances of implanting a listening device. The latter, a spike microphone of some description, would enable them to monitor conversations inside the house. They'd done it on a number of previous occasions, and it enabled them to gauge exactly where everyone was, at any given moment. More than helpful, if they expected any kind of welcome.

Miller parked his car beside the ticket machine, and got out. Charlie went through the usual motions.

"Change?"

"What do you want?"

"Pound."

"*Pound?*"

Miller fumbled in his pockets. Routines like this were costing him a fortune. He found a pound and gave it to Charlie. Charlie put twenty pence of his own in the machine, and extracted a ticket. He pocketed the pound, claiming that Miller owed it to him anyway.

Miller looked at him, saying nothing. He'd liked the quiet young Irishman on sight. The boy had begun service life in a regular unit, the Irish Fusiliers. Then, a year back, he'd taken the six-month course at Hereford, and had acquired a generous helping of the usual SAS skills. At this point, Charlie had opted for promotion and a return to his regiment in BAOR, but the MoD, impressed by the end-of-course reports from Hereford, had invited him to London for a chat.

As far as possible, the Army tried to keep serving Irishmen out of Northern Ireland but there were talents in this young captain which deserved, in their estimation, specialist application. For one thing, he had the perfect Republican camouflage: an Irish childhood, a soft Galway accent, even a modest command of Gaelic. For another, he had a real gift for acting, the kind of personal diffidence that made it easy to shrug on another man's clothes, another man's accent, another man's beliefs. For a third, he was – as far as anyone could reasonably determine – entirely without fear. At Hereford, in the end, they put it down to physiology. Charlie, wrote the training sergeant, had the lowest blood pressure of anyone he'd ever met.

For Miller, the boy was already irreplaceable. He had brains, and limitless courage, and a real talent for the war of shadows they fought every day of their working lives. Charlie's appearance and his manner – the roll-ups, the pony tail, the drawers full of T-shirts – suggested a refugee from the late sixties. But all of that was a blind. Because Charlie had come up with a stream of ideas, and the best of them – the counselling clinic in West Belfast – had tapped a very rich seam indeed. He now commuted to the city twice a week. He rented a small, bare room over a launderette in a street off the Springfield Road. He'd befriended the local GPs, and showed them his CV, his degree in psychology from London University, and offered them a service they could no longer provide themselves. He would be available, he said, simply to listen. Patients for whom medication was a waste of time. Housewives who were simply at their wits' end. Teenagers who couldn't cope any more. Men whom the Troubles were turning inside out. These people he could offer an hour or so each week, no charge, total privacy. He could give them sympathy, and attention, and try and return them to their families a little stronger, a little more intact. The doctors, most of them, had leapt at it. It was, they said, a wonderful initiative. Charlie was *accessible*. He was the right age. He had the right qualifications. The right temperament. Even the right religion. They called him a Counsellor, and with a glad heart they sent him patient after patient, the richest source of raw intelligence anyone had yet had the wit to locate.

Thus, through one of his patients, the first warning about Leeson. Charlie had spotted the potential there, straight off. He'd seen what use the man might be in the right hands, and he'd run the operation ever since. That was how they'd got to Reaper. That was how they'd flushed the man out.

Now, Charlie looked at Miller and smiled. "Well, sir?" he said. "You've news?"

Miller shook his head. Moments before leaving Lisburn and driving south, he'd checked again, by phone. "Nothing," he said.

"No booking?"

"No."

"Not even provisional?"

"I've told you. There's nothing on the computer. The BA people have checked twice. Same for Aer Lingus."

Charlie nodded. "It's Thursday," he pointed out. "Leeson's due Saturday."

127

"I know," Miller smiled. "He'll turn up. I know he will."

Charlie looked at him a moment, then shrugged. "OK," he said, "as long as you're sure."

He hesitated a moment, then peeled the sticky grip from the back of the parking ticket, and stuck it on the front of Miller's raincoat. What could, in most armies, have been insolence, was – instead – a gesture of quiet affection.

"They've a fierce wee warden here," he said, "you'll best not get caught."

Connolly sat in the back of the plane, waiting for the stewardess to answer his call. They'd been airborne now for nearly ten minutes. The coast of County Down was behind them, the BAC I-II still climbing through heavy cloud, the rain beating on the windows, Ulster's eternal farewell. In an hour, they'd be landing at Gatwick. From Gatwick, he'd take a series of trains to Carshalton, his parents' house, his neat little suburban childhood, shelter from the growing storm. He'd phoned them from Aldergrove Airport. His mother, surprised and delighted, said she'd find something special for supper.

The stewardess walked down the aisle towards him. On midday flights, he knew, they didn't automatically serve alcohol. Oblivion was strictly on request. He asked for a large Scotch and soda. The stewardess reached over and cancelled his call button. He watched her walking back down the aisle, bodychecking slightly as the plane hit turbulence. A woman in the next row reached for her husband's hand. His head turned towards her, and Connolly could lip-read the conversation, the husband reassuring his wife that everything was OK. He wondered, for a moment, whether it was true. And if it wasn't, then whether or not he really cared.

He'd spent two days sharing his life with a brown envelope full of twenty-pound notes, and the growing conviction that events were fast spooling out of control. His academic work had all but ceased, his lectures delivered from the remains of last year's notes, his voice barely rising above a mumble, the essays of his small tutorial group returned late,

scarcely marked. Evenings, when normally he'd take the
bus up to Mairead's, help with the supper, put the kids to
bed, watch telly together, stay over, he now spent by himself,
locked inside the bare, empty flat, dreading the footsteps
that paused on the pavement outside, the shadow falling
over his curtains, the brisk tap-tap at the door.

A prisoner of his own making, he retired early, creeping
into the tiny bedroom at the back, climbing into the narrow
iron bed, listening for hours to the steady drip-drip of the
cistern overflow outside his window. From time to time,
down towards the City Centre, there'd come the familiar
howl of the police sirens, or the ambulance, or the fire
brigade, and he'd close his eyes, and picture the buses over-
turned in the road, the flames licking up round the big, fat
tyres, the litter of half-bricks and broken milk bottles.
Images from the early seventies, images he knew were
largely out of date, were returning to haunt him. Kids with
Armalites. Hooded faces over open graves. Belfast, once the
perfect setting for an ambitious young historian with an
interest in the twilight of Empire, was fast becoming a nightmare.

The stewardess returned with a miniature of Scotch and
a tin of soda. He decanted the whisky over the ice cubes in
the clear plastic beaker, and added a similar measure of
soda. The whisky torched the back of his throat, making his
eyes water. Tasting it, he thought once again of Leeson.

He'd tried to phone him twice during the day, home
number, but there'd never been a reply. In the evening,
once, he'd ventured down the street, using the pay phone
in a busy bar on the corner, preferring the swirl of other
people's conversation to the terrible isolation of the phone
box on the Ormeau Road. Using the phone box, after dark,
was an open invitation. He'd be exposed, perfectly lit, the
easiest target of all. Whoever they were, they'd get him.

But Leeson hadn't been in the night he'd phoned, and
hugging the shadows on his way back to the flat he began
to wonder whether he'd already left for Washington. It was
possible, certainly; some sudden change of plan, an earlier
summons than he'd been expecting. But Connolly knew as
well that the results of his medical tests were due any time,

and even Leeson would see the merits of waiting to find out exactly what was wrong with him. Those results might mean a great deal to Connolly, too, and so in the end he'd decided to fly anyway, blowing sixty quid on a one-way ticket to Gatwick.

He sipped the whisky, rehearsing it all in his mind again. Travelling on a Thursday would give him two nights and a day to get Leeson to Dublin. Quite how he was going to do it, he didn't know. Maybe he'd dress the thing up, pretend it was a trip to see an old friend, appeal to his sense of adventure. That, of course, would hardly prepare the man for the meeting itself, for an hour or so with the cold, pale face he'd met across the table, but it would at least discharge his own obligations. His duty done, Leeson delivered, he could safely return to Belfast, and Mairead, and the oh-so-simple life he dimly remembered from last year, before Christmas, before Danny's alleged friends shattered the fantasy, and everything had gone black.

He pondered the plan. He'd no idea what would happen to Leeson, what they'd do to him, but he didn't anticipate violence. Whatever they had in mind presumably depended on Leeson remaining in one piece. Who knows? Maybe he'd even enjoy it.

He gazed out of the window. They were up at cruising height now, the late afternoon sun slanting down on the tops of the clouds beneath them. He felt better with the whisky inside him, warmer, more optimistic. Maybe he'd simply tell Leeson the truth. Tell him everything. Tell him what had happened, Mairead, her dead husband, their own long courtship, his need for her, his longing, the way she made him feel. Maybe that was the answer. He considered the proposition for a moment or two then shook the memories away. Leeson, he knew, was a realist. He had no use for fairy-tales.

The plane dipped a wing, and began a long, slow descent, in towards London. Connolly glanced out of the window, as the cloud reached out for them, parting in a blur of white. For the first time, he wondered whether he'd ever go back to Belfast again, whether it might not be wiser to simply draw a line and rule it out of his life. Then he remembered the man in the front of the Cortina, inspecting his driving licence in the light from the glove box. He'd made a note of the Carshalton address. And he'd smiled, handing the licence back.

Connolly shook his head slowly, draining the last of the Scotch. The rain was smearing the window again, and the turbulence was back.

Leeson sat in the clinic, one leg crossed over the other, waiting for a verdict.

He'd taken the tests ten days earlier, largely at Connolly's prompting. They'd helped themselves to two separate blood samples, the inner surfaces of both forearms. They'd excised tiny chunks of skin from the raised, purplish blotches on his chest. They'd poked around the glands in his neck and armpits where he'd complained of pain. And they'd taken a careful history of his sexual encounters, partner by partner, covering half a dozen sheets of foolscap paper with the answers to their endless questions.

Now, alone in the consulting room, he waited. He had no idea what had been wrong with him, and a week of feeling much better had quickly persuaded him that he was probably cured. But the purple rash was still there, the strange blotches, and the last couple of days he'd begun to suspect that they were spreading. What that meant, God only knew, but he'd had another call from his American friend, and the news was far from cheerful. The poor man was back in hospital. By the sound of his voice, he'd aged a decade. The doctors had stopped answering his questions. They said they'd done everything they could. At the end of the call, he'd begun to cry. "I'm dying," he told Leeson, "I know it." At the time, Leeson had put the tears down to stress and the man's appetite for dramatic gestures. Later in the day, though, he'd been sufficiently alarmed to phone the clinic and remind them of the phone number of the New York hospital where his friend was being treated.

Now, Leeson thought about the American again, and the implications of this last conversation. Personally, he'd never had the least interest in immortality, preferring massive

131

helpings of the here and now to any prospect of life after death. Nor had the realities of dying ever bothered him. On the contrary, it always seemed an utterly mundane business, no different – in essence – to any other function. You ate. You drank. You made love. You took a shit. And one day the whole Godforsaken routine came to an end.

He'd watched his own father die, sitting at the bedside with his mother, holding her hand, trying to comfort her, wondering quite what his father made of it all. He'd had cancer of the liver. He was very thin, especially hollow around the eyes, permanently tired, but utterly cogent. Towards teatime, one afternoon, he'd yawned a couple of times, and peered at the clock on the bedside cabinet, and then laid his head on the pillow. "God, I'm bored," he'd said, shutting his eyes. At this stage, his mother had left the room to prepare a little soup, and it was a good half-hour before anyone realized that the old man had died.

So that was it. When your train was due to leave, they blew the whistle, and banged the doors shut, and that was it. No dramas. No bedside speeches. Nothing spectacular. Just an old man's face on the pillow, the flesh tinged yellow, the eyes shut, the train gone. His father had played the scene well. He'd rather admired him for it.

A door opened across the room and a doctor appeared. She was young, and serious, and her face told Leeson every-thing he wanted to know. She was preparing the ground. She sat down and put a foolscap pad on the desk in front of her. She looked uncomfortable. She cleared her throat. Leeson smiled at her.

"Cancer," he suggested, making it easier for her.

She looked at him in surprise.

"Yes," she said. "How did you know?"

"I didn't. I guessed."

She nodded.

"It's skin cancer," she said quickly, "not as serious as you might think."

"Oh?"

"No." She glanced down at the pad. "We call it Karposi's Sarcoma. It's very rare, but perfectly curable."

Leeson nodded, looking at her, thinking about it.

"Is it catching?" he said. "Can you pass it on?"

The doctor bit her lip a moment. Then she pulled the pad towards her and fumbled for a pen in the top pocket of her white coat.

"This cough you had . . ."

"Yes?"

"Did it hurt at all? When you coughed?"

"Yes."

"Did you get breathless?"

"A little, yes."

She nodded, writing down the answers. She sucked the top of the pen. Then she looked up.

"Have you had diarrhoea at all? Bad diarrhoea?" Leeson shook his head.

"No," he said.

"How about thrush? Do you know what thrush is?"

"No," Leeson said again.

She explained the condition quickly, a fungal infection in the mouth and throat. Leeson began to shake his head, but then he remembered a time, back at the end of the summer, when he'd awoken with a thick white coating on his tongue. It had tasted slightly metallic. It had stayed with him for nearly three weeks. At the time, he'd thought nothing of it. Now, he nodded.

"Yes," he said slowly, "last year."

The doctor nodded and bent to the pad again. Leeson watched her writing.

"I asked you a question,' he said. "I asked you if this . . . thing . . . was catching."

The doctor's hand paused on the pad. She looked up. "We don't know," she said. "That's the truth."

"But you'd have an idea?" He paused. "Or a name for it?"

She nodded. "I told you," she said, "Karposi's Sarcoma."

"Does that cover it all? The cough? The white stuff?"

She blinked at him, slightly discomfited by this strange man in the newly pressed suit, the eyes behind the glasses, his refusal to accept the normal reassurances. She shook her head.

"No," she said slowly, "it doesn't."

Leeson smiled at her. "Gay plague?" he said. "Does that ring a bell?"

She nodded. "It might," she said, "if we knew what it was."

There was a long silence. She began to write again, checking her watch for the date. Leeson looked at her for a while, then cleared his throat.

"You'll have talked to the people in New York," he said. "How's my friend?"

The pen hesitated for a moment, then began to move again. She didn't look up. "He's dead," she said quietly. "He died last night."

The newest member of the Foreign Office Planning Group was a young Third Secretary called Diane. Diane was one of Whitehall's new-style diplomats, products from the provincial universities, first-class degrees, first-class brains, and an urge to confront the old certitudes. Small, neat, slightly shy, she'd met Leeson twice, once at a diplomatic reception, and once in a queue in the Foreign Office canteen. On both occasions, they'd talked for perhaps five minutes, and she'd been intrigued enough to enquire further. From what she could gather, he was clever, original, and a bit of a maverick. On all three counts, she rather liked him. He was, she told her best friend, a bit of welcome exotica.

He phoned her about four in the afternoon. She was sitting at her desk, having trouble with a rock cake.

"Diane . . ." he said, "it's Francis Leeson. I'm at a restaurant called the Mandarin. It's in Poland Street. I'd like you to come and meet me. Take a cab."

She was about to laugh, to protest, to tell him she was a third of the way through an important briefing paper, deadlined for midnight, when he hung up. She gazed at the phone, still buzzing in her hand. Then she carefully blotted the ink on her handwritten draft, reached for her coat, and headed for the door.

Ten minutes later, a cab dropped her outside the restaurant. Leeson was sitting at a table in the window. He was still wearing his coat, a thick black cashmere. He raised a hand to her, nodded a greeting, and got up as she stepped in through the door. She hung her handbag on the back of her chair. There were two glasses on the table, and a large flask of wine. The flask was nearly empty. She sat down. Leeson looked at her. The rest of the restaurant was empty. He didn't seem remotely drunk.

"Thank you for coming," he said, sinking into his chair again, and tucking his coat around him. "It was kind of you."

She nodded, not knowing quite what to say. She unbuttoned her coat and crossed her hands on her lap, feeling faintly uncomfortable. Leeson leaned back in his chair. He made no attempt to offer her what remained of the wine. Instead, he took a thick sheaf of paper from his pocket and laid it carefully on the table between them. She glanced at it. There were two pages of type and what looked like a four-page photostat. The photostat had come from a magazine. Even upside down, she could see it was in Spanish. Leeson followed her eyes.

"Do you read Spanish?"

"A little."

"Well enough to understand?"

"Depends. What is it?"

Leeson showed her the article from *Siete Días*. She scanned it quickly, picking up the salient points, following the drift of the argument, upwind, to where it stopped.

"The Malvinas," she said, looking up.

Leeson nodded. "Yes," he said, "we owe them. And they know it. And soon they're going to take them back."

He sat back in his chair, and she looked at the article again, wondering where all this could possibly lead, the empty restaurant, the distant waiter, half of Chinatown tramping home past the window outside. Leeson began to talk, utterly cogent, offering her his analysis, names and dates, key meetings, other excerpts from other magazines, the Brits throwing sand in the wheels at the UN, the Argentinians no longer hiding their impatience, the muted call for a military solution, and finally today's little surprise: the C–130 criss-crossing East Falkland, sophisticated photoreconnaissance, a prelude to invasion.

135

"You know what you're saying," she said. "That would mean war."

Leeson nodded. "Exactly."

"You think they'd do it?"

"Yes."

"You think they *will* do it?"

"Yes."

There was a long silence. Then the obvious question.

"So why me?" she said. "Why this?"

"Because it's your job to get us off the hook," he said. "The regular machine doesn't work that way. We don't expect it to. We're too close to it all." He shrugged. "We look for order, of course. Patterns. Coherence. A bit of sense. But mostly it's bits and pieces. Business. Memos." He smiled at her. "And the odd bottle or two."

There was another silence. He asked her if she'd like a drink. She said no. She looked him in the eye.

"What we do is confidential," she said, "you know that."

"Yes."

She nodded, still not quite sure of herself, still missing a piece of this strange conversation. Leeson sensed it, hunched in his coat on the other side of the table. He leaned forward, very slowly, very carefully. He looked older than she somehow remembered, that last time, in the canteen queue.

"In confidence?" he said.

She looked at him, surprised, then nodded.

"Of course," she said.

Leeson studied his hands for a moment. What he had to say might sound theatrical but in his heart he knew it was probably true. No real evidence. No proof. Just the deepest, and most instinctive, of convictions. He looked up.

"I suspect I have a terminal disease," he said. "The diagnosis is confusing but the outcome is quite clear. Under the circumstances, I felt I owed you five minutes of my precious time." He smiled thinly. "And yours."

He sat back. She looked at him for a moment, and then said she was sorry. He shrugged the thought away, genuinely indifferent. She looked at him for a moment or two, making up her mind.

"You'll be relieved to know there is a plan," she said at last.

Leeson nodded. "I'm glad to hear it," he said. "What does it comprise? Exactly?"

She hesitated a moment, leaning in towards the table, lowering her voice.

"A Task Force would be organized. It could put to sea in sixty hours. Possibly sooner."

"How many ships?"

"A handful. To begin with. More later."

"Capital ships?"

"At least two."

"Purpose?"

"Deterrent."

"Big stick?"

"Exactly. A public display. Television. Radio. The press. For Argentinian consumption."

Leeson nodded slowly. There was relief in his voice, but surprise as well. Organizing a Task Force wouldn't be easy. Especially in a country where even the trains had trouble leaving on time. He frowned.

"Who dreamed up this . . . plan?"

"Our Lordships. The Naval Chiefs of Staff. They have no doubts that it's viable." She smiled. "In fact they're rather proud of it."

"And the Cabinet?"

"Officially . . ." she shrugged, "they welcome the provision. But then they would. Plans cost nothing. Paper's cheap. As you know."

"And unofficially?"

"They don't give it much thought. They think Galtieri's bluffing. They think he's a reasonable man. At least they assume he is. Either way, they can't see him rocking the boat. He'll get the islands in the end. All he has to do is wait."

"For the Islanders to change their minds?"

"Precisely."

"They won't."

"I know they won't," she said. "And so does he."

There was a silence. Leeson ran a finger round the rim of his glass, then licked it. "So what happens next?" he said.

"Galtieri will help himself."

"And?"

"A war will start."

"And?"

"And . . . ?" She looked at him, conceding the point, a weary smile. "My sailors will get your politicians off the hook."

Leeson nodded slowly, returning the smile. "I think you're right," he said slowly. "Thank God for your sailors."

It was nearly six o'clock by the time Connolly got to Victoria Station. The trains from Gatwick had been delayed by a signals failure. Before he took another train out to Carshalton, he phoned Leeson. Maybe they could fix to meet.

Leeson picked the phone up on the third ring. He sounded distant, a strangely hollow voice, not the usual drawl.

"It's me," Connolly said. "How are you?"

He heard Leeson laugh. "Fine," he said, "under the circumstances."

There was another silence. A black woman with two kids was waiting patiently for the phone. Connolly looked at the meter. Ten pence left.

"Listen," he began, "we ought to meet . . ."

"Come round."

"Now?"

"Yes."

Connolly glanced at his watch. His mother was fussy about mealtimes. After eight o'clock, she'd be less than cheerful. He hadn't seen her for nearly five months. Spending Christmas away hadn't gone down well. He began to make his excuses, to suggest that they meet tomorrow, for lunch, but half-way through he realized it was pointless. Leeson had hung up.

Connolly took a cab to Chiswick. Leeson opened the door at once. He smiled a welcome, standing aside as Connolly stepped in. At once, he noticed a difference about the place.

It was clean. It smelled fresh. Someone had been tidying up.

They walked through to the sitting room. Leeson waved Connolly into a chair. Connolly looked round. The room had recently been redecorated, a quiet regency stripe, not unpleasant. Connolly offered his compliments. Leeson shrugged.

"The agent organized it," he said, "not my doing."

"Agent?"

"I was going to rent the place out."

"Of course." Connolly frowned. "So what's the matter? Have you changed your mind?"

Leeson said nothing for a moment, then told Connolly about the Washington job, the news he'd received that morning, his career hitting the buffers with a jolt. He limited himself to the facts. No bitterness. No self-pity. Just another awkward day at the office. Quite possibly his last. Connolly was appalled.

"So where do you go from here?" he said. "What happens next?"

Leeson smiled thinly and disappeared into the kitchen. He returned with a bottle of red wine and a corkscrew. He uncorked the bottle and poured the wine into two thin-stemmed glasses. Connolly tasted the wine. It was Rioja. Leeson was sitting across from him, his favourite armchair. He cupped the wineglass in his hand, saying nothing at first, gazing down at it, then he cleared his throat and began to tell Connolly about the visit to the clinic, his twenty-odd minutes with the woman in the white coat, what she'd said, what it might mean. When he'd finished, he looked across at Connolly.

"They don't know what's wrong," Connolly said. "It could be some virus."

"Of course."

"And they'll treat you for it."

"Yes."

"Get you better again."

"Yes."

"Get rid of the rash."

"Hmm . . ."

139

Connolly looked at him, slightly irritated by his deadpan tone of voice. "You don't believe me?" He paused. "Is that what you're trying to say?"

Leeson smiled, one finger circling the top of his glass. "What I'm trying to say," he said slowly, "is sorry."

Connolly shrugged again. He was glad Leeson had been to the clinic. It was, after all, his idea. But his own tests had all been negative. Nothing wrong at all.

"What are you sorry for?" he said.

"For putting you . . ." Leeson frowned, searching for the word, "at risk."

"But I'm not at risk."

"No." He smiled again. "Let's hope you're not."

"You think I am?"

Connolly looked up. Leeson was watching him, perfectly still in the chair, and for the first time he began to feel worried.

"My American friend is dead," Leeson said at last, "and he had exactly the same symptoms as me."

"But you said you've got better."

"I have. I feel better. Much better."

"Then you're cured. You've got over it. It's gone away."

"That's what he said."

"Who?"

"My American friend. When he first phoned me."

"And?"

"It came back again." He paused. "He had other friends . . . lovers, out on the west coast . . ." He paused again. "Evidently two of them are dead as well."

Connolly looked at him for a long moment, beginning to understand. Then he closed his eyes. "Oh, shit," he said softly.

They sat in silence for a while, listening to the low hiss of the gas fire. Then Leeson changed the subject and told Connolly again about the letter he'd received, the abrupt withdrawal of the Washington job. He mused on the irony of it all, a single day putting paid to his career, and leaving a large question mark over the rest of his natural life. He'd had fresh news about the Falklands, though, and that had offered some modest consolation.

Connolly listened to him, trying to forget his own anxieties, letting the wine envelop him. The room was warm, and somehow friendlier than he ever remembered. Leeson, too, seemed a changed man. The old acid, the old mockery, had gone. In its place – within the space of a handful of hours – was an odd, slightly wistful, detachment, an acceptance of the facts that displaced any other emotion. He didn't seem angry, or bitter, or even afraid. On the contrary, Connolly had rarely seen him so benign, so sympathetic. The wine in the glass at his elbow was barely touched. For the first time, their conversation appeared to be leading somewhere other than bed. The man was sorry, and he meant it, and he wanted – if possible – to make amends. Not to put the clock back, to pretend somehow that nothing had ever happened. But to shift the relationship onto a new basis. Simple friendship.

Connolly, watching him, listening to him, could scarcely believe it. Getting the man to Dublin might, after all, be a simpler proposition than he'd thought.

Leeson reached across with the bottle and recharged his empty glass. He'd been talking about money. He wanted to make a will. Under the circumstances, he considered it a useful precaution. He put the bottle on the table beside his chair. His own glass was still full.

"So . . ." he said. "Do you want your money now? Or later?"

Connolly shook his head, told him to keep the money. Leeson shrugged, asking him what else he'd like. Connolly studied him for a moment. Then swallowed another mouthful of Rioja.

"There's a man in Dublin I'd like you to meet," he said simply. Leeson looked up.

"Oh?"

Connolly nodded. "I don't know his name. But I know where he lives. We'd fly out on Saturday morning. You'd be back by Saturday night. I'll take care of everything."

Leeson considered the proposition for a moment. "Do you want to tell me why?" he said.

Connolly hesitated. There was a long silence. Then he looked up. "No."

"Is it important to you?"

"Very."

There was another silence. Miles away, a church bell chimed the hour. Nine o'clock. Connolly remembered his mother, sitting by the stove, nursing the remains of supper. He'd meant to phone her, but hadn't. Leeson smiled at him, lifting his glass for the first time.

"OK," he said, "let's do it."

TEN

The three cars from Nineteenth Intelligence left Bessbrook Barracks at dawn on Saturday. Miller and Charlie rode in the first car, a VW Scirocco. Two other men travelled behind them, a newish Vauxhall, red Republic plates. A blue Ford Escort, with a single driver, brought up the rear.

The convoy travelled south, towards the border. Five miles short of Dundalk, they split up, putting distance between them, the third car slowing. They tested the comms, using a very high frequency waveband on the specially installed dashboard sets, carefully disguised to resemble any other car radio. The call signs had been agreed at the final briefing the previous evening. Like the Provisional ASUs, they used cab language on the air, wary for the chance listener, scanning the airwaves, listening in. Unit One was "One Zero". Unit Two was "Two One". Unit Three was "Three Two". Reaper, the primary target, was referred to as "The Fare". While Leeson, the mystery guest from London, was "Yer Man". The street outside the target house was called "The Rank", and a successful snatch would, logically enough, be registered as "a confirmed pickup". In the unlikely event of an abort, Miller would radio "Out of hours" to the other units.

Miller and Charlie, Unit One, crossed the border at eight fifteen. The main Belfast–Dublin road was already busy, trucks mainly, and Charlie settled the VW to a steady sixty. He'd driven back from Dublin only the previous evening with a roll of shots of the target house. Developed in a small darkroom at Bessbrook, the best of the photos had been distributed at the briefing. They showed a modest detached house, single storey, with a dormer window. There was a small garden between the front of the house and the road,

143

and a concrete driveway up the side. The windows at the front of the house were heavily curtained, and there was a newish Ford parked outside. Thick hedges shielded the house from the neighbours on either side. Charlie had toyed with installing a spike microphone and a tiny radio transmitter, driving the spike mike in beside a window frame, or through an air brick, but a cautious recce after dark had left him no wiser about exactly which room was most often occupied, and in the end he said he'd decided not to risk it. Better to rely on surprise and firepower than hazard the operation before it had even begun.

Now midmorning, the three cars met at Swords, a small town ten miles north of Dublin. They parked in separate areas of the municipal car-park, meeting for breakfast in a small café next to the town's supermarket. Charlie bought a copy of the *Irish Press* and studied the afternoon's racing, while Miller outlined elements of the attack plan for the last time. Like Charlie, he was dressed in workman's overalls, frayed at the collar, splashed with paint.

They were, he said, slightly ahead of schedule but there'd be no problem soaking up the time. Special Branch surveillance in London had just confirmed that Leeson had left his home in Chiswick and taken a cab west, out towards the airport. With him had been another man, younger. Special Branch had accessed the British Airways computer and found a name. The name was Connolly. The Dublin flight was due to land at twelve fifteen. Unit Two should be in position thirty minutes in advance. With the airport five minutes down the road from Swords, they'd have ample time to recce the Arrivals hall and assess the best place to park the car. Leeson would either be picked up or take a taxi. At all costs, they were not to lose him.

The snatch itself would take place seconds after Leeson entered the target house. That way, they could take advantage of the diversion his arrival would create. Charlie would come in through the back. Miller and Thompson, the back-up in Unit Three, would take the front. Unit Two would stand by to receive the target. The target would go into the boot of the Vauxhall. With the usual hoopla, and a little luck, they'd be in, out, and away within a minute or so.

The men around the table nodded, stirring demerara into their coffees, trying to avoid the thin curls of smoke from Charlie's second roll-up. The men had drawn weapons the previous evening. There was a machine-gun, a Heckler and Koch MP5, clipped beneath the dashboard of each car. There were stun grenades, and smoke grenades, and a modest allowance of plastic explosive for emergencies. In addition, each man carried a handgun of his personal choice. Most opted for the standard issue Browning 9mm Parabellum. Thompson, the back-up, preferred a revolver, a Smith and Wesson .38 with minor modifications to the barrel and firing mechanism. Miller had often queried the choice – too heavy, too slow – but the man had shrugged off his doubts. The Smith and Wesson, he said, had simply had a bad press. For serious money, he'd drop a row of bottles, in bad light, at twenty metres. In the right hands, there was no better weapon.

Now, leaving the café, Thompson fell into step beside Miller. Ahead of them, pushing an overloaded supermarket trolley, was a woman doing her weekly shop. She walked slowly, rolling her hips. She had a child in one arm, and used the other hand for pushing the trolley. Thompson shook his head. He was a Cockney, East Ham accent, eternally cheerful.

"Magic," he said.

Miller looked at him in surprise. The woman must have been eighteen stone. Thompson grinned and patted his shoulder. He kept the gun there, in a holster he'd treasured for half a decade.

"The Smithie," he said, "the fuckin' shooter."

Leeson and Connolly landed at Dublin Airport at three minutes past twelve, slightly ahead of schedule. Ten minutes later, they were off the plane and queueing for Immigration. The officer behind the desk glanced briefly at Leeson's diplomatic passport and waved him through. Connolly caught him up by the baggage carousel. Neither man had checked anything in.

Leeson looked at him, a glance of enquiry. Connolly had

picked him up in a cab at eight in the morning, having made peace of a kind with his mother in Carshalton. Leeson had been ready and waiting, bathed and shaved, dressed in brogues and a pair of old flannel trousers and a favourite tweed jacket over a blue denim shirt, and a darker blue tie. There was a Burberry folded over his arm, and he carried an umbrella. Watching him from the cab as he stepped carefully out of the house, pulling the front door shut behind him, testing the lock, Connolly recognized at once how he'd decided to play it. The day would be an adventure, a treat, a rather special excursion. They'd have a plane trip, and something nice to drink. They'd meet one or two interesting people, and doubtless spend an hour or two in some restaurant or other, and then – in due course – they'd come home.

On the plane, Leeson had sat by the window, nursing a gin and tonic, reading the *Daily Telegraph*. As Connolly had sensed, he was perfectly relaxed, perfectly content. Not once had he asked for details, for names or a briefing, or some small clue as to what they might be doing. He owed the boy a favour or two, and if settlement meant the day in Dublin, then so be it.

Now though, standing by the carousel, there was a decision to be made. He beamed at Connolly.

"So," he said, "what next?"

Connolly looked round. He had the map from Mairead in his pocket, and plenty of money for a cab, but he somehow expected something else to happen. They were far too well organized to simply leave him to it. Soon, now, someone would make an approach.

He glanced round the busy concourse, spotting the Customs exit in the far corner. He nodded towards it, setting off, Leeson walking behind. They went out through the green channel. On the other side, in the Arrivals hall, there was a small crowd. Some of the people in the crowd held up cards with names on, Irish names, O'Dowd, O'Leary, Flynn. He scanned them quickly, stopping, giving whoever might be waiting a chance to register his presence.

In the corner, beside a pillar, a man in his middle twenties recognized Leeson's face. He gave the trolley he was guarding a gentle push, and stepped towards the door. The white Vauxhall was parked across the access road, double yellow lines, engine running, bonnet up. The driver was bent over the engine, facing the airport building, screwdriver in his hands, eyes on the door. He acknowledged the signal with a nod, and closed the bonnet.

Connolly and Leeson crossed the Arrivals concourse, heading for the door, and the taxi rank outside. A woman intercepted them. She was in her early twenties, attractive, well-dressed. She had a clipboard. Attached to the clipboard was a biro on a piece of string. Connolly looked at the biro. The biro was empty. She smiled at him.

"Mr Connolly?"

"Yes."

"My name's Maura."

She smiled again and led them out of the building. They paused on the kerbside. A hundred yards away, a dark blue Datsun flashed its headlights and pulled out onto the service road. Connolly watched it accelerating towards them, signalling right, slowing to a halt at the kerbside. There were two men in the front. The woman opened the back door and Connolly and Leeson got in. The door closed. The car drove off.

Across the road, the white Vauxhall pulled out behind it, tucking in behind, twenty yards back, the passenger in front already bent to the radio, confirming contact.

In the Datsun, Connolly watched the airport buildings disappear as the car swung left towards the main dual carriageway, the road into the city centre. There was no conversation in the car, no words of welcome, no names, no clues, just the backs of two heads, men in their late twenties, early thirties, one well shaven, the other with a day or two's growth of beard. Connolly looked up at the driving mirror. From where he was sitting, he could see the driver's eyes, flicking up, time and again, checking behind, watching.

At the dual carriageway, he signalled right, in towards the city. There was a gap in the traffic. The driver did nothing, waiting until a big truck was barely twenty yards away, then abruptly pulled out, tyres squealing, revving the engine hard, working the gears, ignoring the angry blare of air horns only feet behind. Connolly glanced at Leeson. Leeson, imperturbable, was gazing out of the window, his Burberry folded in his lap, his umbrella wedged between his knees. He might have been on a church outing. He looked utterly content.

The car accelerated away, 60 m.p.h., 70 m.p.h., then settled back. Connolly looked up at the mirror again. The eyes were still there, still watching, but there was something else, too, the beginning of a frown. Connolly looked back, through the rear window. The truck was a dot in the distance. In the inside lane fifty yards back, was a white Vauxhall. It had red number plates. There were two men inside. He frowned, turning his head again. They were a hundred yards or so from a roundabout. The Datsun slowed, then joined the traffic on the roundabout. Connolly braced, expecting to exit at the second turn, in towards the city centre, but the Datsun stayed on the roundabout, circling it twice. On the second circuit, even Leeson looked surprised. Connolly glanced over his right shoulder. The white Vauxhall was still with them. For the first time, he began to feel the old taste in the back of his throat, the dry lips and the long slow sinking feeling, stomach in his boots, events running out of control.

The two men in the front were talking now, low voices, half-sentences, coded exchanges that made little sense. The man in the passenger seat half-turned. He had a young, swarthy, pockmarked face, the acne clearly visible under the growth of beard.

"There's belts," he said to Connolly. "You'll be best off using them."

Connolly located one end of a seat belt, wedged between his body and the door. He found the other end, and clipped in. Leeson, slower, did the same. They were still circling the roundabout. The driver looked up in the mirror. The beginnings of a smile narrowed his eyes.

"OK?"

Connolly nodded assent. The driver checked the mirror again, indicated for the next left, ignored it, then accelerated hard at the following exit. The Datsun began to slide across the road, but he checked it quickly, a deft flick of the wheel and a stamp of brakes, before he dropped another gear and accelerated again. They were moving fast now, 60 m.p.h., plunging into the heart of a housing estate. There were blocks of flats, five or six storeys high. Cars half-parked on the pavements. Kids on bikes. The driver worked the horn, scattering the kids, urging the car past 80 m.p.h., setting himself up for a long, shallow bend to the left. The back began to slide again, but he let it go, knowing the worst of the bend was over, trusting the camber and a solid burst of third gear to sort the car out.

After the bend, the road narrowed, running straight for half a mile between rows of small, shabby, semi-detached houses. The houses flashed by. Thin, bare hedges. Abandoned trolleys. The odd dog. The driver was checking his mirror again. Way back, in the distance, the white Vauxhall was emerging from the bend. At the end of the straight, the road angled sharply to the right. The driver left his braking late, the car shuddering under the discs, then dipping quickly to the right, the offside wheels losing adhesion, the car beginning to tip. Connolly grabbed Leeson. Leeson looked at him, amused. Then they were round the corner, and the car was level again, the smell of rubber and burning oil.

Fifty yards down the road, there was a gap between two houses. The driver wrenched the car left, no warning, mounting the kerb, crossing the pavement, relying on sheer speed to cross the ten yards or so of soft, rain-soaked grass before they were onto beaten earth. Over the scream of the engine, Connolly could hear the sound of rubble and broken glass beneath the wheels as they bumped across the waste-land and pulled hard left again, over the pavement, and back onto a road.

The car accelerated, tyres screaming. Then, quite suddenly, the estate had gone, and the road had widened, and they were amongst larger houses, walled gardens, pedestrian crossings, and a long set of railings encircling a park. Connolly lay back in the seat as the speed dropped. He looked round, checking the road behind, wondering whether he might, after all, avoid throwing up. The road behind was quite empty. Of the white Vauxhall there was no sign. He turned round again, checking the eyes in the mirror, curious about the noise from the front. The noise was strange, unexpected, not part of the scene at all, and it took him several seconds to work out exactly what it was. The eyes were narrow again. The noise was laughter.

Twenty yards up the street from the target house, Miller bent to the message from the white Vauxhall.

"Yer man's away," the voice said. "We lost him."

Miller acknowledged the call with a single touch on the transmission button, then sat there, gazing down the street, hardly believing it.

"Shit," he said quietly.

Charlie glanced across at him. They'd been parked in the street for nearly two hours. During that time there'd been plenty of movement, dads ferrying kids around, wives away for the weekly shop, but nothing of interest from number 112, the target house. The curtains remained drawn. The Ford was still outside. Nothing came and went.

Miller bent to the radio again. "Units Two One and Three Two," he said, "stand by."

He paused, biting his lip, peering back at the target house. Whatever else he did now, he knew he had to move quickly. They'd never have lost Leeson unless they'd been spotted. If they'd been spotted, the word would be passed. He'd no idea what comms they used, but three years in Belfast had left him with a healthy respect for their operational tradecraft. The best of them, he knew, rarely got it wrong. Miller glanced at Charlie again. Charlie, with some foresight, had carefully folded his paper and stored it in the side pocket.

"We'll take him now," Miller said, "we have no choice."

Charlie nodded. "OK," he said simply.

Miller bent to the radio. "Unit Two One," he said, "you're off the clock." He paused. "Unit Three Two. The fare at number 112 picking up now."

He waited a moment while both units acknowledged the message. He could imagine the atmosphere in the Vauxhall, the two men stony faced, heading back north, putting the best gloss on it, getting some kind of story straight. He leaned back in the seat, easing his Parabellum out of the shoulder holster, checking the breech.

The third car, the blue Escort, appeared at the top of the road and cruised slowly past them, Thompson at the wheel, ignoring them completely, parking two houses down from number 112. Miller looked at Charlie. Charlie started the engine and eased the car into a careful three-point turn. Then he coasted down the road, stopping opposite number 112.

Miller opened the plastic bag at his feet. The bag was full of stun grenades for close quarters work. They produced a deafening explosion, but no real danger of permanent injury. He gave three to Charlie.

"Only if we have to," he said. "Nothing flash."

Charlie nodded, but said nothing. They both put on gloves, tight black leather. For the first time, Miller realized he was sweating. He reached back and retrieved a big canvas holdall, the kind used by plumbers and carpenters. He put four stun grenades and his own gun inside, leaving the top open for easy access. He looked at Charlie for the last time. Then they both got out of the car, two workmen, calling at the wrong address.

They walked across the road, Charlie whistling, Miller carrying the canvas holdall. They pushed in through the creaking gate. Miller could hear the Escort's engine starting again, and the whine of the transmission as it slowly backed up towards the house. Miller and Charlie paused on the front path. Miller glanced across at Charlie, and nodded at the narrow line of paving stones that led to the side of the house. Charlie did his bidding, strolling towards the side entrance, gazing up at the paintwork, assessing the job. Miller gave him a moment or two to step through the wooden gate at the side, hearing the Escort stop on the other side of the front hedge. Then he stepped towards the front door, high profile, wide open, wondering how many eyes might be watching.

He rang the door bell. Nothing happened. He rang again, and then a third time, cursing the sudden change of plan, the risks he was forced to take, the lives he was putting at stake. Finally, deep in the house, he heard footsteps. He lifted the canvas holdall, frowning, the frown of a man who's suddenly realized he might have forgotten something vital. He began to rummage in the holdall, shaking his head, hearing the scrape of bolts, and the creak of an unoiled hinge as the door swung open, then the gun was in his hand, and his body was down at the half squat, and the hand was way out in front of him, the big black muzzle of the Parabellum, his other hand down in the bag at his feet, feeling for the stun grenade. He paused for perhaps a tenth of a second. An old man was standing in the doorway. He must have been eighty. He had a round face, and wispy grey hair, and a pair of ancient horn-rimmed glasses. He had a hearing aid, and his body was bent over a walking stick that had seen better days. He wore an old cardigan. He stood in the doorway, blinking in the low winter sunlight.

"Yes?" he said blankly.

Miller pushed inside. The house smelled faintly of breakfast: bacon and burnt toast. In the kitchen he found an old woman in a chair. There was a cat in her lap. She was trying to knit. Back in the hall, he met the old man again. The old man was peering at him. Then he turned and opened the door to the living room at the front of the house. Miller stepped quickly past him. The room was empty, a heavy, dark, well-furnished room, with brocade curtains and a huge brass fender around the fireplace. The walls were lined with framed photographs, mainly portraits, heavy-set men in suits and ties. Over the mantelpiece was an oil painting. It showed a large chamber, lined with benches, crowded with men, one or two on their feet, makers of speeches, passers of laws, legislators, politicians. For the first time, Miller began to feel uneasy. He turned to the old man.

"Who else is here?" he said, not bothering to disguise his accent.

The old man gazed at him, his mouth catching up with his eyes.

"My son," he said.

"Where is he?"

"Upstairs." He put a hand on Miller's arm. "Careful now," he said, "the boy's ill."

152

Miller nodded. Back in the hall, he mounted the stairs. A single door faced him. He turned the handle. It was locked. He took a step back, and kicked it in. There was a splintering of wood, then a roar of anger from the other side. Miller stepped into the room. A man of about forty was sitting up in bed. He wore a T-shirt and a cardigan. There were a pile of books by the bed. He looked at Miller, the gun, the overalls, the eyes. He didn't seem remotely frightened. And he definitely wasn't the target in the briefing photos.

"Who the Jesus are you?" the man said.

Miller looked at him for a moment. Downstairs, there was a deafening explosion. Miller turned, taking the stairs at the run. There was smoke everywhere. Then Charlie emerged from the living room.

"Some old man," he said briefly. "On the phone."

Miller looked at him for a moment, the anger flooding through him, the certain knowledge that they'd been set up, that they'd stepped into a neat little trap, and turned a mistake into a disaster.

"Out," he said softly. "Get out."

The two men ran from the house. Miller paused briefly at the kerbside while Charlie sprinted for the VW. The Escort's engine was still running. Thompson was bent over the open boot, the car between him and the house, waiting. Miller could see the gun in his hand.

"On yer bike," he said.

"What's the matter?"

"Wrong fare."

Thompson looked at him, pure disbelief. Then he pocketed the gun, slid into the driving seat, and accelerated away. Miller watched him go. The boot was still wide open.

The blue Datsun eased off the main road, drove slowly up the long drive, and came to a halt outside the hotel's main entrance. The whine of taxiing jets was clearly audible from the airport, barely a mile away. The driver glanced over his shoulder. He looked pleased with himself. He nodded at the big, revolving doors, and Leeson followed his gaze. What

153

he could see of the hotel lobby was dominated by a huge chandelier.

"Interesting drive," he said drily, "I take it we've arrived."

The driver's smile widened. "My pleasure," he said, "gentlemen."

Connolly and Leeson released themselves from the seat belts and got out. The girl they'd met at the airport appeared from the revolving doors. The clipboard had gone.

"Mr Connolly," she said.

Connolly nodded. He felt like the man from Federal Express. "This is Mr Leeson," he said, "I think he's expected."

The girl smiled, but said nothing. They followed her inside. The hotel smelled of money. The carpets were thick, and the porters' uniforms were brand new, and even the flowers looked real. The girl led the way across the lobby, towards the lift. Connolly glanced at Leeson. Leeson, he could tell, approved. He was back in his element. Decent hotel. Proper service. People who obviously understood what they were doing. They got in the lift. The girl pressed the button for the fourth floor. She was wearing a wedding ring, third finger, left hand. She had nice nails, no varnish. The lift whirred upwards, stopped. They got out, following the girl along the corridor, to a room at the end. Connolly made a mental note of the number. 416.

The girl paused for a moment outside the door, knocked twice, and went in. Connolly and Leeson followed. The room was large, a sitting room, well furnished, acres of carpet, full-length windows, and a small balcony beyond. There was a drinks cabinet, a television, a couple of deep armchairs, and a three-seat sofa. By the window was a round table. At the table sat the man Connolly recognized from the evening at the cottage. He got up. He was wearing a plain dark suit, with a dark green tie. Except for the tie, he might have been dressed for a funeral. He extended a hand to Leeson. It was the first time Connolly had seen him smile.

"Mr Leeson?"

Leeson nodded. "The same," he said softly, the diplomat's tilt of the head, the slightest touch of flesh on flesh.

154

The man at the table looked across at Connolly, no hint of recognition, no word of welcome, no thanks. "There's a meal for you both downstairs," he said, "in the dining room."

Connolly looked at the table. The table was set for two: full dinner placing, two kinds of wine glass, a basket of fresh bread rolls, generous swirls of butter. He glanced across at Leeson, marvelling at the man's composure. He looked flattered and pleased, the distinguished guest, duly impressed by the scale of the hospitality.

Maura, the girl, touched Connolly lightly on the arm and led him back towards the door. As they left the room, he could hear the man in the suit inviting Leeson to take a cocktail, a quite different tone in his voice to the one Connolly remembered, respect as well as authority.

Connolly and the girl returned to the ground floor. In the hotel dining room, they shared a table next to the window. Outside, there were peacocks strutting between empty flower beds, and a croquet lawn, ready mown, waiting for spring. At the girl's insistence, they ordered wine, a good Chablis, which they drank between courses while she told him about Dublin, the sights, where to go, what to eat, where best to see the real city, the Dublin they never told you about in the brochures.

Dazed by it all, by the wine, and the food, and the starkness of the contrast with the last time, out in the country, the gun on the table, the chill in the man's eyes, Connolly did his best to keep up. Once or twice, Maura hacking at her Beef Wellington, he tried to prise a little of the truth from her, what they were here for, where it might all lead, but the only answer he got in response was a warm, practised smile, and yet another enquiry about the Irishness of his own name. Sure now, he might indeed have come from Clonmel. There were a thousand Connollys down in that part, so there were, and a beautiful part it was too. Connolly listened to it all, letting it wash over him, knowing only too well that the day had slipped out of his control, and that his sole remaining duty was to survive it.

Over coffee, an hour and a half later, Leeson appeared in the dining room. He was unescorted, quite alone. Of his host, there was no sign. He paused by the table, and beamed down. He'd clearly enjoyed himself.

"OK?" Connolly said blankly.

"Extremely civilized."

"Finished now?"

"I suspect so."

The girl organized a cab to the airport. There was no bill for the meal, no cash, no credit card. The cab arrived within five minutes. The girl escorted them both to the hotel lobby. She might easily have been a tour guide, the luxury end of the market, real class. At the kerbside, she extended a hand.

"Thanks," Connolly said.

"You're welcome."

They got in the cab. Looking back, Connolly answered the girl's departing wave with a limp movement of his right hand. Only an hour later, twenty thousand feet over the Irish Sea, did he finally coax any sense from Leeson.

"So what did you talk about?" he said. "What did he want to know?"

Leeson toyed with the last of his complimentary cashews, and took another sip from his second Scotch and water.

"In the end," he said, "or to begin with?"

"Either. Both."

Leeson smiled, gazing out of the window.

"In the beginning there was the usual nonsense. The kind you'd expect. Bombs in briefcases. Access. Names. You know what I mean . . ." he trailed off and yawned. "Not my game, really. I think he understood that."

"So what did you discuss? Afterwards?"

Leeson's head sank back against the seat. The eyes were half closed.

"Afterwards?" The smile softened. "Afterwards, we talked about the Falklands. He was a perceptive man." He looked at Connolly. "He understood it all."

"Did he?"

"Yes." He licked the last of the salt from his fingers. "The folly. The blindness."

"And does that . . ." Connolly frowned, hunting for the right word, "matter?"

Leeson said nothing for the moment. Then he reached for

156

the Scotch and emptied it at a single gulp. "I don't know," he said, wiping his lips.

ELEVEN

Miller held the post-mortem the following day, Sunday. It was a private affair, just the five men on the unit, the ad hoc team he'd put together to lift the man they called the Reaper, and bring him safely home for supper. In theory, it had seemed the simplest of operations, a clean, surgical incision, the heart torn out of the Provo's Away Teams. In reality, as he now knew, it had been a disaster.

He'd received the worst of the news past midnight, back at Bessbrook, on the secure line to London. The home they'd targeted had belonged to a Mr O'Donovan. Tommy O'Donovan had, in his time, been a leading Fianna Fail politician on the Dublin City Council, highly respected, much loved. His son, Kieron, had inherited his father's mantle, and now represented his City ward. He still lived with his parents, and had been housebound for the last week or two with a bad attack of flu. There was one other fact about the O'Donovans Whitehall had thought worth a mention. Both father and son were implacably opposed to the Provisionals and seized any opportunity to say so.

Sunday morning, a grey day, Miller recited the facts without comment. The men sat around him, on the hard, grey, Army-issue chairs, studying their hands. They'd all got back to Bessbrook after dark. They'd had a few drinks. They'd not said much. And then they'd drifted away and gone to bed. Now, one of them looked up, Thompson, the Cockney, Unit Three, the only man to drive through central Dublin with his car boot wide open.

"So what happened?" he said.

Miller looked at him. There was nothing in his face to suggest that he hadn't slept for over thirty-six hours. "What happened to who?" he said.

"The old man. Tommy O'Donovan."

"He died."

Thompson blinked. "You stiffed him?"

"No," Miller said drily, "Charlie blew him up."

Thompson whistled softly. "Nice one," he said.

Charlie was staring at Miller. "You're joking," he said. "It's a joke."

Miller shook his head. "No. He had a heart attack. By the time they got him to hospital, he was dead."

"Natural causes?"

"Hardly."

Charlie nodded. He began to roll a cigarette. Miller watched him, the long fingers working the shreds of tobacco along the thin tube of Rizla, the slightest tremor as he lifted the paper to his lips, licked one edge, reached for his matches. Then he looked up, his face clouded in tobacco smoke.

"So the old fella's dead," he said. "Is that the worst of it?"

Miller shook his head. "No. The son's raising hell. He's got a story about wild Brit soldiers. Some kind of hit squad." Miller paused. "He has credibility, this man. His own people believe him. Potentially, it's . . ." He shrugged. "Explosive."

"And what are London saying?"

"London are denying all knowledge."

"What about the evidence?"

"What evidence?"

"The stun grenade. What's left of it."

"Ah . . ." Miller sighed. "I gather we're awaiting the forensic. When they give us the details, then we'll be able to confirm where it came from."

"Where did it come from?"

"Part of a consignment that went missing," he smiled thinly, "last week."

"Ah." Charlie nodded. "Clever."

"Obvious."

"Will they believe it?"

"Probably not. But that doesn't matter. That's not what really bothers me."

Miller paused and got up. He walked to the window. Outside, it had begun to rain. He turned, and looked at them all. Unit Two, the heroes in the white Vauxhall, had already been debriefed. They'd offered no excuses. The guys in front had simply got the better of them. They'd taken every risk in the book, and they'd driven like maniacs, and they'd been lucky. At those kinds of speeds, in that kind of area, they'd had a choice between maintaining their cover, or keeping up. Not that there was any cover left to blow. The blokes in the blue Datsun had spotted them from the off. The interesting question, the real question, was why.

Miller leaned back against the window sill, the word echoing in his skull. He'd lived with it all night. Soon, he had to find an answer. Otherwise, Whitehall might get there first.

"So," he said to Charlie, "why . . . ?"

"Why what?"

"Why did we go to number 112."

Miller looked at Charlie. Even within Nineteenth, even within this room, just the five of them, sources were sacrosanct. If you were wise, you never told a soul where your information came from. When you found a source, you kept him strictly to yourself, your tightest secret. You gave him money, and bought him drinks, and nurtured him, and won what little confidence he had. He became your friend, this man. You had a pact, mutually acknowledged. He kept his ears and eyes open, and went along with the plot, and told you everything he knew, and in return, you offered him protection. That meant total anonymity. No names. No photos. Not one single clue.

The system was far from perfect, but when the information was kosher, the facts correct, then everyone was happy. Now, the information was dud. They'd been sent to the wrong house. And in the wrong house, they'd played it like infants, doing the opposition a grand favour, disposing of one of their sternest critics. The results, an old man dead, his wife and son in mourning, were already in the Dublin papers. Soon, there'd be the makings of a scandal. For public consumption, the Brits would doubtless shrug the incident aside – black propaganda, yet another spoiling raid by avenging Provos from the North – but that was hardly the point. The point was that he, Charlie, this protégé of his, had found himself downwind of the Reaper.

The Reaper was the man they'd been after for nearly two years. He had a name now, and – all too briefly in a suburban Dublin street – an address. At least there'd been a way to get at him, to lift him, to knock him off the plot. Only the Reaper, somehow, had spoiled the party. Instead of a thirty-second snatch, and the Intelligence windfall of a decade, they'd been had. Their target had vanished. The Reaper had gone. Why?

Charlie looked up at Miller. His roll-up had gone out. "You're saying I should have checked the place out? Gone to Special Branch? The London boys?"

"No."

"That's what I thought." He paused. "They might have told me, though. They might have known who really lived there."

"I'm sure. But then they'd want in. All of them. Death or glory."

Charlie nodded. "That's what I thought," he said, "that's why I – " he shrugged " – played it the other way."
- He frowned and studied his fingernails. Then he looked up, resigned.

"Listen," he said, "there's someone I ought to talk to."

Miller looked him in the eye. "You're right," he said, "and quickly."

The man they called the Reaper left Dublin on this same Monday morning in the passenger seat of a newish Ford Escort.

Beside him, at the wheel, was McParland, his bodyguard. By noon, they were crossing the rich flatlands of Carlow and Tipperary. They took a light lunch at a fish restaurant in Limerick, and continued south-west, towards Tralee and County Kerry. By dusk, they'd arrived at their destination, a small modern bungalow overlooking the sea at Caherdaniel, on the Ring of Kerry. Here, they would meet three other members of the Army Council, newly arrived from Belfast.

161

With the mainland campaign beginning to falter, Scullen knew that the time had come for a fresh initiative. The Army Council, like the rich multinationals it affected to despise, had little patience with failure.

Bumping down the narrow track towards the bungalow, Scullen gazed out at the sudden expanse of ocean, thinking again of Leeson. He'd spent the weekend pondering the consequences of the diplomat's visit, their lunch together, what the man had told him, the things he'd left unsaid. He'd sensed at once that the intelligence was genuine, no plant. He'd recognized the anger that lay behind the easy diffidence, the man's impatience and contempt for the politicians he was paid to serve. They're like barnacles, he'd said. They're brainless, and gutless, and they'll do anything to cling to power. In the South Atlantic, to no one's surprise, they'll soon be facing a war. The war will be short, and nasty, the outcome almost impossible to predict.

The word had stuck in Scullen's mind. War. It left no room for ambiguity, or argument. The Argentinians, Leeson had remarked over the oysters, will push and push. Because we don't take them seriously, we'll leave them no option but to invade. After the invasion, we'll protest. There'll be the usual exchange of ultimatums. Then we'll go to war.

They'd discussed the notion for a while, two middle-aged men with a decent bottle of wine and a mutual appreciation of the absurdities of it all. Scullen had asked about details, scenarios, and Leeson had warmed to his theme, describing the plans for the Task Force, the Queen's writ carried to the bottom of the globe by a handful of warships and a couple of thousand troops. It would, he'd said, be a last spasm of gunboat diplomacy, the final twitch of the Lion's tail.

At first, listening to Leeson's acid exposition, Scullen had found the story difficult to believe. Would the Brits really go so far for half a dozen islands and a couple of million sheep? Hadn't the new Nationality Act just *denied* the Falkland Islanders the right to carry a British passport? But the more he listened, the more he understood Leeson's central thesis. That the coming war would be fought not to defend any great principle, or any vital slice of national interest, but to keep the ruling clique in power. He'd made the point several times, letting the mask slip, leaning in over the table. Sending a Task Force, he'd said, would get them out of the hole they'd dug for themselves. It would demonstrate decisiveness, iron will, the triumph of good over evil. It would proclaim those two great principles: patriotism and the rule of law. It would raise the debate above narrow party advantage. It would overshadow the real story of inertia and incompetence and sheer blind folly. It would line the country up against the forces of darkness, and it would look marvellous on television.

The last phrase struck Scullen with some force. The mechanics of the operation would call for air cover and the landing of a sizeable expeditionary force. That meant aircraft carriers and amphibious assault ships. Both kinds of warship were based in Portsmouth, and it was from Portsmouth – therefore – that the Task Force would probably sail. It would, Leeson remarked, be a rare pageant. Crowds would line the harbour walls. There'd be tiny kids, waving their fathers goodbye. There'd be young wives, stalked by the terrible prospect of widowhood. There'd be flags in the wind, tears and farewells. There'd be bands on the decks of the departing warships, and the country's finest, dressed to attention, at the rail. The lump would rise in the national throat, and the images, live on television, would be beamed round the world in seconds. It would be grand opera, scored for Queen and country. It would be the photo-opportunity of the decade.

Scullen had nodded, saying very little, giving nothing away. How, he'd wondered at the end, would the crisis now develop? How would the world get the first real clues that Leeson's careful fantasy was in some danger of coming true? Leeson had shrugged, toying with his coffee. It was now, he'd said, very simple. The players were in place. The orchestra was warming up. The curtain would shortly rise. For anyone with an interest in getting to their seats in time it was only necessary to buy a national paper. One day soon, the Argentinians would invade. Leeson's best guess, given the circumstances, was May. But it might well be sooner.

Scullen had noted the date, and now, the car bumping to a halt outside the bungalow, he realized again what a profitable weekend it had been. Leeson's thoughts on events in the South Atlantic were, to say the least, provocative. But there'd been the other business, too. The cowboys from Nineteenth stepping mob-handed into the little house in Garville Street. Giving the boy, Connolly, the address had been an elementary bluff, and to be frank he was astonished that the bait had been taken. That alone said a great deal about the state of the Brit Intelligence services, always at each other's throats, always battling for territory and advantage. But it meant something else, too. It meant that someone, between Thursday night in Belfast and Saturday morning in Dublin, had talked to the Brits. News of the address had got out. They'd been ready and waiting. Quite who that someone might be was still a matter of conjecture, though the obvious candidate was Connolly. Soon, they'd have to pull the boy in. Soon, he'd have to answer the harder questions. For now, though, he had a battle of his own to fight.

Scullen got out of the car and smelled the clean salt air. The tiny bay, perhaps a mile across, was dotted with bungalows, recent constructions in rendered breezeblock, each with its own half-acre or so of carefully tended garden. The climate was mild down here, and stuff grew well, and even the garden at his own place, the farmhouse he'd bought, ten miles inland, up in the mountains, was already thick with early spring flowers. He paused a moment, wondering whether he might not have done better down here, on the coast, with a view of the ocean. But then he remembered the handful of nights he'd already spent at the farmhouse, camping in the empty rooms, Handel and Bach on the radio cassette player he carried everywhere, the wind in the chimney, the view down the valley into the last of the sunset, and he knew he'd made the right decision.

He pushed in at the gate and walked up the path towards the bungalow. Like most of the places in the bay, it had been built as a second home. It belonged to a prosperous businessman from up in County Longford, a republican sympathizer who owned a string of garages, and it was on open loan to the Movement for occasional meetings, and the odd spot of enforced convalescence.

Scullen rang the bell, smelling already the peat from the fire. The door opened, the familiar smile, and the tight, curly hair, and the bright intelligent eyes behind the thick glasses. The Chief of the General Staff was, as ever, wearing battered old corduroys, and the same plaid shirt, and a cardigan of the kind that even Dunn's had given up stocking. He grinned at Scullen and pumped his hand.

"You did famously," he said, "famously. Come in. Tell us the heap of it."

Scullen stepped into the living room. The room ran the length of the bungalow, kitchen at one end, open fire at the other, the big picture windows making the most of the view. There was a table, and a couple of sofas, and scatter rugs on the polished wooden floor. There were good quality water-colours on the walls, and a big, red-framed corkboard hung over the worktop in the kitchen. The corkboard was covered in bits and pieces – photos, cartoons from local papers, a tide table, shopping lists, kids' drawings, layers of cheerful family graffiti that accumulated every summer. Scullen had never met the man who owned the place, but he'd been in the bungalow twice before, and he felt that he somehow knew him. From the snaps on the corkboard, he was a big man, with a belly, and a holiday beard, and a passion for deep-sea fishing, and a face full of mischief. The face, and the cottage, were a world away from Belfast.

Scullen accepted a mug of tea and sat down by the fire. Besides the Chief, there were two other men from Belfast. He knew them well, and he told them exactly what had happened in Dublin, the raid on the house in Garville Street, Tommy O'Donovan, Tommy the Tout, expiring at the cough of a Brit firework. They enjoyed that, old scores settled, one enemy seeing off another, the neatness of it, and they enjoyed, too, what Scullen could tell them of the car chase, concluding – like him – that the rendezvous must have been blown between Belfast and London, and that their young Belfast academic probably knew how. The conversation went on for an hour or more, and at the end of it

– curtains pulled against the darkness, more turf on the fire
– the Chief turned at last to the real issue.

"So," he began, "this man of yours, your diplomat, what
does he do for us?"

Scullen took his time before answering. Then he gave
them the meat of the conversation at the hotel, filleting it
of unnecessary detail, confining himself to the raw facts. The
Brits, he told them, were shortly going to war. The war
would begin with the dispatch of a Task Force. Probably
from Portsmouth. Probably in May. The Task Force would
sail south, and try and recapture the Falklands Islands from
the Argentinians. Historically, it would be an anachronism.
The expedition would belong to another, colonial age. As
such, it perfectly suited what he had in mind.

There was a silence in the cottage. The wind sighed softly
in the chimney breast. The ocean lapped the rocks at the
foot of the field. The Chief, like the rest of them, looked lost.
"So," he began, "this man of yours, this diplomat; why
interest? What's in it for us?"

Scullen shrugged at the question, and the men in the
room knew at once that he considered it naïve. "He's nicely
placed," he said, "and he has a fine sense of history."

The Chief leaned forward. The bonhomie, and the smiles,
had gone. "Does he have access?" he said.

Scullen nodded. "Yes."

"But I thought you said he'd resigned?"

"He has."

"Then what use is he to us?"

Scullen looked him in the eye. He'd inherited from his
predecessor a certain degree of independence. Over two
busy years, he'd enlarged these freedoms, protected from
his enemies by the very man he now faced. The Chief trusted
him. The Chief watched his back. But the Chief's patience,
clearly, was far from inexhaustible. Now, he put a careful
hand on Scullen's knee.

"Padraig," he said. "We want her dead. I thought you
knew that."

"I do. Of course, I do."

"Then why are we fucking about with some burned-out
diplomat? What is he to us? Does he sleep with her? Read

166

her stories at night? What's so special about the fella? Justifies all this?"

He withdrew his hand, and Scullen crossed one knee over the other. The others were watching him closely, and he knew it. As long as he carried the Chief with him, everything would work. But once the Chief was lost, he'd be dead in the water. He gazed at the fire for a moment or two.

"I agree," he said at last, "we're after killing her . . ." He paused. "But believe me, humiliation will hurt her more."

There was a long silence. The Chief, like the rest of them, was waiting.

"So what *do* you have in mind?" he said at last.

Scullen gazed at the floor for a moment. Then he offered a rare smile.

"We sink one of the Brit ships," he said, "live. On television."

There was a long pause. Then the Chief began to laugh. Good crack.

"Sure," he said, "and how in God's name do we do that?"

Scullen looked at him. The smile had gone.

"I don't know," he said. "But I'll find a way."

The local Southampton paper published the article about Jude Little that same evening.

Buddy read it at home, sitting alone in the kitchen, preparing a pot of hummus to take to Jude the following morning. He cooked for her regularly now, shipping up baskets of her favourite foods in the back of the Jaguar. He enjoyed the work, the challenge of it, the pleasure it gave her now that she was off the powdered foods. It was something positive, something real, a way forward.

He bent to the article, sitting on the kitchen stool, stirring a pot of boiling chick peas. He'd met the journalist only three days back, before the weekend and had waved away her offer of a fifteen-minute interview in the office in favour of a restaurant meal, with fresh pasta and glasses of good Chianti while he told her everything. He told her the story in outline first; then in detail where it seemed to matter. She'd been genuinely interested, he was sure of that, and in his gruff, direct way he'd made a reasonable job of getting the important bits across. What appealed most was Jude's age – still in her early thirties – and the fact that she was well known in riding circles around the Forest. The journalist herself had heard of her – she had a friend who was taking lessons – and she nodded when Buddy talked about Jude's personality, her sheer physical zest, and the appalling prospects that lay before her, now that most of her body was dead.

"I know," she said, "I can imagine."

At this, Buddy warmed to his theme, drawing on this two weeks at the Regional Unit. Spinal injury, he told her, always cut down the ones who had most to lose. It took the guys in the very middle of the rugby scrum, the bravest gymnasts, the highest divers. In Jude's case, it had been a riding accident, not her fault, some bloody dog, but those three or four seconds, a blink of time, had put her on her back for the rest of her life. Where was the justice in that, he asked her. And what would any bloke, any husband, not do to try and get her back on her feet?

The journalist had nodded, agreeing, writing down the odd phrase of Buddy's. Her own boyfriend, it turned out, was a sports parachutist. The stunts he pulled scared her stiff, and she'd make sure he read the piece and understood what it meant. She couldn't tell exactly how long that piece would be, and she'd have to be careful about saying too much about the American neurosurgeon, but she'd already got the go-ahead from the Features Editor, and the piece would definitely make the paper. All she needed now was a recent photo of Jude, and a forwarding address for any correspondence.

Buddy had queried this latter point. Did articles like these get a big response? Did people write in with cheques? Postal orders? Offers of limitless help? The journalist had smiled and said there were no guarantees. Sometimes it worked. Sometimes it didn't. She'd include the fact that he was appealing for funds, and he'd simply have to wait and see.

Now, the lid on the saucepan, he finished the article. It was longer than he'd expected, a good half-page. It was headed "Unlucky Break", and there was a blow-up of the photo he'd found: Jude on Duke, a year back, when they'd trailed the horses down to Dorset and ridden all afternoon on the cliffs east of Weymouth.

He read the text of the article. The girl had woven in most of his best quotes, taking out some of the anger, underlining the pathos. She'd pointed out the obvious paradoxes – men walking on the moon and coming back to tell the tale, a lady falling off a horse and never lifting a finger again – and she'd wondered why it was that medical science couldn't cope. She'd said that Jude would be back home soon, and that her husband planned to take her to America for a pioneering operation. She explained that the operation might not work, but that it involved no life-threatening risks. She used the word "miracle" a lot, but reminded readers that miracles didn't come cheap. Buddy Little was trying to raise $80,000. Readers might think him a gutsy bloke for trying. It was as simple, and as bold, as that.

Buddy read the article again. There were a couple of paragraphs about his own background, and the girl had gone into some detail about the tough, seasoned ex-Navy diver who'd faced the worst the North Sea could offer, yet couldn't come to terms with his wife's paralysis. That seemed to Buddy to be stating the obvious, but it gave the piece an added poignancy of sorts, and he imagined that was the way they always did it. Maybe it was more effective with a bit of flannel. Maybe that's what it took to get people to reach for their cheque-books. On the pavement, outside the restaurant, Buddy had asked her how soon he could expect any kind of response, and she'd said that was an easy one. With this kind of piece, she told him, it would be a question of days. People either gave at once, or they didn't give at all. By the end of the week, he'd know either way.

Buddy looked at his watch. Monday. Until Pascale had completed his assessment, he'd no idea whether Jude would even be suitable for surgery. That would take at least three weeks, and by then he'd certainly know whether or not this newspaper appeal had worked. If it did – if it raised the money, and got them over in one piece, and paid Pascale's fees – then he'd at least have done his best. If, on the other

169

hand, it didn't work, then he'd simply have to find some other way of raising the money.

He got off the stool and went across to the window, staring out into the stable yard. Friends of Jude's from the village had taken over the riding school for the time being. They mucked out the horses in the morning, and fed them at night, and they did what they could with the programme of outstanding lessons. Their kindness was unending, and Buddy was duly thankful, but he knew from the steady list of cancellations that they didn't have Jude's talent for the job, her infectious enthusiasm. She'd taught by example. She'd befriended her pupils and made light of their clumsiness or fear. She'd put kids on horses, and housewives, and grandfathers, and she'd made them feel utterly at home up there. She'd even taught *him* to ride, for Chrissakes. But would she be able to do that in a wheelchair? With nods of her head?

He turned back into the kitchen and checked the chick peas. Soon, he knew, they'd have to think of selling the horses. He hadn't raised the issue with Jude, fearing the consequences, but the stable's current income was barely enough to cover running costs. Long term, that kind of arithmetic made no sense, and whatever happened next – whether Jude had the operation or not, whether it worked or not – there was no way she'd be able to run a riding school. Even Buddy had been obliged to admit that. No. What they'd do later, for the rest of their lives, was anyone's guess, but it certainly wouldn't include horses. Ever.

He turned the gas down under the chick peas and wandered slowly round the cottage. Room by room, he tried to visualize what it might be like, Jude back again, all the necessary adaptations in place. If he believed the people at the hospital, if he did it their way, the place would look more like a recovery ward than a home. She'd need a room of her own, somewhere on the ground floor. She'd need a bed, and a special mattress, and some kind of apparatus for getting her into a wheelchair, a block and tackle arrangement, vintage North Sea stuff. She'd need a wheelchair, probably motorized, and they'd have to do something about the bathroom.

At the moment, the bathroom was upstairs, beside the tiny bedroom. For Jude, that was hopeless. She'd need somewhere downstairs, wide access, fully tiled. Somewhere she could be washed all over, minimum fuss, lots of room. Because she'd be incontinent, she'd have to have nappies, or a colostomy, a hole in her belly with a bag attached. The bag would need regular changing. Hygiene would be all-important, lots of antiseptic, the smell of it everywhere. Her body would need to be lifted, and turned in the bed every two hours in case she developed bedsores, and then ulcers, big black holes in the flesh, going rotten at the edges. He'd seen a couple in the hospital and smelled them. They smelled of a butcher's stall in the market at the end of a hot day. They smelled of death and decay. That's what you couldn't let happen. That's what you stood guard against.

He could do it, of course, and he would. He'd tackle it methodically, one job after another, twenty-four hours a day. He'd fill her up in the morning, and empty her at night, and attend to the endless routine maintenance she'd need, just to keep her alive. That would be no problem. On the contrary, it would be like diving on the rigs again, fighting the daily battle, patching up the stuff underwater, keeping the elements at bay, never winning, but never losing either. God knows, with the right mix of State benefits and other handouts, they might even have enough for the odd bottle of Guinness, the odd shampoo.

No, the mechanics would be OK. What really worried him was the insides of her head, the one cubic foot of her that still worked. What would happen in there? The days unspooling? The endless indignities? The utter reliance on someone else? The sense of total helplessness? With anyone, that would be depressing enough. But with Jude, being Jude, he just couldn't believe she'd survive. Or want to.

He wandered back into the kitchen and sat on the stool again. The nurse he'd befriended at the hospital had told him Jude would probably be in for three months. That was how long it would take to complete the physiotherapy programmes, and relearn the handful of tasks that special aids might still make possible. Reading. Eating. Drinking. Maybe even writing. After three months, she'd have

171

mastered all there was to master, and the rest would be down to them. Here. In this tiny cottage. With no money, and no prospects, and a future that simply promised more of the same.

Buddy brooded, eyeing the article, the picture of Jude, remembering again the day on the cliffs. The girl in the paper had written of a miracle. For miracles, Buddy had no time at all. Miracle was the word you used when everything else had failed. No. What Jude needed, what they both needed, was some luck. The rest – the vision to know what to do, the money to make it possible, the guts to see it through – was down to him. Somehow, he'd get her to the States in one piece. Of that, he was quite certain.

Ten miles away, in a small terraced house in the middle of Southampton, a woman of twenty-nine opened her kitchen drawer and removed a pair of scissors. She took the scissors next door into the tiny living room. On the table, beside a plateful of cooling spaghetti, was the local paper.

She'd already ringed the article about the girl who'd fallen off the horse. Now she read it again, then scissored round her carefully pencilled line. She folded it twice into a small square and slipped it into an envelope. Reaching for a pen, and a piece of paper, she began to scribble a note, trying to remember the name of the guy who'd been in charge of the ASU, here, in Southampton, nearly a decade back. The Quartermaster, she remembered, had called him Crossbones. It had been worth a laugh at the time, amongst the four of them, but she'd been impressed by the man, the way he conducted himself. Intellectually, he'd been head and shoulders above the rest, and when they'd blown the *QEII* job, saddling themselves with 400lbs of nitroglycerine and a sackful of detonators, he'd been the last to leave for Fishguard, and the ferry.

She sat at the table, searching for the name, picturing the man, a face older than his years, the way he ate the meals she'd prepared, kept himself spotless, his careful, fastidious ways. She smiled, the name finally coming back to her. Crossbones . . . Scullen . . . Padraig . . .

She wrote his name at the top of the page, the simple letter "P", and paused, thinking again about the *QEII*. She'd always regretted not seeing it through. The ship, its name, had been the perfect symbol. The plan, then, had hinged on smuggling the explosives aboard. Now, looking at the article, she began to wonder whether they hadn't missed a trick or two. Maybe they should have gone underwater, used a specialist, blown the boat up as it sailed away down the Solent, the usual gaggle of TV cameras on the dockside, the usual line of cars on the beach, a ready-made audience. In a couple of brief paragraphs, nothing too explicit, she floated the idea. Captain Harrison, she wrote, has probably retired. But his good lady sails on, ever the temptress . . .

She left the rest to Scullen's imagination, and recommended he read the enclosed article. She sealed the envelope, and turned it over. From memory, in black capitals, she wrote a Dublin address, and then concealed the envelope inside the pages of a much-thumbed Russian novel. She returned the novel to a shelf of books above her ancient radio, and fed the rest of the newspaper, page by page, into the fire. The flames licked up at the chimney breast, and she watched them for a moment before returning to the table. Tomorrow, she thought, she'd post the thing. Maybe Scullen would find a use for it. Maybe someone else. If it came to anything, if they liked the idea, then maybe they'd give her a call again, add a little spice to an otherwise dull old life.

She smiled, thinking of the old days again. They'd called him something else, too. Reaper.

TWELVE

Connolly stood in the tiny, shadowed antiquarian bookshop off the Charing Cross Road, looking for a present for Leeson.

He'd been back in London for a week now, staying with his mother in the neat little house in Carshalton. It had been the briefest convalescence, hours of sitting around in the dusty snug at the back of the house, a pile of newspapers at his elbow, familiar smells, the same old dents in the same old buttoned cushions, and a stream of constant chatter from his mother, next door, in the kitchen.

She'd fed him huge meals, and incessant cups of tea, demanding – in return – some small clue to what he got up to, back at the University, in Belfast. He'd told her about the job, about his students, about the lighter side of college politics. He'd explained that his courses had gone down well, that he was making a bit of a name for himself, and that there was every chance that his probationary period as a lecturer would lead to the offer of a full-time job. When she enquired about the rest of it – his private life, what he did evenings and weekends – he said it was a busy place, lively people, and that he was never short of friends. Beyond that, he wasn't prepared to go. That other life of his, Mairead and the handful of relationships that had gone before, at Cambridge, he'd never shared with her. Not then. Not now.

Connolly selected a book of letters home from a remote hill station in Southern India, late nineteenth century, and joined the queue at the table at the back of the shop where the proprietor sat over the cash box. Outside, the book wrapped in old newspapers, he walked the length of Charing Cross Road, thinking again of Belfast. He'd already phoned Mairead a couple of times from Carshalton, waiting until his mother was off for her daily shop. Mairead, at first, had been guarded. She'd been waiting to hear from him, she'd said, and he hadn't phoned, and in the end she'd begun to fear the worst. Connolly, his feet curled under him on the dusty old sofa, had wondered what the worst might be, but he hadn't pursued the thought, telling her instead that everything was fine, the job done, and that he'd be back in a couple of days. Whether, at first, she'd believed him, he didn't know, but he'd prattled on about this and that, and it was his tone of voice, sunny again and upbeat, that broke the ice. He'd felt the temperature between them warming. She'd told him about her Da's win on the pools, £145 for a 20p stake, about a new jumper she'd found for Bronagh at the Social. She'd said that it hadn't stopped raining since he'd left, and there was ice in the lavatory in the mornings, and by the end of the second call they were back to the way it had always been. She'd missed him, and so had the kids, and she couldn't wait to have him home again. Home. He'd smiled at the word, putting the phone down, gazing round.

Now, he sat on the tube out to Hammersmith, the book in his lap, his single bag between his feet. He'd spend an hour or so with Leeson, have a pot of tea, make his excuses, and leave. The Dan Air flight to Belfast was scheduled out of Gatwick at ten past six. With luck, he'd be back in Belfast, at Mairead's, in time for a late supper.

At Hammersmith, Connolly ducked out of the station and walked the mile and a half to Leeson's house. For late January, the weather was warm, a hint of spring, snowdrops dusting one or two of the better-kept front gardens. Connolly smiled, glad that the winter was three-quarters gone, glad that the nights were drawing out, glad to be spared so much darkness.

Outside Leeson's house, he paused, then stepped through the gate and rang the door bell. A black cat looked up in the next garden, watching him. He meowed at it, softly. The cat yawned, and disappeared. He rang the bell again. Nothing happened. Connolly glanced at his watch and frowned. He'd phoned Leeson from Victoria Station only two hours ago. He knew the man should be in. He lifted his hand to ring the bell a third time, and as he did so he

realized that the front door was slightly open, just an inch or
so. He pushed it gently. The door swung inwards. Connolly
paused, then stepped inside.

"Francis?"

There was no answer. He walked slowly along the hall.
The door to the kitchen was closed. He paused at the end
of the hall. The door to the living room was open.

"Francis?"

Again, nothing. Connolly hesitated. There was something
about the house, the tick of the clock, his own voice, the old
questions, his voice less sure of itself.

"Francis?"

He stepped into the living room and looked round. The
room was empty. The gas fire was on and there were a
couple of tea cups and a milk jug on the table. Beside the
tea cups was a willow-pattern plate. On the plate, neatly
arranged in a circle, was a small pile of ginger biscuits. His
favourite. Connolly stood by the fire for a second, then
looked down at the milk jug. It was empty. Leeson, ever
careless, had gone out in search of milk.

Connolly loosened his anorak, put the book carefully on
the table, and went back out into the hall. At the most,
Leeson would be ten minutes. By the time he came back,
Connolly would have the kettle boiled, and the teapot full.

He opened the kitchen door. The kitchen was small and
narrow. The sink and the cooker and a fitted unit ran the
length of one side. The rest was occupied by a table, two
chairs and a tall fridge. Leeson was sat against the fridge.
His jacket was off, and his tie was loosened, and there was
a small black hole where his left eye had once been. There
was blood on his chest, and blood on the lino, and blood –
still fresh – on the side of the fridge. His glasses lay in pieces
on the floor.

Connolly blinked, feeling for the edge of the table, steadying himself. Then he stepped forward, knowing in his heart
that Leeson was dead, but knowing too that he should check.
He touched him lightly, then eased his body away from the
fridge. His body was heavy, deadweight. Most of the back
of his head was missing, and the hole in the fridge was
crusted with hair and pieces of brain. Connolly closed his

eyes a moment, letting Leeson's body slump against the fridge. Then he stepped back.

There was a movement behind him, in the hall. Connolly stiffened, feeling a new chill steal towards his heart. He'd left the front door open. Someone had come in. Slowly, he turned round. A big man stood in the hall. He was about thirty. He had long, lank, greasy hair, and a flat face, and he needed a shave. His hands were in his pockets, and he was smiling.

"Name's Ingle," he said pleasantly, "Special Branch."

They took him to Paddington Green police station in the back of an unmarked Vauxhall Cavalier. He sat between Ingle and another man. He asked Ingle twice whether he was under arrest. The first time Ingle just smiled. The second time he asked why. Connolly said he'd get out otherwise. Ingle said nothing. The car drove on.

At Paddington Green, the car drove into the police station. The police station was large and modern, iron grilles over the windows, a large pair of electronic gates at the foot of a vehicle ramp. The gates swung open as the car approached, and closed again behind them.

Ingle got out first, and held the door open for Connolly. Connolly followed him into the building, along a corridor, down a flight of steps, into the basement. The driver of the car walked behind him. Connolly could hear him whistling. Something topical. "Physical." Olivia Newton John. Leeson's dead, Connolly wanted to say. Leeson's dead, and the best you can do is whistle.

The basement housed the holding area. There was a row of cells with modern reinforced steel doors and a long flap in the middle. Ingle pushed a door open with his foot and peered inside. The cell was empty. Connolly stood in the corridor.

"No," he said.

Ingle smiled again. "For your own good," he said.

"I want a solicitor."

The other man, the driver, hit Connolly hard on the side of his head. The blow came from behind and took him by

177

surprise. He staggered for a moment, and then recovered his balance. There was a ringing in his right ear. The driver hit him again, from the front this time, a short, vicious jab, central solar plexus. Connolly doubled up under the blow, hearing his own gasp of pain, the breath driven from him. He stayed on his knees on the floor for a moment, waiting for the third blow, fighting for breath. Ingle bent over him, helping him to his feet. He smelled of cheap cigars and something else, an aftershave of some kind, a sharp chemical smell. He was still holding the door open.

"In," Ingle said.

Connolly tried to protest, to demand a solicitor again, but no sound came out. He looked at Ingle for a moment, then shrugged, and limped into the cell, hearing the door shut behind him, the automatic locks engaging, the sound of footsteps disappearing down the corridor. The driver was suggesting a cup of tea. Ingle was declining the offer.

Connolly stood in the middle of the cell. There was a toilet and a raised area of concrete. The concrete was covered with wooden boards and obviously served as a bed. Connolly stumbled across to the toilet. There were two cigarette ends in the bowl. He shut his eyes for a moment, and he saw Leeson's face again, the blood on the fridge, one eye pulped, and he began to vomit, holding his stomach as he threw up, trying to ease the pain. After a while, he stepped back wiping his mouth. The smell was already filling the cell.

He sat on the wooden boards for perhaps five minutes. High on the wall, there was a window, squares of thick bubbled glass. He got up and tried to look out. There was daylight beyond the glass, but no view. He sat down again, his ear not hurting quite so much, the pain in his belly ebbing away. Surreal, he thought. Pure Kafka.

After a minute or so, he called out. He called his name. He asked for someone to talk to him. Nothing happened.

The footsteps returned an hour later. The door opened and Ingle stood there. He'd taken off his coat. He was wearing a big sloppy pullover, no shape whatsoever, and a pair of jeans. The jeans had a patch on the knee. He held the door open and handed Connolly a cup of tea. Connolly looked at him. "What is this?" he said.

Ingle smiled. "Milk, guvnor. Two sugars."

"I meant all this. What's going on?"

Ingle gave him the tea. "Drink it," he said. "Make you feel better."

Ingle sat down on the floor, back against the wall. He took out a packet of thin cigars and offered one to Connolly. Connolly shook his head.

"Mind if I do?" Ingle said, nodding at the lavatory in the corner. "Might help."

Connolly shrugged and sipped the tea. It was too sweet for his taste but it was better than nothing. Ingle watched him, blowing small imperfect smoke rings and playing with a box of matches. He had big hands, spade nails, very dirty. Connolly finished the tea. "Just tell me what you want," he said. "Please."

Ingle looked at him for a moment, coal black eyes under a curtain of greasy hair, and Connolly realized exactly what it was that was strange about the man. Despite the circumstances – Leeson, the cell, the pain in his ear – he exuded no menace. On the contrary, he was detached, almost sympathetic. His whole manner invited intimacy. Connolly should trust this man. He should talk to him.

Ingle stirred. "My friend's upstairs," he said. "He has an ulcer. Gets bad sometimes. Makes him unreasonable." He nodded towards the lavatory again. "He gets wound up about results. Meant no real harm."

Connolly said nothing. Time passed; perhaps a minute. Then Ingle got up with a regretful sigh and gestured Connolly towards the door. Connolly shook his head.

"OK," he said.

Ingle sat down again, his knees up around his chin. One of the seams on the pullover was coming undone, the wool beginning to unpick itself. In a couple of days, the thing would be in pieces. Ingle stifled a yawn, holding the cigar at arm's length, contemplating the end through narrowed eyes.

"Your name's Connolly," he suggested. "You live in Belfast."

"That's right."

"You're friends with matey back there. Mr Leeson."

"Yes."

"Mr Leeson's dead."

"Yes."

"Murdered."

"So I gather."

"Yes." Ingle nodded. Then he looked up. "You kip with him a lot?"

"I don't have to answer that."

"You're right." Ingle smiled. "Shall I show you the records from the clinic? We've got them ...' he paused. "Upstairs."

There was a long silence, then Ingle began to talk again, musing, the flat South London voice, reflective. "Bad prospect, Mr Leeson. Couple of years. Couple of months. Who knows?" He paused again, and looked at Connolly. "Did he tell you? As a matter of interest?"

"Tell me what?"

"That he had this pox of his? That he might have given it to you?"

Connolly looked at him, frowning, trying to work out the drift of his questions, the traps he was baiting, what he really meant.

"Is it an offence," he said, "being ill?"

"Not at all," Ingle grinned. "But that's not the point."

"It isn't?"

"No. You're right. Getting poxed isn't an offence. But it might be a motive."

"*Motive?*"

"Yeah ..." He inhaled a lungful of cigar smoke and expelled it in a long thin stream. "Think about it. You're with him for a while. You like him. You don't like him. Either way, it makes no difference. You fuck around together, and he's got some dreadful disease. That means you've probably got it too. That's all you need to know ..." he looked up, "isn't it?"

"To do what?" Connolly said.

"Kill him."

Connolly gazed at him. The pain in his head was getting worse. "That's absurd," he said.

Ingle shrugged. "I'm a simple man. I read comic books.

Detective stories. I know about motive. Opportunity." He smiled again. "So do the blokes on the jury."

"You're crazy."

"Yeah?"

Ingle got up and crossed the cell, dropping the remains of the cigar into the lavatory. Then he turned round, his back to the window, his face nearly invisible. "Actually, I'm being kind," he said. "Most juries hate faggots. They think they're at it all the time. Bitching and screwing and tearing each other's eyes out. Goes with the plot, doesn't it? You standing there, bits of your lover all over the fridge . . ."

Connolly blinked, trying to keep up. "So where's the gun?" he said. "What am I supposed to have done with the gun?"

Ingle nodded slowly. "Ah . . ." he said, "the gun."

There was a long silence. Connolly shook his head.

"I didn't kill him."

"So you say."

Connolly turned away and sat on the wooden boards. Ingle didn't move. Dimly, Connolly began to detect a pattern in the questions, some faint glimmer of sense. He wasn't, after all, about to be arrested. Nor, with luck, was he in for any more violence. No, it was something more complex. Something infinitely nastier.

"What do you want?" he said dully.

Ingle didn't say anything for a moment. Connolly heard the rattle of matches as he lit another cigar.

"I want you to go back to Belfast," Ingle said at last, "and I want you to tell me what happens."

"Nothing'll happen. I've got a job there. I'm working most of the time."

Ingle shrugged.

"Then we'll have a quiet old life," he said.

"You think something will happen?"

"Yes. To be candid."

"What?"

"I don't know. That's why we're here." He paused and produced a small notepad and a pen. He scribbled a number and gave it to Connolly. Connolly glanced at it. Seven digits. He looked up.

"That's a local number," he said, "Belfast."

"Yes."

"You'll be there?"

He nodded. "On that number," he paused again, "there'll be a series of places we can meet. The first'll be the Central Station. Upstairs. Outside the Whistle Stop bar. Can you remember that?"

"Upstairs," Connolly repeated, "outside the Whistle Stop bar."

"Right."

There was another long silence. Connolly began to frown. He looked at the piece of paper Ingle had given him, the phone number.

"What does that make me?" he said. "If something does happen?"

Ingle put an arm on his shoulder, a surprisingly light touch. He was smiling again, the daylight back on his face, the big flat Slavic features, the cigar in the corner of his mouth.

"A tout," he said cheerfully.

Connolly nodded, remembering a hundred Belfast headlines.

"Touts die," he said, "all the time."

"So did Leeson's American chum." He smiled. "According to the files I've seen."

"Thanks."

"Pleasure."

Ingle stepped back, towards the door. Connolly stopped him.

"And Leeson," he said, "what about Leeson?"

Ingle frowned a moment, removing his cigar, rubbing his eyes with the heel of his hand, a gesture of perplexity or faint regret. "Mr Leeson . . ." he said finally, "is now the subject of a murder investigation. Should there be any progress in the investigation, I imagine you'll be the first to know." He shepherded Connolly towards the door, and drew it shut behind them. "Fair enough?" he said, heading for the stairs.

Scullen got the cutting from the Southampton paper in the post. It had been forwarded from Dublin. Pinned to it was a terse note from whoever had sent it on. The Army Council Secretariat, it implied, was not a branch of the Post Office.

Scullen read the note and dropped it in the bin. Then he unfolded the article. The brief covering letter fell out and he opened it, recognizing at once the careful script. He read the letter, remembering the girl in the purple jeans and the black fingernails. She'd been German, a student. Her name was Eva. She'd had a tiny bedsit up near the University. She'd been ultra-left, and she'd been reading philosophy, and she cooked truly terrible omelettes.

She'd come to them through Dublin. She'd taken a ferry, and knocked on doors, and persisted and persisted until they'd had no choice but to take her seriously. She'd said she wanted to help. She was fluent in three languages, and she knew her way round Europe, and Operations had used her in the recces for a couple of arms runs, Belgian stuff, shipped out through Le Havre. The girl had done well. She'd learned the fundamentals at the edges of the Baader-Meinhoff group, and Dublin had been impressed, letting her closer and closer to the real action, watching her carefully, setting the usual traps, fully expecting her to be a Brit plant, gradually convinced that she was nothing of the sort.

By the time Scullen met her, she'd been fully vetted. She had genuine cover at the University, and pursued her studies with the same combative vigour she brought to everything else. Scullen had liked her, enjoyed her company. She was a very different proposition from the Volunteers he was used to. She was highly educated in the formal sense. She was strong willed, and hot tempered, and refused to defer to the usual Catholic notions of a woman's proper place. She organized a safe house, and laid in food, and once the ASU had moved in she swopped a large handful of used notes for – at last – a decent car.

Scullen smiled, remembering the car. It had been a Volkswagen. The lads had laughed, making the inevitable digs. They wanted a Cortina or a Vauxhall, cars they were used

183

to. She ignored them. She told them to get on with it. She was only, ever, interested in results. To that end, she'd bend all her best efforts. If a Volkswagen could do the job better than a Brit car, then so be it. VWs worked. *Nein?*

The Southampton ASU, in the end, had been disbanded. Their plans for the *QEII* had been betrayed by a tout, and the rest of the southern strategy – the raid on the oil refinery, the car bomb outside the Tank Museum – had come to nothing. That, for Scullen, had been a matter of some regret, but not once had he blamed the girl. On the contrary, Eva's work had been beyond reproach, and if he had a single memory of the night they'd baled out, minutes ahead of the squad cars from the special unit at Lyndhurst, it was of her face. She'd been disappointed. She'd expected more of them. In certain operational ways, they'd let her down.

He'd occasionally thought of her since, what might have happened to her. Her studies had been important to her, he knew. She wanted to go on and do a doctorate. She wanted to teach, spread the word. If high explosives wouldn't do the job, then perhaps – after all – it would have to be books. The written word. A process of careful argument. A lifetime's work.

Now, though, looking at the cutting from the paper, thinking of his own plans, he wasn't so sure. He read the article carefully, then again. He read the paragraph about the husband a third time. A diver, he thought, with naval experience. He glanced at the letter again, checking Eva's address, and he began to smile, remembering again the purple jeans, and the black fingernails, and the incessant battering the lads had taken. When the old debates had started, sitting in the safe house, a couple of glasses down, she'd put them right on every detail, every date. She never let up. Ever. Even their washing up, she'd said, was a disgrace.

There was a phone number at the top of the letter. He committed it to memory, then reached for the pile of coins he always kept in the drawer of his desk. The nearest pay phone was down the street, towards the town centre. He used it for the calls he couldn't afford to have compromised. He paused, looking at the letter again. She'd used his name on the envelope. That was regrettable. She must have forgotten what little he'd been able to teach her about fieldcraft. He smiled. A mild rebuke, he thought, the faintest slap on the wrist.

THIRTEEN

Buddy Little was late for the appointment, something he always tried to avoid, and it made a bad mood worse.

He'd driven over from Southampton in the Jaguar, stopping at a pub en route to phone Jude with the news. "Pascale's come through," he told her, "he says you're fine. He'll take you. You're on the list. We made it . . ." Jude had said she was pleased for him, for Buddy, an odd reaction, and Buddy had known at once that she was still in two minds about the whole thing, unconvinced by Pascale, by his operation, but grateful that Buddy had taken the trouble to find him. She ended the conversation by asking again about the money, and he'd told her not to worry. There'd be a way, he said, and he'd find it.

Looking at his watch, he'd rung off, more frustrated than ever, with a tiny voice at the back of his brain asking him whether it wouldn't be simpler just to give in, to accept it all, to lay Jude down for the duration and somehow make the best of it. The response to the newspaper article had been pathetic. He'd had a couple of phone calls from mutual friends – lovely picture, such a tragedy – and four letters. Three of the letters had been expressions of sympathy, and the fourth, from a pensioner, had included a book token for £3.

Buddy had answered all four letters as best he could, and given the book token to one of the girls from the village who was helping out with the horses. He'd yet to tell Jude about the newspaper appeal, and the way it had turned out, he decided he never would. With his own savings fast disappearing, money was now a real problem. At this rate, he'd soon have to start looking for work. Unless, of course, Harry came through.

Buddy drove fast, outside lane, keeping the Jaguar above ninety, still ten minutes from Brighton, where Harry lived. Harry, he knew, was a long shot, a retired diver of fifty-eight who now ran a small company based in Shoreham. Buddy had worked for him on a number of jobs, a month here and a month there, local stuff, piers, and sewage outlets, and the odd wreck. He'd liked the man on sight, the way everyone did, the strong bony face, the shock of wild hair, the inexhaustible fund of stories. He'd built a business from hard graft and tough negotiation. He knew the diving world inside out, and he loved it with a rare passion.

More to the point, Harry was himself handicapped. An explosives accident in the fifties had blown off both his legs. He'd lost them beneath the knee, but gone back to diving with a special suit and an extra set of weights. His exploits in the water were legendary, and he still dived alongside the men he employed, checking their work, sharing the risks they took. If anyone could see the logic of getting to Pascale, of never giving up, it would be Harry.

Buddy drove into the outskirts of Brighton, following the instructions Harry had given him on the phone. He hadn't seen the man for three or four years, but Harry had recognized his voice at once. "Little place in Portslade," he said, "don't be put off by the colour."

Buddy found the address. It was a terraced house in a modest street near the docks. There were empty milk bottles outside the front door, and the paintwork around the windows was peeling. Once the house had been simple brick, like the rest of the street, but someone had since added a coating of thick stucco. The stucco was bright pink.

Buddy got out of the car and rang the bell. As he did so, he noticed a piece of paper wedged in the letter box. The paper had his name on it. He unfolded it. A handscrawled message, in pencil. "Gone swimming," it said, "end of the road. Then left. Look for the statue of Queen Vic."

Buddy folded the note into his pocket and got back in the car. A mile or so along the seafront, he found the statue of Queen Victoria. He parked again and got out. There was a keen wind, blowing in from the east. The sky was grey, and there were the beginnings of a big sea running down the

Channel. The water looked ugly, a heavy brown flecked with white.

Buddy shivered, standing on the promenade in his jeans and sweater, remembering Harry's daily ritual, the afternoon swim. He'd done it since he'd known the man, probably a lot longer, and he stuck to the routine regardless of the weather or the season. He was famous for it. He claimed it kept him going, opened up his blood vessels, did him good. Buddy shook his head, turning his back to the wind. Nutter, he thought.

He descended a flight of steps and tramped across the beach. Near the water's edge was a small pile of clothes. He stood over them, recognizing Harry's false legs, the straps at the end that buckled around his knees. They looked bizarre, lying there on the wet pebbles, half hidden by the old plaid shirt and the torn flannel trousers.

Buddy looked up. The wind was blowing even harder here, the beach more exposed, and the waves were building steadily as they rolled in, serious waves, rearing up for the final roaring lunge at the gleaming shingle. Buddy gazed out to sea, looking for Harry, wondering for a moment whether the old boy could cope with the conditions. Then he saw him, a tiny white dot about fifty yards out, Harry's head, rising and falling. Buddy waved, and he saw Harry waving back, a cheerful lift of the arm, before the next wave rolled in and smothered him in foam.

Harry began to swim back, a long slow methodical crawl, surfing on the bigger waves until he was within reach of the beach. Buddy watched, anxious, as Harry paused, treading what little water he could, waiting for the wave that would deliver him to the beach in one piece. Finally it came, a beast, eight foot or so of towering brown water, and Harry ducked into its belly as it sucked back the remains of the wave before, and reared up, and then dumped him on the pebbles. Harry shook the water from his eyes, and began to crawl slowly up the beach, away from the next wave. He'd been a big man before the accident, well over six foot, powerfully built, and even now his chest and shoulders were broad and strong, compensating for the lack of legs.

Buddy walked down the beach with the towel. It was

raining now, the rain cold on his face, and he draped the towel round Harry's shoulders, much to the old man's amusement. "Found me then," he said.

Buddy nodded. Harry was still kneeling on the beach. He'd cut himself and there was blood running down his left thigh. He mopped his face with the towel, and dried the water from his ears. His hair was everywhere, fine and white, already blowing in the wind. Buddy watched him for a moment or two, marvelling at the man's resilience, his total indifference to the weather, and the waves, and the hard pebbles beneath his knees.

"You're nuts," he said fondly, "fucking barmy."

They went back to Harry's place. Inside, it was a wreck. There were books everywhere, and piles of diving magazines, and a scattering of clothes, and bits and pieces of food. Harry poked at a packet of crumpets and told Buddy to light the gas fire. Buddy did so, finding the matches in one of Harry's shoes. The gas fire roared into life, and Buddy turned round to find Harry extracting a bottle of Scotch from a drawerful of socks. He'd put his legs back on by now, and moved around the room stiffly, occasionally reaching out for support, a chairback or the corner of a cupboard. Buddy couldn't remember him doing that before. A sign of age, he thought. Not immortal, after all.

They had toasted crumpets and mugs of whisky around the fire, Harry his old gruff self, the abrupt one-line questions, the wind-ups, the slow mischievous smile. He was pleased to see him, he told Buddy. Later, they'd go out for a proper drink. Meanwhile, they'd polish off the Scotch. Buddy nodded, eyeing the half-empty bottle, knowing what an evening with Harry meant, glad of the invitation. He'd get the business over and done. Then they'd get truly rat-arsed.

He told Harry what had happened to Jude. He explained about the accident, and her paralysis, and the line the doctors were taking. Harry listened, gazing at the fire, his mug cupped in his hand.

"Fucking doctors," he grunted. "Don't know fuck all."

Buddy warmed to his theme, loosened by the Scotch, heartened by this glorious old villain who'd never listened for a moment to anyone in authority. Harry had always done things his way. He'd invented new machines, perfected new techniques, allegedly made a small fortune from a handful of registered patents. Some blokes said he was brilliant. Others said he was a lunatic. Either way, you had to love him, the sight of the man, the hair, the steam rising from the ancient flannels, soaked by the rain.

Buddy came to the point of his story. Pascale. The offer of an operation three thousand miles away. Harry looked over at him. Age was tightening the flesh around his head and neck. He looked almost gaunt in the light from the gas fire. He took a pull of the whisky, and wiped his mouth with the back of his hand.

"What do you think?" he said. "Trust the bugger?"

"I dunno." Buddy paused. "What do you think?"

"Me?" Harry looked at him again. "How would I fucking know?"

Buddy shrugged. The question had come out wrong. It sounded indecisive, faintly pathetic. He hadn't come for advice. He'd come for money.

"I want to do it," he said. "We need to do it. She'll go barmy otherwise."

"Will she?"

The old man raised an eyebrow. Around his mouth was shiny with butter from the crumpet. Buddy nodded.

"Yeah," he said. "She will."

"You sure?"

"Yeah. As sure as I can be." He paused. "Wouldn't you?"

Harry turned his head and lifted his legs away from the fire. First one. Then the other. Bonk. Bonk.

"Yeah, I expect I would," he said at last.

There was a long silence. The gas fire popped and roared. Buddy could hear the wind outside.

"Harry . . ." he began, "I need money."

The old man grunted. "How much?"

"Fifty grand."

"That's a lot."

"I know. You'd get it back. In time."

"Yeah?"

190

He looked up. Buddy nodded, leaning forward.

"Yeah," he said.

There was another silence. Harry farted quietly, moving his body in the chair. There was colour back in his cheeks. He looked thoughtful.

"I haven't got fifty grand," he said. "I haven't got twenty grand. Or ten. Or five. In fact I haven't got fuck all."

Buddy nodded slowly. Looking round the room, he could believe it.

"I'm sorry," he said, "I didn't know that."

Harry grunted again. "Doesn't matter," he said, "money's no answer anyway." He smiled at the thought, then glanced at his watch and drained his glass. "Six o'clock," he said. "Time for a quick one."

They went to a pub a couple of miles away, back in Shoreham, round the corner from Harry's business. Harry drove a big old Rover, automatic gearbox, specially adapted brakes. In the pub they drank pints of Guinness with Jameson's chasers and the landlord kept a slate behind the bar.

Harry talked about his business, the recession, the collapse of a major contract after a client went bust. His exposure was huge, and he'd been left owing tens of thousands to suppliers of his own, with his last two stage payments unmet. He'd paid off most of his debts, but his business was close to collapse. He'd sold his house to preserve his good name, and with luck he might survive until the summer. In July, he was on the promise of a big offshore contract in the Bristol Channel. If he got it, if the client came through, his problems might be over. But these were difficult times, and it was a fool who relied on anyone. In the meantime, he lived from day to day, swim to swim. The business was down to a permanent staff of three, and he took whatever tiny jobs turned up.

He looked at Buddy, picking at a plate of sausage rolls that had appeared from nowhere.

"Doesn't help you at all, does it," he said, grinning, "all my problems?"

They got very drunk. They told stories about the old days, runs ashore in the Navy, blokes they'd known, strokes they'd pulled. They relived the first wild seasons on the North Sea rigs. Americans off the plane from Texas, holding court in the big Aberdeen hotels, open cheque books at their elbow. Harry chuckled, remembering his first big job, the breakthrough, inventing a new strain container for the huge concrete caissons, kidding the Yanks along, telling Buddy the story he'd heard a million times before, drawing the old, old diagrams on the bar top, a fingertip moistened with a dip of Guinness. They'd been good days, great days, brilliant money, real laughs, and at half past ten Buddy settled the slate, and ordered a taxi, holding the door open for Harry, helping him across the wet cobbles. Harry stood by the waiting cab, swaying slightly, the rain flattening his hair.

"Love and war," he said cheerfully, "real bastards."

Buddy thought nothing of the comment, folding Harry into the taxi. Back at the house, he stirred instant coffee into mugs of hot water and carried them through to the living room. Harry was back in his chair by the fire. His legs were propped on a pile of magazines and his eyes were closed. Buddy put the coffee beside his chair, making no sound. He moved across the room, thinking he'd find the spare bed Harry had promised him for the night. He had the door half open when he heard the old man's voice.

"Buddy . . ." he said, "I've got no fucking money but one day you'll need gear. I know you will. I've got the gear. Piles of it. You can take what you want. It's all in the yard. It's yours . . ."

Buddy looked at him, wondering what on earth the old man meant. The evening had been wonderful. He'd forgotten he'd come for help. "What do you mean?" he said. "Gear?"

Harry opened one eye. He was smiling. "You name it," he said. "It's yours."

When Miller suggested they take a walk on the golf course, Charlie knew it was serious. Miller hated golf, and didn't much like walking. Crisis time.

The two men drove out of the big grey barracks at Castlereagh. They'd spent the morning at yet another interagency conference, Miller scribbling laconic notes to himself on the pad he always carried, while the three-man team from the RUC got more righteous than usual about yet another security débâcle.

UK Special Branch had been running a series of surveillance operations across the Irish Sea, Stranraer to Larne. The operations had been innocuous enough, low grade stuff, but someone had forgotten to tell the locals. The result had been a run-in on the dockside at Larne. An over-zealous RUC man, plain clothes, had pulled a gun on one of his Special Branch cousins from over the water. The Special Branch man, a thick-skinned Scouser with fifteen years' service, had told him to piss off. It wasn't very friendly, but it hardly warranted a knee in the groin. The Scouser had retaliated, and they'd had to go through the usual charade – caution, arrest, interrogation – before the Scouser was allowed a phone call and the penny had dropped.

At the conference, the incident had been recounted in exhaustive detail, yet more evidence that Whitehall's declared policy of police primacy – RUC up front – wasn't working the way it might. The security agencies had to get their act together before something really nasty happened, and the locals – the RUC man repeated – should be calling the tune. It was, after all, their bloody country. Miller had nodded, smiling his non-committal smile, wondering what he'd make of the Dublin fuck-up, if he only knew.

Now, Miller parked the car beside the Fortwilliam Golf Club. He and Charlie got out of the car and began to walk. The course was virtually empty, midweek, a fine rain drifting in from the west. Miller put up a borrowed umbrella, pulling in Charlie beside him. They were still abreast of the first tee when he got to the point.

"You'll have seen your source," he said.

Charlie nodded. Despite the umbrella, there was rain on his face. It ran down his forehead and began to form a drip on the end of his nose. He could feel it there, hanging. "Yes," he said.

"And?"

Charlie shook his head. The drip flew into nowhere. "That's all there was," he said. "Just the address."

"Where did the address come from?"

193

"Character named Dermot McGee. Fit little bugger. Works out a lot. Moustache. He took his wife and kids over the border. He's been living in the south for a bit. Never gaoled. Never injured. Works with Scullen. Good operator."

"Have you seen the file?"

"Yes."

"What else does it say?"

"Not much. He's been pulled in a couple of times but they never got anything out of him."

"How hard did they try?"

"Oh . . ." Charlie glanced sideways at Miller, "hard enough."

Miller nodded, absorbing the information. He rarely enquired about sources, trusting his men. Unless circumstances were especially dire, sources were sacrosanct. He plunged on down the first fairway, Charlie in step beside him.

"McGee contacted your source in the first place?" he said.

Charlie nodded. "Yes."

"Wanting to know about Leeson? Our diplomat friend?"

"Yes." Charlie frowned. "They wanted to find out more about him. A local had passed the word through. Scullen thought he sounded promising."

"And your source knew Leeson?"

"Knew of him," he nodded, "yes."

"How?"

Charlie didn't answer for a moment, looking out across the sodden greens. Miller stepped in front of him. They'd both stopped walking.

"Tell me, son," Miller said. "Tell me how your source got to know."

Charlie glanced at him. Then he shrugged. "Her boyfriend knows him," he said, "English fella. Name of Connolly."

Miller frowned. "But Connolly's not the source?" he said.

Charlie smiled. "No," he said. "She is."

Connolly found Mairead in the launderette up in Andersonstown. She was sitting by the window reading a copy of the *TV Times*. Bronagh was with her, sitting at her feet with a one-armed doll, gazing at the swirl of dirty clothes going round and round in the washing machine.

Connolly closed the door and stood beside her, looking down. She was half-way through an article on Tommy Cooper.

"Hi," he said, "it's me."

Mairead looked up with a start. She'd had her hair cut since he'd seen her last. It was cropped short, and took some of the softness from her face. It made her look slightly aggressive. She smiled at him, folding the magazine.

"Hi, yourself," she said, "we've been waiting."

Connolly helped her carry the laundry home, the two big dustbin liners, the rain beginning to fall again. Mairead always dried the clothes at home, shaking out the wrinkles, pegging them up on the line in the garden. She always said they came out better that way, smelling of God's fresh air, but Connolly knew different. The drying machine cost an extra seventy pence. And seventy pence, on a bad day, could buy the evening meal.

They pushed in through the front door, Connolly man-handling the big plastic bags down the narrow hall, up the stairs, and into the bathroom. He'd done it before. He began to unpack, emptying the wet clothes into the bath, hearing Mairead in the kitchen below. He heard the pop of the gas as she put the kettle on for tea, and then a squeal from Bronagh, and a clap of the hands, and footsteps back down the hall. The front door opened again, and then closed behind them, and he heard their voices receding down the street, Bronagh excited, Mairead – as ever – telling her to calm down.

Connolly glanced at his watch. It was barely midday. He wondered where they were off to, the kettle on the stove, himself in charge of the weekly wash. He shrugged, unfolding the clothes horse, balancing it on the top of the bath, arranging the clothes and opening the window to let the chilly air get at them.

Mairead was back within minutes. The kettle had started to whistle in the kitchen, and she turned off the gas, and poured the hot water into the big china teapot she'd inherited from one of her aunts, and piled cups on a tray, and mounted the stairs. Connolly met her at the bathroom door.

Mairead smiled at him, kissed him lightly on the lips, and took the tea-tray into the bedroom. Connolly watched her, his list of carefully prepared questions beginning to dissolve. He followed her into the bedroom. The bedroom was freezing. Mairead was turning down the bed. The tea tray was on the window sill, the steam clouding on the cold glass. Mairead finished with the bed and looked at him, his expression, the slightly frantic look of a man who can't believe his eyes. She began to laugh.

Connolly stepped forward. Mairead nodded at his anorak. "You'll be taking that off?" she said.

Connolly peeled off the coat and hung it on the nail on the back of the door. When he looked round Mairead was putting the tea-tray on the carpet beside the bed. Then she pulled the curtains, and stepped round the bed towards him. Close up, Connolly smelled perfume, something nice. It was his turn to laugh.

"Christmas is over," he said.

"I know. But I thought you deserved it."

"It?"

"Me."

"Why?"

She smiled at him again, her finger on her lips, and he wondered what had happened since he'd been away. She had a girlishness about her that he hadn't seen for months. The reserve and the caution had quite gone. She began to unbutton his shirt. Her fingers were warm on his chest. Connolly looked down at her.

"Why?" he said again.

She shook her head, easing his shirt away from his shoulders, folding it carefully, putting it to one side. "Come to bed," she said, "it's all over. Make love to me. Tell me what you really think."

She kissed him again, softly, on the belly, then stepped away and pulled her T-shirt over her head. She took off her bra and began to unzip her jeans. Connolly watched her.

196

"What's all over?" he said.

Mairead grinned. "All that nonsense," she said. "Going to see your friend. Whatever they wanted. It's finished. Gone. The wee boys are happy. Whatever you got up to in Dublin – " she shrugged – "it's done the trick."

Connolly nodded, saying nothing. Mairead was naked now, except for her knickers, standing on the square of worn carpet, her flesh beginning to pimple in the cold. She had a beautiful body, long and lean, big breasts, flat belly. She looked at him a moment longer, then the smile began to fade.

"What's the matter?" she said. "Can't a good Catholic girl say thank you?"

Connolly shook his head, caught in the trap of his own making. He opened his mouth, looking for a place to begin, not finding one. Mairead sat down on the bed. She was beginning to shiver.

"What is it?" she said again. "Don't you want me?"

"No. Yes." Connolly shook his head. "It's not that. It's not you."

"What is it then?"

"I . . ." he stopped, and abruptly he began to cry, confused now, and frightened, and worn out. The last few days, he'd thought about the very end of the road, where he'd find it, what it would feel like, and he realized now that it was here, in Mairead's bedroom, another of life's little surprises.

He blinked at her through the tears, nowhere to hide. She was on her feet again. She put her arms around him. She took him to the bed. She undressed him. She folded the sheets over him, and pulled up the blankets, and slid in beside him, cradling his head in the crook of her arm. She asked no questions. She dried his tears. And then she seduced him, very slowly, with an expertise he'd never before associated with her, this mother of three, centre of his life, always busy, always on her feet. She danced her fingers down his belly, and teased and kneaded and ducked her head, pushing him gently back on the sheets when he tried to respond, to reciprocate. The pressure inside him grew and grew, and she knew it, her breasts cupping him, her fingers working underneath, her eyes looking up at him, along the length of his body, bigger than he could ever remember. Moments before he climaxed, she began to straddle him, but he shook his head, groaning under her, and she nodded, not understanding, not knowing why, but happy to settle again, easing her breasts backwards and forwards, pleasing him, saying a personal thank you, making it all good for him.

Afterwards he reached for her hand, and held it tightly, his eyes still half closed, the blood still pumping in his head.

"No?" she said.

He shook his head, explaining nothing, remembering only the woman on the phone from the clinic, the obvious advice, keep yourself to yourself for a while, just in case. He looked at Mairead. "No," he said.

They lay together for perhaps half an hour. The tea went cold on the tray below. Quite empty, quite at peace, Connolly looked at her.

"I love you," he said. "Whatever that means."

Mairead nodded. "Whatever that means," she agreed.

"I mean it."

"Yes," she smiled, "I think you do."

Connolly went quiet for a moment. For most of the last twelve months, he'd been imagining this very scene, this very bed. Mairead. Beside him. Beneath him. All over him. When it had finally happened, the very last thing he'd expected, it had exceeded his wildest expectations. Now, he was quite lost in a feeling of semi-narcosis, a lovely feeling. Nothing could touch him now. Nothing could hurt. He'd been there. And she'd been there with him. And it had mattered for both of them.

"Leeson's dead," he said blankly. "Someone killed him."

He felt Mairead stiffen beside him. He reached for her hand again. Squeezed it. He might have been describing an event in the newspapers. The words had no meaning.

"They tried to arrest me," he said. "They tried to make me think I did it."

"Who?"

"Special Branch."

"Who are they?"

He looked at her. "God knows," he said.

Mairead began to shiver, and Connolly pulled the blankets tighter around them, knowing now why Mairead had taken him to bed, why she'd made the space for them both. The pressures were off her. Danny's friends had come and gone. She thought it was over. But she was wrong, and now she knew it, lying beside him, her eyes wide open, staring at the ceiling. He bent to her ear.

"It's all shit," he said softly, "all of it."

She nodded. "It is," she said, "you're right."

"So . . ." he got up on one elbow, looking down at her, the smell of him all over her, "tell me this."

"What?"

He smiled, savouring the pause, aware of the questions circling urgently behind her eyes, but not knowing what they were, and not caring. He traced the outline of her mouth with his fingertip.

"Tell me something," he said.

"Sure."

"But the truth."

She nodded, the old caution back.

"Sure."

"Promise?"

"I promise."

He bent and kissed her on the lips, amazed – in the end – at how simple it all was. She half closed her eyes, still watching him.

"Do you love me?" he said.

She didn't answer for a long time. Then she nodded.

"Yes," she said, "that's what makes it so horrible."

199

FOURTEEN

Three days later, Buddy Little went for his annual medical. With the newspaper appeal dead in the water, and Harry out of funds, he knew it was his only option. He had to find a big, big job, and he had to find it quickly.

He'd seen Jude four times in the past week, and each fresh visit convinced him yet again that she was losing her belief in herself, losing the battle to hang in there, mutely accepting what the doctors assured her was the certain prospect of the rest of her life in a wheelchair. Intellectually, it was a proposition she could well understand, one event leading to another, falling off a horse, breaking her neck, waking up paralysed, not getting better. But that wasn't the same as coming to terms with it, living with it, this slow, slow death of a thousand helping hands.

Already, in the hospital, Buddy had watched her slipping further out of reach, not answering questions, not picking up a conversation, removing what little was left of her body to the very edges of everyone else's world. The nurses had noticed too, of course, and they were worried about it as well. One of them had taken Buddy aside, asked him whether there wasn't anything he could suggest, some little present that might cheer her up. Buddy had thought hard about it. He'd gone out one lunchtime, and bought ribbons for her hair, and a large bottle of the most expensive shampoo he could find, and a tiny vanity mirror the nurse could hold up when she'd finished brushing her hair in the mornings. The presents helped. Jude was grateful. But the bedside silences got longer, and when the same nurse had put the question again – what else can we do? – Buddy had simply smiled, and suggested an airline ticket to Boston and a cheque for fifty grand. The nurse had looked puzzled at this, and slightly hurt, and Buddy had apologized, telling her it was a joke. Buddy had stayed late that night, sitting at the bedside, but for the last hour of the day Jude had simply closed her eyes and drifted away, ignoring him, ignoring everything.

Now, sitting in the doctor's waiting room, Buddy bent to a questionnaire he had to fill in. Every year, professional divers had to go through an exhaustive medical. Without the medical, his licence to dive would be revoked. And without a current licence, no commercial firm would touch him. No licence, no job. It was as simple as that.

Buddy's medical fell due in February, and had Jude not had the accident he wouldn't have bothered to apply for a renewal. His month in Saudi would have been over, and he'd be back at the stables, two thousand pounds the richer, ready to tackle the extension. Now, though, he had no choice. If he was to start to put the money together, enough to convince some bank or other he was worth a loan, then he had to have another medical.

Already, he'd spent the morning at a nearby private hospital, submitting himself to a series of X-rays: chest, shoulders, hips, knees. The service had been brisk and efficient. For one hundred and fifty pounds, a steely radiographer had run through his check list of required films, arranging Buddy in pose after pose, adjusting the arms of the X-ray machine, retiring behind a screen while the machine hummed and clicked, and red lights winked, and Buddy lay gazing at the ceiling, wondering what this year's map of his body would reveal.

For nearly a decade now, Buddy's speciality had been saturation diving, a system much beloved by the oil companies because it worked the divers to the absolute limit, avoiding the lengthy and costly decompression stops every diver must make on his return to the surface. The theory, in essence, was simple. They stuck you in a Sat-System, a complex of pressure chambers on the deck of the oil rig, and wound up the pressure until it reached the pressure on the seabed where the work was to be done. You were fed a mixture of oxygen and helium to breathe, and once every twenty-four hours you crawled out of your living quarters and into a diving bell. They winched the diving bell off the rig and into the water. Down you went until the bell settled at working depth. Then you and your number two spent eight hours doing the biz, just like any other navvy.

At the end of it all, the job done, they winched you up again, and you crawled back into the Sat-System on deck where you lived. Food and magazines and the odd letter came in through a small airlock on the thick steel walls of the pressure chamber. Telly you watched through one of the viewports. Paperbacks you consumed by the dozen. It was often boring, and just a little claustrophobic, but they paid you the earth and after twenty-eight days they decompressed the whole system, and you returned to the real world.

Sat diving, though, took its toll, and the annual checkups were more than usually rigorous.

So far, Buddy had been lucky. He'd logged thousands of hours underwater, more – sometimes – than he liked to remember. But he'd stayed fit, and gone easy on the drinking, and avoided silly risks, and his annual medical had so far revealed no major problems. At thirty-eight, though, he knew his working days underwater were numbered, and he'd no desire to end up like some of the men he'd dived with: crippled, semi-deaf, permanently breathless, very rich invalids, set up nicely for the rest of their brief, brief lives.

A door opened, and the surgery nurse appeared. She said that the doctor was ready. Buddy folded the completed questionnaire, picked up his envelope of X-rays, and followed her into the surgery. He knew the doctor as well as the annual check-ups permitted. He was a thin, nervous man, ex-Navy, with a habit of coughing before each new sentence. Buddy had often thought of recommending a good linctus, but had never got round to mentioning it.

He gave the doctor the X-rays. The doctor emptied them out onto the desk and held the first of the films briefly up to the daylight. In a moment or two there'd be more tests: blood pressure, ECG, eyes, ears, teeth, chest, and four minutes or so of heavyish exercise on a cycling machine before Buddy would be told to expel one deep lungful of air into an analyser. Quite what this revealed, he'd never understood, but it was infinitely more knackering than anything he'd ever been asked to do in the North Sea.

For now, though, the doctor was still examining the X-rays. He clipped the first of the films to a light box, and looked hard at the image on the screen. Buddy recognized the shape of his upper thigh, the ball and socket joint in his hip, the lines of the bones a denser grey than the surrounding flesh. The doctor was still peering at it. He glanced at the nurse. She handed him a small magnifying glass. With the glass tight to his eye, he took another look. Buddy frowned. He could see nothing wrong. His hand began to crab up along his thigh, an instinctive gesture, curiosity and self-defence. The nurse, watching him, smiled. The doctor turned from the light box and selected another film. He clipped it beside the first film. He bent towards it again, the glass to his eye. Then he coughed, and turned round, as if to check that Buddy was still there.

"Any pain at all? Any niggles?" He tapped the first of the images. "Round there?"

Buddy shook his head. "No," he said.

"Sure?"

"Positive."

The doctor grunted to himself and checked the image again, a hiker in unfamiliar territory, looking for a long-forgotten footpath. He found it at once. He coughed.

"You'll know about bone necrosis."

Buddy nodded. Bone necrosis was an occupational hazard for divers. It had something to do with the blood supply. The bones began to crumble at the edges. It meant they were knackered. Some men likened it to metal fatigue. He looked at the doctor.

"How bad?" he said.

The doctor peered again at the X-ray, though without using the glass.

"Bad enough," he said.

"Bad enough to affect the licence?"

"Depends." He paused and looked round. "What plans might you have?"

Buddy hesitated a moment. The temptation was to tell him everything. Jude. The accident. Pascale's operation.

What the whole thing would cost. Put the right way, leaning on the man, trading on his sympathy, he might just suspend his medical judgement and give Buddy the benefit of the doubt. But that, he knew, would be unfair. Better to play it straight. Give the man an objective decision. Take whatever was coming. He shrugged.

"Dunno," he said, "more of the same, I suppose."

"Sat diving?"

"Maybe."

"Hmm . . ."

The doctor checked the rest of the X-rays. In Buddy's shoulders and knees, and the long bones of his lower leg, he found the beginnings of more necrosis, tiny irregularities on the smooth grey surfaces of the bones. Buddy, watching him, began to feel uncomfortable. The nurse, he noticed, had stopped smiling.

When the doctor got on with the rest of the tests, Buddy's eyes strayed constantly back to the images on the light box. Finally, an hour later, he stepped off the exercise bike, accepted a towel and a glass of water from the nurse, and tottered back to the chair in front of the desk while the doctor quickly tabulated the results.

Buddy watched him closely, the pen racing across the page, forgetting for a moment the moneys he needed to raise, the need to get Jude to Boston, the whole point of the exercise. The next five minutes, he knew, might end his diving career for good. He'd spent more than half his working life underwater, first in the Navy, then in the civvy world. He'd known all the time that one day it would come to an end. But that wasn't at all the same thing as actually being there, in this stuffy airless room, the smell of antiseptic, a towel round his shoulders, waiting.

With Jude fit and well, with plans to make, and extensions to build, and two lives to get on with, diving was something he'd have barely missed. But Jude was far from fit and well, and diving – his career – was suddenly all-important again, his only real handle on the world.

The doctor looked up. Buddy waited for the cough. It came and went, an apologetic flap of the hand. Then the doctor ducked his head again, looking at the pad.

"In most respects, you're very fit," he said carefully.

"But?"

"But . . ." He shrugged, throwing a regretful glance at the light box. "But you've got necrosis. I make no bones about it."

He paused, waiting for Buddy to acknowledge the ritual joke. Buddy looked at him, expressionless.

"So?" he said.

"So . . ." he shrugged again, "you definitely won't be going sat. Definitely not. No question of that."

Buddy nodded. "So what are you saying? What do you recommend?"

"Me?" He got up and stretched, running a tired hand over his face. "If I were you?"

Buddy nodded again. "Yes."

The doctor hesitated. He switched off the light box and wandered over to the window. He gazed out for a moment at the apron of concrete that served as a car-park. Buddy's Jaguar was out there, his precious XJ6. The doctor was looking at it, the ghost of a smile on his face.

"I'm no diver," he mused, "but I know you blokes. How you miss it all afterwards. So . . ." he turned back into the room, "I'd go for one last job. Not sat. Maybe nothing worth a great deal. But something *really* interesting." He paused. "That sound good advice?"

Charlie picked up Mairead at the usual place, outside the travel agents in Great Victoria Street, half a mile from the Europa Hotel. She was waiting by the bus stop, umbrella furled, shopping bag at her feet. She saw his car, the tan Ford Escort, and she picked up the bag. Minutes later, they were heading north, out past the Harbour Airport, out towards Bangor.

Charlie offered her a wine gum from a packet on the dashboard. He didn't smoke in the car any more, not since she'd said it made her feel sick. He glanced at her. She'd phoned at nine on the special number he'd given her. She looked terrible. He wondered about Connolly, the mystery guest in Dublin.

"He's back?" he asked. "Yer man?"

Mairead nodded. "He says he loves me," she said, "it's very difficult. What am I supposed to do now, for God's sake?"

Charlie said nothing for a moment. They were following a removals van. The road was still wet after the overnight rain, and there was stuff all over the windscreen. Charlie put the wipers on and indicated to overtake.

"And you," he said at last, the van receding behind them, a dot in his mirror, "how do you feel?"

"I've got three kids," she said automatically.

"But do you love him?"

She hesitated a moment, then nodded.

"Yes," she said, "I think I do."

"So . . ." Charlie shrugged, "what's the problem?"

Mairead looked across at him. She'd been up most of the night. The boy couldn't stop talking, hours and hours of it, and she'd listened, lying beside him, the light off, the curtains open. How do you explain all that, she wondered. How do you do it justice?

"Something's happened to him," she said, "he's made a decision in his life. It's not a small thing, Charlie."

"What decision?"

"I don't know. It's hard to explain. He can be a strange wee fella sometimes. He doesn't know what he wants. Who he is. But something's happened. I can see it in him. He's changed. He's put all his money on one square."

"Which square?"

"My square. Me."

"Oh." Charlie smiled. "And does he know about . . . this? Us? Me?"

She shook her head. "No," she said.

"Then it's simple. You tell him. You tell him how you feel. About what happened to Danny. About the movement. What it's done to your family." He paused. "He's a Brit. He'll understand. It's nothing to be ashamed of."

"It's not that simple. I live here, God help me."

Charlie glanced across the car. The girl on the radio was warning of rain.

"We could help you," Charlie said, "you know that. We could move you away."

"Yeah . . ." she laughed, a small bitter laugh, "afterwards."

Her hand disappeared up the sleeve of her coat and she took out a small crumpled ball of Kleenex. She blew her nose. "Anyway, that's not the point," she said, "he wouldn't want me talking to you."

"Why not?"

"Because he's started to believe it all, God help us."

"All what?"

"All the Republican squawk. All the mumbo-jumbo. I tell you. The man's made a decision. He's turned a corner. He's been reading about it for most of his life. He teaches it up at that University of his. Now he believes it, too."

"He does?"

Mairead looked at him quickly. There was something in his voice, a question behind the question. For once, he sounded surprised, even uncertain. Despite everything, she liked Charlie. There was a softness about him. Something about the eyes, the pony tail. God knows why he'd joined the Army. He might have been her brother. Easily. "So," she looked him in the eye, "he tells me I should support the cause. He's doing a Danny on me. It's happening all over again." She sniffed. "So . . ." she said again, "what do we do?"

"We?"

"Yes. Me and Derek."

Charlie thought about it for a moment.

"My boss . . ." he began slowly.

"I don't want to know about your boss. I'm asking you. You understand that?" She paused. "Real people, Charlie. Me and Derek. Remember?"

Charlie nodded, reaching for a wine gum. He sucked it for a moment, then glanced across at her.

"I can tell you now," he said, "we won't let you go. It gets very territorial. We need to stay in touch. Believe me."

"But what about Derek?"

"What about him?"

"This man Ingle he's supposed to meet."

Charlie's eyes went up to the mirror. "Ingle?" he said. "Who's Ingle?"

"Special Branch." She frowned. "Isn't that your lot?"

Charlie looked at her a moment, then pulled the car off the main road, away from the coast, into the country.

"No," he said at last, "it's not."

"Oh." She nodded. "I see."

They drove on in silence for a while, narrow country lanes, the odd bungalow. Mairead blew her nose again.

"Derek doesn't like Ingle," she said at last, "he wants the man off his back." She glanced across at Charlie. "Can you fix that for us?"

Charlie shook his head, revolving the wine gum slowly beneath his tongue.

"No," he said, "I can't."

"Why not?"

"Different branch of the family."

"But you know them, don't you? Talk to them? Same side?"

Charlie said nothing, reaching for the wipers again. The girl on the radio had been right about the rain. They drove in silence for a while, corner after corner. Mairead began to wonder whether Charlie hadn't got them lost. Finally, they came to a crossroads. The signpost indicated right for Belfast. Charlie turned right. The car settled down again, a steady thirty-five.

"So," Mairead said, "what do you want from me?"

"Yer man, Derek," he said, "he'll tell you everything? About Ingle? And whatever else happens?"

"I don't know," she said, "I can't say. He might. He might not."

Charlie smiled. "He will," he said.

"And if he doesn't?"

Charlie glanced at her. "Then I tell them," he said, "everything."

"Who?"

"Dermot. Those fierce neighbours of yours. The boyos."

"About us? This?"

Charlie nodded, sucking on the wine gum, saying nothing.

Mairead stared ahead, through the windscreen, the country-side a green blur in the rain. Liam, she thought, the kids.

"You're as bad as they are," she said softly.

The car stopped at a main road. The signpost said Belfast. Charlie shook his head. The pony tail. The soft Irish brogue.

"No," he said grimly, "we're worse."

Scullen met the Chief in the bus station at Dundalk. There was a small café beside the waiting room. Scullen ordered the teas. The Chief paid.

They sat at a table next to the window. Mid-afternoon, the light was already fading, a grey premature dusk falling on the half-acre of oil-stained tarmac outside the window. One of the buses was going to Dublin. Another was headed for Belfast. One day, thought Scullen, there'll be no border in between. Just a single country. And a single people.

The Chief leaned in, across the table, beckoning Scullen towards him. The rendezvous had been at his invitation. Scullen had been driven down from Sligo, where he was currently headquartered. There'd been a big shipment of arms come in. The Quartermaster was working day and night, supervising the dumps out in the country, keeping them all busy. He'd begun to tell the Chief about it, but the Chief – unusually – wasn't interested. He was less cheerful than usual. He had something else on his mind. He looked Scullen in the eye.

"I want to know about Qualitech," he said.

Scullen nodded. "Aye?"

"I'm told it wasn't one of ours."

Scullen nodded again. "That's right," he said, "I got a call."

"Who from?"

"O'Mahoney." Scullen frowned, remembering the half-minute of conversation on the phone at Buncrana. O'Mahoney was the point man on one of the ASUs. He'd recognized the voice. "He said they'd nothing to do with it," he told the Chief, "he was quite categorical."

"So why the headlines? Why our name on the fucking bomb?"

"I don't know."

The Chief nodded. "Neither does O'Mahoney," he said. Scullen stared at him for a moment. "You've seen him?"

"Yesterday."

"Where?"

"Belfast."

"What's he doing back?"

"He wanted to talk to me."

"Why you?"

The Chief recognized the tone in Scullen's voice, the wounded pride, the anger, O'Mahoney stepping out of line, going behind his back. He reached across and put a gloved hand on Scullen's arm.

"Padraig," he said, "the boy's worried. That's why."

Scullen nodded, unconvinced. "What did he say?"

The Chief spooned sugar into his tea and stirred it, thoughtful. Scullen began to understand why they'd met, the urgency of it.

"He got to talk to somebody who knew a journalist. Brit journalist. This fella had gone to the press conference. They had the device there. The fella knows a thing or two about our stuff, the way we do it – " he looked at Scullen – "the way you do it."

Scullen nodded. Every bomb had its trademarks, its special features, its clever little short cuts. They told an expert where the device had come from, even who'd made it. If you knew what you were looking for, they were as good as fingerprints. Scullen looked up.

"So?" he said.

"So . . ." the Chief shrugged, "the thing was definitely ours. The fella swears by it."

"He's winding us up."

"Maybe." He paused. "But O'Mahoney believed him. That's the importance of it. O'Mahoney believed him and he wants to know what the fuck's going on."

"So he talked to you."

"Yes. He thought I might know."

"And do you?"

"No." He shook his head. "That's why I'm here."

Scullen leaned back in his chair, and pulled his coat

around him, gazing out of the window. Currently, he had two ASUs on duty on the mainland. One was O'Mahoney's. The other was based in the West Midlands. He'd checked the Qualitech job with them, using a courier on the Birmingham service out of Dublin Airport. She'd reported back that they, too, had no knowledge of the hit. On the contrary, they'd assumed that it had been O'Mahoney's work. Nice stroke, they'd said. Shame it hadn't worked. Scullen glanced back at the Chief and bent to his own tea.

"I don't know . . ." he shrugged, "the thing's a mystery."

"Doesn't that bother you?"

"No." He stirred the tea. "Should it?"

There was a long silence. Then the Chief leaned forward across the table again, one elbow in a puddle of spilled tea.

"There's another thing about O'Mahoney," he said.

"There is?"

"Yes," he nodded, "he did a head job for you. Quick in and out. He didn't tell me all the details but he wasn't very happy."

Scullen glanced up. He'd sent a courier to O'Mahoney with orders to kill Leeson. He'd supplied the address and told him the job was priority. Under the circumstances, there'd been no choice. Apart from Connolly, Leeson was the only Brit who might spoil the plans he was laying for the Portsmouth job. Supplying the germ of the idea in the first place didn't protect him from the operational consequences. O'Mahoney's hit, though, had clearly been less than simple. Scullen looked at the Chief.

"Why?" he said mildly. "Why is the man upset?"

"The target was under surveillance. And you never told him." He paused. "Luckily, he went in through the back. Otherwise it might have been nasty."

"Maybe I didn't know," Scullen paused, "and maybe he should have checked."

"Yeah. Maybe you didn't. And maybe he should. But these fellas get jumpy. You know that. They need support . . ." He paused, making the point, then his hand disappeared beneath the table. "Here," he said, "it's a present. From yer man."

"Who?"

211

"O'Mahoney."

Scullen nodded, taking the plastic shopping bag. It was heavy. He could guess what was inside.

"OK," he said.

A silence settled between them. Then the Chief leaned across again, driving home his point.

"Support, Padraig. Not my job. Yours."

"Mine," Scullen agreed.

The Chief nodded. "Secrecy's a fine thing," he said. "But people get nervous. They need talking to sometimes. You should remember that."

"I will."

Scullen looked at him a moment, and then ducked his head, a stiff gesture of submission, accepting the reprimand, recognizing the conversation for what it was, a formal warning. He stirred his tea slowly.

"About Qualitech," he said, "that bomb."

The Chief looked up. "Yes?"

"There are two possibilities." He paused, frowning. "The first is obvious."

"What's that?"

"There never was a bomb."

"Then what did they show? At the press conference?"

"A mock-up. They could do it in their sleep. They've got enough examples. They know what they're up to."

The Chief nodded. "And the rest of it?" he said. "Your other theory?"

Scullen sipped at his tea. Then patted his mouth with a small white handkerchief.

"They might have planted it themselves," he said.

The Chief frowned.

"Who might?"

"The Brits."

"Yes, but who? Which Brits?"

There was a long silence. A bus coughed, out in the semi-darkness. Then, for the first time, Scullen smiled.

"Exactly," he said, "*which* Brits?"

212

Buddy Little flew back from Aberdeen two days later. He'd spent the best part of a week knocking on doors, meeting old contacts, sounding out prospects, enquiring about work. The start of the North Sea season was still a couple of months away, but with a full sat medical clearance he could have been out on a plane already, any number of destinations, Middle East, Caribbean, even Australia. Any of the jobs would have given him a fat wodge of money, swopping a month on the seabed for at least a partial solution to his problem. As it was, though, his licence ruled him out. No one would touch him. He was just too old.

In desperation, towards the end of the week, he began to listen to the offers of shore-based work, a white collar job, something supervisory, something that would put him behind a desk and make the best of his experience, but the more interviews he had, the more hands he shook, the more he realized that this simply wasn't his world. They were nice enough people, and the money was tempting but the work was high pressure, incessant, governed by the kind of impossible performance targets he'd always fought against as a professional diver. Looking through the other end of the telescope, putting on the company tie, it wasn't hard to see the rationale – lower costs, bigger profits – but he knew too much about the realities of diving, about the million silly things that could go wrong and kill a man, to simply join the bosses. No, if they wanted a gamekeeper, then they'd have to look elsewhere. Even for Jude, he wouldn't screw his mates.

And so he came home, empty handed, unlocking the back door of the cottage and stepping into the tiny kitchen. The place was getting a little shabby now, he knew. He was doing his best to give things a wipe or two every week, but huge chunks of his time were swallowed up by trips to the hospital, and bids to find work, and if he was honest, his heart was no longer in it. The cottage had been home with Jude around. With Jude gone, it was simply a pile of bricks, a collection of rooms, and with the heating off to save on the bills, the place beginning to smell of damp.

213

There was a letter on the mat for him. He recognized the writing on the envelope, stooping to pick it up, wandering into the kitchen to read it. The letter was from Gus, his mucker on the rigs. It said that near Easter he was due a spot of leave. That Marge and the kids would be away at her mum's place in South Wales. That he might drop by for a day or two to catch up on the news, share a pint or two, take them both out. Buddy read the letter quickly. He'd never told Gus about the accident. He'd thought about it once or twice. He'd even tried to start a letter of his own. But in the end he'd screwed it up and thrown it away. Gus, he knew, would be on the next chopper out, the next plane down. He was that kind of bloke. He'd be very upset, and very supportive, and very sensible, and he'd drive Buddy mad within hours. Just now, he could do without all that. Better, he thought, to leave Gus in the dark just a little while longer. He folded the letter and stuffed the envelope into his back pocket, forgetting it.

He took a chocolate biscuit from the tin beside the fridge and wandered through to the living room. The answerphone lay on the table under the window. There were half a dozen messages on the tape. He spooled quickly through them. Four were enquiries about the riding school, and he made a note of names and addresses to call back. The fifth was an American voice, someone from Pascale's clinic, someone he'd never met before, wanting him to call about dates and availability. Evidently there'd been a phone conference with Bishop. The English doctor thought Jude would be discharged in March. Buddy listened to the voice, noting the details, wondering if it wasn't already too late.

The tape stopped at the last message. He pushed the cue button. There was a burst of static, then a female voice he couldn't quite place. The voice asked him to phone as soon as he could. There was a ten-digit number and a name. Sheila Rogers. The voice rang off.

Buddy looked at the number, recognizing the hospital's STD code. Then he looked at the name again, at last putting a face to the voice. Sheila Rogers. The pretty young nurse in Jude's ward.

He dialled the number. The number answered. He asked

214

for the nurse. There was a silence, then the nurse came on. Buddy said who he was, and there was a brief pause. He could hear a door closing in the background. Then the nurse came back. She sounded slightly out of breath.

"It's your wife, Mr Little," she said.

"What's the matter with her?"

There was another pause, the length of a heartbeat. Then the nurse again. "I'm afraid she's tried to kill herself," she said, "you ought to come up."

Buddy got to the hospital in a fraction under the hour. He pulled the Jaguar into one of the consultants' parking bays, and ran the length of the main corridor. He found the nurse in the small office at the head of the ward. She told him to sit down. She closed the door. He stared up at her.

"What happened?" he said.

She told him the bare facts. How she'd been on duty the previous evening, midnight to eight. How she'd checked the ward every half-hour or so, keeping an eye on the patients throughout the night. And how she'd found Jude, three in the morning, lying on her back, blood everywhere, choking. Somehow she'd managed to hide the small vanity mirror inside the top of her pyjamas. The nurse gone, she'd retrieved it with her mouth, broken it with her teeth, and tried to swallow it. Fortunately, the pieces had been too big, and the muscles of her gullet too weak, for her to swallow properly. She'd begun to choke, cutting herself badly, the noise unmistakable. The nurse had been at her bedside in seconds, retrieving the shards of broken glass with her fingers. Buddy listened, sick at heart, believing every word of it, only surprised that it hadn't happened before.

"How is she?" he said.

"Furious."

"I meant inside."

The nurse shrugged. "She was bleeding. They had to suture. But it was nothing too serious. She'll live."

"Yeah." Buddy nodded. "After a fashion."

He left the office, thanking her, and walked the length of the ward. Jude saw him coming, and Buddy knew from her expression that she'd have turned over, her face to the wall, had she been able.

He sat at the bedside and kissed her on the forehead.

"My bloody mirror," he said softly, "cost me a fortune."

She looked up at him, still angry. There was a cut at the corner of her mouth, and she was obviously finding it difficult to swallow. Her voice, when she talked, was very low, the words coming out slowly, through God knows how many stitches.

"At least I tried," she said.

He looked at her for a while, fingers through her hair.

"So how do you feel?" he said.

"Lousy."

"I meant about Boston?"

She said nothing, just blinked, and he bent very low, to her ear, and said he loved her. Her hair smelled of shampoo. The nurse again. An act of simple charity. Some small consolation.

Buddy withdrew slightly, gladder than he could say that she was still alive, that circumstances – for once – had frustrated her. He repeated the question. Pascale, he said, Boston? She smiled up at him, for the first time, a small, wan smile, the faintest curl of the lips.

"OK, Buddy," she whispered, "we'll do it your way."

BOOK THREE

BOOK THREE

FIFTEEN

Six weeks later, eight and a half thousand miles away, four British scientists set out on a routine field trip from the British Antarctic Survey base at Grytviken, on the island of South Georgia. They carried with them a radio, binoculars, an assortment of scientific apparatus, and enough food and fuel to keep them alive for a week.

They made their way up the rocky north coast, and established camp at the deserted settlement of Leith, once a prosperous whaling station. Amongst the gaunt, abandoned sheds, and the litter of old steam winches, they settled into a daily routine. They recorded the wildlife. They took soil and ice samples. They monitored the notoriously treacherous weather.

On March 19th, they awoke to find an Argentinian warship anchored in the harbour. They watched, as about fifty men began to unload supplies. Some of the men wore paramilitary uniforms. A small party left the whaling station, and soon the scientists could hear the crack of high-powered rifles echoing amongst the surrounding mountains. Hours later, the men were back again, dragging behind them the corpses of slaughtered reindeer. By this time, a blue and white flag was fluttering over the abandoned town. The flag belonged to Argentina.

The scientists did what they could. They told the captain of the warship that no one could land on South Georgia without British permission. They pointed out that it was illegal to shoot reindeer. And they said that the men had no right to fly a foreign flag on British territory. The captain shrugged off their protests. It had all, he said, been taken care of.

Returning to their camp, the scientists passed a notice,

219

recently pasted on the wall of one of the whaling sheds, warning intruders against unauthorized landings. Across the posters, in Spanish, someone had scrawled "*Las Malvinas son Argentinas*". Only one of the scientists spoke Spanish. The others looked at him. He shrugged.

"It's the Falklands next," he said. "The buggers think it belongs to them."

Scullen, in Dublin for a couple of days, read the news over his second cup of coffee in a small café near Heuston Station. He'd bought a copy of *The Times* at the airport, inbound from Galway. He read the paper every day now, Leeson's parting recommendation after the lunch they'd shared way back in January.

The report was on page six. It was headed "Argentinians hoist a flag on South Georgia". The intruders, it said, had been asked to comply with immigration procedures, or leave. Since they'd done neither, the Foreign Office had responded by dispatching the survey ship HMS *Endurance*. The ship carried a detachment of twelve Royal Marines. The island was British sovereign territory. If all else failed, the Argentinians were to be thrown off.

Scullen read the reports twice. Then he folded the paper carefully and laid it on the table beside his empty cup. Leeson had mentioned South Georgia during their lunch in Dublin. He'd said there was a chance it might start there. Not the invasion itself, but the sequence of events that would lead to the invasion. Diplomacy, he'd said, is like chess. You make your opening gambit on one side of the board. And win the game on the other.

Now Scullen picked up the paper again and scanned the article for a third time, making quite sure. "Argentina," it warned at the end, "will soon seek other means of solving the dispute, unless there is a speedy settlement." Scullen read the phrase, and then pushed the paper away again, a gesture of quiet applause for the English diplomat. Like the man in the dress circle, he'd got the plot exactly right.

He got up and paid for the coffee. McParland joined him on the street outside. They drove to a hotel half a mile away where Scullen had booked a room. Later, God willing, the boy Connolly would be joining them. Then he planned a trip round the zoo, an appropriate backdrop, he thought, for yet another survey of the goods on offer. First though, there was South Georgia to attend to. The Falklands. The looming hostilities. Scullen stepped into the hotel, and found the tiny phone booth at the end of the hall. He dialled a number from memory and glanced at his watch. Finally a woman's voice answered. She had a faint German accent.

"It's me," he said carefully, "I think the answer's yes."

Jude Little had been at the house just one night when Buddy took the phone call.

Friends had surprised them both, the evening the ambulance had brought them back from the Regional Spinal Unit. There'd been flags around the door, little Union Jacks tucked in amongst the Virginia creeper, and food and drink laid out in the kitchen. There'd been sausage rolls, and baked potatoes, and a huge bowl of hummus – enough, said Jude, to keep her going for a month. There'd been wine, and music, and the party had gone on long past midnight. Jude had been installed in the living room, the conversation and the laughter swirling around her, old friends on chairs circling the bed, kids too, their chins on the blanket, their eyes wide. Auntie Jude, they'd thought. Off to bed so early.

Jude had cried at it all, total surprise, an easier homecoming than she'd ever anticipated, and Buddy, too, had been moved to tears. Towards midnight, everyone a little drunk, he'd slipped out into the darkness. Only one of the horses was left now, Duke. Buddy had found him in his box in the stable yard, a cloud of white breath on the cold night air. The big horse had ducked his head and shaken his ears, seeming to sense that his mistress was finally home, and Buddy had looked at him, stern, real eye contact.

"Your fault," he'd said, "your bloody fault."

Next morning, Buddy had got up early, meaning to clean the house and finish the washing up before Jude awoke. But when he tiptoed quietly downstairs, her eyes were already open. She could move her head now, in any direction, and she watched him through the open kitchen door as he filled the sink with water and began to soap the dirty dishes.

"Me next," she said.

The washing up done, and the tea brewing, Buddy switched on the electric fire and began to warm the living room. The busiest month of his life had included installing central heating, essential – said the hospital – if Jude was to be safe from chest infections. One of the side effects of paralysis, Bishop had explained, was a general lowering of resistance. From now on, Buddy was to be the guardian at Jude's gate, scourge of the world's known germs. Nothing, he'd determined, would get past. No chest infections. No kidney infections. Nothing that might steal through and take her from him. The central heating, though, was proving temperamental. Overnight, for some reason, it had switched itself off. Thus the need for the electric fire.

They had breakfast while the room slowly warmed. Buddy propped Jude's body up against a stack of pillows, and fed her porridge by the spoonful. He decanted tea into a baby's plastic cup and held it to her lips while she sucked and rolled her eyes and made loud gurgling noises. She'd had three glasses of wine the previous evening, the first alcohol for three months, and the booze had left her dehydrated. They had a second pot of tea. And then a third.

By now, the room was warm. Buddy offered the plastic cup a final time. Jude shook her head.

"Bolt the door," she said.

Buddy looked at her, not quite understanding.

"The door," she said again. "Bolt it."

Buddy went to the back door and locked it. The front door was already bolted. He was back by her bed.

"Curtains?" he enquired.

Jude nodded. "Close them," she said.

Buddy pulled the curtains. The room sank into semi-darkness, shafts of daylight down the stairs, the hum of the electric fire in the hearth. He looked at Jude again. Some new hospital routine, he thought, something they never told me about.

"Now what?" he said.

She looked up at him. "Take your clothes off," she said.

"Me?"

She rolled her eyes again. "Who else?"

Buddy hesitated. "Why?" he said at last.

She looked at him. There was a comma of porridge at the corner of her mouth. Buddy lifted a finger and wiped it off, and her tongue caught him in the act. She sucked the end of his finger for a moment or two, still looking at him. Buddy smiled at her. He felt uncomfortable. She let his finger go.

"Off," she said, "get your clothes off."

Buddy smiled, wiser now. "There's no need," he said softly, "honestly."

"Who says?"

"I say."

"And me? Do I get a say?"

"You're . . ."

He stopped and shrugged, embarrassed at what he'd so nearly said. Then he shrugged again and began to loosen the zip of his jeans. Jude nodded, her point made.

"Thank you," she said, "Mr Do-It-All."

"I'm sorry. I only meant . . ."

"I know what you only meant."

"Oh?" He looked down at her.

She nodded. "You only meant to tell me to go easy. Little Miss Cripple. Know my place . . ." She smiled tightly up at him, angry. "Right?"

He nodded. "Right," he said.

She looked away for a moment.

"At least you're honest," she said.

"I'm sorry."

"You said that before."

"I meant it."

She nodded and said nothing for a moment. Then her head turned back on the pillow.

"OK," she said, "now the rest."

Buddy took his pants off, then his sweat shirt. He could feel the electric fire against the backs of his legs. She gestured him forward with her eyes. He stood by the bed. It was a very high bed, designed to make nursing easier. She grinned.

"You're going to need a stool," she said. "Short ass."

Buddy closed his eyes for a moment. Ridiculous, he

thought. He fetched a small wooden box from the kitchen, stood on it beside the bed. Jude examined him closely.

"Beautiful," she said, "come here."

Buddy glanced down. Nothing happened. Jude looked up at him, a request, a favour.

"Help me," she whispered, "please."

Buddy did so. It took a long time. Finally, she kissed him, softly, on the tip. Then she looked up again.

"You could fuck me properly," she said, "only I won't feel a thing."

Buddy nodded, but said nothing. "So this'll have to do. My treat. OK?"

The phone call came an hour later. A woman's voice, a strong Irish accent.

"My name is O'Hara," she said, "I work for a Catholic charity organization." She paused. "It's about your wife. I wonder whether I might come and talk to you both."

She arrived within the hour in a small white car. She parked outside the stable yard and picked her way down the muddy path, a stout, bulky figure in a long black coat. Buddy met her at the front door. She stepped inside and Buddy took her straight through to the living room. There was a new fire in the hearth and the smell of air freshener, something lemony. He introduced her to Jude. He felt wonderful.

"Exhibit A," he said. "My wife."

Jude smiled a greeting. The woman reached forward and touched her face, a rare, intimate greeting, someone who knew about paralysis, someone without embarrassment or fear.

"I'm pleased to meet you," she said, unbuttoning her coat, "my name's Mary O'Hara."

Buddy looked at her. She was middle aged, about forty. She was stockily built with a warm, dimpled face, framed with red curly hair. She wore a crucifix at her neck, and no rings on her fingers. She accepted Buddy's offer of tea, and sat down beside the bed. She looked at Jude. She had very pale grey eyes.

"I've read about you," she said.

Jude blinked. "You have?"

"Yes."

Out in the kitchen, pouring the tea, Buddy closed his eyes. He'd never told Jude about the article. He'd never thought he'd have to. The appeal, the money, even Pascale's operation, had just disappeared, past tense, something they didn't even discuss any more. He stepped out of the kitchen, interrupting the conversation.

"The local paper did an article," he told Jude quickly. "About you."

"They did?"

"Yes. They got in touch. Asked me lots of questions."

"What did you say?"

"Oh," he shrugged, "this and that." He looked at the woman. "You read it?"

"We did."

"We?" Buddy frowned, moving the conversation on. "Who's we?"

The woman sat back a moment, one leg crossed over the other. She explained that she represented a big Catholic charity. The charity was based in Dublin. They'd read about Jude's accident, and they knew about Pascale, and under certain circumstances, they were prepared to help. Buddy stared at her. He was still carrying a dishcloth and a wet tea-cup.

"Help?" he repeated blankly. "What kind of help?"

The woman looked at Jude and smiled at her. "We'd pay," she said. "For your wife to have the operation."

The woman stayed an hour. She said that her charity was amply funded and that its job was to relieve individual suffering. To this end, she travelled widely, assessing individual cases. Discretion in this matter was entirely her own. Religion or race were no bar. She'd made enquiries elsewhere, and she knew about the circumstances of the accident, and – standard procedure – she'd already cleared Jude's case with the charity's trustees. The only stipulation they wanted to make concerned her fitness for the journey and the operation. They wanted to be sure that Jude could cope physically, and to this end they proposed to fly her to

Dublin for an assessment by designated physicians. With that single promise, they'd be happy to meet Pascale's bill, and additional expenses, in full.

"Why?" Buddy asked.

She looked at him. "Because it is God's will," she said.

There was a silence. Buddy swallowed hard. Jude looked up at her.

"Is this God's will?" she said. "Me? All this?"

The woman glanced down at her. "Yes," she said, "it is."

Connolly met Scullen by the Monkey House in Dublin Zoo. He'd phoned the number he'd been given from the station, and McParland had answered. Over the past four weeks, he'd managed to get on terms with the man. False or otherwise, he'd even been permitted to use his Christian name.

"Thanks, Sean," he said, "the Monkey House it is."

Connolly found Scullen sitting on a bench eyeing a cage full of chimpanzees. He'd bought a bag of peanuts, and he was shelling them methodically, one by one, tossing them into the cage. The smaller of the two chimps was always the first to the peanuts. The fat one couldn't be bothered.

Scullen moved up the bench, and offered Connolly the last of the peanuts. Connolly shook his head.

"No thanks," he said.

Stooping from the bench, Scullen began to tidy the semi-circle of shells around his feet into a neat pile, collecting them up and shovelling them into the empty bag. He'd had Connolly picked up five weeks ago. Two men had gone to his flat in the Ormeau Road, and waited in a car outside. When Connolly had arrived, midday, they'd intercepted him before he got to the door, and driven him south, across the border, into the outskirts of Dundalk.

There, in a small council house, they'd taken him upstairs to a bare back room, lino on the floor, two chairs, and some rope. They'd tied him to one of the chairs, and left him for three hours. There were splashes of blood on the skirting board, and a battered wooden box in the corner. In the box were an assortment of blunt instruments, and an old Black

226

and Decker drill. There was a clear plastic case for the drill bits, but most of the bits were missing. The bit in the drill itself was on the large side. There was blood on that, too, though from a distance it looked like rust.

Late afternoon, Scullen had arrived. He'd gone straight up to see the boy. When he'd met him before, in the cottage, down in Armagh, he'd smelled the fear on him. Now though, to his surprise, there was something else entirely, a sense of composure rare to this terrible room. Connolly had looked him in the eye, steady as you like.

"Get these off," he said, nodding at the ropes, "and then we can talk."

Scullen had looked at McParland, and said OK, and McParland had obliged. The ropes off, Connolly had shaken the stiffness out of his wrists and asked for his pullover back. McParland had given him the pullover. Connolly had dragged it over his head, and stood up, and swung his arms round for a while, and then sat down again.

For the next fifteen minutes, no interruptions, no promptings, he'd told Scullen exactly what he'd wanted to know. He'd told him how Mairead had given him the rendezvous in Dublin, how he'd persuaded Leeson to fly over with him, how they'd taken the Saturday flight. He described the girl that had met them at the airport, and the car chase that followed. He told Scullen about getting Leeson back to London, the state of the man – cheerful, content – and his own brief few days out at Carshalton with his mother. On his way back to Belfast, he said, he'd called in to say goodbye to Leeson and found him dead in his own kitchen. He explained about Ingle, about the afternoon in the police cells, and about the deal he'd been obliged to strike. He held nothing back, and at the end – when Scullen asked him why the Brits had staked out Dublin Airport, who'd told them – he simply shrugged.

"Obvious," he said.

"Not to me."

"Obvious," he repeated. "They knew about Francis."

"Francis?"

"Leeson. They knew he was gay. They knew he was a security risk. They simply followed him."

"But they were waiting. At the airport."

"Then they must have checked the flights. His phone's bugged. Bound to be. I'd have talked to him about it. They'd have known."

Scullen had nodded. Saying nothing.

"Who's they?" he said at last.

"Ingle's lot. Special Branch."

Scullen had nodded again, musing, wondering how much – if anything – the boy knew about Nineteenth Intelligence, the real threat. Back by the window, Connolly had broken the silence.

"There's a point to all this," he said.

"All what?"

"All this stuff I'm telling you. Ingle. Special Branch. The Brits."

"Oh?" Scullen had looked enquiring, his big black coat wrapped tightly around him. "And what might that be?"

Connolly had hesitated a moment, hating the melodrama, but knowing exactly what he wanted to say. Ten years of study, of books and essays and conversation. Two years of lecture work, tight little tutorials up at Queens, the chance to explore it all first hand. A year of Mairead, a pace or two behind the front line, the framed pictures of Danny, the widow the movement never forgot. And now this, at last, the real thing. He'd looked up at Scullen.

"I'm supposed to be touting for Ingle," he said. "Doesn't that excite you?"

Scullen had nodded. "It might," he said.

"There must be things you want to tell them? The Brits? Ingle? There must be things you want them to believe?"

Scullen had acknowledged the point with the merest nod.

"Then I'm your man. Your delivery boy. Federal Express. Whatever you say, goes."

"To Ingle?"

"Yes."

Scullen had nodded, looking for the trap. "A conversion," he'd said at last. "Remarkable."

In the five brief weeks since, Scullen had met Connolly on a number of other occasions. Each time, the meetings had been over the border. Each time, the invitations had been unannounced, the precautions watertight, the field-work immaculate. Not once had there been any suspicion of surveillance, not a shred of evidence to confirm Scullen's innate conviction that he was being set up. When they met, they talked about the broad issues – nothing specific, nothing operational – and Scullen had begun to warm to the young academic. He was quick. He was sympathetic. He was witty. And he was remarkably compliant, a good listener, a willing ear. Scullen's tastes weren't the same as Leeson's. He had little sexuality of any kind. But none the less, he began to understand what it was that had attracted the older man. Connolly, in a curiously attractive way, was extraordinarily naïve, a blank sheet of paper on which the next man – or the next woman – scribbled whatever they chose.

Now, walking slowly past the alligator pit, Scullen paused. "Tell me," he said, "why this decision of yours? Why come to us?"

Connolly thought about the question for a moment. The longer answer he'd been formulating for several years. It had provided a raft on which they'd floated their conversations over the past month. It had to do with the covert exercise of state power, the animal that lurked in the deepest recesses of Whitehall, the depth and complexity of the con trick that had begun to envelop the England he thought he knew, the fingerprints of the State he'd come to hate. But there was another reason, too, a bit closer to home, the practical application of all that theory. He glanced up at Scullen.

"They killed Leeson," he said simply. "I know they did."

Charlie knew it had got personal the day the photograph appeared on Miller's office wall.

He saw it when he went in for the morning update, the head and shoulders shot, Scullen sitting in a car, slightly out of focus, staring straight ahead through the windscreen. Miller had pinned it to the noticeboard across from his desk. If he looked up, he couldn't fail to see it, a reminder, a taunt.

Charlie sat down in front of the desk. Miller had his head in the paper. He didn't look up. Charlie opened the file in his lap. He'd spent the best part of the previous evening with an agent he was running in Londonderry. They'd met in a big DIY store on the outskirts of the town, and driven in Charlie's car to a remote part of the Sperrin Mountains. The road was bare and exposed, winding up the mountainside. They'd talked for an hour and a half, the window an inch or two open, Charlie listening for movement in the windy darkness. Anyone driving up the road, he'd spot several miles away. Anyone approaching on foot might be a trickier proposition.

Miller, in the office, looked up. His eyes, Charlie noted, went straight to the photo of Scullen.

"What happened?" he said.

Charlie told him. The source, highly placed in the Derry Brigade, had the confidence of some key people. Over the past six months, since the deaths of the Hunger Strikers, he'd kept Charlie briefed on the biggest of the current issues: the strength of the call for revenge, and precisely what shape that revenge might take. The conversation had ranged far and wide, but the name that came up time and again was Scullen's. He'd become a very powerful man. He'd secured a perch for himself at the very top of the organization. He'd been given a large budget, and the pick of the best men, and remarkable freedoms. He'd rebuilt the ASUs, and insulated them from the home-based Brigades. He'd created an army within an army, and placed himself at its head. So far, so good. But Scullen had enemies in the movement, increasingly powerful, and in the judgement of Charlie's source, these enemies were close to having Scullen by the throat.

Miller looked up.

"Why?" he said.

Charlie's finger found a phrase he'd noted from the cassette recording in the car. It had struck him at the time.

"Because he thinks he's the Crown fucking Prince," he said. "Direct quote."

Miller nodded, unsurprised. "So what?" he said. "He's very good. Better than the Chief."

"The rest don't see it that way."

"They don't?"

"No. The word they're using is undemocratic."

"Undemocratic?" Miller laughed. "Since when have the Provos been interested in democracy? Is this something new? Have you briefed me on this?"

Charlie smiled for a moment, then returned to the file. "There's more," he said, "which might help. Apparently there's another big row. About means and ends. Chiefly means."

Miller nodded again, impatient now. "They want her dead," he said, "we know that. That's what it's all about. That's why we're here."

"Ah . . ." Charlie held up a cautionary finger, "but how? How will they do it?"

Miller looked at him. "If I knew that," he said, "the game would be over. We'd all be back home. Doing something half useful." He paused. "So what are you telling me? What did your man say?"

Charlie shrugged. "The word is, Scullen has something big in mind. Something a bit special."

"What?"

"I don't know."

"What *kind* of thing?"

"I don't know."

"Does *he* know? Your source?"

"No." He paused. "That's the point. No one knows. Scullen's stepped right out of channels. Not even the Chief knows." There was a long silence.

"The Chief protects him," Miller said. "No Chief. No Scullen."

"Precisely."

"So what does he think? The Chief?"

Charlie's head dipped towards the file again. "I gather he's reserving judgement."

Miller nodded. "Makes a change," he said tartly.

There was a long silence. One of the Unit's three-tonners ground past outside. Miller leaned back in the chair and gazed up at the ceiling.

"So what do *you* think?" he said at last.

231

Charlie hesitated a moment. "I think we need him off the plot," he said, "fast."

Miller let the chair tip forward again and looked him in the eye. "That's what Dublin was about," he said, "in theory . . ."

"I know."

There was another silence. The truck had come to a halt several blocks away, the engine still running. Miller was still looking at Charlie.

"So where do we go from here?" he said. "What about your young lady? Up in Andersonstown? What's she been telling you?"

"Nothing."

"*Nothing?*"

"No," he shrugged, "she says there's nothing to tell."

Miller watched Charlie for a moment longer. Then he folded his paper and put it carefully to one side. He opened a drawer and produced another file. Charlie looked at it. Miller had stencilled the word "Reaper" on the front. The file was no fatter than a month back. Miller opened it, checked something, and glanced up.

"We have a friend in the Garda," he said, "you'll know that."

Charlie nodded. There'd been talk of a source in the Irish police for a while. He even had a name. The Badger. "Yes," he said, "I'd heard."

Miller nodded. "Our friend has been involved in the Garville Street inquiry. Evidently they've put the forensic together and one or two other clues we left around. Our friend has lifted a copy. He sent it through."

"Nice of him."

Miller nodded. "Yes," he said, "the job's got our signature all over it. The Garda knew we were there. They're livid."

"How livid?"

"They've sent a copy to Downing Street. Back door job."

Miller leaned back, watching Charlie carefully, letting the implications sink in. To date, with backing from the very top, they'd got away with it. But now it suddenly looked very different. If the Garda really did go public, there'd be some hasty realignments. Nineteenth would be for the chop. The RUC would have a field day. MI5 would nod wisely and permit themselves a discreet smile. Special Branch would piss themselves. Horrible. Quite horrible.

Charlie glanced up. Miller was still looking at him. The two men said nothing, then Miller's eyes strayed again to the picture on the wall, and Charlie began to understand the way he'd been lately, withdrawn, watchful, quiet. Miller got up and walked across to the window. He had his hands in his pockets. He sounded tired.

"We need some action, Charlie," he said quietly. "We have one or two things to prove." He glanced round. "You get my drift?"

Charlie nodded. "Yes," he said.

"Talk to the girl again." He paused. "And try to forget you're bloody Irish!" He glanced round. "That possible?"

Charlie looked at him, saying nothing.

SIXTEEN

It took an hour for Buddy to make the arrangements for Dublin, and a day to convince Jude it was worth going.

The arrangements couldn't have been simpler. Mary O'Hara had left a card with a Dublin number. Buddy was to book a flight, ring the number, and everything would be taken care of. The ticket would be paid for, a hospital would be alerted, and an ambulance would meet the flight at the airport.

Putting the phone down, he told Jude the good news. She nodded, a small white face on the pillow, a towel still wrapped around her head after the morning shampoo.

"Fine," she said, "have a good time."

"You're coming with me." Buddy frowned. "That's the whole point."

She shook her head. "No," she said, "I'll stay here and tidy up."

"Ha, ha."

"I mean it." She smiled. "The first bit, anyway."

Buddy, astonished, had gone through it all again. He reminded her about Pascale, her suitability for the operation, the efforts he'd made to try and get them both to the clinic. He told her about his visit to Harry, his bid to borrow fifty grand, his tour of the oil companies up in Aberdeen, the journeys he'd made, the hands he'd shaken. He even told her, in detail, about the interview he'd given to the girl at the local paper. He found a copy of the article. He showed it to her. She glanced at it, read the headline, gazed for a moment at the shot of herself, sitting on Duke.

"You had no right," she said, "without asking me."

Buddy looked at her. He was furious. "I was trying to help," he pointed out, "I was trying to get you better."

"But you just went and phoned this girl up? My wife's a cripple? Help us make it through? Was that it?"

"Something like that."

"Wonderful."

Buddy walked into the kitchen. Counted to ten. Walked back again. She was watching his every move from the bed, determined to finish what she'd started, no matter where it led.

"So what did she say? This . . . girl?"

"She listened. I did most of the talking."

"I bet."

He rounded on her. "What does that mean?"

"It means I bet she sat there, listening to you talking about me." She paused. "You tell her about the old days? The horseriding? All that shit?"

"Yes."

"What else did you tell her? You tell her how we screwed? What kind of positions? How often? How horny I was? Always bothering you?"

"I told her I loved you."

"Yeah?"

"Yeah!"

There was a long silence. Buddy circled the bed. At the hospital, they'd warned him that this would happen, that Jude – one day – would offload all the bitterness, all the rage. At the time, he'd nodded, accepting it, a perfectly reasonable reaction, easy to understand, easy to forgive. Now, he wasn't so sure.

"I'm sorry," he said, "I shouldn't have done it."

She looked at him. The last thing she wanted was an apology.

"It was my body," she said bitterly.

Buddy nodded. "Yeah . . ." he said, "and my life."

There was another long silence. Buddy sat down. Miles above them, he could hear the thin, high whine of a passenger jet. The main airway to the States lay over the house. During the summer, lying on his back in the garden, Buddy had often watched the planes, tiny silver fish in an ocean of blue. Jude had been there too, bikini and garden gloves, squatting amongst the flowers, up to her elbows in soil, grubbing out the weeds. They'd have tea together. They'd talk. They'd laugh. Later, they'd go to the pub, roll back late, tumble around. Now, Buddy studied his hands, not looking at her. Where did all that go, he wondered, what kind of people were we then? He sat back in the armchair, letting the anger drain out of him. Jude was crying, big tears, rolling down onto the pillow, anger and frustration, not grief. Buddy watched her for a moment, then began to get up, reaching for the ever-present box of Kleenex.

"Don't," she said, "I don't want you to."

Buddy shrugged, collapsing back into the chair. The row had exposed them both, and he knew it. "I'm sorry," he said again, "I mean it."

Jude sniffed. "Doesn't matter," she said. "There's nothing we can do about it."

"I don't believe that."

"I know you don't. But it's true, my love."

"Who says?"

"Everyone. Everyone you talk to. The doctors. The physios. Even the nurses. People know. They just know." She paused. "That's the shame of it. If I was a pet, you'd have put me down by now. Put me out of my misery."

"I love you."

"Yeah . . ." she nodded, blinking, "I know. That's *why* you'd have put me down."

They talked all day. What began as a row became, in the end, a debate, Buddy the reluctant participant, Jude forcing him time and again to acknowledge the facts. Her life was effectively over. It had become, in essence, a list of jobs, someone else's jobs, Buddy's jobs. She took no pleasure from that, from the knowledge of it. Buddy listened to her quiet analysis, recognizing it for what it was, careful, emotionless, quite empty of bitterness or self-pity, but at the end of it all he simply shook his head, and said there was no argument. Everyone had a right to life, he said. Even her.

Jude had smiled at this. It was, she said, a very unhandicapped view. He ought to try it one day, try getting into her bed, or her wheelchair, cutting off nine-tenths of his body, compressing a fifteen-hour day into movements of his head and neck. Life, she said, was a gift. But if the thing didn't work any more you could send it back. That's where she was. That's what she thought. And if he really loved her, really wanted to do what was best for her, then he'd buy several bottles of decent champagne, and a dozen or so tablets, and they'd get smashed first, so the rest of it wouldn't feel so deliberate. Buddy watched her, nodding in mock agreement.

"OK," he'd said. "But I'll come too." He smiled. "That OK?"

"You're crazy." She smiled a small smile. "Crazy man."

"I mean it."

She looked across at him and shook her head.

"You don't," she said, "you're just confused."

"Wrong."

"Right. You're confused because you can't get the rest of it out of your head. The way we were." She paused. "The way we were was great. I mean it. It's never been better than that. Never. But this—" she turned her head away — "this is a joke."

Late in the evening, drunk again, they arrived at a deal. Jude would consent to go to Ireland, and on to Boston. Pascale would operate, the Irish charity would pay, and if nothing happened afterwards — no sensation, no movement — they'd order the champagne and the pills. The champagne they'd split. Jude would have the pills. This arrangement might be painful to discuss upfront, so from now they'd refer to it by code. The codeword would be Bollinger. Bollinger, insisted Jude, would be exactly what the word suggested. There'd be lots of fizz, lots of bubbles, an hour or two's dreamy conversation, and then she'd go to sleep.

Watching her talking, past midnight, stretched out beside her on the bed, Buddy yawned.

"End of story?" he suggested.

Jude grinned, life not quite so bad anymore, remembering the first time, in the horsebox, miles from anywhere, Duke outside, tied up to some tree or other.

"Yeah," she said, "happiness always smelled of horseshit. You know that."

*

Back in Belfast, Connolly phoned the number Ingle had given him.

He'd been living with Mairead full time for three weeks now, using the flat off the Ormeau Road as a study during the day. The arrangement was working well, better than he'd ever anticipated, and even Liam was beginning to accept it. The wooden glances over breakfast were becoming rarer, and the boy had even enquired about the possibility of Connolly joining him for a game of football. There was a park down the road. He played there with his mates. They sometimes needed a referee. Connolly would do nicely. Connolly, flattered, had exchanged glances with Mairead and said yes. He knew nothing about football, but he suspected that was irrelevant. Rules had ceased to matter in West Belfast for more than a decade. Having a referee was simply a passing whimsy, this season's little joke.

Connolly phoned Ingle from a call box opposite the City Hall. When he got through, there was a recorded message referring him to another number. Connolly wrote it down and looked at it. 0836, he thought. One of the new mobile phones. He dialled the number. It answered on the second ring, and Connolly recognized Ingle's voice at once, the flat South London accent. There was music in the background, something heavy, Led Zeppelin.

"Yes?" Ingle said.

"It's Connolly."

"Yes?"

"We need to meet."

"When?"

"Tonight. Half past five."

"OK."

The phone went dead and the music stopped. Connolly hung up and left the booth. On a news stand beside a chemist was a billboard for the evening paper. In heavy black scrawl it read "Informers Crippling IRA – Say Police".

Connolly left the University at five o'clock, and took the bus to the Central Station. The station was busy with commuters leaving the city for the suburbs and he had to push his way up the escalator and onto the crowded concourse. Ingle was standing outside the Whistle Stop bar. He was wearing a long, grubby raincoat, and a pair of plimsolls. His hair was as lank as ever, and he needed a shave.

"Terrible weather," he said, "always fucking raining."

Connolly shrugged. "You get used to it,' he said, "after the first ten years."

They walked back down to ground level. Ingle's car was parked beside the station. They sat inside, the engine on, the heater running. Connolly could hear the rumble of trains leaving the station near by. He looked across at Ingle.

"Been here long?" he said.

"Five minutes."

"I meant Belfast."

"Oh," Ingle shrugged, "a while."

There was a silence. The windows of the car had clouded with the warmth. Connolly wiped a small square in the cold glass. Coats and anoraks strode past outside. Ingle shifted his body in the seat. The car was too small for him. He turned sideways, his back to the window, looking at Connolly.

"Well?" he said.

Connolly took his time, remembering Scullen's careful instructions.

"There's some people I met . . ." he began.

"Yeah?"

Connolly nodded.

"Yeah," he said, "Republicans. Highly placed."

"Names?"

He glanced across at Ingle. Ingle had a small notepad out. His pencil broke on the first letter. He fumbled for a biro, and took the top off with his teeth.

"Well?" he said.

Connolly shrugged. "Dunno."

"They don't have names? Nicknames? Nothing?"

Connolly frowned, remembering the way Scullen had put it. Give him a taster, he'd said. Give him one name. Just one. Give him mine. Connolly looked up.

"There's one name," he said, "might be useful. Bloke called Scullen."

Ingle stared at him. "Scullen?" he said. "This kosher? Or a piss-take?"

"I don't know," Connolly said, "but that's his name. Or he says it is."

There was a long silence. Then Ingle shrugged and wrote the name on his pad.

"So what does he tell you?" he said. "This Scullen?"

"He doesn't tell me anything. It doesn't happen that way. You listen. You deduce. You work one or two things out. And then," he shrugged, fingering the window again, "I give you a ring."

"And?"

Connolly looked across at him. "There was an incident recently," he said, "a bomb scare. Something to do with the Prime Minister."

"Qualitech," Ingle said quickly. "They mention that? Factory place? Basingstoke?"

"That's it." He paused. "Someone found a bomb there."

Ingle nodded. "That's right," he said, "someone did."

Connolly glanced across at him. "Do you know who?"

"Yes. As it happens."

"Who was it?"

Ingle didn't answer. The pen was back in his hand. He was looking at Connolly. He wasn't smiling.

"Don't fuck around," he said. "Just tell me what you want to tell me. Someone knew about the Qualitech bomb. One of your lot–" he corrected himself – "their lot."

Connolly smiled. "Yes," he said, "their lot."

"So?"

There was a long silence. "It wasn't a Provo bomb," Connolly said at last, "someone else put it there."

"INLA," Ingle said quickly, naming a Republican splinter group, even wilder than the Provos.

"No."

"Who then?"

Connolly smiled again. Ingle was watching him carefully now. "Who?" he said again.

240

Connolly hesitated a moment, then nodded at Ingle's notepad.

"My impression," he said, "is that whoever found it, knew where to look."

"So?" Ingle frowned, his irritation beginning to show. "Someone touted. It's fucking obvious."

"Not necessarily."

"No?"

"No." Connolly paused. "Whoever knew where to look may also have planted the bomb in the first place." He smiled. "That make any sense to you?"

Ingle gazed at him for a long time and Connolly knew at once that he wanted to believe him. Maybe the seed had been planted way back. Maybe he knew all about it already. Either way, Connolly was bringing him good news. The biro had disappeared now, back into Ingle's pocket. Ingle was studying the pad. The single name. Scullen.

"So tell me," he said, "how come they're so fucking open with you around?"

Connolly shrugged. "I've joined the movement," he said. "Like you told me to."

"And they trust you?"

"Who knows?"

"But they think you're for real?"

"Yes."

Ingle reached forward, wiping the windscreen with his big hands. Then he stopped and looked at Connolly again.

"Are you?" he said. "For real?"

Connolly opened the door. There was a blast of cold air from the car park. "Dunno," he said vaguely. "What do you think?"

Connolly got back to Mairead's at seven. The kids were in the living room. They'd eaten already, and Mairead was in the kitchen, cheering up the remains of the shepherd's pie with a thin coating of grated cheese. The worst of her haircut had grown out now. It was longer, and already curly. Connolly kissed her at the kitchen door and sat down at the tiny table. He could tell at once that something had happened. Mairead had been talking to somebody. Or, more likely, somebody had been talking to her.

She bent low over the oven and lit the gas. Connolly had told her nothing of his contacts with Scullen, and she'd not asked. The way they were playing it – no questions, no answers – reminded him of Danny again, that same pattern, except that Mairead had known from the start that he'd joined the movement, taken the big step, pledged his Oath of Allegiance. The rest, though, had been silence. A conspiracy of which she was – however tacitly – a part.

She slid the remains of the shepherd's pie into the oven and closed the door. Then she sat down opposite him, the dishcloth folded neatly in front of her.

"You never told me," she said carefully, "that your wee dead friend was sick."

Connolly blinked. "You never asked me."

She laughed, a short, curt laugh. Then she fell silent.

"Are *you* sick?" she said at last.

"No."

"Are you sure?"

"Yes." Connolly returned her look, unblinking.

"This sickness . . ." she said slowly, "what do you have to do to get it? From other men? It'd be best if you told me."

Connolly shrugged. "I don't know," he said, "no one knows. It's a mystery."

"Do you have to sleep with . . ." she frowned, "another man?"

"Maybe. I don't know."

"Did you ever sleep with your friend?"

Connolly looked at her. There was a long silence. Then he nodded.

"Yes," he said.

"Why?"

"I don't know. I . . ." he shrugged again, "I just did."

"Do you sleep with all your friends? Your man friends?"

"No." He paused, looking at her. "He was the only one."

"Why?" she said again. "I don't understand."

Connolly reached forward, detecting the tone in her voice, distress and bewilderment. She moved back from the table, not wanting him near, not now, not during this conversation.

"Well?" she said at last.

Connolly said nothing for a moment. He could hear the gas roaring in the oven.

"It's difficult," he said at last. "He was an older man. He was a bully. He knew what he wanted –" he shrugged – "and he got it."

"Did you like him?"

"Not much. Not at first."

"When was first?"

"At University."

"Dear God. How old were you then?"

"Nineteen."

"And you didn't know any better?"

"I didn't know anything. Except that I was frightened of him. It was fear more than anything else. Fear and a kind of . . ." he shrugged, "I dunno. Politeness, I suppose."

"Politeness?" Mairead shook her head. "Did you say please? Thank you?" She paused. "Did you enjoy it?"

"No."

"Ever?"

"No."

"Truly?"

"Yes."

She looked at him. "You're very mixed up," she said, "aren't you?"

Connolly nodded, back on safer territory. "Yes," he said, "I was. Then."

There was another long silence. The dog began to scuff at the door. Connolly leaned back, letting him in. He shuffled across the kitchen and sat down beside Mairead. Mairead reached down for him, patting him, not taking her eyes off Connolly.

"Should I have told you?" he said.

She thought about the question. Then shook her head.

"No," she said.

"Why not?"

"Because we wouldn't have been sitting here. Like this. Now."

Connolly nodded. He wanted to agree, to confirm it, to get close to her again, physically, to tell her everything. But

243

there was another question first, and he knew he had to ask it.

"So how did you know?" he said. "How did you find out?"

Mairead got up and checked the shepherd's pie. Then she sat down again.

"You want the truth?" she said.

"Please."

She nodded. "OK." She frowned for a moment, collecting her thoughts. Then she looked up again. "You remember Danny's friends?" she said. "The first time? When they came calling?"

"Yes."

"It scared me. You know that. I told you."

"You did."

"I was frightened. Dear God. Liam. The kids. You. I could see it all happening again." She paused, studying her hands. "So . . ." she shrugged, "I did what we all do round here. I took myself off."

"Where to? The priest?"

"No," she smiled. "The doctor."

"What for? Aspirin?"

"Advice. Depression." She shrugged again. "They give you stuff sometimes. Special tablets."

"And?"

"He told me I needed help."

"What sort of help?"

"Counselling."

Connolly nodded. "So what happened?"

"I went off to find a counsellor. Like the doctor said."

"Who did you see?"

"The doctor gave me a name. Young guy. Up from the south. He had a degree in psychology or something. He was very sympathetic. He had a room and everything. I believed in him . . ."

"And?"

"I told him everything. That's the way they do it. You tell them everything. Every last detail. Then they say they'll help you." She paused. "His name's Charlie. At least that's what he says he's called."

244

"And did he? Help you?"

Mairead looked at him for a long time. "Hardly," she said at last.

"Why not?"

"He works for the Brits. He's a soldier or some bloody thing." She shrugged. "I dunno."

Connolly nodded slowly, beginning to understand.

"And you told him about me?"

"Yes."

"And Danny's friends?"

"Yes."

"And Leeson?"

"Yes."

"I see." He paused. "And now he's told you the rest? Leeson? Me? This . . ." He shrugged. "This *sickness*?"

"Yes . . ." She hesitated. "He had a name for it. He called it gay plague. He said it comes from America."

Connolly nodded, saying nothing. Then he frowned. "So why," he said, "why did he tell you all this? Why did he bother?"

There was another long silence. "Because he wants me to tout for him. He wants me to find out about you. What you're up to. Where you go. Who you see. He thinks you tell me. He doesn't believe it when I say you don't."

"So he told you I was sick?"

"He said you could be."

"To let you know what kind of man I really was?"

"Yes."

"So you'd do a proper job for him? Winkle it out of me?"

"Yes."

Connolly nodded, and pushed his chair slowly back from the table. Mairead bent to the dog. The dog could smell the food in the oven. Finally Mairead looked up.

"So what do we do?" she said.

Connolly looked at her for a long time, speculative.

"I don't know," he said, "I'll take advice."

Buddy and Jude left Hampshire for Dublin the following morning. A private ambulance arrived at nine fifteen, and two men lifted Jude's wheelchair carefully into the back. They secured the wheelchair to the floor, and folded down a small jump seat for Buddy. The last thing Jude saw before the back doors closed was Duke, tethered in the stable yard, his nose in a bucket of feed.

Two hours later, they arrived at Gatwick Airport, a bright sunny day, the first real warmth of spring. The ambulance drove round the big South Terminal, and they stopped for Immigration and the ticketing procedures at a gate manned by two armed policemen. The tickets were handled by a plump, friendly Dan Air official with a broken nose and a fresh spray of carnations. He clambered into the back of the ambulance, gave the flowers to Jude, and took the tickets from Buddy.

"How are you travelling?" he said. "Which class?"

Jude smiled up at him. "Cargo," she said drily.

The flight over was uneventful. The airline had stripped out the first row of seats, and Jude, strapped in her wheelchair, was anchored to the floor by the window. As the plane lifted off, she gazed down at the patchwork of fields and farms. Her hair was newly washed, Buddy had taken greater care than usual with her make-up, and as they headed north, climbing through a thin layer of cloud, she wondered whether she wasn't beginning to enjoy it all.

An hour later, the engines throttled back and the plane dipped its nose for the long descent into Dublin Airport. Jude gazed out at the twin arms of Dublin Bay, the docks at Dun Laoghaire beneath them, the low swell of Howth to the north. The aircraft slipped in over the city, and touched down five minutes early. The Catholics aboard crossed themselves as the tyres hit the tarmac. Buddy did the same.

The aircraft taxied to a halt at one of the terminal piers. Jude was first off, the wheelchair in the hands of a porter, Buddy walking behind. He was carrying two bags, one for each of them. A single night, the woman from Ireland had assured him on the telephone, then you'll have her home again.

They wheeled through the Immigration and Customs procedures, at the head of every queue. Outside the terminal building, there was another private ambulance. It looked brand new, smoked glass in the windows, an electric lift at the rear door. They paused for a moment on the pavement while Buddy tipped the porter, then the front door of the ambulance opened, and a man in an anorak got out. He nodded at Buddy. His accent was harsher than Buddy had heard before.

"Hello," he said, "welcome to Ireland."

The passenger door opened, and another man stepped round the bonnet. He was wearing a long white coat. He might have been a doctor. He held out his hand.

"Mr Little?"

Buddy nodded, and introduced Jude. The two men wheeled her round to the back of the ambulance and tapped on the door. The door opened. A third man, younger, leather jacket, jeans. He, too, smiled.

"You're early," he said.

From the airport, they turned right, towards the city. A mile or so down the road, they turned right again, cutting west, across miles of bleak, grey suburbs. There were three of them in the back. Buddy, Jude, and the man in the leather jacket. The man in the leather jacket said his name was Joe.

They made small talk for a while, desultory, the weather, the rain they'd had all winter, the prospects for the coming summer. After a time, through the window, the suburbs thinned, and disappeared, and they were out on a main road, still heading west, through a succession of small, ugly villages. Buddy watched the countryside roll by, wondering how far the place could be. Mary O'Hara, on the phone, had never been specific, but somehow he'd assumed that the hospital she'd mentioned would be in Dublin itself. It had sounded like an institution of some kind, a place you'd find in a big city. Not here. Out in the sticks.

Once, he asked the man Joe. Joe smiled at him, a slow country smile, and said it wasn't far. An hour later, they were still on the move, smaller roads, rocky verges, wild, bare country, the driver taking care on the bends. By now, Buddy was bemused. He sensed something wasn't quite right, the ambulance too new, the journey too long, Joe too unforthcoming.

Finally, the ambulance slowed. The driver indicated left,

and pulled carefully onto a stony track that led towards a fold in the hills. They bumped slowly along the track. Soon, looking back through the rear windows, Buddy had lost sight of the road. Then quite suddenly, there were trees, pine trees, a forest of some kind. The ambulance stopped. Buddy peered out. There was a low stone hut beside the track. The hut had a wooden door and a corrugated iron roof. There were two cars parked beside it, an old Mercedes, and something modern, a Ford.

Buddy frowned. The scene, the destination, made no sense. They'd come to find a hospital, not some logging hut in the middle of nowhere. He turned back into the ambulance to ask the obvious questions – where are we? what the fuck's going on? – but as he did so, he realized that the questions were academic. Joe was still sitting beside Jude. He was watching Buddy carefully. And the small black object in his right hand was a gun.

"Welcome to Ireland," he said again. "Tiocfaidh Ar La."

SEVENTEEN

At about the same time, late morning, a shift leader at the Government's listening post at GCHQ in Cheltenham lifted the telephone and asked for a secure line to his counterpart in the National Security Agency, at Fort Meade, in Washington.

For the last three hours, he'd been studying the mass of material that had been chattering in over the transatlantic telex lines. The bulk of it came from listening posts in southern Chile, raw intercepts from Argentinian radio traffic. The sheer volume of the stuff had taken him by surprise. He'd been monitoring the South Atlantic for a year, but he could never remember a period quite so busy. Now, waiting for the line to be established, he leafed back through the logs, a simple quantum comparison, making sure he had his facts right. A month back, comparable signals activity had been down by a factor of four. A month before that, barely anything had happened. He shut the log book, and turned again to the morning's intercepts. No doubt about it. Something was up.

The line finally cleared and he found himself talking to Fort Meade. He recognized the voice at once, a woman he'd spoken to a number of times over the past week. She was cheerful and businesslike and never wasted a moment of the Agency's time. As ever, she beat him to the punch.

"Pretty dramatic stuff, huh?"

The GCHQ man smiled. "You're right," he said. "Are we sure it's all naval?"

"Most of it," she said. "There's a bunch of intercepts in there from the Aerea Fuerza boys, but most of it's seagoing. Boats out of Porto Belgrano and that place down south."

"Ushuaia."

"Right."

"So," the GCHQ man glanced at the growing pile of intercepts, "what are we saying?"

The woman laughed. "I guess we're saying they got boats out there. Lots of boats."

"They'll call it exercises."

"Sure. And when the shit hits the fan they'll call it something else."

"Surprise me," he said.

"Hey," the woman chuckled, "I don't get paid for thinking. I'm just the humble clerk. Have a nice day, now. And . . . er . . ."

"Yes?"

"Watch Red Route One, eastbound."

The line went dead, and the shift leader pushed his chair back from the desk. In the corner, there was a bank of telex machines. Red Route One, eastbound, was the designation of the machine on the left. The shift leader got up and walked across to the machine. It was spilling out more intercepts, the green light winking on the status panel. He watched for a moment, recognizing the coding groups, the tell-tale chatter of individual Argentinian warships, very definitely at sea. The stuff went on and on, pages of it. He lifted a telephone and pushed three buttons. The line went straight through to a desk in the Cabinet Office. There, he knew, was a duplicate of Red Route One.

"GCHQ," he said briefly. "Are you seeing what we're seeing?"

Buddy Little sat in the back of the grey Mercedes, watching the ambulance bump away through the trees, back down the track they'd taken, back towards the road. Inside was Jude. The last he'd seen of her before they'd closed the doors had been a faint tip of her head. It was a way she had of saying goodbye.

Now, the ambulance gone, he turned back into the car. Joe, with the leather jacket, was leaning on the front passenger seat. He was still holding the gun. The gun was pointing at Buddy's throat. Buddy looked at him.

"If she comes to any harm . . ."

Joe was eating an apple. He nodded, registering the unspoken threat, but made no comment.

They waited in the Mercedes for perhaps five minutes. No one said a word. Then the driver started the engine, and they took the track back to the road. They turned left, heading west again, and Buddy sat in the back, watching very carefully, looking for landmarks, registering every curve of the road, every fold of the landscape. After a while, he looked at Joe again. He'd finished with the apple and was winding down the front window. The window open, he threw the apple core out. Buddy watched it bouncing into the ditch. Whatever else was happening, they sure as fuck weren't going to a hospital. Not now. Not without Jude.

"She needs special nursing," he said, "you know that?"

Joe said nothing. He had a brown paper bag. The bag was full of apples. He offered the bag to Buddy. Buddy just looked at it.

"Special nursing," he said again, "you understand English?"

Joe nodded. "Sure," he said.

"So where's she gone? Who'll look after her?"

"I dunno."

Buddy looked at him a moment, wondering whether to press the point, deciding against it. The thing had been too well organized, too elaborate, not to have an explanation. Quite who these people were was beyond him, but soon – no doubt – he'd find out. He settled back into the seat, and nodded at the brown bag.

"OK," he said. "Sort me out a ripe one."

Half an hour later, they reached the outskirts of a village. The sign beside the church read "Kiltyclogher". They drove down the main street and stopped outside a small terraced house, slate roof, two tiny windows at the front and an old wooden door in between. There was another car parked outside.

Joe motioned Buddy out of the Mercedes. "We're going inside," he said. "It's best if you talk to the man yourself."

He put the gun away, and opened the passenger door. Buddy got out of the back and stood beside the car for a moment. Down the street there was a crossroads and a tall grey statue. There was a bunch of dead flowers at the foot of the statue, and a dog, sprawled across the pavement, asleep. There were curls of smoke from a long terrace of houses, but no other signs of life. The place was utterly silent, like a page from a pre-war picture book.

Joe knocked twice on the front door. The door opened. Buddy stepped inside. There was a small parlour, with a wooden floor, and a table, and a couple of armchairs. There was a cat on one of the armchairs, and a man in a dark suit in the other. The man got up and extended a hand.

"Mr Little," he said, "I'm pleased to meet you."

Buddy ignored the proffered hand. "Who are you?" he said.

The man in the suit ignored the question, shooing the cat off the other armchair and inviting Buddy to sit down. Buddy shook his head, and asked the question again. The man in the suit looked at him for a moment. He had a long pale face. His hair was parted on one side.

"You're hungry?" he said. "A little lunch, perhaps?"

"I've eaten."

"You'll take some tea? Coffee?"

Buddy glanced round. Joe was by the door. His gun was out again, and another man had appeared from the kitchen. He, too, was armed. Buddy shrugged and sat down in the armchair.

"Tea," he said briefly, "two sugars."

The man in the dark suit sat down in the chair opposite. He had the manner of a schoolmaster, stern, fastidious, slightly removed. Long, thin fingers plucked at the creases of his trousers.

"You've come a long way," he said, "I won't waste your time."

For the next ten minutes or so, Buddy listened while the man in the armchair outlined what he had in mind. Buddy listened to him, making no comment, expressing neither surprise, nor disbelief, nor even disapproval. At the end of it, the explanation over, the request on the table, Buddy laughed, striking a new note in the conversation. Derision.

"You're mad," he said, "I couldn't do that."

"Why not?"

"It's not possible."

"I don't understand."

"The gear you'd need. The explosives. The preparation. Security. Everything." He shook his head. "No . . ." he said again, "it's a fantasy."

There was a long silence. The cat stalked the length of the room and wound itself around the other man's legs. The cat knows him, thought Buddy. He's been here before. The man in the armchair picked at a thread of cotton on his trousers. The fingers again, long, thin, bony, just like the rest of him.

He looked up. "Supposing," he said, "you *had* to do it."

Buddy frowned. "I'm not with you," he said.

"Supposing . . ." the other man shrugged, "you had no choice?"

"But I do have a choice. You're giving me a choice. You're saying here it is, here's the job, here's what we want you to do. Now I'm saying it can't be done. I'm saying it's impossible. If you think different, *you* do it. But I tell you now. You'd be off your trolley to even try." He paused. "That's leaving out the rest of it, of course."

The other man looked up. "Rest of it?" he said mildly.

"Yeah." Buddy nodded. "I'm not just talking technique. Details. Small print." He paused again. "It's my country, for Christ sake. I'm British. I won't do it." He shook his head. "No way."

The other man nodded, but said nothing. The cat was in his lap now. Buddy could hear it purring. Buddy watched it a moment. Then he looked up again.

"Who's talking about a war anyway?" he said. "Who are we supposed to be fighting?"

"Argentina."

"Oh?" Buddy frowned. "Something I missed?"

"It's a prediction," the other man said, "not a fact."

"Who says?"

The other man looked at the cat, not answering the question. Buddy's tea arrived, a big brown mug. He took it from the man who'd been standing in the kitchen door. The gun was still in his other hand, an automatic of some kind. The man had blue letters tattooed on his knuckles. Buddy could read an "L" and an "O". The man returned to the kitchen. Buddy sipped at the tea.

"My wife," he began, "what's happened to her?"

"She's in good hands."

"Where?"

The other man looked up. "You'll see your wife again," he said carefully, "when you've finished the job."

There was a long silence. The cat had stopped purring. Buddy was looking hard at the mug of tea in his lap, measuring the distance between himself and the man in the dark suit, remembering where the others were, computing the angles in the room, the scope he had for serious violence. Seldom in his life had he ever been roused. On one of the three occasions it had happened, another man had died. It hadn't been entirely Buddy's doing, but afterwards he'd realized what a simple, logical process killing can be. The snuffing of a candle. The flick of a switch. Now, he looked up. Part of the trick was to keep your head. And the odds, he knew, were against him. He looked at the man in the armchair.

"If you hurt my wife," he said softly, "I'll kill you."

"Your wife will come to no harm," he repeated, "as long as you get the job done."

"I've told you. That's impossible."

The man in the suit turned his head and looked out of the window beside the fireplace. Miles away, there were hills. Further still, the hard grey shapes of a mountain range.

"Pity," he said at last.

Buddy stared at him, recognizing the threat, quite explicit.

"You wouldn't," he said.

The man in the suit looked round at him. "We might," he said. "And that's a risk you wouldn't want to take." He paused and bent to a briefcase beside the chair. He opened the briefcase and took out a file. "Let's be clear what we mean," he said. "If you do the job, you'll get your wife back. We'll fly you to Boston. You'll meet her there." Buddy looked up, surprised. He'd forgotten about Pascale.

"Boston?" he said.

The other man nodded. "That's right," he said, "I understood you'd already been told." He looked up. "We pay for the operation. The expenses. The travel. Everything." He gestured at the file. "We're not ungenerous."

Buddy frowned. "But where's Jude?" he said. "Where's my wife?"

"She's in good hands. We have access to doctors. I understand she has a spinal lesion. She isn't the first in the world." He smiled thinly. "Even the Irish break their necks."

"So you'd look after her?"

"Certainly."

"Where?"

The other man looked at him, saying nothing. Then he closed the file.

"You have the right background," he said, "the right training. Perhaps even the right access. Your only problem is motivation." He paused, consulting the file again, and Buddy caught a glimpse of the article he'd planted in the local paper. The other man was studying it. "She's a handsome woman," he said, "takes a fine photograph." He looked up. "Get the job done for us, she could be back on that horse. Say no, turn us down . . ." He shrugged, closing the file.

Buddy gazed at him for a long time, recognizing the trap they'd so cleverly baited. Provisional IRA, he thought, the lunatics in the black balaclavas, the monsters savaged by the tabloid press, so very different in the flesh.

"But what do you think you'll achieve," he said, "supposing it all happens? Supposing it can be done?"

The other man shrugged again. "It's a step," he said, "in the long march."

"But you think you'll get us out that way? You think we'll just leave and pack up?"

"Yes," he nodded, "in the end I think you will."

Buddy shook his head very slowly, a gesture he reserved for life's dafter moments.

"You're mad," he said, "you're fucking barmy. North and south, you're stuck with it. You'll never change it. It's there for ever."

For the first time, the other man smiled. One hand crept across to the file again, gave it the softest of taps.

"You have your problems," he said quietly, "we have ours."

Buddy said nothing for a full minute, staring into the middle distance, feeling his options closing around him. This strange cold figure in the dark suit wanted him to blow up one of the Navy's warships. Live. In Portsmouth Harbour. On prime-time television. Twelve years in the service told him that was wrong. Twenty years underwater told him it was probably impossible. But Jude's life hung on his decision. So what the fuck was he supposed to do? He stirred in the armchair. He put the mug carefully on the carpet. Then he looked up.

"You want a decision," he said.

It was a statement, not a question. The other man nodded.

"We do," he said.

Buddy looked at him, assessing him, wondering whether the impossible might, after all, respond to careful planning and a kilo or two of high explosive. The cat stretched and yawned. Buddy studied it for a moment.

"OK," he said finally. "When?"

Miller got the call he'd been anticipating, on his private number, an hour after midnight. He was in bed, book on his pillow, wondering whether to start another chapter or not. This time of night, Montgomery's memoirs were better than Nembutal.

He lifted the phone. A voice on the other end asked him whether the line was secure. He said it was.

"OK," the voice said, "we've got a problem."

"Who's we?"

"You."

"What is it?"

"Qualitech."

"Really?"

Miller closed the book and reached for a tiny pad he

256

always kept by the telephone. "What's the problem?" he said, non-committal as ever.

"There's word it wasn't as simple as it sounds."

Miller smiled. "I'm sure," he said, "but what's that got to do with me?"

"Word is, the bomb was a Brit plant. Someone wanted leverage. Someone put the bomb there, or had the bomb put there, then took the credit when the bomb was found."

Miller nodded. "Neat," he said, "almost plausible."

There was a pause. Miller had still not been able to place the voice. His private phone number had a strictly limited circulation, two dozen or so people, some of them MI5, some of them MI6, some of them Special Branch or RUC. The voice came back. It was a flat, South London voice. With a hint of amusement.

"There's a source in Belfast," he said, "boy named Connolly. Special Branch are running him. He seems to know a great deal."

Miller scribbled the name on his notepad and looked at it. Connolly, he thought. The boyfriend of Charlie's source. He bent to the phone.

"Anything else?" he said. "While you're on?"

The voice hesitated a moment. "Yes," he said, "the suits are taking it to the top."

"Really?"

"Yes." He paused. "Whoever you've upset, you've done a wonderful job."

"I see." Miller gazed at the phone. "So what's your angle?" he said at last. "Why the favour?"

The voice laughed, a long chuckle, real humour. "They're wankers," he said. "All of them. That's why."

The phone went dead and Miller stared at it a moment longer, uncertain what his brain was trying to tell him. Then he had it. The bloke was pissed. Had to be.

Next morning, half past seven, Miller got Charlie out of bed. The boy opened the door to his room and stepped out onto the landing, his toes curling on the cold concrete.

"What's the matter?" he said. "What is it?"

Miller stepped past him, into the room. "Shut the door," he said.

Charlie shut the door. Miller glanced round the room. The place was a tip, ashtrays overflowing, records everywhere, Charlie's dirty washing spilling out of a black laundry sack. Miller stood by the bed. Charlie plugged in the electric kettle.

"There's a bloke called Connolly," he began, "you've mentioned him."

Charlie nodded. "Mairead's fella."

"How much do we know about him?"

Charlie hesitated, spooning instant coffee into two mugs. "He was Leeson's pal," he said, "turned up with him in Dublin."

"I know that. What's he at now?"

Charlie shrugged. "I don't know," he said.

"Why not?"

"She won't tell me."

"How hard have you tried?"

"Very."

Miller looked at him for a moment, then walked to the door. "Try harder," he said. "And sort your bloody self out."

Mairead took the call at half past nine. Connolly had been away early, swallowing a round of toast and two cups of tea before heading for the door. He'd muttered something about an early lecture, and she'd kissed him in the hall, knowing that Tuesdays he never lectured until the afternoon.

"Be careful," she said, "all those students."

Now, the kids away at school, Bronagh tucked up with a cold and a drawing book, Mairead answered the phone. She thought for a moment that it might be Connolly. Her smile faded when she recognized the soft Irish brogue.

"Charlie," she said flatly.

"Me," he agreed.

"What do you want?"

"We have to meet."

"I can't."

"I said we— "

"I can't. Bronagh's not well."

258

"Then I'll come and see you."

Mairead gazed at the phone. Under any other circumstances she might have laughed, the absurdity of the proposition. Instead, she got angry.

"You won't," she said, "not now. Not ever. Anyway," she shrugged, "there's nothing to say."

"I don't believe you."

"It's true."

There was a long pause. In the living room, Mairead could hear Bronagh singing to herself in front of the fire, under the eiderdown, the child's voice huskier than usual. Charlie, she thought, here, in her own street, her own house. She shivered at the image, hearing his voice again on the phone. The tone of his voice had changed. It was harsher, more impatient. In ten brief seconds, he'd reverted to type. Bossy Catholic male. Laying down the law.

"Listen to me," he said, "you've got twenty-four hours to talk to that man of yours. I'll pick you up tomorrow. Usual place. I'll be there at one. And again at two. We'll have all afternoon. I'll look forward to it."

"I won't be there," she said automatically. "There's nothing to say."

"Talk to your man," Charlie said again, "ask him about a place called Qualitech. Ask him tonight. Ask him what he knows, and how he knows it. I want names, Mairead, and places I can find people. I want to know who he's been seeing, who's been talking to him." He paused. "What was the place I mentioned now?"

"Qualitech."

"Good. See you tomorrow. Tiocfaidh Ar La."

Charlie rang off, and Mairead stood for a moment in the hall, holding the phone. So much for the listening ear, she thought bitterly, and the soft Irish eyes.

Connolly joined Scullen for lunch at a café in Letterkenny, a small Irish town at the crossroads between Strabane and Rathmelton, just over the border from Londonderry.

He'd been driven the hundred-odd miles from Belfast in a brand-new Ford. He'd rung the local number Scullen had given him, and explained where he wanted to go, and the car had arrived outside the flat off the Ormeau Road within the half-hour. He'd never met the driver before, a well-dressed young guy from Ballymurphy, but the man was pleasant enough and they'd spent the journey talking about the situation in the Falklands. There was talk of the Argies getting stroppy about British claims in the South Atlantic, and as a fellow Catholic, the driver thought they had a point.

"Same old story," he said, "the Brits only understand violence."

They crossed the border at Strabane. Connolly had half expected trouble, but the RUC and the Garda had waved them through with barely a second glance. As the car settled down to a steady sixty on the main road into Donegal, Connolly had relaxed. Working for Scullen, he'd concluded, was like working for a large multi-national. The back-up seemed limitless, the travel arrangements were a delight, and with luck there might even be a spot of complimentary lunch.

Scullen was already in the café at Letterkenny when they arrived, occupying a small table by the window. The table was set for two. Scullen glanced up, his finger in a copy of *The Times*. Connolly nodded a greeting, looking at the paper. "Falklands tension grows," ran the headline, "Carrington to issue statement".

Scullen folded the paper and the two men sat in silence for a moment while the woman behind the counter asked them what they wanted. Scullen ordered chicken soup. Connolly settled for a toasted cheese sandwich. The woman disappeared into a back room.

Scullen leaned back in his chair and listened while Connolly told him about Mairead. The Brits, he said, had been screwing stuff out of her for months. They'd got to her through a counselling service, and before she'd realized the implications, they'd tucked her away. She had a single handler called Charlie, and Charlie was now tightening the screws. He wanted to know all about Connolly, about what he did, who he talked to, and he'd taken certain steps to make sure Mairead obliged. Mairead, thank God, didn't know what Connolly was up to, but the situation was now critical. Charlie was threatening to expose Mairead as a tout, and if that happened, God knows where it might lead. Mairead had kids, as Scullen knew, and the last thing Connolly wanted was to see them hurt.

Scullen listened carefully. When Connolly had finished, he looked away, gazing out of the window.

"You say she's not a tout?"

Connolly shook his head. "No," he said, "she's meat. In the sandwich."

"That's what all touts say."

"Not this one. Not her."

There was another pause. The woman arrived with the food. Scullen raised a spoonful of chicken soup to his lips and blew on it.

"You're talking about Danny's wife," he said at last. "We know her. Remember that. We know the way the woman thinks." He paused. "She's no friend of ours."

"I know." Connolly nodded. "But that doesn't make her a tout. Mother, yes. Widow, yes. But no tout." He paused. "Political commitment's a bit hard to come by when you've lost your husband."

"If we're talking about loss," Scullen said, "perhaps we should talk about Danny. They took his life. Remember?"

"Danny was a Volunteer. That's different." Connolly paused again. "I'm telling you. She's no tout."

Scullen nodded, swallowing the soup, appearing to accept the point. The two men ate in silence for a moment or two. Then Scullen looked up.

"So you're worried about her?" he said.

"Yes."

"And you want me to do something about it?"

"Yes." He glanced across at the older man. "I thought it might be an opportunity, as well as a problem."

"Quite," Scullen said drily, tipping the soup bowl back to trap the fleshy remains of the chicken.

After lunch, they left the café, driving north, around the head of Lough Swilly, Scullen's car in the lead. McParland at the wheel. Half an hour later, they arrived in Buncrana, parking outside a small timberyard. Scullen got out, wrapping his coat around him. There was a cold wind, north-west, off the lough. Gulls were wheeling over a distant dinghy. Two men with rods, one of them standing up.

Connolly followed Scullen into the timberyard. They mounted a narrow flight of steps beside the racks of newly sawn deal and pine, and Scullen unlocked a door at the top. Inside was an office. There was a large metal desk by the window and a couple of filing cabinets. Scullen sat down behind the desk. Through the window, Connolly could see the lough again. The dinghy was still there. Both men were now sitting down and the gulls had gone.

Scullen reached for a piece of paper and scribbled a number from memory. Then he opened a drawer in the desk and took out a gun. The gun was an automatic. Connolly looked at it. It was big. It was wrapped in a dirty piece of cloth. Scullen put it on the blotter and searched in the drawer again. After a while, he produced a box. Inside the box, there were two dozen bullets, brass jackets, snub nose. He counted the bullets, and then looked up at Connolly. Connolly couldn't take his eyes off the gun.

"Have you ever used one of these?" Scullen said.

Connolly shook his head. "No."

"The boy outside will take you to the coast. He'll show you the way it goes. Use both hands." He looked up at Connolly again. "Do you have a pair of gloves?"

"Yes."

"Wear them. Never handle the gun without gloves."

Connolly nodded. "No,' he said, "of course not."

There was a silence. Scullen pushed the gun across the desk. Connolly felt in the anorak for the gloves he always carried. He put them on. He picked up the gun. The gun was heavy. Oil glinted on the breech mechanism. He put the gun in his pocket and picked up the box of bullets. They, too, were heavier than he'd expected. He cleared his throat, looked at Scullen again, nodded at the gun.

"Tell me," he said, "what am I supposed to do with it?"

Scullen leaned back in his chair, hands clasped behind his neck, his face quite impassive. "Mairead's worried about . . .?" he paused, pretending to be hunting for the name.

"Charlie."

"Charlie." He nodded. "Charlie will doubtless get in touch." He leaned forward, picking up the piece of paper with the number on it. "When he does so, you phone this number. Tell them the time of the rendezvous. Arrange for them to pick you up. They'll know what to do."

Connolly nodded. "I give them the gun?"

Scullen shook his head. "No," he said. "The gun's yours. They drive the car."

Connolly frowned. "So what do I do?"

Scullen looked at him for a moment. Then he stood up, turning to the window, gazing out at the view. The dinghy on the lough was back on the move at last, the two men in the stern, bent against the wind. Scullen yawned, a hand to his mouth.

"You kill Charlie," he said, glancing over his shoulder, "and then we talk again."

EIGHTEEN

Buddy Little was back in England by ten that night. The Mercedes had taken him on, across Ireland, to Shannon Airport. Joe had given him a ticket for the eight o'clock flight to Heathrow, and had wished him luck. Buddy had refused the proffered handshake, and the murmur of reassurance about Jude, and had turned his back and walked away. His ticket, when he presented it, entitled him to Club Class travel. He drank free Scotch most of the way home but refused the plate of fresh salmon. His appetite had quite gone. Only the anger remained.

Now, back home, nearly midnight, Buddy stepped out of the taxi, paid the driver, and walked the last ten yards to his own front door. Coaxing the key into the lock, his eyes beginning to adjust to the darkness, he noticed the car. It was parked beside the stable block. It looked like a small Volkswagen. There was someone sitting behind the wheel.

Buddy let himself into the house and switched on the hall lights. He closed the front door, and drew the curtain in the adjoining window. Then he switched on the lights in the living room, stepped back into the hall, and through to the kitchen. The kitchen was still in darkness. He felt his way to the back door, eased the bolts, and stepped out into the stable yard.

The back of the car was visible across the yard. Hugging the shadows, Buddy skirted the yard until he was only yards from the car. He paused a moment, then peered carefully round the corner. The car was empty.

Buddy blinked, and checked again, and then slipped round the corner. He was now back at the front of the house. The distance between the car and the house was perhaps twenty yards. Keeping his body low, following the line of the hedge, Buddy began to approach the house. He'd covered half the distance when a voice came out of the darkness. It was a woman's voice, low, the English faintly accented.

"Mr Little?"

Buddy froze. The voice again, closer.

"Buddy?"

Buddy stood up, feeling faintly ridiculous. A figure stepped out of the shadows, not tall. He saw teeth in the darkness, the middle of a smile. The figure stooped quickly and picked up a rucksack. He saw a hand outstretched and wondered briefly whether it was holding a gun. The figure advanced, the hand still outstretched, into the pool of light from the door. A woman of about thirty. Small. Black hair. Denim jacket. Jeans.

"My name's Eva," she said, "you're supposed to be expecting me."

Buddy looked at her, remembering Scullen's departing words. Someone, he'd said, someone will make contact, sooner rather than later. At the time, Buddy had assumed he'd get a call over the next day or two. An invitation to meet some place, to find out about the next bit of the jigsaw. The last thing he'd expected was this, some woman, nearly midnight, in his own front garden.

Buddy shook the hand briefly and gestured towards the house. "I was looking for you," he said gruffly, "I didn't know who was in the car."

The woman nodded. "I know," she said. "That's why I went to the back door."

"You followed me?"

"No," she smiled, "I was waiting for you. The house has only two doors. You were bound to use the other one."

They went inside. Buddy closed the front door. The woman put the rucksack beside the stairs. Buddy looked at it.

"What's that for?" he said.

"I'm staying the night. We have to talk. It's better we take our time." She paused. "No?"

Buddy hesitated a moment, wondering whether to throw the woman out, to bolt the door behind her and start the day all over again, no Dublin, no ambulance, no stranger

265

in a dark suit offering him impossible deals. Then he glanced down the hall, and into the living room, and knew that he couldn't. Jude's bed was still there, the sheets rumpled, the night dress over the pillow. This strange woman, the jeans, the jacket, was all part of it, the package deal, the price he had to pay to get Jude back, to get them both to Boston. He shrugged, and walked into the kitchen, flicking on the lights.

"Tea?" he said. "Or coffee?"

The woman was a step behind him.

"Coffee," she said, "and I'll make it."

They stayed in the kitchen for an hour, the woman effectively in charge, Buddy too exhausted to argue. They drank coffee and ate the last of the flapjacks Buddy had made the previous week. The woman said she was German. She'd studied for her degree in Southampton, and now she had a house of her own there. She worked part-time at the University, taking conversation classes in German, and she gave extra lessons on the side to make ends meet. Nights and weekends, she worked on her doctoral thesis, something to do with a German writer called Günter Grass. She said he was German literature's sole remaining hope in an increasingly bourgeois world, and hoped one day to meet him. She had his telephone number and his home address, and had written him a number of letters. To date, he had yet to reply, but she lived in hope.

Buddy half listened to her, chewing his way through the flapjacks. She had a plain, round face, and a snub nose, and short black hair. She talked non-stop, with her whole body, arms, hands, the lot. She swayed and bent on the kitchen stool, going on and on about herself, that single-minded preoccupation with the small print of her own life that Buddy had met – occasionally – in others. It meant she was probably single. It meant she was serious about more or less everything. And it meant that, deep down, she'd be impossible to touch.

The flapjacks gone, Eva pausing to drain her coffee, Buddy yawned.

"You with them, then?" he said.

Eva looked at him over the rim of her cup. She'd found the best china in minutes.

"With who?" she said.

"This lot. The lot I met today."

Buddy gestured over his shoulder with his thumb. Ireland, the thumb said. The Provos. The men with the guns, and the bags of apples, and the big ideas. Eva smiled, balancing the cup and saucer on her lap.

"Yes," she said, "when they need me."

Buddy frowned. "How does it work then?" he said. "You freelance? A freelance terrorist? Yellow Pages?"

Eva got off the stool and ran the dirty cups under the tap. She didn't answer his question for a moment and he knew why. He had, after all, touched a nerve in her. He'd questioned her faith. He'd caused her offence. He yawned again.

"Don't believe it all, do you?" he said.

"All what?"

She didn't look at him. She washed the cups with fierce energy. Lots of water. Lots of suds.

"All this Provo crap. One country. Brits out. All that."

She wiped the last cup and put them carefully back on the shelf.

"Yes," she said, "but I wouldn't expect you to understand."

She reached up to the shelf, her face inches from his, confronting him, urging him on. Buddy obliged.

"So why's that, then?"

"Because you're English. Being English, you don't have a point of view. You don't think yes, and you don't think no. You just think everything goes on for ever, the same old way. You have your weather. Your dogs. And if something goes wrong, really wrong, you just grin and bear it." She smiled. "Isn't that the way it goes?"

Buddy frowned. Now, against his better judgement, the woman was engaging him, joining battle, getting under his skin.

"Bollocks," he said briefly.

"Oh?" She folded the dishcloth and laid it carefully on the side. "So what makes you so different?"

"I don't grin and I don't bear it," he said. "If I think something's wrong, I say so."

"Like what?"

Buddy looked at her. Jude, he thought. Jude on her back, numb from the neck down.

"My wife's a cripple," he said. "But that's their word, not mine."

"Whose word?"

"The doctors. They say she's incurable. They're wrong."

The woman looked at him for a long time. Then she nodded, very slowly.

"I know," she said, "I read the article in the paper." She paused. "They say she'll never get better. Never be whole again. Isn't that what they say?"

"Yes."

"So . . ." she shrugged, "it's the same with us. The Brits tell us we're crazy. They say we're lunatics. They tell us no one else sees it our way. They say we're . . ." she paused, frowning, looking for the right phrase, finding it, "flogging a dead horse."

Buddy nodded. "They might be right," he said, "have you thought of that?"

She shook her head. "No."

"Why not?"

"Because we can't afford to think of the alternative . . ." She paused again, her eyes going to the tiny framed picture of Jude, propped amongst the jars of beans. "And neither can you."

Connolly and Mairead finally got to bed past midnight. They lay together, the light off, the cat from next door yowling at the tom across the road.

Connolly put his arm around Mairead's shoulders, kissed the soft triangle of skin at the base of her neck.

"When will you meet him?" he said. "This Charlie?"

Mairead was silent for a while. Connolly could feel the blood in her veins, her pulse quickening slightly.

"Tomorrow afternoon," she said at last.

"Where?"

She opened one eye and looked at him in the darkness.

"Why?" she said. "Why do you want to know?"

"I might come too." He paused. "Wouldn't that help?"

He could sense her thinking about it, weighing the proposition up. Finally, she nodded. "It might," she said.

"I could tell him whatever he wants to know," Connolly said, "get him off your back."

"Would you?" She frowned. "Would that do it?"

"Yes."

She nodded, falling silent. The cats across the road were at it again. Full moon, Connolly thought. Mairead stirred beside him.

"He'd never come back?" she said. "Never again?"

Connolly smiled at her. "No," he said. "Never."

She thought about it a bit more. Then she nodded.

"There's a travel agency in town," she said. "Great Victoria Street. It's called Pegasus. He's to pick me up outside. He has a car." She paused. "I've told him one o'clock."

Buddy Little woke late, with a headache and the memory of a dream. In the dream, a door had opened and a figure had stolen across the room and bent low over the bed and gone away again. He opened one eye, wondering about the time. In front of the alarm clock was a cup of tea. He reached for the tea. The clock said ten to eight.

Downstairs, he found Eva back in the kitchen. She'd spent the night in a sleeping bag on the floor in the living room, but the bag was back inside her rucksack, and there was no other sign of her presence in the room. Now, she was cooking bacon and eggs. Buddy warmed to the smell, reaching for the cupboard where he stored the aspirin.

"This is a fantasy," he said, "and you're the au pair."

After breakfast, Eva washed the dishes, sluiced the sink with bleach, wrote Buddy a shopping list, and told him they were going to Portsmouth. Buddy looked at her across the kitchen, recognizing the shape of the relationship, yet another order masquerading as simple conversation.

"Portsmouth," he said wonderingly. "What a surprise."

They took her car. She drove. Portsmouth lay thirty miles

to the east, at the end of the coastal motorway. It was a big city, a naval city, nearly a quarter of a million people packed onto a low, flat island, a city of terraced streets, and chimney pots, and flat-capped men on bicycles. Buddy knew the place well. He'd learned his diving there, way back, at the Navy's school at HMS *Vernon*, and the city had felt familiar from the start. In some ways, it reminded him of his own childhood in Camberwell Green. The place seemed instantly recognizable, a chunk of inner London transplanted to the south coast. It was scruffy, and working class, and quite poor. The people had no side, and little money. At nights, the going could be rough, but there were plenty of laughs, and the locals had a kind of stoic cheerfulness. Just like home, Buddy thought.

Ten miles short of the city, Eva signalled left, taking the motorway exit for Gosport. Gosport was over the water from Portsmouth, duller, slightly more genteel, a smaller town that had also made its living from the Navy. Between Gosport and Portsmouth lay Portsmouth Harbour, a huge expanse of water reaching five miles inland. The upper reaches of the harbour had become an anchorage for moth-balled warships, but the seaward end remained what it had always been, home base for the Navy and the dockyard, and the dozens of warships that returned from duty for overhauls and resupply.

Eva drove the VW down through Gosport, and parked a hundred yards from the waterfront and the ferry terminal. The ferry ran a regular service across the harbour, connecting the two towns, and Eva bought two return tickets. Buddy followed her down to the pontoon, gazing around, remembering the countless times he'd used the ferry before, runs ashore to Gosport's wilder pubs, evenings with an agile divorcee who'd tired of her ever-absent submariner husband, and found aerobics no substitute for the real thing. Waiting for the ferry, Buddy smiled at the memories. On a good night, no beer, he could keep up with her for a couple of hours. After that, she'd give him the fruit bowl and tell him to keep at it. She had a limitless appetite, and no shame, and Buddy had avoided bananas ever since.

The ferry arrived, and Buddy and Eva joined the queue

as it shuffled forward. On board, Buddy gestured at the upper deck. Since yesterday, in the cottage back home, he'd been waiting for this, the chance to explain why – in principle – the plan might seem a great idea. And why – in practice – it would never work.

The ferry cast off and nosed into the harbour. The tide was at full ebb, the water racing seawards, tugging the red and green buoys against their mooring chains, lapping against the side of the ferry as it crossed the tidal stream. Buddy stood at the port rail, Eva beside him. A couple of hundred yards away were the first of the dockyard berths, the grey warships double-moored, side by side. The dockyard stretched up-harbour for about a mile, berth after berth, hundreds of acres of repair sheds, workshops, warehouses, dry docks, and the huge grey cranes that dominated the skyline. Today, there were perhaps a dozen warships tied up alongside: frigates, a couple of destroyers, one of the new mini-carriers, HMS *Invincible*, and the familiar shape of the warship she'd soon replace, HMS *Hermes*, an ancient aircraft carrier newly tarted up to take a squadron or two of helicopters, and the Navy's latest fighter, the vertical take-off Sea Harrier. Buddy gazed at it all as the ferry butted across the harbour. He'd loved the Navy, loved his years aboard these ships. They'd been home to him, more important than any other place he'd ever lived, and it was bizarre to be here, thinking of them with anything but affection. To do what they wanted, to turn his working life on its head and sink one of the buggers, was out of the question. Now, he thought. Now is the time to bury it. To expose the plan for what it is. Pure fantasy.

He glanced at Eva. She had a small camera. She was taking photographs. He tapped her on the shoulder. She lowered the camera.

"Listen," he said, nodding down at the tidal stream, the slate grey water foaming past the ferry, "number one, the current. You're looking at four knots of tide. That's a joke, for a start." He looked up, redirecting her attention to the dockyard, the massive cranes, the incessant clank of heavy metal. "Number two, the place is sealed as tight as a parson's arse. They guard it night and day. You have to

271

have passes. Special permission. You can't just walk in there . . ." He paused. "OK?"

Eva nodded. "OK," she said.

Buddy paused for breath, working steadily down his mental check list.

"Number three," he said, "I'll need gear. Loads of it. Specialist stuff. Closed circuit breathing sets. Explosives. Detonators. Timing devices. This stuff doesn't grow on trees. You can't buy it at Woolies."

He paused, looking over his shoulder, down the harbour towards the sea. The harbour mouth was narrow, barely three hundred metres across, guarded on the eastern side by an old fortification, the Round Tower, and on the other side by HMS *Dolphin*, the Navy's submarine base. Eva was following his eyeline, keeping up with the arguments, saying very little. Buddy looked at her.

"They want it done when the ships are leaving," he said. "Isn't that right?"

She nodded. "Yes," she said, "that's the whole point. There's bound to be television. Press. All kinds of coverage. He wants the whole world to see."

Buddy looked at her a moment.

"That means radio detonators," he said briefly, "button job."

"Of course."

"You think that's simple?"

Eva shrugged, saying nothing, and Buddy let the silence speak for itself before gesturing at the dockyard again, closer now.

"OK," he said. "Let's imagine I get hold of all this gear. Get it into the dockyard. Wait until they're looking the other way. Get kitted up. What then?"

"You swim."

"Sure. But there's a war on. Remember? That's what I'm told. I'm told we're off to beat the shit out of the Argies, and the Navy's going to do the job, and half the world's going to watch it all on television." He paused. "That's the plot . . . isn't it?"

"Yes."

272

"So you think they're just going to leave me to it? Not take precautions?"

"What precautions?"

Buddy gazed at her. "Are you asking *me*?" he said.

"I thought you were in the Navy."

"I was. It was a while ago, though. Things change."

"So . . .?" she shrugged, "how did they used to protect their ships? When you were there?"

Buddy frowned. "That's classified," he said.

"You mean they didn't."

"It's classified," he repeated, knowing only too well that she was right.

The ferry began to turn for the run in towards the Portsmouth terminal. Buddy turned to talk to Eva again. Her camera was back up to her eye. She was taking more photos. He watched her for a moment, shot after shot, then shrugged. The thing was impossible. There was nothing left to be said.

Five minutes later, the ferry cast off again, nosing back out towards Gosport. Eva put the camera away and took Buddy by the arm, walking him around the deck to the starboard side. From here, on the return journey, they had the same view of the dockyard. She settled him against the rail, and he realized yet again how businesslike she was, how organized.

The ferry gathered speed. She nodded down at the water. "The tide," she said, "is slack for eight hours a day. Two hours either side of high water. Two hours either side of low water." She looked at him. "OK?"

Buddy nodded, said nothing. She reached in her bag and took out a tide table. She showed him the tide table. She put it back in her bag, very patient, very methodical. Then she looked up again, back, towards the dockyard.

"Number two," she said, "you'll never need to be in the dockyard in the first place."

Buddy gazed at her. "You want me to swim? From Southampton?"

"No." She pointed to a marina on the Gosport side of the harbour, a forest of yacht masts. "You swim from there."

"It's private," Buddy said automatically.

"You're right," she smiled, "but they hire out berths. To visiting yachts. At a price."

"So?" Buddy shrugged. "What does that solve? You need a yacht."

She smiled again, reaching in her bag for the third time. "I've got one," she said.

She produced a packet of photographs. She slipped off the elastic band and quickly sorted through them. Towards the bottom of the pile she found what she wanted. She gave it to Buddy. Buddy looked at the photo. It showed a three-quarter stern view of a yacht. The yacht was white, tied up alongside a river pontoon. It had a cockpit aft, and a small three-rung ladder over the stern. The sails were furled, and a woman of about forty was beaming at the camera. Eva looked at Buddy. "Note the ladder," she said.

Buddy nodded. "Who's the woman?"

"She's the owner's wife. The yacht's up for charter. We've chartered it."

"Who's we?"

"Me."

Buddy looked at her, then shook his head.

"You can't have," he said.

"Why not?"

"You need a certificate to do that. A yachtmaster's certificate."

"I've got one."

Buddy blinked. "You know how to skipper a yacht?"

Eva shook her head. "No," she said.

"Then where does the certificate come from?"

She looked at him, saying nothing. There was a long silence. They were half-way across the harbour. Buddy looked at the water bubbling past.

"Where is this yacht?" he said at last.

"On the Hamble. At Warsash."

Buddy nodded. The Hamble was a river about ten miles away. It ran into Southampton Water, and Warsash was at its mouth. Sailing from Warsash to Portsmouth would be a doddle. They could do it on the engine alone. They need never raise the sails. It would take a couple of hours. Three at the most. Buddy looked at the picture one last time and then gave it back to her.

"OK," he paused, "so who supplies the gear? The explosives? The set?"

There was another long silence. The ferry began to turn again, the skipper juggling the throttles, bringing the hull beam-on to the approaching pontoon. Tricky manoeuvre, Buddy wanted to say. Needs a real expert. Just like any other boat on the harbour. Eva looked at him for a moment, then produced the article from the local paper. She unfolded it. Buddy glanced down. Jude. On Duke. Eva was still looking at him. She didn't need to check the small print. She'd been word perfect for a month.

"You said you'd do anything to get your wife back on her feet," she said, "you said you'd go to the ends of the earth." She paused. "It also says you've been diving for most of your working life . . ." She began to fold the article. Then she looked up. "I can't believe you don't know where to find the gear," she said slowly, "and I can't believe you don't know how to handle a boat."

Buddy leaned over the rail. He looked across at the dock-yard. At the great cranes. At the big diving tank at Vernon where he'd done his first emergency ascents. At the long line of sleek grey warships. There was a matelot aboard one of the destroyers. He was scrubbing down the afterdeck. After a while, he disappeared.

"OK . . ." Buddy said quietly, "suppose the plan's possible. Suppose it might even work. How do you suggest I handle the rest of it?"

Eva frowned, genuinely puzzled. "Rest of it?" she said.

"Yeah . . ." Buddy looked round at her, "me?"

They came for Connolly at twelve o'clock. He'd been waiting in the cold, bare flat off the Ormeau Road for over an hour. He'd phoned the number Scullen had given him at nine. The man at the other end had grunted. He'd given the man his address, and the spot where the hit was to take place, and the time, and the barest details. It felt mechanical, cold, like ordering a pizza.

There were two of them, both unfamiliar. They were young. They didn't say very much. They took him down to the car and put him in the front, beside the driver. They checked the gun, and told him the way it was to be.

They would park in the street, upstream from the travel agency. They'd scouted the street already. There was a spot that would do, single yellow line, waiting permitted for half an hour. The target would pull in at the kerbside to pick the girl up. They'd stop alongside, hemming the target in, trapping him behind the steering wheel, making it impossible for the man to get out. Connolly would be nearest to him, in the front passenger seat. He was to keep firing until the man was down. He should aim for the head. When the man was down, he should fire through the door. The big automatic took a fourteen-shot magazine. Fourteen shots should do it. Easy.

The briefing went on, the older of the two youths, fish and chip complexion, greasy skin lightly crusted with acne. He had a low, flat, toneless voice and didn't look Connolly in the eye.

After the hit, they'd drive out of the city. After a mile or so, there'd be another car waiting for them. There'd be a driver at the wheel. They'd swop cars again, a third driver, on the way down to Armagh. If the thing went right, he'd be over the border in time for tea.

The other youth asked Connolly whether he understood it all. They went over the details again, and Connolly got it right first time, all of it. They told him he was bright, unlike others they could name. He said it was simple, a good plan. He smiled at them, complimenting them. They didn't smile back.

At half past twelve, they set off. Connolly sat beside the driver. The driver gave him a black balaclava. He held it for a while, then stuffed it between his knees. Whatever he did, he couldn't stop his hands shaking.

They turned down Donegal Place, watching carefully for the RUC and the Army. The car was stolen, the theft only hours old. They'd taken the car from the station car park at Dunmurray. With luck, the owner would still be at work in the city. With luck, he wouldn't report it until the evening.

They stopped at the junction with Great Victoria Street, turned right, and drove the brief two hundred yards to the place they'd chosen. The driver parked up, killed the engine. They both had newspapers. They opened them, heads tucked well down, faces invisible from the street. Connolly didn't read the paper they'd left at his feet, didn't bother. He'd not be back here. He knew it. No matter what happened, how careful they were, how lucky, he'd not be back. He'd left a note for Mairead. He'd given her an address to write to, his mother's telephone number. He'd told her he loved her. He'd promised they'd be together again one day. He'd said what he'd done was for the best. For her. For them. For the Movement.

He looked at his watch. Five to one. He looked down at the balaclava, wondering who'd worn it last, what his face had looked like, what had happened to him, what he'd done. He looked up again, curious at the way the world outside the car windows had ceased to be real any more. Lunchtime. Pretend people. Shadows hurrying by in dresses and coats. A film without a soundtrack. Make believe. He blinked. A tan Ford Escort was coasting slowly past them. It was indicating left. It stopped outside the travel agency. Connolly lifted the gun from the floor, holding it out of sight. He'd never lifted anything so heavy. He could smell the oil.

He nudged the driver. "He's here," he said.

"I know."

"Why don't we do it?"

"He's looking at us in the mirror."

Connolly glanced up. He was right. The driver in the Escort was studying the mirror. He could see him. He was looking directly at them. Connolly began to panic.

"What do we do?" he said.

"We wait."

"How long?"

"Until he stops looking."

Connolly nodded. Of course, he thought. Of course that's what we do. He swallowed hard, wondering about the balaclava. When should he put it on? Now? In a minute or so? Under the dashboard? So his head wasn't visible? Looking straight ahead through the windscreen, trying to think it through, he saw Mairead. She was a figure from a dream. She was hurrying along Great Victoria Street. She was wearing the coat he'd bought her for Christmas. She'd seen the Escort, Charlie, and now she was looking round. For him. For Connolly. He watched her, scarcely daring to breathe. She'd slowed down. She was trying to hang it out. She obviously wanted him there, needed him there, believed he'd do as he'd promised, turn up.

The car's engine started. The car began to move. The driver wasn't looking at him.

"OK?" he said. "Are you fucking ready for it?"

Yes, thought Connolly. Yes, I am. Yes, I am ready for it. For the man Charlie. Killing him. Doing it. The Escort nosed into the road. The driver was looking at the approaching traffic. He'd need a U-turn in a minute, a space to swing the car round and head back out of town. He was planning ahead, the deed done, the target dead.

The car began to slow. Connolly watched the Escort drifting towards them. It seemed disembodied, quite unreal. The man inside, Charlie, was looking at Mairead. Mairead was ten yards away. He must like her, Connolly thought, he must fancy her. He's smiling at her. There now. A little wave, even. The car stopped. Mairead paused. Charlie looked round. Connolly gazed at him.

"Do it," the driver shouted. "Fucking do it. Shoot the bastard!"

Connolly raised the gun and pulled the trigger. There was a deafening bang. The glass in the window shattered. Charlie pitched sideways across the width of the car. His face wasn't there any more. Connolly pulled the trigger again, and then again, smelling the cordite. Someone began to scream. Charlie had disappeared and Connolly lowered the gun, putting the last six bullets through the door, just as the man had said. He felt the car pitch forward, then swerve violently to the right. He heard the scream of the tyres biting on the tarmac, and there was a new smell, burning rubber, along with the cordite. A bus loomed up. It blocked the street. The car hit the kerb. He saw people diving for cover, an old woman, slower than the rest, her body tossed onto the bonnet, her face pressed against the windscreen, looking at death. Then she was gone, and they were back on the road again, the speedo way up, sixty, seventy, the traffic scattering in front of them, bicycles, vans, cars, a lorry.

A minute later, they were in a side road. They left the car. They ran to another, Connolly in the back, lying on the floor, the car beginning to move already, the distant wail of sirens. Connolly shut his eyes, trying to make the noises go away, trying to forget the smells, trying to rid his head of that single image. Charlie's face. Gone.

After a while, the car slowed down. Normal road noise. The low burble of conversation in the front. Connolly began to relax. His hands were still pushed down hard between his thighs, foetal position, the ultimate crouch. He unclenched his hands, letting the gun fall to the floor, realizing for the first time what it was that he'd been holding between his knees. He looked down, making sure, knowing already that he'd blown it.

The balaclava, for God's sake. The fucking balaclava.

NINETEEN

The naval dockyard at Gibraltar lies on the western side of the Rock. The long seaward breakwater offers protection against the heavy Atlantic swells rolling in over the Bay of Algeciras, and there's a fine view of the entire base from most of the hotels that dot the Rock itself.

On the late afternoon of Monday 29th March, much to the surprise of a visiting Ministry of Defence civil servant making a routine call to his office back in London, the long black shape of a submarine appeared from the south and tied up alongside. The call over, the civil servant rummaged for his battered Zeiss binoculars and returned to the balcony of his room. The submarine, nicely in focus against the rough grey stonework of the quay, belonged to the Swiftsure class, fast-attack boats, hunter-killer, nuclear powered. The number on her conning tower identified her as HMS *Spartan*. *Spartan*, he knew from the briefing notes in his attaché case, was playing a key role in Exercise Spring Train with the First Flotilla. What, therefore, was she doing back in Gib?

The civil servant went shopping for an hour. When he returned to his room, he could see at once that the submarine was still there. He lifted the glasses again. Dusk was falling, and they'd switched on the big sodium floodlights along the dockyard quays. *Spartan*'s forward hatches were open, and there were dockyard workers on the long slope of the submarine's bow. Tied up alongside was another submarine, and the civil servant recognized the outline of an "O" class boat, one of the smaller, diesel-powered craft. He peered through the glasses, scanning left and right. There was a pile of cylindrical objects on the quay behind *Spartan*. The cylinders were packed in crates, and he could clearly see the distinctive red markings of the dummy torpedoes. He scanned left again. The diesel submarine also had her forward hatches open. More torpedoes were appearing, the old Mark Eights, swinging high in the air between the two submarines, then winching slowly down into *Spartan*'s forward compartments. He racked the focus a moment, sweeping up, looking for the one clue he needed. He found it in seconds, a single red flag, flying from *Spartan*'s stubby topside mast.

The civil servant lowered his glasses and retreated to the warmth of his room. The spring days cooled early, and it was already chilly in the wind. He sat down on the bed, a frown on his face, pondering the red flag. Live torpedoes, he thought. She's loading live torpedoes.

The soldiers arrived at Mairead's house an hour past midnight.

Two men pushed around the back, assault rifles at the ready, their faces daubed with greasy stripes of cam cream. One of them kicked over the neat square of empty milk bottles Mairead had left for the morning. Cats scattered in the darkness. A light appeared at the back of the house behind.

Half a minute later, the unit in position, the young captain knocked twice on the front door. Mairead, who'd been waiting for them since dusk, pulled her dressing-gown around her at the head of the stairs. The kids were away for the night. Knowing what would happen, knowing it was inevitable, she'd packed them off to friends.

Mairead put the light on and began to creep downstairs when there was a splintering of wood at the front door. The door burst open and the tiny hall was suddenly full of soldiers. One of the soldiers saw her on the stairs and raised his gun, and she screamed, and turned, and began to run back to the bedroom, but there were hands around her waist, and she found herself slipping down the stairs again, her nightie and dressing-gown riding up over her thighs, the metal treads on the stairs bumping against her shins. She hit out at the figure behind her, a mad flailing in the dim light of the forty-watt bulb, and she felt a sudden sharp pain in the kidneys that took her breath away. Then she was on the floor, in the hall. She could smell the dog on the lino, and there were a pair of boots an inch away from her eye. She looked up, gasping, wondering why the men bothered with the strange green make-up. War paint, she thought to herself. Savages.

The captain took her through to the kitchen. He found some matches and lit the gas under the kettle. He did it at once, without comment, the closest he could get to an apology. Then he told her to sit down at the kitchen table. She did so.

"I've orders to search your house," he said.

She nodded dumbly, knowing she ought to protest, knowing that compliance was as good as an admission of guilt. "Why?" she said.

"Because there's been an incident."

"What kind of incident?"

"A killing. A murder."

"Where?"

"In the city."

He looked at her. It took more than camouflage cream to disguise the contempt in his face. He was young. He had a very English accent. Mairead rubbed her back again, trying to ease the pain.

"But why me?" she said. "Why here?"

"Orders," the officer said.

Mairead nodded, listening to the sound of boots overhead, the rasp and creak of floorboards being pulled up, drawers wrenched open, then a thud that shook the whole house as something heavy was tipped on its side. The officer was watching the kettle. He made no attempt to ask her questions. She began to wonder why.

"I thought the police did this?" she said. "The RUC?"

The officer ignored her. Said nothing. She persevered.

"Why you?" she said. "Why the military?"

The kettle began to sing and the officer reached up for the battered metal tea caddy on the shelf above. Then the door opened and another soldier appeared. He was carrying a white envelope. Mairead had never seen it before. He gave it to the officer.

"Upstairs, sir."

"Whereabouts?"

"Under the woman's pillow."

The officer nodded, dismissing the soldier. The door closed again. The officer glanced at Mairead.

"What's this?" he said.

Mairead looked at the envelope. She recognized Connolly's careful script. Her name. The way he wrote it. The flourish after the final letter.

"I don't know," she said.

The officer opened the envelope. There were two sheets of paper inside, the writing closely spaced. He began to read it, then skipped on, checking the name at the end.

"Derek," he said, looking up. "Who's Derek?"

Mairead stared at the letter, wondering what to say, whether to deny it all, to do what she knew other women had done, to tell these animals to get out of her house and leave her alone. Then the door opened again and there was another man standing there, an older man. He wasn't a soldier. He wasn't in uniform. He wore brown corduroy trousers. He had an old leather jacket on. He had freckles, and swept back hair. The young officer stood to attention and snapped a salute. He was still holding the letter. Mairead just watched.

"Sir?"

The older man nodded, not bothering to return the salute. He looked at Mairead.

"Do you live here?" he said.

Mairead nodded.

"Yes," she said.

"Where's Connolly?"

"I don't know."

"I said where's Connolly?"

"I don't know."

The older man glanced at the young officer. The officer gave him the letter and the envelope and left the room. The door closed behind him. The older man sat down and Mairead looked at him. Connolly's chair, she thought. Derek's favourite spot. The older man bent to the letter. He read it carefully. Then he looked up.

"Do you know where he's gone?"

"No."

"Are you sure?"

"Yes."

He nodded. There was a brief silence. He looked at the letter again.

"When did you last see him?" he said at last.

Mairead hesitated. She knew the question was coming. She'd known all day. She'd made up her mind what her answer was to be. But now, here, with this man in her kitchen, it wasn't so simple. She could feel the anger in him, the rage. He must have known Charlie, she thought. He must have liked him. He was still looking at her, one finger on a sentence in the letter.

"Well?" he said.

She looked at him, seeing it all again, Charlie, the noise, the bangs, the thin film of blood on the window closest to the pavement. Charlie had fallen on his back across the front seats. Wherever you looked, wherever you put yourself, you couldn't avoid seeing him, the mess on the front of his head where his face had been. She blinked, dropping the curtain, shrouding the memory.

"This morning," she said.

"Where?"

She looked at him again, pleading, wanting him to believe her, wanting him to go away, wanting them all to go away.

"Here," she said.

The other man nodded. He proffered the letter.

"Have you read this?"

"No."

"Read it."

He gave her the letter and got up and went to the gas stove. The kettle was boiling. He turned it off and poured hot water into the teapot. Mairead tried to read the letter, tried to get the words in the right order, to shake the sense out of it. Derek had gone. He'd done what he had to do, done what was necessary, and he wasn't coming back. He loved her. They'd be together again. Sometime. She looked up. The man at the gas stove was a blur.

"Sugar?" he said.

She nodded, numbed. She heard him stirring the tea in the pot, brisk, everyday movements, real life. She looked at the letter again, tears pouring down her cheeks. Two deaths, she thought. One public. Charlie. One private. Hers. The man sat down and put the teapot between them.

"Do you love him?" he said.

She blinked at him. There was a new note in his voice, something she hadn't heard before, something close to kindness.

"Yes," she said.

"Does he love you?"

She nodded at the letter. "What do you think?" she said.

There was a long silence. The other man bent towards her.

"Do you know what he's done?" he said at last.

She looked at him for a while. He knows, she thought. He knows I was there. He knows what happened. He's seen Charlie since. He's been to the hospital, the morgue, wherever. He's seen what I saw. She lowered her eyes to the letter, not wanting to look at him any more, ashamed. He leaned forward across the table, his voice quickening, not hostile, not angry, but somehow more urgent.

"You had a meeting, didn't you," he said, "with Charlie?"

She nodded. "Yes."

"This afternoon. One o'clock."

"Yes."

There was another long silence. She reached for the pot of tea, then felt his hand on hers, restraining her. Not yet, he was telling her. Not yet. Soon. But not yet. She looked up, uncertain, knowing full well what his next question would be.

"Who else knew about your meeting?" he said.

She closed her eyes. She shook her head. She'd seen Connolly in the other car. She'd watched him, curious, wondering who his friends were, who he'd got the lift from, where they were going to let him off. She'd seen the car slowing. She'd seen him raise the gun. She'd seen the car stop. She'd tried to shout. A warning. To Charlie. To Derek. To anyone. Anyone who'd listen in this God-forsaken city. But the shooting had started, and the noise, and people running all over the place, bits and pieces of shopping spilled on the pavement, and Charlie not there any more, and she'd known then that it was all too late. No point, she'd thought. No point even staying. And so she'd run, like the rest of them, up the street and away. She opened her eyes. The question lay between them, unanswered. She sniffed.

"Derek knew," she said, "I told him."

The other man nodded. "Did you see it? Did you see what happened?"

"Yes."

"What happened?"

"Derek killed him. Shot him." She closed her eyes again. "Derek did it."

"So where is he now?"

She stared at the letter.

"God knows," she said.

The other man looked at her for a moment, then picked up the teapot. He poured two cups, pushed one across the table. He spooned in the sugar and she told him to look in the fridge when he asked about the milk. The house was quieter now. She wondered whether the soldiers had gone. She reached for the tea. It was sweet, two sugars, the way she liked it. She cupped her hands around it, shivering.

"What now?" she said.

The man leaned back. "You've got a choice," he said. "There'll be a police investigation. They'll want to talk to you. Maybe not tomorrow. Maybe not this week. But soon enough." He shrugged. "So you can stay here and wait for the phone to ring . . ."

"Yes?"

"Or we can do something else."

"We?"

"Yes." He looked at her. "You and me."

There was a long silence. Mairead sipped at the tea again.

"What's that, then?" she said. "What can we do?"

"We can get you away from here."

"I've got kids."

"I know." He paused. "We can set you up somewhere else."

"Where?"

"UK. Mainland. Somewhere nice."

"Why should we want to do that?"

The man looked at her, not answering. She asked him the question again. He reached for his tea. She picked up the letter and read it again slowly. Then she looked up.

"If we stayed here . . ." she said, "what would they do to us?"

"Who?"

"The police."

The other man shrugged. "I don't know," he said. "But the police would be the least of your problems. You were off to meet a Brit. You were consorting with the enemy." He paused. "I don't think it's the police you should be worrying about."

She stared at him. "Would that come out?" she said. "Would everybody know that?"

"Almost certainly."

She swallowed hard, reaching for the tea again, the warmth, the comfort. She thought about it, the neighbours, the kids, Danny's friends, the old nightmare. If they knew about Charlie, about the meetings . . . If she was to stand up in court and have the truth come out . . . She shuddered.

"When do I have to make the decision?" she said. "When do you have to know?"

"Now."

"*Now?*"

"Yes."

She blinked. "So when would we go? Away?"

The man smiled at her. "Tomorrow," he said. "First light."

Connolly awoke late, eleven o'clock, the sun streaming in through a chink in the curtains. He blinked and sat upright in the narrow bed. Far away, he could hear the sea. Closer, the lowing of cattle. There were gulls, too, wheeling above the cottage.

He looked round. The room was built in the roof. The walls sloped inwards, and there were a couple of small dormer windows. There was a white shag rug on the bare floorboards, and a selection of DIY furniture: a single chair, a chest of drawers, a small wardrobe. The place smelled new, of chipboard and freshly sawn timber. There was a dressing-gown on a hook on the back of the door. The dressing-gown was red.

Connolly got out of bed and pulled back the curtains. From the window, he could see across a meadow to a beach. The beach was cupped in a small bay. Across the bay was a finger of rock that pushed into the sea. The sea, like the sky, was a startling blue. The beach was almost pure white, completely unmarked. To the left, a narrow track ran down to the beach. The track was hedged on either side with fuchsia. Connolly opened the window and took a deep breath. The air was full of farm smells, and there was the scent of the ocean, too. Connolly smiled, leaning on the window ledge. The wood was already warm. There was barely any wind. The air was soft. Paradise, he thought.

After a while, Connolly stepped back into the room, leaving the window open. He got dressed and went downstairs. On the ground floor, the cottage was open plan, a single room running the full length of the place. There were big picture windows and a scattering of cheerful holiday furniture. Last night, arriving, he'd seen none of this. He'd been driven across the border west of Armagh. They'd swopped cars in Dundalk, and yet again two hours or so further south, a small village miles from anywhere with a single shop and a dog with three legs. The last part of the journey had taken place after dark, an ancient Datsun, driven by a small, hunched man who'd barely said a word. The journey had ended past midnight, total darkness, on a road by the coast. There'd been a track of sorts, off the road, and a gate, and the dim outline of a small white cottage, and the man had produced a key, and let him in, and taken him upstairs with the help of a tiny pencil torch. Whether he'd used the torch because there were no lights, Connolly didn't know, but he'd got into bed, and pulled up the duvet and listened to the old Datsun bumping away into the night. The Datsun had taken with it the last of what he wanted to remember about the most terrible day of his life. He didn't need a light. He didn't want to know what the room looked like, where he was, what might happen next. All he wanted to do was to sleep. And to forget.

Now, downstairs, he washed his face in the sink, cold water from the tap, a pebble of soap from the dish on the draining board. He rinsed his face a couple of times, and dried it on a dishcloth. There was a big corkboard hanging on the kitchen wall. It was covered in bits and pieces, old photos, recipes, kids' drawings. A family home, he thought. A place to bring the kids in the holidays.

He wandered upstairs again, glad of the silence and the sunshine puddling the wooden floors. Beside the bed was a plastic bag. Inside the bag was the black balaclava, and the gun, and the box of shells. He took the balaclava out, shaking it into shape, spreading it on the fingers of one hand, like a puppet. He sniffed it. It smelled of cheap tobacco. With the gun, crossing the border, heading down towards Dundalk, it was his sole worldly possession, all he had left. The rest of it – his books, his clothes, years of academic work, even his identity – had all gone, left behind in that other life he'd led, the forfeit he'd paid for three seconds' madness in a busy street in Belfast.

He looked at the balaclava again. Then he went downstairs with it, up to the far end of the big room. Here, there was a fireplace, an open hearth, a working chimney. He found some matches, and a little kindling, and an old newspaper. He arranged a bed of crumpled newsprint on the hearth, and built a tiny cairn from the kindling, and lit it. Then he laid the balaclava on the flames, watching it begin to smoke and burn, the eyeholes going first, and then the mouth, the wool unravelling in the heat, the folds of black moving slightly. It looked like a head, half human, and he knew it, turning away, the sour taste of vomit in his throat, thinking of the man Charlie.

An hour later, lunchtime, dressed, he heard a car. Sitting outside in the sunshine, his back against the wall of the cottage, he was thinking of Mairead. He knew, in his heart, that she must have seen him doing it, killing the man. He wondered what she made of it, what she thought. He wondered whether she knew why he'd really done it, for her, for her Irishness, her legacy, making his own modest statement, his own small contribution to the cause. To begin with, now, she'd be horrified. Later, when they met again, she might understand.

He squinted into the sunshine, watching the car bump into sight, an old grey Mercedes, a big car, two men inside. The car stopped outside the cottage. One of the two men got out. He recognized Scullen's walk, the slight stoop, as he pushed in through the gate. Connolly didn't get up. Scullen's shadow lay over him. He looked up.

"Where am I?" he said.

Scullen thought about the question, recognizing it for what it was, not strictly a matter of geography. Then he peered round, as if he'd never been here in his life.

"Kerry," he said briefly, "heart of the universe."

"Whose universe?"

"Mine."

Scullen looked down at him, the teacher with a disappointing pupil. Neither of them had mentioned the shooting, and Connolly knew instinctively that neither of them would. Scullen began to frown.

"You're a historian," he said, "you've heard of the great man."

Connolly looked away for a moment or two, consulting his mental check list of Irish folk heroes. One of them had Kerry connections. Came from down this way. Must have done. Scullen was watching him, the frown deepening. Then Connolly remembered.

"The Liberator," he said. "Daniel O'Connell."

Scullen nodded, pleased again, peering out towards the west where the mountains shouldered down towards the sea.

"There," he said.

Connolly followed his pointing finger. Daniel O'Connell had been a nineteenth-century lawyer and politician. He'd fought for Catholic emancipation. He'd spoken for the people. He'd taken on the Brits and won. Connolly looked to the west.

"Where?" he said.

"Over there. In the next bay. That's where the man lived. We'll see it later. I'll take you round."

Connolly got up and wiped the dust from his hands. "We're not staying, then?" he said.

Scullen looked at him. "No," he said, beaming, "I've more work for you."

Buddy got the letter from Jude in the late morning post. He collected it as he was leaving. He recognized the Irish stamp, and he peered hard at the postmark. Cahersiveen, it said, County Kerry.

Buddy read the letter once he got to the motorway, heading east again, towards Brighton. The letter was brief, two paragraphs, and had obviously been confected by whoever had typed it. The odd phrase he recognized as authentically Jude's, but for the most part it read like the kind of statement policemen extract from interviewees, a flat, formal prose, no smile, no lift. The letter said that Jude was OK. It said that she missed him, and wanted to be back with him. It said she was looking forward to going to Boston, and that she was sure he'd be able to make it work for them both. At the end of the letter, also typed, it said: "All my love, and whatever else you need . . . Jude." Instead of a signature, it carried the imprint of a pair of lips. The lipstick was the right colour, a deep red. Buddy lifted the paper to his nose and sniffed it. It smelled of Jude. He slipped the letter back into the envelope, keeping his eye on the road. He'd packed her make-up in the overnight bag, he remembered. They must have found it.

An hour later, he turned onto Brighton seafront, and parked the Jaguar about a quarter of a mile from the Palace Pier. He'd phoned Harry before breakfast. The old man was on his way out of the house. Buddy had said he needed equipment – breathing gear, some specialist stuff – but Harry cut him short, telling him to put it all on a piece of paper and send it along. Better still, he said, come on down and do it in person. Harry was supervising a piling job on the end of the pier. One o'clock sounded a sensible time for lunch.

Buddy checked his watch. 12.30. He locked the car, fed the meter, and strolled along the prom towards the pier. It was a glorious day, late March, the sky the cleanest blue, the faintest lop of the water between the two piers. Already, there were a handful of picnickers on the shingle, wicker baskets and plaid rugs and kids shredding bread rolls for the squadrons of wheeling gulls.

Buddy walked the length of the pier. Painters were at work on the cast-iron balustrades. There was a smell of popcorn and warm timber, the scents of early summer. At the end of the pier, there were amusements, and a bar, and a small gate marked "Private. No Admittance". Buddy pushed through it, clattering down a flight of steel steps towards the pier's lower deck. From here, Harry's men were diving, the long air-hoses snaking down another flight of steps to the sea. Buddy leaned over the rail and gazed down. The visibility was excellent for the time of year, a good ten feet, and he could see the shapes of the divers working around the base of the big supporting pillars, the tell-tale column of bubbles breaking surface beneath his feet. Buddy watched the men for a moment, enjoying the sun on his face, wondering whether he really missed it after all, even this kind of thing, kids' stuff, then he dismissed the thought, and went looking for Harry.

In the long, dark locker room the divers were using for Control, they told him that Harry was still down. The Diving Superintendent on the job, a big Geordie in a singlet and a pair of jeans, bent to the intercom on the operations panel and told Harry he had a visitor. Buddy listened for a moment, recognizing Harry's voice, disembodied, slightly metallic.

"Tell him to fucking wait," the voice said. "He's early."

Buddy waited outside, on the lower deck, leaning over the rail, warming his body in the sun. There were a couple of other divers there, already suited up, waiting to relieve the men in the water, and the three of them talked about the Falklands. Rumours were surfacing in the papers now, talk of sovereignty, and ultimatums, and possible moves against the Falkland Islands. There was nothing definite, nothing firm, but one of the men had a brother in the Navy, and he'd been recalled from leave at twelve hours' notice. Buddy shot him a look.

"Diver?" he said.

The other man shook his head. "Submarines," he said, "*Conqueror*."

Harry surfaced ten minutes later, wallowing beside the landing platform in a tangle of lines. One of the two divers went down to help him, and Buddy watched as he eased the old man's helmet off, and unbuckled his harness and his air bottles and the thick belt of weights he wore around his waist. Suddenly diminished, a stocky, white-haired old man in a black rubber suit, he looked up at Buddy and waved. Then he began to crawl up the iron steps on his hands and knees, trailing seawater behind him.

Buddy threw him a towel at the top. "Lunchtime," he said briefly, "and I'm buying."

Harry mopped his face and dried the water from his ears. "Thank Christ for that," he said.

They had lunch in the bar at the end of the pier. They sat at a small table near the door. The sun had come round a bit, and there was no wind, and it was pleasantly warm. Buddy fetched and carried from the bar, steak and kidney pie for Harry, fish and chips for himself, and two pints of Guinness. They said nothing for a while, eating the food. Then Harry looked up.

"You need some stuff," he said, as if he'd suddenly remembered.

Buddy nodded. "I do."

"What sort of stuff?"

Buddy hesitated a moment. He'd spent a couple of days drawing up a comprehensive list, and he'd brought it with him now. It included a closed circuit breathing set, twenty kilos of RDX explosive, a set of special magnetic clamps, a pair of detonators, and an underwater transmitter adjusted to a special sonic frequency to trigger the blast. The list was detailed, with careful specifications, and to anyone with Harry's experience it told its own tale. Yet he knew he ought to have a cover story, something at least half plausible for the moment when Harry asked the obvious question. He looked at the old man, then told him what he needed. Harry listened without comment. Then he raised an eyebrow.

"*How* much explosive?"

"Twenty kilos."

"That's a lot."

"I know."

"Have you got a PE Certificate?"

Buddy shook his head. A Police Explosives Certificate was the piece of paper you needed to handle explosives. On commercial jobs, it was always the responsibility of the diving contractors.

"No," Buddy said.

"You can have mine."

"Thanks."

"Means I'll have to come along, though."

Buddy looked at him. Then shook his head. "No," he said.

"Why not? Is it illegal?"

"Yes."

"Oh." Harry grinned. "*Very* illegal?"

"Yes."

"Good." Harry put his knife and fork down and wiped his mouth with the paper napkin. "Money in it?"

"As much as I need."

Harry stared at him. "Fifty grand?" he said.

Buddy nodded. "Yeah," he said.

Harry whistled, then reached for his glass. The conversation had begun to resemble a game show. Question and answer. Name the job. Harry took a long pull at the Guinness and frowned.

"You're blowing something up," he said.

Buddy nodded but said nothing. Harry looked at him. "A boat?"

"Yeah."

"Big boat?"

"Big enough."

"Here?"

"Across the Channel."

"France?"

"Yeah."

Harry nodded again, a gesture of applause, and bent to his meal while Buddy told him how he'd been hired to cripple a Liberian-registered tanker currently berthed in

minutes, he waited in the office of a junior whip. Finally, near eight o'clock, he joined the council of war.

The Prime Minister's office was crowded. The First Sea Lord counted seven heads. He sat down. The Prime Minister asked him at once whether the Navy could mobilize a Task Force. He said they could. She nodded and asked how quickly it could be done. He hesitated long enough to feel the temperature of the room. There was confusion here, and some anger. The politicians were boxed in. The diplomatic bluff had finally been called, and now the Argentinians were making the running. Years of neglect had come to this: an enemy fleet at sea, an invasion likely within forty-eight hours. The Prime Minister asked the question again: how soon could the Navy sail a Task Force of its own? The First Sea Lord paused for a second. Then he looked at her.

"A balanced force, Prime Minister?" he queried.

She nodded. "Whatever's necessary," she said.

He pursed his lips a moment, long enough to command complete silence. Then he looked up.

"By the weekend," he said.

Ingle, still in Belfast, sat at his desk and studied the telex from Paddington Green. There were no ambiguities, no possibility of mistakes. RUC scenes of crimes men had recovered seven bullets from the Great Victoria Street shooting. They'd run the usual tests and had circulated the results. One copy had gone overnight to Special Branch, Area Three, London. The Met's forensic department had compared the RUC analysis to their own library of spent rounds. Of these, the critical evidence from hundreds and hundreds of other incidents, only one other shooting had emerged from the computer as a perfect match. Francis Gerard Lancelot Leeson. Killed by person or persons unknown. 24th January, 1982. In Chiswick.

Ingle read the telex again, trying to think the whole thing through, trying to patch together enough of the picture to satisfy himself that the scalp in the out-tray wouldn't be his own. It was now confirmed that the victim, Charlie McGrew, had been a serving soldier, working undercover for Nineteenth Intelligence. That, in itself, had been an occasion for discreet celebration in certain security circles, tired of Nineteenth's special privileges, of the space they'd made for themselves, of the short cuts they took, of the aura of quiet invincibility they'd constructed to deflect all criticism. These were guys who thought they were super-human, immune to mistakes or political control. Now the world at large knew different. Charlie McGrew had been nutted on a crowded street in broad daylight – *lunchtime* for Chrissakes – by a guy in a car who'd managed the cleanest of getaways. That wasn't remotely superhuman. That was kids' stuff. That was very careless indeed.

Ingle bent to the telex. He'd already seen the RUC pre-liminaries, and he knew that Charlie McGrew must have been set up. He'd have been stopping for a rendezvous or a pick-up. He'd arranged to meet somebody, and that somebody had invited some other guests to the party. There'd been plenty of witnesses, and the usual flood of conflicting descriptions. Some people had said the gunman had been blond. Others said he had dark brown hair. One old woman even thought he looked like a girl. Age? Some said early twenties. Some said much older. Only on one detail was there any reasonable measure of agreement. At least half a dozen people had said the bloke looked half crazy. Drugs, or booze, or something. Out of his head. The eyes wider than you'd credit.

Ingle shook his head. Nothing there, he thought. Just another lunatic from West Belfast auditioning for the Clint Eastwood role. But what *was* interesting was the witness who hadn't come forward. Two or three people on the street had talked about a woman in a white coat. Youngish girl, black curly hair. She'd been by the car when the firing started. Indeed, one witness said she was about to get inside the fucking thing. Knew the driver. Bloke had waved to her. Just before half his head blew away. Fine. Good lead. Maybe the girl was even the pick-up. But where on earth had she gone?

Ingle didn't know, and in one sense it wasn't his business to find out. The RUC, the local force, were charged with the investigation. They'd do the necessary. They'd do the door-to-doors, and take the car to pieces, and re-examine the recent surveillance analyses, looking for patterns, and repeats, and re-entries, trying to put a name, or some shred of motivation behind the man in the white Ford. They'd be in charge of the job, and the investigation would develop at a pace of their choosing.

But there was another matter that bothered Ingle, and he was beginning to wonder whether the RUC knew about it. Since his meeting with Connolly, Ingle had looked yet again at the Qualitech job. He'd acquired the files from London, and the closer he examined the evidence, the more he was convinced that the job – the threat – had been totally synthetic. A lookalike IRA bomb, plausibly hidden, dramatically revealed, headlines everywhere, much credit. The fact that the IRA themselves had disowned the device Ingle had at first discounted. But now, he'd begun to have second thoughts. The Provos, after all, had a consistent – if somewhat chilling – reputation for putting the record straight. *Post facto*, you could trust their communiqués. If it was their bomb, they generally said so, no matter how ghastly the consequences. If it wasn't theirs, then they simply said nothing. On this occasion, though, two unusual things had happened. Firstly, they'd actually *denied* that it had anything to do with them. Secondly, the bomb itself hadn't gone off. The Prime Minister had thus been granted a stay of execution. And those around her were duly grateful.

To Ingle, that only had one explanation. Whoever had planted the bomb had never intended the thing to ever go off. On the contrary, it was planted with the sole purpose of generating useful credit, of putting the frighteners on Downing Street, and perhaps obtaining some extra leverage. Look, they would have said. Look what we've found. Look how close you've come to getting killed. Look how dangerous these men can be. And look at how good our sources must be if we – and we alone – have saved your precious life.

We? Ingle leaned back in the chair and pushed the telex away for a moment. The Qualitech job had been broken by Nineteenth. They'd found it. They'd taken the credit. And a week or so later, when the shit hit the fan in Dublin, it was fucking obvious why. They'd wanted yet another extension to their licence. Not just a trip across the border. A nut job in some cowshed or other, or a stake-out in some hedge. But the real thing, off in the motors, all tooled up, down to the home of the black stuff for a spot of real mischief. That was something he admired, an appetite for real risks, and talking to the man Miller on the phone in the middle of the night – far too pissed for his own good – he'd tried to pop a bob or two in their collection box, warning him to get his act together before the suits did it for him.

Miller, of course, had said nothing either way, but then he wouldn't. The boys from Nineteenth had long ago burned their bridges to the rest of the intelligence community. They trusted nobody. They were just too smart and too paranoid for their own good, and once they had faith in the Dublin address, once they'd OKed the source, they'd never stoop to cross-checks. For one thing, consultation might have blown their operation. Even worse, it might mean having to share the glory – and these boys were far too greedy for that.

Ingle smiled, staring at the bulletin board across the room. Greed. Glory. That, in a sense, said it all. Nineteenth had become an army within an army. Unaccountable. Out of control. And now, here, in this city, things were going horribly wrong for them. That's why it had made sense to confide his early suspicions about Qualitech to London. And that's why he now had to do something about the girl in the white coat.

He pulled the Paddington Green telex towards him again. It was black and white. The gun that had killed Leeson, killed Charlie McGrew. The common link was Connolly. Ingle, far too down to earth to ignore mundane factors like coincidence, reached for his mac. The boy was staying up in Andersonstown. He had the address. It was time for a chat.

Half an hour later, Ingle stepped out of his pool car and tapped on the door of Mairead's house. The lights were off downstairs, and when he opened the letter box and peered through, he couldn't hear the telly. He knocked again, but nothing happened. He stepped across the tiny apron of worn turf and began to pick his way round the side of the house when he noticed a roll of paper stuffed in a milk bottle. He bent down and picked it up. Under the street lamp on the pavement, it read, "No more milk, thanks. Thanks for everything. Cheque in the post."

Ingle frowned, and looked at the house again. It was obviously empty. Mairead, and her children, and maybe Connolly, had gone. He stepped next door and rang the bell. A dog barked. A door opened inside. Then another. He heard voices, and finally the front door opened and a woman of about fifty peered out. Her hair was in curlers. She was wearing slippers. It had just begun to rain.

Ingle introduced himself as a friend of Derek's next door. He'd come over from England. Derek had promised him a bed. Where was he? The woman shook her head.

"Gone," she said.

"Gone where?"

"Wouldn't say."

The woman peered at him some more, weighing him up, the long hair, the flat white face. Finally, she invited him in, out of the rain, long enough to explain that Mairead had gone off, the kids too, with a van full of furniture, and not so much as a goodbye. The van had come early, big thing, grey. There'd been men in the van, and they'd carried stuff out of the house, and the whole family had been away before even the milkman called. Speaking personally, she'd been insulted. She'd told the rest of the street not to bother with the woman. Nor the milkman, either. Easy come, easy go, she'd said.

Now, to Ingle, she said it again. No offence, mind, but taking up with the English boy when those friends of her husband's had been so good to her. Is that any way for a girl to carry on? On an estate like this? Is it? Ingle, stepping back into the rain, said it wasn't. One foot still in the door, he mentioned his English friend.

"Derek?" he said. "He go too?"

The woman looked at him. "No," she said, "no, he didn't."

Ingle nodded, and frowned, taking his time. "This girl-friend of his . . ." he said, "didn't have a white raincoat, did she?"

The woman looked at him narrowly, knowing at once that he wasn't a friend at all, but someone else, someone official, someone finding out things.

"Why?" she said.

Ingle shrugged. "Just wondered."

The woman looked at him for a long time. Rain began to drip down Ingle's face. Then she nodded. "Yes," she said shortly. "Smart thing. Brand new. He bought it for her. She wore it all the time."

"Who bought it for her?"

The woman frowned at him, impatient now to end the conversation. "That so-called friend of yours." She began to shut the door. "Derek."

The first thing Connolly noticed about Jude was the smell.

He'd driven up into the mountains with Scullen and McParland, away from the coast. They'd followed the course of a river, winding higher and higher, through pockets of forest, up towards the high passes with astonishing views back towards the sea. The roads grew narrower and narrower, the surface pocked with holes, wild sheep looking down from the rocks, and even with the windows up, the car was cold without the heater. Connolly had never known that Europe could be so wild, so remote. It was a forgotten place, miles from anywhere, a place you'd go for silence, and the taste of the wind.

At length, they'd come to a farmhouse in a narrow valley. The sides of the valley were steep and rocky, almost a perfect "U", and the house was without sunshine most of the day. It was stone built, solid, with big thick walls and a newish slate roof. The woodwork around the windows had recently been repainted. There was smoke from the chimney, shredded by the wind, and a huge, slow dog, blind in one eye.

They parked the car. Scullen got out. He wrapped his coat around him and walked straight into the house. Connolly hesitated a moment, hearing the sound of water, looking around for its source, spotting the endless streams tumbling from the mountainside, splinters of sunshine against the yellows and browns of the rocks. He shivered, wishing he had a coat. The air was cold and damp. He followed Scullen into the house. There was a small hall inside the door, flagstones, a low table. There were coats hung on pegs, and doors off the hall. Scullen was already in the room to the left. Connolly could hear his voice. He went in.

The room was big, low ceilinged, stone walls, good quality furniture. Someone had been redecorating recently. The paintwork was new, and the curtains, too. One end of the room was dominated by an open fireplace. Beside the fireplace was a wheelchair. In the wheelchair, sat a woman. She was huddled in a blanket. Her skin was very pale. She smelled of dead meat.

Scullen looked up, seeing Connolly. He stepped back from the fireplace, offering the simplest of introductions.

"Derek Connolly," he said, "Judith Little."

Connolly mumbled a greeting. He couldn't take his eyes off the woman. Her skin was almost translucent. Forget the rest of her – the wheelchair, the blanket – and she had the face of a saint. She looked almost ethereal. She belonged in a stained-glass window, a strange luminous presence, scored for a small choir and one of the softer requiems. She smiled at him. He smiled back, slightly unnerved.

Scullen nodded at them both and made for the door. "I'll be in touch," he said, "you'll be staying here." He glanced back towards the fireplace. "Company for Judith."

A ghost of a smile shadowed his face, and then he was gone, a tall cadaverous figure, clad in black, closing the front door. Connolly heard his footsteps outside. Then the purr of the Mercedes engine, slowly receding as it bumped away, back down towards the coast.

Connolly circled the wheelchair, looking for warmth from the small fire. The place was freezing. He stirred the single log with his foot. Smoke curled upwards. There was a silence in the room, and Connolly suddenly realized what it was about the woman. Her body never moved. Only her head. He looked at her. She was still smiling, twin dimples, bringing her face to life.

"Who are you?" she said.

Connolly thought about the question for a moment or

303

two. In all truth, he wasn't sure. He decided to keep it simple.

"An academic," he said. "From Belfast."

"Are you one of them?"

He looked at her again. Closer, the smell was overpowering.

"Yes," he said, "I suppose I am."

"Then you'll know about my husband." She paused. "And me."

Connolly shook his head. "No," he said, "I know nothing. They're strange people."

"They?"

He looked at her again. The smile had gone. He shrugged.

"We," he said.

There was a long silence, and as he looked around the room again, properly, taking in the rows and rows of books, and the small writing desk, and the tiny gilt icons, and the mawkish painting of the Crucifixion on the wall, Connolly realized that the house must belong to Scullen. The man fitted in here, like a piece of furniture. He was made for the place, its atmosphere of scholarship and piety, its inadequate heating, its sense of permanent chill. It was a house for an ascetic. Full of rectitude. Full of shadows.

The woman coughed, a small dry sound, and Connolly looked round at her, expecting the usual reflex action, the hand to the mouth, but there was nothing, not a hint of movement. Then the woman began to tell him what had happened to her, the flight over, the prospect of an operation, the journey out from Dublin, then her husband abruptly gone, guns everywhere, not the whisper of an explanation. Connolly listened to her, following the story, and then he asked about the operation, what was wrong with her, and she told him about the accident, way back now, three months ago, and her paralysis, and what the doctors had said, and the dangers she faced now, here, a million miles from anywhere. There were two others in the house, she said. A woman in her forties who cooked and cleaned, and a younger man who was supposed to be medically qualified. Connolly looked up.

"Is he?" he said.

Jude looked at the fire. "Yes," she said, "I think he is. But it won't make any difference."

There was another silence. Then the woman began to explain about the care she needed, the two-hourly adjustments to her body; shifting the weight in the chair, the regular bowel and bladder routines, the scrupulous hygiene, the need to keep herself warm. She recited it like a list, the faintest American accent, totally objective, not a shred of self-pity or complaint, simply a page or two from some maintenance manual. The list came to an end. Connolly was appalled.

"There's a smell," he said, "can you smell it?"

She nodded. "Me," she said.

"What is it?"

"An ulcer. It starts as discoloration. Patches of red skin. Tiniest thing. Then it becomes a kind of sore. Then the stuff around it goes black and dies. They call that an ulcer. That's what you can smell. The black stuff . . ."

"Where is it?"

She smiled. "I don't really know," she said.

"You don't *know*."

"No." She paused. "He does a lot around my bum. The left buttock. That kind of area. I've asked him enough times, but he's determined not to tell me. He just says it's OK. I think he's worried. I don't think he knows what to do."

"What can he do?"

"Not much. You just need constant nursing. Real care. It's a tough one."

"So how long . . ." Connolly frowned, "how long will it take? To get better?"

She looked at the fire for a moment. "I told him three months," she said, "maybe four. With hospital care."

"Told who?"

"Padraig. The man you came in with." She paused. "He's had some specialist here. From Dublin. He thinks he should get me into hospital. I told him not to bother."

"No?"

"No."

Connolly stared at her. "So what's going to happen?" he

said. "Here? You?" He nodded vaguely at her body under the blanket. "That?"

She thought about the question for a while. Then she looked up.

"It'll get worse," she said. "It'll get deeper, and there'll be more dead flesh, and in the end it'll kill me . . ." She paused. "It's called gangrene. It's pretty quick, once it really gets a hold . . ."

Connolly blinked, unable to relate what she was saying to her tone of voice. What she was saying was grotesque. A bit of her was dying. Soon it would kill the rest of her. Yet she appeared totally unconcerned, just another of life's little trials.

"You don't mind?" he said.

"Not at all," she smiled. "Apart from the smell."

Miller met the man from Downing Street in a small fourth-floor office in the Ministry of Defence.

They'd agreed lunch on the phone, but a later conversation had cancelled it. Whitehall was in chaos, he'd said. The Argies were thirty hours or so from hitting the beach and the place was thick with headless chickens. At best, they might manage a sandwich. At worst, they'd have to sort the thing out by phone.

In the event, though, the man from Downing Street found time to cross Whitehall, and toss his sandwiches and his briefcase on the desk, and accept Miller's offer of coffee. Miller knew him as Davidson, slight, pale face, rimless glasses, younger than he looked. Amongst other duties, he helped bridge the gap between the Joint Intelligence Committee, the security clearing house, and the Prime Minister's private office. The civil servant whom Miller had previously met was the senior official responsible for the JIC. Miller had originally requested a meeting with him, but under the circumstances it had been judged impossible.

"He's in orbit," Davidson explained, settling into the chair and reaching for his sandwiches. "We've got a war on our hands. It's a nasty surprise."

Miller nodded, spooning powdered creamer into the coffees. "I bet," he said drily.

He stirred the coffee and passed it over the desk. Davidson glanced at his watch. "I've got ten minutes," he warned, "then it's back to the bunker."

Miller sipped at his own coffee, taking his time. He'd known for a couple of days that Nineteenth's very survival was at stake. For the past month, they'd suffered defeat after defeat, a succession of disasters. First the Dublin débâcle, the failure to nail Scullen. Then the rumours about Qualitech. And finally, Charlie, a very public humiliation. Now, above all, Nineteenth needed help. Problem was, Miller had no friends to call on, no credit left. Nineteenth had elected to fight a solitary war, and now they were in danger of being wiped out. He looked up. Attack, they'd always taught him at Hereford. If in doubt, attack.

"The Prime Minister," he said carefully, "is in grave danger."

Davidson nodded. "I understand you've already made that point," he said thinly, "some time ago."

"I meant it then," Miller said, "and I mean it now."

Davidson reached for another sandwich. "Evidence?" he said.

Miller hesitated. "They've been playing with us, and vice versa. Frankly, we could have done better. It happens that we didn't. In fact we lost a man. As you know."

Davidson nodded. "Unfortunate," he said, "I agree."

Miller got up and went to the window. It was a flawless spring day. The river was nearly blue, the first of the season's pleasure boats pushing downstream against the flood tide.

"We have indications," he said, "that they're planning the big one. We've coded it Reaper."

"How picturesque."

Miller glanced round, recognizing Davidson's inflection for what it was, slightly fastidious, slightly disapproving, the tone of a man who bothered about language.

"The big one," Miller repeated, "something special. The hit that evens the score. The one that really matters."

307

Davidson picked a shred of chicken from his back teeth. He looked at it, frowning.

"They all matter," he said.

"Quite."

"But you think . . . ?" He paused.

Miller nodded, emphatic. "Yes," he said, "the Prime Minister."

"Why?"

"Because she's the obvious target."

Davidson looked at him. He was still frowning.

"I understood these people . . . this character of yours . . ."

"Scullen."

"Scullen was good."

"He's very good."

"Then he may do something else." He paused. "May he not?"

"It's possible."

"Something far from obvious?"

Miller shrugged. "Yes," he conceded. "If he gets the chance."

"And will he get the chance?"

"Not if we get to him first."

"And will you?"

Miller looked him in the eye.

"Yes," he said, "I think we will."

There was a brief silence. Big Ben chimed. The single stroke. One o'clock.

Davidson was looking out of the window.

"You said that before," he said, "didn't you?"

"Yes."

"And we had the Irish on. Most of the following week."

"So I believe."

"Extremely tiresome."

"Of course."

Davidson registered the point with another silence. Then he cleared his throat.

"We have procedures already," he looked at Miller, "for protecting the Prime Minister."

"So I understand."

"And there's a lot going on. God knows."

"Agreed."

"But you still think we should be cautious?"

"Very."

"Despite the . . . ah . . . inconvenience?"

Miller nodded. "Yes," he said, "that's why I'm here."

Davidson looked at his briefcase a moment, as if debating whether or not to open it. Then he glanced at Miller again. "If nothing materializes," he said, "she won't be best pleased."

Miller shrugged. "If nothing materializes," he said, "at least she'll be alive."

"Quite."

There was another silence, longer this time, and Miller knew that he'd underestimated the young civil servant, permitted himself to be pushed into a corner of someone else's making. The unspoken warning was quite clear. This time, they were saying, you'd better be right. This time, there'd better be a real threat, a real attack, not some clever props work in the wings, noises off, scaring the daylights out of everyone, crying wolf. Miller glanced up. Davidson was wiping the crumbs from the table and folding his greaseproof paper. The meeting was evidently over. He stood up.

"By the way," he said, reaching for his briefcase, "the RUC have been on this morning. They're apparently missing a key witness. Young woman." He smiled. "Wouldn't have any ideas, would you?"

It took Mairead most of the morning to borrow a washing line.

She tried first at the next billet in the camp, another of the hideous concrete slab prefabs she'd last seen under the bulldozers in West Belfast. The woman next door couldn't stand the Irish, and she saw it in her face as soon as she opened her mouth and the woman heard the harsh Belfast accent, and shook her head at the word "borrow".

Mairead gave up at that point, tugging Bronagh down the road, heading for the NAAFI, her purse still bulging with the twenty five-pound notes they'd given her on the plane over. But the NAAFI didn't stock washing lines either, so in the end, determined to rescue something from the morning, she sat the kids round the brand-new video, and phoned for a taxi, and rode down to the local town where she found what she needed. The local town was called Borden. She hadn't a clue where it was, and she wasn't much bothered. Only the kids, keeping them safe, now mattered.

An hour later, she was back. There were, she had to admit, odd moments of consolation in this strange new life of hers, and this was one of them, the kids sat around on the floor, a cartoon video on the telly, food in the fridge, money in her purse, and the assurance from the man in the leather jacket that they would all – sooner or later – be shipped back to Belfast. She'd no idea who he represented, whether he worked for the police, or the military, or some other organization, but she knew she needed someone to trust, and in the absence of anyone else, it had to be him.

He appeared in the late afternoon. He said he'd been up in London. He stepped out of a small green car and asked where they might talk. Mairead suggested the garden, out the back. The kids were onto their third video. It was a nice day. She'd make him tea.

They talked for nearly an hour. He explained he was Charlie's boss. He said he'd got to know the boy very well, had loved him like a father. He said that Charlie's job was to pass on all the information that she'd been able to give him, either up front, or without really knowing that she'd said anything of value. He said she'd helped them greatly in certain respects, and that they were now closer to finding a man who was causing a great deal of concern, a very dangerous man. She listened to him throughout without making any comment of her own, topping up his tea-cup, passing him the sugar, and when he ended up by saying that essentially they were all on the same side, allies in the same war, against murder and violence and suffering, she nodded.

"They all say that," she said.

"All?"

310

"You. The priests. The doctors. My lot," she paused. "Even Charlie."

"Don't you believe me?"

"Of course," she said, "I believe you all. But it still goes on." She looked at him. "Doesn't it?"

He nodded. "Yes," he said.

There was a long silence. She could hear Bronagh screaming inside. The kids had persuaded her to hire a horror video. Bronagh was easily frightened. She looked at the man in the leather jacket.

"So what do you want?" she said. "Why have you come?"

He bent his head a moment and looked away, realizing for the first time how direct this woman could be, how difficult it must have sometimes been for Charlie. He plucked a blade of winter grass and sucked it. It tasted of nothing.

"I want you to talk to Connolly," he said.

Mairead nodded. "How do I do that?"

"He'll phone. Sooner or later." He nodded towards the house. "Your Belfast number's been transferred. Any calls, they'll ring here." He looked at her. "So don't go out, please. Stay in."

"And?"

"When he phones, find out where he is."

"And?"

"Tell us." He hesitated. "Tell me. I'm staying around for a bit. I may even be here. On camp."

Mairead looked away, squinting in the bright sunshine. Bronagh had stopped screaming.

"But what will you do?" she said. "What will happen to him?"

Miller extended a hand and laid it lightly on her forearm. "Nothing," he said. "Nothing can. Nothing will. He'll be in the Republic somewhere. Bound to be. That's a foreign country. He's abroad. He's safe."

Mairead frowned, confused. "So why bother?" she said. "Why find out in the first place?"

"Because he'll take us to someone else. Someone we want very badly."

Mairead nodded. "And won't he be in the Republic too?"

"Probably."

"But won't that matter? Won't he be safe there?"

Miller looked at her for a long time. Then he shook his head.

"No," he said. "Not this time."

Scullen handled the Great Victoria Street debrief himself.

He went back to Buncrana, and drew up the report, spending even more time than usual getting it exactly right, the prose elegant, the structure tight, each paragraph striking the perfect balance between information, atmosphere, and the remorseless onward march of the narrative. Charlie McGrew. A confirmed member of Nineteenth Intelligence. A target of opportunity. Handed to them on a plate. The operation put together at short notice by the pick of Scullen's Belfast apprentices. And then the hit itself, a masterpiece, a Brit finger on the trigger, one more recruit to the cause, a quite unexpected dividend.

Scullen typed the report himself, and made the phone call. The Chief said he'd come the same day, and bring company.

Company turned out to be O'Mahoney. Scullen hadn't seen him for nearly six months, not since the start of the current mainland campaign. He'd put on weight. Never talkative, he'd become even more withdrawn. He didn't bother to take his coat off. Unshaven, hostile, he sat on a pile of historical reviews in a corner of the office, a brooding presence on the very edges of the conversation.

The Chief read Scullen's report over coffee. Then he put it down.

"It says you did well, Padraig," he remarked, "saves me the trouble of forming my own opinion."

"We did," Scullen nodded. "We did."

The Chief studied the closely typed pages again, then looked up. "The Brits are going to war," he said, "it seems you were right there, too."

Scullen smiled. The Chief was watching him closely now.

"So tell me," he said, "when can we expect some action?"

Scullen shrugged. There was something in the Chief's

312

voice, something close to anger, something perhaps for O'Mahoney's benefit, but he couldn't quite place what.

"Action?" he said.

The Chief nodded. "You promised us an operation. We were going to blow up a battleship or two." He paused. "Wasn't that the heap?"

"Ah . . ." Scullen smiled again. "Yes."

"So when will it happen?" The Chief paused. "And who's in place to do it? Do we get any clues? Only some of the boys are getting confused."

He glanced across at O'Mahoney. O'Mahoney grunted, burying his nose in his mug of coffee. Scullen looked at him a moment, trying to gauge the depth of the man's resentment, the reasons for it. The Leeson hit had been unfortunate. He'd never intended to give O'Mahoney problems, and he'd written to him since, a careful note of apology. Now, looking at him, it plainly hadn't done the trick. The Chief picked up Scullen's report and began to fold it.

"I take it there will *be* a hit?" he said.

"Yes."

"Soon?"

"Yes."

The Chief nodded. "Good," he said, "because you'll fucking need it."

He glanced across at O'Mahoney again and got up. Both men headed for the door. Scullen watched them, not beginning to understand.

"Where are you going?" he said.

The Chief got to the door and paused. He turned round. Scullen had never seen the expression on his face before. It was a dark fury.

"I'm off back to Belfast," he said, "to postpone a funeral."

"You are?"

"Yes."

"Whose funeral?"

"Yours."

"Why?"

There was a long silence. The Chief began to tuck the report into his inside pocket.

"Because Charlie McGrew was ripe for turning," he said,

313

"the boy was a real prospect. And you had him fucking killed."

TWENTY-ONE

The Argentinians had been ashore on the Falklands for twenty-four hours before Buddy next appeared on Portsmouth Harbour.

He'd driven over from the cottage and hired a small speedboat from a yard in Gosport. The boat had a 50hp outboard and a nice turn of speed, though the harbour itself had a tightly policed limit of ten knots. Now, midmorning, he cruised slowly up and down on the edges of the buoyed channel, watching the warships on the Portsmouth side of the harbour, fixing the picture in his mind.

The first Home elements of the fleet, he knew, were due to sail on Monday morning, two days hence. According to the morning's news on the radio, the Admiralty had announced that three capital ships would be involved, the old aircraft carrier *Hermes*, the new jump-jet carrier *Invincible*, and the amphibious assault ship *Fearless*. All three ships were now visible in the dockyard, *Invincible* tied up at South Railway Jetty, broadside on to the harbour, *Hermes* further north, tucked around the corner, with *Fearless* berthed near by.

Buddy took the little speedboat up the harbour, beyond the commercial ferry port, and then cut the engine, letting the ebb tide push the bow round and ease her slowly back down-harbour, towards the open sea. MOD police would, he knew, have men afloat, more vigilant than usual, keeping an eye on the dozens of small craft nosing around the dockyard. There were no restrictions on this stretch of water, no ban on private shipping, but all the same it wouldn't pay to write notes, or stay too long, or appear to be anything but a casual gawper, eager to share the glow of this small moment of history.

315

The speedboat drifted along, Buddy relaxing against the padded mock-leather seat. He'd taken some care to dress for the part, T-shirt, jeans, wrap-around sunshades, and he wondered for a moment whether he shouldn't have let Eva come too. She'd have looked good beside him, completing the tableau. She might even have behaved like a human being, relaxing for an hour or so, instead of playing the tight-lipped full-time revolutionary she felt the job demanded. Funny woman, he thought.

Last night, Friday, she'd stayed late again at the cottage, trying to persuade him to do without an extra pair of hands. He'd gone through the thing time and again, the help he'd need with the boat, with the gear, with the pick-up afterwards, but each time he described a particular task she'd simply said it would be no problem. Taking the yacht round to Portsmouth? She'd do it. Preparing the diving gear? She'd help. Manhandling the explosives, and the other gear, over the side? Her job. In every possible respect, she was totally inexperienced. She'd never sailed in her life, never dived. Yet still she insisted.

Finally, getting to the bottom of it, Buddy had asked her point blank: what's the problem? Why not get help? She'd refused to answer for a minute or two, and then told him it was absurd. They couldn't possibly go out and simply hire someone. He'd said of course not. They'd have to ask the people in Dublin for reinforcement. But this, too, she turned down flat. They were, she'd said, unimpressive. That was the word she'd used. Unimpressive. One or two were good, she'd said, but the rest were *schiess*. Better, and safer, to handle the job themselves. In the end, two in the morning, he'd given up. "OK, then," he'd said, "it's you and me. Versus the entire fucking Navy." She'd shrugged at the odds and reached for her duffle coat. "No need to swear," she'd said, heading for the door.

Now, eyeing the line of grey warships, he thought about the odds again. He'd finally decided to limit the amount of explosives, cutting his order with Harry by half, causing damage, but little possibility of injury or death. By placing two ten-pound charges aft, close to the vital glands that protect the main propeller shafts, he'd guarantee to stop a ship in its tracks. Damage to the steering gear would also be likely, making it doubly certain that the ship would have to return for expensive repairs. This, as he understood it, was the whole point of the exercise. To inflict the maximum humiliation in front of the biggest possible audience at a key moment in the nation's history. The papers were already stirring the national pot, talking about the biggest naval encounter since the Second World War, and he could imagine the kind of capital the Provos would make of a successful pre-emptive strike. The tabloids, of course, would rant and rave about betrayal. Politicians would bang on about the Fifth Column. But most blokes, he knew, would have a quiet think about the reach and the calibre and the motivation of a guerrilla army that could stop the Royal Navy in its tracks. Wouldn't it be simpler, they might conclude, to just get out of Ireland altogether? To leave it to the Irish and come home? That was the real prize. That was why they'd gone to the trouble of kidnapping Jude. That was what they were looking to him for.

Buddy eased the speedboat off to starboard as a big Sea King helicopter clattered in from the west. They were drifting down towards *Invincible*, and the last thing he wanted was attention. He gazed up at the huge hull of the warship. She was almost brand-new, but already under offer to the Australian Navy, part of yet another Defence Review. She was big, nineteen thousand tons, with a ski jump at the bow for the new Sea Harrier STOL jets. She had a bridge, and two funnels, and a massive radar array in a command island offset to one side, while the rest of her deck was dedicated to aircraft. Looking up, he could see men working through the open scuttles on the side, and he could picture the scenes on the quay, the lorries grinding in from the supply depots inland, the big dockyard cranes winching aboard the heavier items, machinery, guns, spare parts, crates of ammunition, the human chains on the gangplanks, passing stores aboard, hand to hand, hour after hour. There'd be Petty Officers on the quayside, clipboards, endless lists of stores. There'd be NAAFI blokes dispensing buns and cups of hot coffee. There'd be dockies running around with spanners and tins of grease, civvy lorry drivers helping with the heavier loads.

God knows, even the police probably had a smile on their faces. Buddy grinned and shook his head. It was a fairytale, he thought. Everyone off to war. Everyone delighted. And here he was, trying to wreck the party.

He glanced across the harbour, back towards Gosport, measuring the distance between *Invincible* and the marina where the girl had booked a berth. He'd already decided that *Invincible* would be the target, chiefly because she was liable to take the lead as the capital ships left the harbour, but also because she was the easiest ship to attack. His plan would call for the yacht to drift slowly down the middle of the harbour after dark on Sunday night. At half past midnight, the tide would be slack high water. Abeam *Invincible*, he'd slip into the water on the blind side, and swim submerged on a compass bearing to the carrier's stern. The charges would be magnetic, already shaped and prepared. He'd attach them both and prime the detonators. The detonators he'd asked for were sonar-sensitive, tuned to a frequency he suspected was never used. After he'd planted the charges, he'd return underwater on a back bearing. With no tidal flow, he'd only need a time estimate to the marina. The girl would have returned the yacht to the marina, and he'd join her there. Ten hours later, with *Invincible* slipping out through the harbour narrows, he'd detonate the charges with a single press of a single button. An underwater sonar signal, and the watching television cameras, would do the rest.

Buddy eased the speedboat's outboard into reverse and drifted back until he was abeam *Invincible*'s stern. By looking at the markings on the ship's hull, he could gauge the depth of the water she drew. He'd already guessed twenty-four feet. At eight metres, he was only about two feet out.

He turned the speedboat to starboard again, and headed for the marina, glancing over his shoulder as he did so. When he was exactly on course, he checked the tiny portable compass he'd suckered to the dashboard. Returning to the marina, underwater, he'd need a course of 260 degrees magnetic. He checked the course against the chart he'd already bought at the marina chandlery. The course was spot on. He then measured the distance between the two points, estimating it on the chart at a little over five hundred metres. Swimming in slack water, with full gear, five hundred metres would take about twenty-five minutes. With two bottles, and a maximum work depth of twenty-six feet, that would give him a residue of fifteen minutes to find the ship, locate the target area, and plant the charges. Fifteen minutes. He glanced over his shoulder at the huge warship, wondering whether it would be enough, marvelling at how cool he was about it all. Just another calculation. Just another job.

It was nearly lunchtime on the second day before Connolly realized how badly Jude needed help.

He'd taken her out in the morning, pushing the wheelchair up the narrow road beside the farmhouse. They'd walked for perhaps a mile, the road getting steeper and steeper, a cold damp windy day, the tops of the mountains hidden in cloud. Scullen's male nurse, a dim, rather sullen man of about thirty, had dressed Jude for the trip. She was wearing an extra pullover, and a heavy green anorak that didn't quite fit. She looked paler than ever, and she didn't bother to answer the odd question that Connolly addressed to the back of her head.

After a while, they stopped. Connolly had made some sandwiches from a loaf he'd found in the kitchen, and a couple of tins of sardines. He unwrapped them, offering one to Jude. She nodded, and he knelt by the wheelchair, feeding them to her. She chewed for a moment, and then swallowed the first mouthful.

"Nice," she said. "Real good."

They talked for a while about picnics they'd enjoyed, Connolly sitting on the ground, leaning back against one of the wheels. She told him about holidays she'd taken as a kid, out on a bunch of islands off the North Carolina coast, place called Cape Hatteras. They'd had bake-outs on the beach. They'd eaten clams and fresh mullet. It had seemed a rare adventure. She asked for another bite of sandwich, and Connolly reached up. The skin on her face was cold to the touch. She bit the corner off the triangular sandwich and played with it in her mouth, and Connolly found himself wondering what kind of woman she really was, she'd really been, when her body worked properly, and life wasn't the gift of passing strangers.

She fell silent and he glanced up. She was staring down at her lap.

"Is it me," she said, "or do I hear water?"

Connolly smiled. Ireland was full of water, especially round here, out in the west. The mountains were criss-crossed by streams, ribbons of water tumbling down the rocks. The previous night, the sound had sent him off to sleep, water in a gully outside his window. He smiled.

"You hear water," he confirmed.

"No. Look. Underneath. Please."

He glanced up at her. She looked frightened. He turned round, and looked beneath the wheelchair. She was right. Water was dripping through the canvas seat, onto the gravel beneath. He dipped his finger in the puddle and smelled it.

"Yours," he said, "sorry." He got up. "What do you want me to do?"

She looked round. Fifty yards away there was a clump of pine trees in a hollow amongst the rocks. The wind had stripped the pines and the ground beneath was soft with needles.

"Take me there," she said. "We have to do something. It's bad otherwise."

Connolly pushed the wheelchair to the trees. The wind felt cold on his face. He stopped. "What now?" he said.

"You lift me off," she said, "you bend down and I fall forward over your shoulder. Grade One stuff. Fun if you're into contact sports."

Connolly smiled at her. "I'm a humble Volunteer," he said. "That's the last thing I'm into."

She looked at him.

"OK, wise guy," she said, "just do it."

Connolly did what she asked, folding back the footrests on the wheelchair, getting down on his hands and knees, and pulling her body towards him. She fell over his shoulder, slack, like a bag of coal. In the open air, the smell wasn't quite so bad. He laid her body gently on the pine needles. She looked up at him. She winked.

"You've done this before," she said, "for real."

He returned the wink. "Maybe," he said. "What now?"

"Take my bottoms off," she said, "roll up my sweater. You'll find a tube and a plastic bag. The tube comes out of me. The bag's full. There's a valve on the tube. You seal the valve and change the bag." She smiled. "Like I said. Grade One."

Connolly rummaged in the holdall they'd brought with them. He found two spare bags. They were marked "Sterile", sealed in Cellophane. They were about the size of a paperback book. He turned back to her and unzipped her anorak. Underneath, she had two sweaters. He rolled them both up. Then the T-shirt. Then, finally, the tops of the tracksuit trousers. He glanced up at her face.

"Everything's soaking wet," he said.

"Yuck."

"I mean it."

"OK." Her eyes flicked left, to the holdall. "There's spares in the bag. Change the sweaters and the tracksuit. There's no spare T-shirt. Forget it."

Connolly nodded, arranging the dry clothes on the pine needles beside her body. Then he turned back to the bag. The bag was full, seeping urine at one corner. He found the valve on the tube and shut it. He moved her body slightly, easing it to one side. Then he saw the bandage.

It was huge. It was high on her left buttock, an untidy oblong of lint, taped at the edges with sticky brown plaster.

"Your bandage," he said, "that's wet too."

"Shit."

"What shall I do?"

He glanced up at her. Her eyes were closed. If she could die, he thought suddenly, if it was within her grasp, under her control, this would be the moment, half naked, up some freezing Irish mountain, in the hands of a man she didn't even know. She opened her eyes. Her voice was very quiet. She didn't phrase it as a question. She just told him.

"There's a fresh bandage," she said, "in the bag."

Connolly reached for the holdall again. He found the bandage. He used a towel to mop her dry. He glanced at her face. She was staring up at the trees.

321

"Change the bag first," she said quietly, "before you do anything else."

Connolly did what she asked, removing the full bag of urine, and attaching one of the new ones. He put the full bag beside the wheelchair.

"OK?" she said.

He nodded, opening the valve again, and watching the thin trickle of urine emerge from her belly and trickle through to the new bag.

"OK," he said.

"So now take the bandage off," she said, "and clean it up."

Connolly nodded, glancing up at her. Then, as carefully as he could, he began to ease the wet bandage off, loosening the strips of plaster inch by inch.

"Be brave," she said. "Rip it. I can't feel a thing."

He looked at her for a moment. Then he did as he was told, pulling the bandage diagonally, one corner to the other, a single movement. The bandage came off. Underneath, there was a hole the size of a tea-cup. It was black and yellow at the edges. It went deep. He could see glimpses of bone at the bottom.

"Shit," he said quietly.

He folded the soiled bandage and buried it under the pine needles. Then he returned to the ulcer. He'd never seen anything like it. It looked like a war wound, the kind of hole a lump of shrapnel makes, cratering the flesh. Here and there, the flesh was still healthy, still red, but for the most part, the wound oozed pus, the tissue turning to yellowish slime, and then dying completely as the infection bit ever deeper.

There were balls of cotton wool in the bag. Connolly took a handful and began to clean out the wound, scouring out the pus and slime, trying to get down to the healthy tissue. He had no idea whether what he was doing was medically recommended, or even safe, but the stuff offended him. It represented death and decay. It *was* death and decay. He looked up. "This hurting?" he said.

Jude looked at him and shook her head. "Wish it did," she said.

Connolly registered the answer and mumbled an apology, working as fast as he could, knowing that a chill could be as dangerous as gangrene. Jude had given him a brief account of the conditions that could hurt her the previous evening. He'd asked for it because he had some dim belief that he was now responsible for her well-being, perhaps even her survival. She'd gone through the list without any evident emotion – damp, cold, kidney infection, bladder infection, chest infection, bedsores, ulcers, gangrene – smiling at the end when he'd asked her how badly each of these afflictions could affect her.

"Affect me?" she'd said. "They'll kill me. Any one of them."

Now he scissored an oblong of lint and laid it carefully over the ulcer. The lint dimpled in the middle where the hole was. He taped it round the edges, noticing that even here the flesh was beginning to yellow.

The bandage secure, he quickly checked the new bag for drips, and then changed her trousers and her top. She was thinner than he'd imagined, the bones of her rib cage noticeable beneath the pale flesh. He pulled down the bigger of the two replacement pullovers and nodded at the wheelchair.

"Party's over?" she said.

He smiled. "Afraid so."

He lifted her up, very slowly, and folded her over his shoulder, careful to avoid touching the top of her left leg. He carried her back over the pine needles to the wheelchair, and settled her as comfortably as he could, only realizing at the end of it that comfort was irrelevant. She could feel nothing. She was dead. He kicked the full pack of urine over the edge of the road, watching it bounce for twenty or thirty feet, and then burst on a rock. Then he began to push the wheelchair back down the mountain towards the house. Off to the right, the flank of the mountain fell away, nearly sheer, to the valley floor. The weather was clearing a little now, shafts of yellow sunlight spearing through the ragged overcast. He could smell heather, after the rain, and peat. The wind keened as they left the last of the trees.

They walked in silence for a minute or two. Then Jude asked him to stop.

"Tell me something," she said.

"What?"

"How bad is it?"

"What?"

"The ulcer."

Connolly stepped round the wheelchair, and chocked one of the wheels with a rock. It seemed rude talking to the back of someone's head.

"It's terrible," he said. "It's very bad."

She nodded. "Yeah?"

"Yeah." He looked at her. "You need help. Proper help. You need a hospital. I'm going to fix it."

"How?"

"I'll phone."

"There is no phone."

"I'll find one." He shrugged. "Somewhere else."

"Really?"

"Yes."

He looked at her, recognizing the tone in her voice. It began as scepticism, but it ended up as something else. She didn't want a hospital. She wanted out. She was eyeing him, anticipating him, enjoying the brief telepathic comforts of this unspoken conversation of theirs. She turned her head to the right. The road clung to the side of the mountain. There was nothing between this thin ribbon of pocked tarmac and the drop to the valley floor. She glanced up at him.

"Well?" she said.

Connolly shook his head.

"No."

"Wouldn't it be simpler?"

"Maybe."

"But you won't do it?"

"No."

She thought about it for a moment or two. It started to rain again, a thin fine drizzle. Then she looked up at him.

"You're like Buddy," she said glumly, "you have absolutely no imagination."

When Buddy finally got down to the yacht, midafternoon, Harry had been waiting for nearly an hour. The old man emerged from the cabin and levered himself carefully onto the marina pontoon.

"Bloody silly boat," he said, "to go across the Channel.' Buddy shrugged.

"Beggars can't be choosers," he said.

"I thought they were paying you?"

"They are."

"Then get yourself something half-decent. This thing belongs in the bath."

He looked Buddy in the eye and grunted, and Buddy watched him limp off towards his van, wondering what he was doing in the cabin in the first place. The boat was supposed to be secure. There were charts in there, the whole story mapped out in pencilled lines and tide tables and scribbled estimates of bottom time. Harry opened the back of his van. It looked nearly as old as he was. There was a skirt of rust around the bottom, and one of the tyres was completely bald. He glanced back over his shoulder.

"You want this stuff," he said, "or not?"

Buddy walked across. The gear he'd asked for was piled neatly on the floor of the van. There was a closed circuit diving set with twin cylinders and a dive vest. There were two metal boxes about the size of cake tins, and a pair of magnetic clamps. There was a rubber dry suit, and a couple of face masks, and a weight belt, and a pair of flippers. Buddy looked at it all.

"I don't need the suit," he said.

"You sure?"

"Yeah. I'll use my own."

Harry nodded, tossing the suit towards the front of the van. His hand strayed to the dive set.

"You know this one? The Mark Six?"

Buddy looked at it. The Mark Six was an American design, US Navy issue. Two cylinders of oxygen sat in a back frame. The back frame attached to a dive vest. At the front of the dive vest were two pockets. Each of these pockets contained a breathing bag. The diver inhaled air from one bag, and exhaled air into the other. The exhaled air was passed into a scrubber, which removed all the poisonous carbon dioxide, and was then recirculated into the inhalation bag. Oxygen from the cylinders at the back was carefully fed into the circuit, topping up the recirculated air. Buddy had used the system on a number of jobs, and liked it. It was efficient and it was safe. You stayed down longer and you didn't produce bubbles. He smiled. Bubbles underwater would give him away in seconds, leaving a tell-tale trail on the surface. He looked at Harry and nodded.

"It's fine," he said.

Harry frowned. "You going deep?" he said. "Big tanker?"

Buddy shrugged. "Deep enough," he said.

"How deep?"

"Thirty feet." Buddy looked at him. "Why?"

The old man shrugged. "Nothing," he grunted. "Piece of piss."

He picked up one of the oxygen bottles.

"They're both fully charged," he said, "one's oxygen. One's oxy-helium. You set the flow rate yourself."

"OK."

Harry gave him the cylinders. Between the two cylinders was a smaller bottle, black. Harry touched it.

"I did the Baralyme this morning," he said, "if you have to do it again, make sure the stuff settles. There's more Baralyme in the box there." He nodded at a small cardboard box in the back of the van. "Keep tapping the cylinder when you put it in. Otherwise you'll be in the shit."

Buddy nodded. Baralyme was the chemical you used to fill the scrubber. The stuff removed all the carbon dioxide, and it came in granular crystals. If you weren't careful when you refilled the scrubber, you got holes between the crystals, which meant you ended up breathing your own exhaust. He'd worked with a guy in the Middle East who'd done just that. The funeral had been a quiet affair.

Buddy stepped away from the van for a moment. He could see Eva walking down the pontoon. She was wearing an oilskin and a pair of yellow wellies. Just like any other weekend sailor. He looked at Harry.

"What about the explosive?" he said.

Harry nodded at the metal boxes. "You've got two charges," he said, "RDX. Five kilos each."

"Detonators?"

"They're in the front."

Buddy looked at him for a moment. "How did you get aboard," he said, "into the cabin?"

"I knocked on the door."

"And?"

"Your friend let me in."

"Ah," Buddy nodded, "my German friend."

"Yeah. She went off for a while and left me to it." He paused. "Who else is going?"

Buddy shrugged. "Couple of guys," he said, "no one you know."

"Need any help?"

"No." He smiled. "Thanks."

The old man looked at him for a moment or two, and then nodded, and Buddy sensed that something was wrong. Eva joined them. She'd bought fresh milk and some biscuits. She asked Harry whether he'd like a cup of tea. Harry shook his head and said no thanks. She smiled at him, and stepped aboard the yacht, disappearing into the cabin. Harry watched her go.

"Shame about the Falklands," he grunted.

Buddy nodded. "Yeah."

The old man looked at him for a moment, a look of frank curiosity, then he limped around the van and returned with a shoe box. On the outside, in black stencil, it read "Plim-solls, white, size ten".

"Detonators," Harry said briefly, giving the box to Buddy. Buddy took it.

"What about the transmitter?" he said.

"That's in there too. I've left you a note about the frequency."

Buddy looked in the box. It was quite heavy. "OK," he said, "thanks."

The old man grunted, reaching for the explosives, transferring the gear out of the van, piling it neatly on the quayside. "Pleasure," he said, nodding at the yacht, "I just hope the fucking thing gets you there."

It was dark by the time Connolly found a telephone.

He'd slipped out of the house after tea, an hour before nightfall, leaving Jude with a huge fire and the company of an old television. The reception, so far west, was appalling, but she said it was better than nothing. Her attempts to talk to the people who looked after her had finally collapsed. Both of them thought her days were numbered, and one of them, the woman, had asked her cautiously about a priest. Jude had smiled at her, and said no thanks, she was trying to give them up. There'd been a silence, and the woman had stared at her, uncomprehending, and then crossed herself quickly, and left.

Now, Connolly hurried down the mountain, following the road, trying to remember from his journey up in Scullen's Mercedes how close the next house might be. They'd certainly passed a place, he knew that. He remembered kids in the road and an old horse, tethered to a tree, curls of smoke from a stubby chimney. Whether the house would have a telephone, he didn't know, but even if it didn't he could maybe hitch a lift, on down the valley, back towards the coast. Sooner or later, he was bound to find a phone. And then he'd start to put things right.

He plunged on, through the windy darkness. It was squally now, sudden pockets of wind, and even up here he could taste the sea in the occasional showers of rain that came sideways at him, out of the night. Soon, he lost track of time. The road wound on. Sometimes trees, and shelter, and a sudden silence as the wind dropped. Sometimes a glimpse of the stars as the clouds parted, and a little moonlight spilled through. Finally, miles later, he saw a light. He slowed, then stopped, making out the shape of a low cottage, off to the left. There was the sound of running water again. A dog began to bark.

Connolly approached the cottage. There was a low stone wall. He felt along it in the darkness. It felt mossy and wet. He found a hole where a gate had once been. He stepped through it, hearing his feet squelch in the mud, the rain dripping from the trees, the dog going mad round the back. He knocked on the door. He could hear music inside from a radio. The door opened. A big man stood there. He peered at Connolly.

"Yes?" he said.

Connolly introduced himself. He said he was a visitor. He said he had a sick friend up the road. He said he needed to phone for help. Under the circumstances, there seemed nothing much wrong with the truth. The man at the door stood aside and invited him in. The cottage smelled of damp and lamb fat. He pointed to a telephone on a pile of old newspapers on the floor.

"Sure," he said, "you're welcome."

Connolly smiled. "Thanks," he said, "only one problem."

"What's that?"

"Where are we? What's the place called?"

The man looked at him, pure wonderment. "You don't know?"

"Haven't a clue."

"Well now . . ." he frowned, "there's a road up from the coast. You go to Waterville. That's the town. And then you take the road in towards Lissatinnig Bridge. Then you turn right, by the signpost, up the hill. Keep the wind at your back. Glannadin's the place. You want Glannadin . . ."

Connolly thanked him. He picked up the telephone, watching the man retreat into another room. There were kids around. He could hear them. He dialled the operator, and asked for Mairead's number in Belfast. The door to the other room was still open. He heard the line connecting. The burr-burr of the phone ringing at the other end. Then Mairead, Mairead's voice, clear as a bell.

"Hallo?" she said cautiously.

Connolly smiled, imagining the scene up in Andersonstown, Liam sprawled on the floor, Bronagh poking the dog, Mairead pulling the door shut on it all, bending to the phone. He asked her how she was. She paused for a moment, long enough to place his voice, then she said she was fine. She sounded cautious, not the Mairead he'd left three days back, and he knew at once that she must have seen him in Great Victoria Street, the car, Charlie, the gun, and known it was him. He hesitated a moment, wondering whether to go into it all, to explain why, and how, and what next, but

329

he knew that was a week-long conversation, and that here and now there were more urgent things to do. A woman was dying. She needed help. And only Mairead could deliver.

"Do you have a pen?" he asked.

"No." A pause. "Yes."

"Write this down." He closed his eyes, remembering the man's instructions. "Waterville," he said, "County Kerry. Find it on the map. Then take a road inland. Up into the mountains. You're looking for Glannadin. The house is white. Two storeys. There are pine trees across the road. It's miles from anywhere . . ."

He paused for a moment, giving her time to write the names down, then he told her that she had to drive down, bring a van of some kind, borrow one, hire one. It was all a bit complicated, but he wouldn't bother her unless it was important. Would she do it? Could she do it? He bent to the phone, waiting for an answer. There was someone else in the room with her, a male voice. He could hear the murmur of conversation. He frowned, knowing what a problem he'd set her, how she hated driving, wondering whether she could dump the kids. She'd every right to tell him no, to remember those three terrible seconds outside the travel agents, and simply put the phone down, severing the conversation, the relationship, for ever. He waited, hearing the wind stirring the trees outside. Then there was a clatter on the line as she picked the phone up again.

"Waterville," she said carefully, "a place called Glannadin."

"That's it."

"You're alone up there?"

"No."

"There are others?"

"Yes."

There was a pause. Connolly could see a child's face at the door along the hall. Then Mairead came back.

"OK," she said briefly.

Connolly smiled, and turned his back on the half-open door.

"I love you," he said.

He hesitated, waiting for a response, the old affirmation,

but nothing happened and after a while he realized she'd gone.

Buddy Little spent the evening in Portsmouth.

He went from pub to pub in a long zig-zag that took him from the Victory Gate to the city centre. It was an old route, a route he'd taken a hundred times before, a pint here, a pint there, pubs full of sailors, music, the laughter louder and more frantic than usual. He occupied corner after corner, stool after stool, the small stocky bloke with his glass full of Guinness and his elbow on the bar. In one or two pubs, he got talking, conversations of his own making, conversations with strangers, young skates off to war. They blustered about the headlines, the invasion, the Argies, and what a dose or two of high explosive would do to Galtieri's boys. They made it sound like a football match, a fixture they couldn't afford to miss. They said they were well tooled up, the best gear in the world. They said it would be a doddle.

Buddy listened to it all, understanding it, this blind primitive bloodlust, patriotism in the raw. But he knew the realities better than the kids. He knew that war, any war, meant slaughter. He knew that soon the music would stop, and that some of these blokes would be shipped back early, zipped into body bags, ready for collection. He knew that families would be left without dads, that wives and girlfriends would have to trade in their man for a line of his own on some war memorial or other. But none of that mattered, because the call had come, and the blood was up, and the fleet was ready, and the flags were snapping in the wind.

It was a big feeling, this feeling of Buddy's, a lump in the chest feeling, and when the singing began, and the arms linked, he joined in. Everyone was part of it. Everyone was in there. Someone started "Don't Cry For Me Argentina", the obvious taunt, and Buddy sang along, not knowing the words, swaying on his bar stool, moist eyed, choked. The song ended in a torrent of cheers, glasses raised, an ocean of sweaty faces, and when Buddy lifted a hand, and mopped his own eyes, he realized that he, too, was crying.

A bit later, a woman appeared at his elbow, local accent, heavy make-up, and Buddy knew at once that she was a whore. She leaned into him, pissed out of her head, her face tilted up.

"You off too?" she kept saying. "You off too?"

Buddy just looked at her, too muddled to answer, and she reached up to him, and pulled his face down to hers, and said it was free tonight, a special night, something to take away with him, something to keep him warm. He gave her a kiss, and told her no thank you, and good luck, and she gazed drunkenly after him as he made his way through the crowd to the door.

Outside, round the corner, someone was being sick in the street. He was bending over the gutter, spewing all over the cobblestones. Buddy went up to him, put his arms round his shoulders, comforting him. A face looked up. He was a kid. He must have been eighteen. Buddy looked at him.

"It'll be OK," he said, "honestly."

The kid shook his head, and began to lurch off into the darkness, wiping his mouth with the back of his hand.

"I'm going to fucking die," he said. "I know it."

Buddy drove home. By Southampton, he'd decided that he couldn't go through with it. No way. The thing had been a fantasy from the start. However good a diver he might be, however great the gear was, he just couldn't do it. Not here. Not now. Not to them.

He pulled off the motorway at the New Forest exit, and followed the road home. He half expected the girl to be there, his minder, but when he turned in at the gate, the house was dark. He parked the Jaguar, and looked for her car. It wasn't there. He fumbled for his keys and let himself in. The place smelled of polish. He frowned, finding the lights. He looked round. The girl must have cleaned up, he thought. She must have spent the evening here, giving the place a proper going over, Kraut efficiency, Kraut standards.

He reached for the phone, meaning to ring her, tell her about his decision, call the thing off, but then he saw the door to the living room open. He walked down the hall, switched on the lights. Jude's bed had gone. Just disappeared. He looked round. Her clothes had gone, too, tidied up, stored away, sensibly pushed to the edges of this home of his. He felt the blood rising again, the choke in his throat. His house. His woman.

He went through to the kitchen. Everything had been rearranged, Jude's jars of beans, her photographs, the old letters he'd clothespegged together, the ones he'd written when he was still out there, out on the rigs, and paradise came in three weekly doses, largely horizontal, whenever the mood caught them, sometimes here, in the kitchen, on the rush mat floor.

Buddy sank onto the kitchen stool and closed his eyes. He felt dizzy. He felt slightly sick. Miles away, he heard the phone begin to ring. He let it go for a full half minute, and when it didn't stop he went back into the hall. He picked it up. It was Eva.

"You OK?" he heard her say.

He looked at the phone. "You had no right," he said thickly.

"Back in one piece?"

"You had no right," he said again. "My house. My wife."

He looked at the phone again, held it at arm's length, hearing her voice, a jumble of nothing. Then he put the phone down, cutting her off. Jude, he thought. For Jude.

BOOK FOUR

BOOK FOUR

TWENTY-TWO

Miller flew to Belfast the same evening. He took with him a sheaf of maps of south-west Ireland, on extended loan from a small office in the basement of an address in Curzon Street. To acquire the maps, he'd had to complete the standard withdrawal form. Under "Reason For Loan", he'd written – in terse capitals – "Reconnaissance".

The flight landed late. Despite a phone call from Heathrow, there was no one to meet him at Aldergrove. He waited the standard ten minutes, then hired a Group One Metro from the Europcar desk. He gave the girl at the counter his driving licence and watched her transfer the details onto the booking form. On the plane, sitting in a row by himself, he'd studied the maps. He'd found the road up from Waterville. It led inland, away from the coast, up into the mountains. The map was large scale, updated in 1968. Tiny black squares denoted houses. A mile or two from the coast, the black squares got fewer and fewer. On the phone to the Irish girl, Connolly had said at least ten miles. That had been the phrase. At least ten miles. He'd blocked the distance out on the map, using the side of his biro. Ten miles inland, the black squares were practically non-existent. In a five-mile radius, he had a choice of four. Only one of them could be white, two storeys, with pine trees across the road. There, God willing, they'd strike lucky.

He picked up his licence, and put it in his pocket, waiting for the car keys. Twenty-four hours in Whitehall had taught him a great deal. Nineteenth, as he'd suspected, was under the cosh. Even in Army circles, they'd been less than popular – an over-protected species – but now it was plain that they were facing a powerful alliance of enemies. The RUC had long wanted them reined in. MI5, undistracted for once by the feud with MI6, regarded them as unaccountable, and therefore inherently dangerous. Special Branch told all and sundry they were "cowboys". Even the SAS, once a reliable source of nourishment, were beginning to have second thoughts. Miller pocketed the keys to the hire car, and walked across the concourse towards the main exits. Maybe, after all, Qualitech hadn't been such a great idea. Maybe there'd been cleverer ways of acquiring Prime Ministerial credit. Like keeping his head down, and doing his job, and waiting like the rest of them for the inevitable headlines. One day, Scullen would get to her. He knew it. One day he'd get to her. And then it would be too late.

He drove south, to the barracks at Bessbrook. He turned the car in at the gate and told the Duty Sergeant to sort it out with the hire company. He walked the quarter of a mile to Nineteenth's makeshift HQ. They'd been here for six months now, far longer than any other posting, and he believed that operationally it had begun to show. They'd got sloppy. They'd trusted assumptions, instead of facts. They'd made a virtue of short cuts, and they'd paid the price. First Dublin. Now Charlie. Dublin, just, they'd get away with. Over the last twenty-four hours, he'd knocked at the right doors, sat at the right desks, thrown a big, heavy fire blanket over the worst of the damage. It would smoulder on for a while. There'd be a wisp or two of smoke and the usual smell of burning but that would be all. Charlie, though, was different. Charlie was personal.

It was nearly midnight when he finally got the men together. Including himself, there were four of them, the Dublin squad minus Charlie. He closed the door in the upstairs briefing room and drew the curtains. Thompson, the Cockney, had taken Charlie's place in the pecking order. The other two were Camps and Venner. Camps was a big man, spare, lean, dark. He had a wife in Cardiff, and another woman in Wiltshire whom he occasionally described as "rough". She had a child by him, and he wrote to her weekly, enclosing money. Venner was an ex-truck driver from Cornwall. His family ran fishing smacks out of Newlyn, and he'd joined the Army to get away. He was small, and broad, and tight with his money. He was the toughest man Miller had ever met. He had a real talent for violence.

Miller spread the maps on the floor. Thompson was the first to ask the obvious question. "So what's it like," he said, "back home?"

Miller looked at them. The Government had yet to declare war on Argentina, but the invasion had made hostilities a virtual certainty. Action, when it came, would be very different from the kind of war they fought in Northern Ireland, and these blokes quite fancied being part of it. Thompson asked them again. What had he left? Back in London?

"Chaos," he said.

Thompson grinned. "Bit sudden," he said, "isn't it?"

Miller nodded. The Falklands situation had been a godsend. It had blown up in days and caught everyone by surprise. Most of Whitehall, still digesting the latest round of defence cuts, had suddenly been ordered to tool up for a shooting war, eight thousand miles from home. As a result, the military machine was totally preoccupied. The priorities were ships, helicopters, artillery support, heavy lift. The last thing on anyone's mind were the ethics of a spot of private enterprise in the mountains of south-west Ireland. Miller reached forward and tapped the map. He'd chinagraphed the road from the coast in red.

"I've found the guy that did Charlie," he said. "His name's Connolly. He's holed up in a farmhouse . . . round here."

Thompson looked at him. Never shy, he'd become a kind of spokesman for the group. Now, he needed persuading.

"No offence," he sniffed, "but who says?"

"I do."

"Kosher?"

"Definitely."

"That's what you said about Dublin."

Miller looked at him. "No," he said quietly, "that's what Charlie said about Dublin."

There was a brief silence. Miller offered no more information. Thompson looked at him again, checking, then shrugged.

"OK," he said.

Miller glanced at the other two.

"OK with you?" he said.

Camps nodded. Venner leaned forward. "I'm not with you," he said, "who are we after? This bloke? Connolly? Or someone else?"

Miller looked up from the map. "Both," he said.

"So who's the other one?"

"Scullen."

Venner nodded.

"And what do we do? When we find them?"

Miller paused. "Depends," he said. "Either we bring them back. Or— " he shrugged. "Depends . . ."

Miller turned back to the map and ran quickly back through the operational details. They'd leave at first light. They'd motor south. They'd rendezvous at a small town called Cahersiveen. They'd recce after dark. And then they'd go in. He looked up.

"Dublin," he said, "all over again."

Thompson frowned. "Yeah," he said. "Except we won't fuck up."

Miller looked at him. "You're right," he said quietly, "we won't."

Camps was still studying the map. "What are we taking," he said, "in the way of precautions?"

Miller looked at him for a moment or two. It had been a long day.

"Everything," he said. "I want an Armalite each. A couple of pairs of night glasses. We'll need the Brownings. Plenty of spare clips. We'll take stun grenades, usual issue, and the sat link as well. Oh . . ." he smiled, "and some plastic."

Camps nodded, ever patient, misunderstood.

"I meant cover stories," he said, "fall backs."

Miller nodded, still smiling at him. "I know you did," he said. "We all have a point to make."

Buddy woke up with the eight o'clock news on his alarm radio. His head was splitting and he had trouble remembering which day it was. The BBC pips came to an end, and the lady in Broadcasting House helped him out. Sunday 4th April, she said: And the crisis in the South Atlantic deepens.

Buddy lay there for the duration of the bulletin. The Argentinians were consolidating their hold on the Falkland Islands. Major Gary Noote and his luckless Marine garrison would shortly be repatriated. Delirious crowds were flooding into Buenos Aires. The UN Security Council was in emergency session. The Prime Minister has pledged a restoration of British rule. The Naval Dockyard in Portsmouth was working round the clock to prepare the Task Force for sea.

Buddy turned over, shutting his mind to it all, reassembling bits and pieces of the previous evening, thinking again of Jude. The job done, he'd fly to Dublin. There'd be chaos in Portsmouth, a massive manhunt nationwide, but the IRA would be claiming responsibility and the first sweeps would be targeting Irish suspects. Naturally the security people would assume that the attack itself – the diving, the knowledge of underwater explosives – was a specialist job, but the support would have come from normal terrorist sources, and that's where they'd be looking first. In this respect, Buddy had to admit that the plan was clever. To date, he'd left no trail because there was no trail to leave. Only later, if they recovered enough evidence from the explosion itself, would the net begin to close, and by that time he and Jude would be three thousand miles away, spending his earnings on a miracle.

Buddy smiled at the irony, wondering yet again whether the operation would really work. The last three months, he knew, had robbed him of his sense of perspective. The shock of Jude's accident, of the sheer scale of her loss, had slightly unhinged him. His life had acquired the dimensions of a tunnel. At the very end of it, thousands of miles away, was a tiny disc of light, and his sole job, his sole duty, was to somehow make it through the dark. That he'd do it, that he'd get them both there, he'd never doubted. But the risks were enormous, and the final bill the accident had presented – to cripple a capital ship, at a time like this – had become utterly surreal.

In his saner moments, lying in bed on a Sunday morning, remembering the pubs he'd drunk in the previous evening, he found it hard to believe. But circumstances had given him no choice. He had to do it. And doing it, he had to think of it simply as a sequence of tasks, entirely logical, entirely under his control. Put this way, it was a far simpler proposition than hundreds of other jobs he'd done. He had the gear. He had the know-how. The depths were child's play. The thing was a doddle. There'd be lots of drama. Lots of headlines. But no one would die, and afterwards, with luck, his woman would re-occupy a little of the body that those same circumstances had taken away from her. The end, in short, justified the means. Nothing else mattered.

Buddy reached out and switched off the radio, knowing in his heart that this rationale of his was nonsense. What he was doing was wrong. He knew it, and it hurt him, but it still didn't matter. Life had confronted him with a choice – his country or his wife – and he'd gone for Jude. Or what was left of her.

He gazed up at the ceiling, wondering vaguely what would happen afterwards, after Boston, once they were back again, here, in this cottage. By now, the chances of detection might be high. They might have linked the gear to Harry. The old boy might have blown the whistle. They might have traced the booking on the yacht, searched it, found evidence of explosives, arrested the girl, investigated her background, drawn the obvious conclusions. They might be waiting here, at the cottage, ready for their return, Buddy Little and his lovely wife Jude, the well-known walking miracle. They might greet him at the door, arrest him, interrogate him, squeeze the truth from him, present him with the evidence, tell him it was all over. There'd be a trial, more headlines, and countless years in some prison cell or other. Buddy thought about it, getting out of bed, and as he did so he realized that he didn't care. For the last three months, he'd been in a cell of his own making anyway. Coming to terms with the real thing would be the merest formality.

Below him, downstairs, he heard a knock at the front door. He frowned, and reached for his dressing-gown. He made his way downstairs. In the living room, the curtains were still drawn tight. He walked through to the hall, hearing more knocks. On the mat inside the door was his one weekly extravagance, a copy of the *Sunday Telegraph*. "Fleet Assembles for Falklands Action", went the headline, "Navy Prepares for War".

Buddy looked at it briefly, recognizing the familiar lines of HMS *Invincible*, then opened the front door. A man in his early forties stood in the sunshine. He had a round, cheerful face. His hair was receding. He was wearing a blazer with an open-necked white shirt. He was carrying a large holdall. There was a smile on his face. Inwardly, Buddy groaned.

"Gus," he said.

The other man stepped into the house, uninvited. He put his holdall on the carpet by the stairs.

"Nice," he said, looking round, taking stock. "Very nice."

Buddy closed the front door, remembering the letter he'd never answered, the threat that Gus might one day hop on a plane, and fly down from the oil fields, and stay over for a day or two. He leaned back against the wall, closing his eyes for a moment, waiting for the sudden gust of nausea to pass. When he opened his eyes again, Gus was inches away. He looked concerned. Of all the roles he played, older brother was his favourite.

"Mate," he said, "you look terrible."

Buddy muttered something about a night out and retreated to the kitchen. He put the kettle on and checked the fridge for fresh milk, wondering where to start. Gus saved him the trouble.

"OK, then," he said, "where is she?"

Buddy reached for the teapot. "Who?" he said hopelessly.

"Jude. The little woman. My favourite girl."

Buddy gave him a look and told him to sit down. It took him several minutes to explain. By the time he'd finished, Gus was close to tears.

"Fuck me," he kept saying, "fuck me."

Buddy poured out tea for them both, wondering whether a shot or two of whisky might help their separate problems. He went into the lounge. It took him several more minutes to discover where Eva had hidden the booze. He returned to the kitchen with a litre of Johnny Walker and two glasses.

Gus was sitting where he'd left him, anchored to the kitchen stool, white faced, shaking his head.

"So where is she?" he asked.

Buddy poured two large shots of Scotch. He gave one to Gus.

"Nursing home," he said briefly.

"Where?"

"Miles away."

Buddy waved the bottle vaguely towards the west, amused for a second or two by the small truth of his answer. Gus gazed into his glass.

"When can we go and see her?" he said.

"We can't."

He looked up. "Why not?"

Buddy paused, cupping the glass in his hand, wondering where the conversation might end.

"Visiting hours," he said. "They're very strict. Have to be."

Gus nodded, gazing around the kitchen, thinking about it.

"So how come you got shit-faced last night?" he said at last.

Buddy looked at him. Gus was an intensely practical man. He had the most logical mind he'd ever encountered. It made him a fine diver, and a good bloke to have around when things got tough. It also, now, made him dangerous. Buddy swirled the Scotch around his glass, saying nothing, then downed it in a single gulp. Time to play the widower, he thought, time to bid for sympathy. He put the empty glass on the dresser.

"You wonder why I get pissed?" he said, feeling the warmth spreading upwards from his belly.

Gus frowned. "Must be terrible," he said.

"It is. It's fucking awful."

"I meant for her."

"Yeah." Buddy glanced up at him. "That's what I meant, too."

They had breakfast. Buddy stirred hot milk into porridge oats and fed slices of brown wholemeal into the toaster while Gus circled him with more questions. How, exactly, had it

344

happened? Where was the break in her neck? What did the doctors have to say? What was life like in this nursing home of hers? And why, in God's name, hadn't Buddy had the sense to write and tell him? The last question Buddy had anticipated.

"I wanted to spare you," he said, "I thought it best you didn't know."

Gus looked hurt. "I'm a mate of yours," he said, "I was best man, for fuck's sake."

"Yeah," Buddy nodded, "you'd have been bloody upset."

"Too right."

"So what's the point?" Buddy spooned a small mountain of porridge into a bowl and passed it to Gus. "Why wreck someone else's day?"

Gus looked at him, not saying anything, reaching for the sugar bowl. Always had a sweet tooth, Buddy thought, watching him tip the bowl over the porridge and shake it gently. Gus glanced up.

"Must get lonely," he said, "Just you. On your tod."

"It does."

"You miss her?"

"Yeah."

"Don't blame you." He paused and sniffed. "I would, too."

Buddy nodded, saying nothing. Gus began to eat the porridge, blowing on each spoonful, ever cautious. "So what are you doing," he said, "to make ends meet?"

Buddy deflected the question as best he could. He'd had another Scotch, and he felt much better.

"This and that," he said, "bits and pieces."

"Local stuff?"

"Yeah."

"So you can be with her?"

"Yeah."

Gus nodded, approving, the older brother again. He swallowed another mouthful of porridge.

"You need money?" he said at last. "You want a cheque?"

Buddy smiled, remembering Pascale. Maybe Gus was right, he thought. Maybe I should have written, touched him up for the odd loan. Fifty grand. Repayable whenever. He glanced across at Gus, shaking his head.

"It's OK," he said, "I manage."

"No need to go short. You know that."

"Yeah. Thanks."

There was a silence. Buddy poked at the porridge with his spoon. Gus looked up again, with his slow grin.

"Listen," he said. "You need a lift. Real night out. I got paid off yesterday. Six weeks' work. Serious money. We'll really go to town."

Buddy tried the porridge. It was scalding hot.

"Sounds great," he said, fanning his open mouth, "only I can't."

"Can't?"

"No." He paused. "I'm on a job at the moment. It's tidal. We're working nights."

"Oh?"

"Yeah."

There was a brief silence. Then Gus was back. Another idea.

"I'll give you a hand," he said. "We'll see it off together."

Buddy shook his head. "It's a sewage outfall," he said, "you'd hate it."

"Really?"

Gus looked at him, alarmed.

"Yeah," Buddy nodded, remembering how fastidious Gus could be, how obsessed by bugs and hygiene. "Turds everywhere," he said. "Huge brown fuckers."

There was the sound of a car engine. Buddy glanced out of the window. A small VW was bumping down the track. He shut his eyes a moment. The last thing he wanted was Eva in here. He turned back to Gus.

"Listen," he said, "you must be busy. Marge. The kids."

Gus shook his head. "They're in Wales," he said, "that's why I thought I might stay a couple of nights. Keep you company."

Buddy looked at him a moment, knowing it was hopeless. Gus was here for the weekend, come what may. He turned to the sink, abandoning his bowl of half-eaten porridge. Eva was walking briskly up the garden path. He'd given her a key. She'd be inside in seconds. Gus was eyeing the teapot. He drank the stuff by the gallon.

"Where is this job?" he said idly.

Buddy hesitated a moment, not wanting to be contradicted by Eva.

"Down on the Hamble," he said, "Warsash way."

"Oh," Gus nodded, "handy."

Buddy heard the door open, footsteps up the hall. Then Eva was standing there, in the kitchen doorway. She was wearing her oilskin again, and she was carrying an empty wicker basket. She was looking at Buddy. She couldn't see Gus.

"Hi," she said, a smile in her voice, "I made a sponge cake last night. I thought we might take it with us. It's in the larder. Up on the back shelf."

Buddy looked at her for a moment. "Wonderful," he said, "I love sponge cake."

Ingle found the GPO intercept the same morning, Sunday. The list had been forwarded from Paddington Green, one of a dozen or so, and he only bothered to read it because the newspaper shop on the way to the Special Branch offices off Royal Avenue had run out of copies of the *News of the World*.

Now, half past ten, he lifted the phone and dialled the number of his other office in Paddington Green. The number answered at once, the new boy, Kee.

"It's me," Ingle said briefly, "I want you to do us a favour."

Ingle explained what he wanted, quoting the reference number of the intercept, and Kee went away to find another copy of the master list, and confirm the date. The Post Office intercepts centre at Mount Pleasant was authorized to open and photograph all mail *en route* to certain addresses. These addresses, known as the "A" list, covered seven sheets of foolscap paper and included a number of addresses in Dublin. Every two days, a list of intercepts was circulated to a smallish circle of subscribers on the Intelligence and Counter-Terrorist circuit. Only on application would the relevant photocopies be forwarded, a recent economy measure that would, the Treasury said, save tens of thousands of pounds.

Kee came back. Ingle could tell by his voice that the boy was frowning.

"It's a while back," he said, "23rd January."

Ingle scribbled the date, then paused, his pencil in mid-air.

"They keep these things for ever?" he said. "I can't remember."

"No. Only for three months."

"OK." He paused again. "Get over there and get hold of it. You'll need a chit."

"Sure."

Ingle looked at his watch. There was a British Midlands flight, Saturdays only, at noon. With luck, he'd just make it.

"Listen . . ." he said, returning to the phone, "stay in the office when you get back. I'll be over."

Kee, a dedicated Spurs fan, grunted. He was planning on yet another afternoon at White Hart Lane. There was a postponed Cup match against Everton. He began to suggest an alternative but Ingle ignored him, gazing at the name he'd underlined on his copy of the intercepts list.

"Scullen," he said down the phone, "that's the bugger we want."

Scullen arrived at the farmhouse half an hour before noon. He'd driven up from the coast with McParland. McParland sat outside in the Mercedes, while the older man shook the rain from his coat and shut the front door carefully behind him.

Connolly met him in the hall. He'd been up half the night with Jude. She had a high temperature and she'd been sick several times. After daybreak, Connolly had moved his chair to the window, half expecting Mairead to turn up with a van. But nothing had happened, and when Scullen's nurse had finally appeared – nine o'clock – he'd looked down at Jude, and yawned, and said it was probably indigestion.

Now, Connolly followed Scullen up the hall.

"She's ill," he said briefly, "she needs help."

Scullen folded his coat over the banister. Underneath the coat he was wearing a dark suit, and Connolly sensed at once that he'd been to church. Scullen smoothed his hair.

"What kind of help?" he said.

"Proper help. Medical help. She needs a doctor."

Scullen looked puzzled.

"But I thought you'd telephoned already?" he said. "Last night?"

Connolly blinked. "I did," he said, "you're right."

"Then surely help will come?"

"I . . ." Connolly shrugged, "I don't know."

"You don't?"

"No."

Scullen nodded, and Connolly wondered how on earth he'd found out about the phone call. Then he remembered the open door along the hall in the cottage down the road, the kids' faces, the listening ears. They're all in it, he thought. The whole valley. The whole peninsula. All Kerry belongs to Scullen. He looked at the man. Scullen, to his surprise, seemed unmoved.

"I had to," Connolly said quietly, "I had to do it. I had no choice."

"No?"

"No." He shook his head. "The woman's dying. She has an ulcer the size of your fist. We need to get her to hospital."

Scullen nodded and glanced at his watch.

"When are you expecting your . . . ah . . . friend?"

Connolly shrugged. "I don't know," he said. "She may not come."

Scullen looked at him for a moment. "Where is our guest?" he said.

Connolly indicated a door at the end of the hall. Scullen walked down the hall, knocked briefly, and went in.

The room was tiny. There was a small, deep window, and a view of the mountainside and the valley below. Beside the window was a high single bed. Jude lay in the bed, her head turned towards the window. There were spots of high colour in her cheeks, and she was having trouble breathing. Her breath rasped in and out, irregular. Hearing the door open, she turned her head. Sweat glistened on the pale skin. The pillow was visibly damp. Scullen stood by the bed for a moment. The smell of dead flesh was overpowering.

"Good morning," he said quietly.

Connolly watched him from the hall. He might have been the priest, he thought, or the doctor, a grave, professional presence at the bedside, someone to banish doubt and disease. Jude was looking up at him. She was finding it hard to focus. She obviously didn't have a clue who he was any more. She licked her lips.

"Water?" she whispered.

Scullen gazed at her for a moment, then laid a hand beside her cheek. He held it there for a moment or two, then stepped out of the room. He glanced at Connolly.

"She needs a drink," he said, "I'll be back in a moment."

Connolly nodded and began to say something, but it was too late. Scullen was already at the front door. Connolly heard the front door closing behind him. He went out, into the hall. Through the window beside the front door he watched Scullen open the boot of the Mercedes. He took out a long canvas carrier with a buttoned flap at one end, and a white plastic bag. Connolly stared at the bag, recognizing it. It was the bag he'd brought south from Belfast. He'd given it back to Scullen only the previous day. It had the handgun inside it, and the box of shells.

Scullen closed the boot of the car and walked back towards the house. Connolly met him in the hall. Despite the hour, it was nearly dark in the narrow passage. Scullen handed him the long canvas carrier and told him to give it to the nurse. The nurse's name was John. Connolly nodded, taking the carrier. It was surprisingly heavy. He leaned it carefully against the panelling in the hall. Scullen smiled, watching him. Then he gave Connolly the plastic bag. Connolly opened it. The automatic was in there, and the shells, too. He looked up.

"What do I want this for?" he said.

Scullen was still watching him. He began to do up the top button of his coat, the long white fingers searching for the hole.

"You may need it," he said.

He nodded solemnly, the usual farewell, and turned to the door, pausing only when he'd opened it.

"Don't forget the drink," he said. "Water may well be best."

Back in Jude's room, a glass of water in his hand, Connolly knelt by the bed. Jude's eyes had closed now, but her breathing had quickened, tiny, shallow gulps of air. He moistened his finger in the water and held it to her lips. Her lips were dry and cracked. She began to lick his finger. Her eyes opened. He offered her the glass. She shook her head. She was smiling.

"Strange, huh?"

Connolly leaned in, towards her. Her voice was nearly inaudible.

"What," he said, "what's strange?"

She looked at him. She was still smiling.

"Dying," she said.

TWENTY-THREE

Buddy arrived at Warsash at noon, parking the Jaguar on
the waterfront and carrying his diving gear in a holdall
down onto the pontoon where the yacht was moored. Eva,
he knew, would already be there. She'd stayed at the cottage
for no more than five minutes, picking up the sponge cake
and offering a wary hand to Gus when Buddy did the formal
introductions. Gus had watched her walking back down the
path towards the car.

"Friend of Jude's," Buddy had told him, "keeps an eye
on me."

He'd left the cottage an hour or so later, abandoning Gus
with his feet up in front of the telly. Stepping out of the
house, his holdall looped over his shoulder, he'd left him
with final instructions on where to find the rest of the booze.
Help yourself, he'd shouted through the living room
window, but leave enough for a decent wet. He'd be back,
he said, sometime Monday. And he'd probably need a drink.

Now, he clambered aboard the yacht, and down into the
tiny cabin. Eva was bent over the stove, coaxing a flame
from one of the Calor gas rings. There was a small fold-
down table set for two. There was a red gingham tablecloth
and a basket of black German bread and a plate of thinly
sliced cheeses. There was salami and two other kinds of
sausage and newly boiled eggs, fresh coffee on the stove,
and two Sunday papers neatly folded on the bench seat
beside the table. Buddy stood in the open doorway and
shook his head. For a terrorist, Eva was remarkably suburban.

They ate in silence. Buddy read the papers, keeping to
the sports reports, trying to avoid the pages and pages of
analysis. The only photo that interested him was an aerial

352

shot of Portsmouth Harbour. He studied it over the last of the salami, wiping the grease from his fingers and marking the halftone with a pencil. According to the text, the photo had been taken at six o'clock the previous evening. The three capital ships – *Invincible, Hermes* and *Fearless* – were still moored alongside at their respective berths. Overnight, he knew, nothing would have changed. With deadlines this tight, the last game the Navy would play was musical chairs. He gave the photo a final glance and pushed it to one side. He looked across at Eva. She was reading one of the arts pages. She didn't look up.

"What will you do with all the gear," she said, "afterwards?"

Buddy smiled. It was true what they said about the Germans. They never got off the job. "Which bits?" he said.

"The vest. The bottles. The stuff the old man gave you."

"I'll dump it. Before I get back on board."

She nodded, still deep in the article. After Buddy's return from planting the charges, they'd agreed to lie up for the rest of the night beside the marina pontoon. Then, come daybreak, Eva would take the yacht back to Warsash, single-handed. She'd go through it inch by inch, wiping every surface, removing every last trace of their presence. Then she'd return the keys to the office with a smile and a thank-you and drive back down to Portsmouth. Buddy, by now, would be over the water, waiting for the Task Force to leave. The job done, they'd meet up. He'd collect his car from Warsash. And his responsibilities would be over.

The plan, like anything on paper, seemed foolproof. He and Eva had spent the previous afternoon practising basic manoeuvres with the yacht: casting off, making way against the tide, then nudging back in against the pontoon. It wasn't a big boat – no more than twenty-seven feet – and they'd be using the engine throughout, but after she'd dropped him in the harbour, she'd have to get the yacht back into the Gosport marina single-handed, and in the dark that wouldn't be simple. But the girl had been remarkably good, and the rehearsals had gone well. She was gentle on the throttle. She wasn't frightened of the odd thump. And she seemed to have an instinctive appreciation of current and tide. Buddy had been impressed, and now he said so.

"You were good on the helm," he said, "for a woman."

Eva shrugged and began to clear the table. "We should go soon," she said. "Is there anything else you need?"

Buddy yawned, folding the paper.

"Yes," he said, "there's a list." He looked up. "And it begins with my wife."

The two cars from Nineteenth set off from Bessbrook at one in the afternoon for the long run down to Kerry. Miller and Thompson led in the first car, Thompson driving. Camps and Venner followed, a mile and a half behind. Both cars, once again, were plated with Republican registrations.

The lead car, a white Ford Capri, crossed the border thirty minutes later, heading south on a small unadopted country road that connects the two villages of Cullyhanna and Mill Town. At Mill Town, a mile into the Republic, Thompson had to slow to a crawl to pick his way around an ancient Fordson tractor with a trailer full of sugar beet. The tractor had broken down, and the trailer had somehow jack-knifed behind it, leaving only the narrowest of gaps. The spot, on a sharp left hand bend overlooked by a big old stone barn, was an ideal location for an ambush, and the two men exchanged glances as Thompson dropped into first gear, ready to accelerate out of trouble. Beside him, Miller reached for the heavy Browning automatic, pushing the seat back against the runners to give himself the maximum freedom of action.

The car edged slowly forward. Then a child appeared in the road, a girl of about seven with a smile and a puppy on a length of rope, and both men relaxed as Thompson threaded the Capri through the gap, and the road opened up, and the car accelerated away again. Turning to wave at the child, Miller failed to notice the dull glint of light on the binoculars of the man in the hayloft of the barn. Neither would he have seen him writing down the registration number of the car, and its colour, and the time it passed by. Elsewhere along the border, there were a handful of other breakdowns, equally innocuous, each with its own small diversion, and its hidden observer, with his binoculars, and his notebook, and his three-digit telephone number in Waterville, County Kerry.

"Thank you," Scullen said carefully, when the phone call came through, "I'll pass the message on."

Ingle got to Paddington Green police station a little after half past two. Kee met him in the office. He'd been to the Mount Pleasant sorting centre and returned with the contents of envelope A 4561. He'd had all the appropriate clearances, but evidently it hadn't been easy.

"Pakistani bloke," he said despairingly. "Tricky bastard."

Ingle ignored the comment, picking up the photocopy. The letter had been handwritten, on a single sheet of paper. It was addressed to someone called "P". It talked of a Captain Harrison. Captain Harrison, it seemed, may have retired. But his good lady, whoever that might be, was sailing on. He read the sentence again, frowning, then finished the rest of the letter. The rest of the letter boiled down to a couple of brief sentences. There was a mention of some article or other, and talk of "a second try". At the foot of the page was a scrawled signature, the single letter, "E". There was a Southampton address at the head of the letter, and a phone number as well.

Ingle read the letter again, then looked up. Kee was deep in the paper.

"There's supposed to be an article in here," he said. "Where is it?"

Kee glanced up, one finger deep in the sports pages. "I dunno," he said, "I noticed that too."

Ingle frowned again. "What about your Asian friend? Didn't he have it?"

Kee shook his head. "It was down in the log. Two items in the envelope. But," he shrugged, "he could only come up with one."

Ingle looked at the letter again. "Shit," he said.

He got up and walked to the window. The letter told him

355

nothing, except the fact that it had been addressed to Scullen. Scullen he'd heard about from Connolly. The boy had met him. Scullen was the man who knew about Qualitech. Ingle had drawn the file that same afternoon, checked him out. He had serious form – nothing in the way of convictions, nothing as careless as a single court appearance – but the man had left a trail through countless Intelligence assessments, a sighting here, a word or two from a tout there, heads put together, conclusions drawn. One of the firmer rumours had the man in charge of a mainland ASU in the early seventies. There was nothing as concrete as an address, or a positive link with a specific operation, but Ingle knew that one of the ASUs had been quartered in Southampton, and had caused more than a little heartache for a month or two. He wandered back to the desk and picked up the letter again. The thing had come from the south. It had a Southampton address. Idly, he dialled the number, listening to the burr-burr at the other end, putting the phone down again after a minute or so when there was no answer.

He sat down behind the desk, deep in thought. Kee mentioned tea. The machine in the corridor was on the blink, but the canteen was open again on-Sundays and he said he'd do the honours. Ingle nodded, saying nothing, reaching for the phone again.

A call to a Scotland Yard number gave him the name he wanted, the officer in charge of the Hampshire Anti-Terrorist Squad in the early seventies. He wrote the name down and picked up the phone again. The girl on the switchboard at Hampshire Force Headquarters, in Winchester, answered on the first ring. Ingle introduced himself. He said he was on a Northern Ireland job. He said he needed to talk to Inspector Wilby. There was a short pause.

"He's Detective Chief Superintendent Wilby," the girl said, "and it's Sunday."

Ingle was patient. He said he knew it was Sunday. He told her again it was important. The girl began to get flustered.

"I'm sorry, sir," she said, "I can't give out private numbers on the phone."

Ingle nodded and gave her a number to ring at Scotland Yard. They'd vouch for him, he said. It was all kosher.

"Then phone Wilby yourself," he said shortly, "and ask him to bell me here."

He put the phone down and reached for Kee's paper. Three minutes later, the boy still in the canteen, the phone rang. Ingle picked it up.

"Ingle," he said briefly.

There was a silence. Then an oldish voice came on, speaking slowly, softish country accent.

"Wilby," the voice said, "I hope this is important."

Ingle pushed the paper away and said it was. He explained again that he worked for Special Branch. He said he'd looked out some files. Stuff from the early seventies. There was a name he needed some help with. He paused, waiting for a response.

"What name?" Wilby said at last.

"Harrison, sir. A Captain Harrison."

Ingle leaned back in the chair, the phone clamped to his ear, hearing the short bark of laughter.

"Harrison?"

"Yes, sir." Ingle paused. "Who was he?"

"A sailor," Wilby said, "used to work for Cunard."

Ingle frowned, looking at the letter again, the mention of the "good lady".

"So why would his name be in the frame?" he said. "Back in your day?"

There was a long silence. Ingle could hear music in the background. Some theme tune. "Desert Island Discs". Then Wilby returned to the phone.

"He was Master of the *QEII*," he said, "the night they tried to blow her up."

"Who tried to blow her up?"

"Scullen's lot." Wilby laughed again. "Doctor Death."

By the time they got to Kerry, Thompson knew Miller was in trouble.

They drove down from Tralee, hitting the Ring of Kerry at Killorglin. From here, the road skirted the southern arm of Dingle Bay, winding steadily south-west, glimpses of the sea on the right, range after range of mountains rippling away inland, the sun beginning to dip towards the western horizon. They drove in silence, Thompson still at the wheel, Miller beside him, gazing ahead, saying nothing.

Thompson had never seen him so preoccupied, so withdrawn. He'd known, of course, that Miller's relationship with Charlie had been close. Everyone had noticed it, and drawn their own conclusions. The man had treated Charlie like the son he'd never had, with trust and encouragement and a slightly exasperated affection. He'd given him free rein, permitting him six- or seven-day absences from base, certain that the fruits of Charlie's latest trawl through the markets and villages of South Armagh, or the pubs of West Belfast, would make their own case. On many occasions, he'd been right. The lad had delivered some real windfalls – scraps of intelligence cleverly jigsawed together, Provo operations anticipated and left to wither on the vine, even half a dozen or so Grade "A" informers, men and women who'd been bribed or blackmailed into a reluctant flirtation with the gentle wee boy with the Galway accent and the pony tail and the nicotine-stained fingers. Charlie had been a priceless asset – no question – but even a covert, undeclared war imposed its own rules, its own obligations, and one of them was never to get too close, to risk too much. It was true of fieldcraft and it was true of the lives they led together, of the ways they got by. If you showed too much of yourself, if you let too much hang out, chances were, you'd pay for it.

Once or twice on the journey Thompson had tried to talk about it, to remember the good times with Charlie, to coax a smile or a shake of the head or even a story or two from Miller. But whatever he said, however he came at the man, the reaction was always the same. Miller just looked at him, a chill emotionless stare, an expression that carried with it the unspoken suggestion that he should keep his mouth shut and his eyes on the road. Charlie, Miller seemed to be saying, had been a part of himself. And now his own war had turned abruptly personal.

They reached Cahersiveen at five fifteen, the other car several miles behind. Miller had already stipulated a rendezvous in the town, and now they drove slowly down the main street. The place was small, and sleepy, an eye not quite open for the start of the tourist season. Many of the shops were closed, last year's wares shrouded beneath sheets of yellowing newsprint. There were dogs everywhere, and ancient cars half-parked on the pavement, and old men in twos and threes, brooding in shop doorways. The light was soft, the beginnings of a fine sunset, and when Thompson pulled in and stopped on Miller's curt instruction, he wound down the window, smelling the bitter-sweet tang of peat smoke in the air.

Miller nodded at a shop across the street. The shop was narrow fronted, a single door and a window. In the window was a cross and a small casket. Across the top of the shop, in fading gilt letters, was a line of Gaelic script. "Sean McGrew", it read, "Undertakers". Thompson looked at it a moment, and then turned back to Miller.

"Are you serious?" he said. "You want us to go in there?"

Miller nodded again. "An uncle of Charlie's," he said. "There's a bar at the back."

"But he's an undertaker. He lays out stiffs."

"Yeah." Miller reached for the door handle. "Mine's a Guinness."

He got out of the car and walked across the road, his head down, his hands thrust deep inside the pockets of the ancient leather jacket. Thompson watched him for a moment, then retrieved his Browning from the parcel shelf beneath the steering wheel, and stuffed the automatic inside the waistband of his jeans. Camps and Venner would certainly spot the van. Whether they'd join them in the undertakers was anybody's guess.

Thompson got out of the car and ran across the road. By the time he caught up with Miller, the older man was opening the shop door. Inside, the place was dark. It smelled, faintly, of embalming fluid. There were three high-backed chairs against a wall, and a low table. On the table was a large Bible, metal embossed at the corners, and a catalogue of coffins. The catalogue was dated 1967.

The two men stood together for a moment. A door opened at the back of the shop and light spilled in. A man emerged. He was old. He was bald. He wore an old black suit, with a cardigan underneath. The cardigan was yellow. Thompson noticed his hands, one held in the other, as if it might fall off. Miller looked at him, saying nothing.

"You have a bar," he suggested at last.

The old man nodded. He had a soft Kerry accent. He spoke in a whisper.

"We do," he agreed.

"My friend and I would like a drink."

The old man nodded again. "Do you have business in here?" he enquired.

Miller glanced at the catalogue, and picked it up.

"No," he said, "not yet."

There was a long silence, Thompson staring at Miller, beginning to wonder about his sanity. Then the door opened suddenly behind them, and Thompson spun round, instinctive, stepping into the shadows, his right hand going down to the waistband of his jeans. Two men walked in, familiar silhouettes against the sunlight outside in the street. One of them was Venner. The other was Camps. Miller didn't even bother to turn round. Thompson looked at them both for a moment, enjoying the expression on Venner's face, bewilderment and disbelief.

"Hi," he said drily, "we're here for a drink."

They went through to a room at the back, darker still, a single table beside an empty fireplace. The floorboards were bare. They'd been painted black. Drinks came from two shelves of bottles behind a tiny bar. Thompson drank lemonade. Venner and Camps settled for lager. Miller ordered a large glass of Guinness.

They sat in silence while the old man found some glasses. When the drinks came, on a battered Aer Lingus tray, Miller distributed them round the table. Then, before the old man had even left the room, he began the final briefing.

Fifteen minutes south was another town called Waterville. From Waterville, a road went east, inland, beside a river. Ten miles up this road they'd find Lissnatinnig Bridge. There, they'd turn right, up towards Knockmoyle Mountain. The target house lay at the end of the road. It was white. There were pine trees opposite. The area was called Glannadin. It would be dark by the time they got there. It would be cold. They'd recce from the south and the east, using the handsets. He paused, and then began to go through the instructions again, entirely unnecessary, a low, slow monotone, dictation speed, as if he were talking to a bunch of kids. The men exchanged glances. Thompson put his pencil down and swallowed a mouthful of lemonade. It was foul. No fizz, and a bitter, chemical aftertaste. He wondered briefly about the embalming fluid, and whether it might not, after all, have been wiser to stick to the black stuff.

He looked up. Miller had come to an end. He was sitting back in the chair, gazing at the bottles behind the bar. No one else said a word. As a briefing, it had been a joke. Nothing settled. Nothing fixed. None of the really important details even mentioned. Just the route they'd take, and the name of the prizes at the end of the road.

"Scullen," he said again, softly, reaching for the last of his Guinness, "and the boy Connolly."

He drained the glass and stood up. The men followed him out of the shop, and across the street. He looked at his watch, waiting for Thompson to unlock the car doors, and then got in. They waited a full minute before Miller gave the signal for the off. Only when they were a mile out of town, heading south again, did Thompson voice the obvious thought.

"Why didn't you write it all out and stick it on a lamp-post?" he said. "Give them all a treat?"

Miller said nothing for a moment. Then he smiled.

"Quite," he said, opening the metal box at his feet and beginning to sort his way through the small armoury of weapons inside.

Buddy found the gun as the last of the sunset expired over Gosport.

They'd slipped from the pontoon at Warsash at three in the afternoon, easing into Southampton Water on the last of the ebb tide. They'd used the motor, hugging the coast, managing a half-decent four knots while the long straggle of weekend sailors beat their way back towards the Hamble marina. Out in the Solent, it was less crowded, and they'd made good time, puttering east past Stubbington and Lee-on-the-Solent, and then dog-legging round the broad shoal of Spit Bank before turning inland again towards Southsea Castle, and the deep water channel that ran in beside the mile of busy promenade.

They'd entered the harbour at six o'clock, the air beginning to chill after the warmth of the day. The harbour had been busy – more yachts, commercial shipping, ferries to the Isle of Wight and France – but they'd found the marina berth and tied up alongside with no real difficulty. As Eva hopped onto the pontoon and threw a perfect half-hitch around one of the big mooring rings, the first of a squadron of Sea Harrier jump jets had appeared from the west, tiny grey dots that grew and grew as the pilots rotated the jet exhausts downwards, keeping the planes airborne on a column of raw thrust. Even a mile away, the noise was deafening and Eva had turned her back and put her hands over her ears as the planes dropped slowly towards the dockyard, one after the other, turning into wind and finally settling, like nesting birds, on the flight decks of the two carriers. Buddy had watched them, looping a second pair of fenders over the starboard quarter, thinking of the guys he'd met in the pub, their songs, their eager, frantic courage. Part of him still wanted to go. No question.

Now, though, he'd something else to think about. The gun was small and black. It fitted snugly into the palm of his hand, and when he worked out how to open the magazine, he emptied seven bullets onto the table. The bullets were small, .22 calibre. To do anything with these, thought Buddy, you'd have to get close. Very close. The boat rocked. Eva had been away, up in the town. She'd said she needed to make a call. She'd said it was important. Now she was back, standing aft, hands deep in her bomber jacket, looking at him through the open hatch. Buddy had found the gun behind a cushion in the cabin. It had been wrapped in a dishcloth.

"Yours?" he enquired. "Or does it come with the boat?"

She looked at the gun, stepping down into the cabin, putting a Waitrose shopping bag on the fold-down table.

"Mine," she agreed.

"You use it often?"

She glanced at him, ignoring the sarcasm.

"No."

"Have you ever used it?"

"Yes."

"And what happened?"

"I missed."

"Thank Christ for that."

She looked at him for a moment, then held out her hand. He gave her the gun, and she examined it quickly, then swept the bullets on the table into a neat pile. Buddy watched her reloading the magazine. Whatever had been wrong with her marksmanship didn't extend to the rest of it. She handled the gun with total confidence, securing the magazine, sliding the breech mechanism backwards and forwards, checking the safety catch. Finally, she wrapped the gun in the dishcloth again and put it back behind the cushion.

"You planning on using it again," he enquired, "this time round?"

She shrugged, starting to unpack the bag of shopping. More cold meats. A container or two of salad. Half a dozen crusty white rolls.

"Hope not," she said.

"But you will if you have to?"

"If we have to," she nodded, "*natürlich*."

Buddy gazed at her for a moment, shaking his head, trying not to think too hard about the implications. He'd signed up to cripple an aircraft carrier. Not play Bonnie and Clyde with whoever happened to get in their way. She turned her back on him, ignoring him, busy with the food, and he looked at her a moment longer before returning to what he'd been doing earlier, laying out his equipment on the triangle of mattress in the forepeak, checking the charges, the clamps, fitting them carefully into the cheap shopping bags he'd bought in the market. The bags were latticed in plastic, strong enough to bear the weight of the clamps and the explosives, but open at the top. He planned to secure the tops of the bags with twists of wire, cocooning the charges inside. With one in each hand, underwater, they'd offer the minimum resistance, yet still be easy to carry. He knew it was a botch, a thoroughly makeshift solution, but twenty years underwater had taught him that the simplest, crudest ideas were often best.

The charges packed, and the sonar detonators tuned to the blast frequency, he turned to the closed-circuit breathing set. On the way over from Warsash, sitting at the table, he'd run through his earlier calculations, checking his input figures – depths, pressures, swim times – making sure he'd calculated the right flow rate, the all-important trickle of pure oxygen he'd need to feed into the circuit to enable him to stay submerged and alive for long enough to complete the task. Now, he did the sums again, using a paper and pencil the first time, and a calculator the second. Both times, the result was the same. Unless there was a sudden need to go deeper, he'd have sixty-five minutes, more than enough to swim to the target, attach the charges, and then return across the harbour to the marina. Of the three elements to the operation, it was the third that worried him the most. Like most divers, Buddy didn't much like swimming. Five hundred metres was a fair distance, and he only hoped he had the stamina to make it.

An hour later, dark outside, Eva served supper. Buddy had thrown a blanket over his equipment in the forepeak, and had retired to the cockpit outside while Eva laid the table. She'd bought some cans of Pils in the supermarket, and he sat in the stern, his legs stretched out, sipping the lager. It was cold now, a brisk wind blowing down the harbour from the north-west, and he was wrapped in a heavy polo-necked sweater and a thick anorak. The water was black, beginning to stir with the incoming tide, the wind pushing against it, pocking the surface with tiny, fretful waves. Across the harbour, the dockyard was ablaze with lights, and he could see figures in blue overalls working around the Sea Harriers. He counted the Harriers. There were half a dozen, and he wondered briefly exactly what difference their temporary loss would make to the Task Force they'd managed to cobble together. Presumably, they'd ship south aboard some other vessel. Presumably, as ever, the Navy would cope.

The door to the cabin opened, and Eva emerged. She had a cup of coffee in her hand, and she shut the door carefully before making herself comfortable on the bench seat opposite. Buddy looked at the coffee for a moment. The second can of lager had warmed him, a blessing, and he felt looser about everything, less anxious, even benign. What he had to do, he had to do. Thinking too hard about the implications was no longer worth the candle. Better, by far, to look ahead, beyond it all.

He looked at her in the darkness.

"Tell me . . ." he said, "about tomorrow."

"Tomorrow?" She glanced across the harbour, towards the carrier. "Tomorrow we— "

"I meant afterwards. Me. My wife."

"Ah," Eva nodded, "your wife."

"Yes."

"She's well."

"You've spoken to her?"

Eva shook her head. "I've spoken to someone who's been with her."

"And?"

"She sends her love."

"Good." Buddy tipped his empty can, a toast. "So when do I get to see her? When does it happen?"

"We phone."

"*We* phone?"

"I phone. I have a number. There's a procedure. It's all arranged."

Buddy nodded, watching her, impatient for the details, the small print that would bridge the gap, back to Ireland, back to Jude.

"So how do I get there?" he said. "Ferry? Take the car?"

"Plane. From Heathrow. You'll need your passport. You'll fly to Cork. You'll be picked up."

Buddy nodded again, warming to the arrangement. Then he remembered the last conversation with the man in the cottage, the shape of the deal he'd offered.

"I thought we were supposed to meet in Boston?" he said.

Eva shook her head. "Ireland. It's changed."

"But we're still going to Boston?"

"Yes. Of course."

Buddy looked away a moment, saying nothing, wondering about another can of Pils. Somewhere in the darkness he heard the sound of laughter, men, distant but distinct. He peered across the harbour. There were no clues aboard *Invincible*, just the silhouette of the Sea Harriers against the black of the night.

"Tell me something," he said at last, "where is she? Where have they put her?"

Eva emptied the mug of coffee. Then she shook her head. "I don't know," she said. "That's the truth."

After dark, lying in bed by the window, Jude felt her head beginning to clear.

Most of the day had vanished, compressed into a meaningless series of hallucinations, the fever lapping at her brain, retrieving memories she'd long forgotten, phantom bodies skipping across rooms she'd known only as a child, up and down an enormous spiral staircase she must once have seen in a movie, the music coming and going, sometimes loud, sometimes indistinct, like a badly tuned radio. Then, abruptly, it had all gone, like summer thunder, rolling away, and she was left with squares of darkness in the window, and a very clear view of the door. She called out. The door opened. A face appeared, the boy who'd arrived later than the rest of them, the young academic from Belfast, the one she'd decided to trust.

She looked up at him. She moved her head on the pillow. She realized that the pillow was soaking wet. She smiled. She could barely speak. He knelt down by the bed, on the bare wooden floor. She closed her eyes a moment, determined to concentrate, now that she could think it all through.

There were details to sort out, important details. There was the question of dispatch. Her body. What she wanted to happen to it. Afterwards. After she'd gone. She didn't want it to go back to the States. She didn't want her family to see her this way, even dead. She pondered the problem. What difference would it make? Dead or alive, nothing worked. She thought about it some more, trying to be sensible, but it didn't help. It had nothing to do with logic, this feeling of hers, this conviction. But then that wasn't the point. She frowned, beginning to lose touch again. What *was* the point, she wondered.

The boy from Belfast, Derek, came closer. She'd got to know him a bit. She liked him. She thought he might like her, might be extending something a little more than sympathy. If she had hands, she'd have touched him now, at the bedside. Instead, she moistened her lips with her tongue. She wanted to share with him something profound. Something important. Something central to her life. Now that it was so nearly over.

"Buddy," she whispered.

Connolly nodded, catching the name. She'd talked about him. Described him. Offered snapshots of the relationship, how it had started, where it had been. Connolly had listened to her, recognizing the memories for what they were, travellers' tales from a land he'd never visited, a country on no map. She'd shared everything with this man of hers, everything it was possible to share. And sharing everything, dividing everything, they'd become one, indivisible.

"Buddy," he confirmed.

She blinked up at him. "Tell him it was great," she whispered, "all of it."

Connolly nodded.

"I will."

"Tell him I'll miss it."

"Yes."

"Here . . ." she closed her eyes a moment, trying to concentrate, "you'll need the number."

"Number?"

"The telephone number."

Connolly stared at her a moment. He'd never watched anyone die before, not the way Charlie had died, the death of the bullet, but the other kind of dying, the slower death, the death of the last vigil, the creak at the door, the sigh in the chimney, the rustle of the curtain, the last goodbye.

People who had, people he'd talked to, read about, said that you knew when it was imminent, a wholly natural thing, complete with its own small surprises, and kneeling beside her now, he knew it was true. This woman was dying. Soon she would be gone. Yet still she had time to share a phone number.

"0703 . . ." she said, counting out the numbers slowly, like coins, "834139."

Connolly wrote down the number. He wondered why it was so hard to keep his hand still. He looked at the number, and repeated it. She nodded, her breathing shallow now, her voice fainter than ever.

"Will you phone him?"

Connolly nodded. "Yes."

"Will you?"

"Yes."

"Good."

She smiled, and Connolly looked at her, realizing what he'd become, the bookend to her life. He bent very low, his cheek close to hers, atoning for Charlie. Her face was very hot.

"What shall I say?"

She frowned for a moment, working it out again. "Tell him to bury me," she said at last, "but here. Not there."

"Not where?"

"Not in the States." She smiled. "He can get as close as he likes but keep this side of the ocean. Eh . . . ?"

She left the sentence in the air and closed her eyes. There was peace in her face and a certain amusement, and when the first shots came out of the darkness, very distant, there was no sign that she'd even heard them.

TWENTY-FOUR

Ingle and Kee were in Southampton by seven o'clock. All the pool motors were out, so they'd driven down from London in Kee's car. Kee had just acquired one of the new Ford Escort XRis. With its go-fast stripes and rear spoiler it was, said Ingle heavily, perfect for surveillance work. Maybe he should have chosen something with a slightly lower profile. Like a Rolls-Royce. Or a Sherman tank.

They found the address on the intercepted letter without difficulty. The house was tucked away up a narrow street in an area just north of the city centre, hemmed in by a grid of new expressways. Judging by the bicycles, and the oriental food stores and the rows of Bengali restaurants, the neighbourhood had been taken over by a mix of students and Asian families. Sitting in the darkened car, gazing down the street, it reminded Ingle of parts of the East End. Same smells. Same curls of dog turd. Same sodden mattresses, abandoned in the tiny oblongs of front garden.

Ingle and Kee got out and crossed the road. Number 20 was neater than the rest of the houses in the street. The pavement outside was swept clean. The paintwork was new. There were even curtains at the window. Ingle knocked at the door. There was no answer. He knocked again. Nothing. He opened the letter box and peered through. The house was dark. There was no sound of television or music. The place smelled, very faintly, of caraway seed. He glanced at Kee. Kee produced an old credit card. Ingle took it and inserted it between the door and the jamb, working it slowly in, feeling for the tongue of the lock. For some reason it took longer than usual, but finally he found it, exerting a gentle pressure, easing the lock backwards. The door opened. Ingle grunted. Kee returned the credit card to his wallet.

Inside, the house was spotless. With the lights on, Ingle pulled the curtains and moved quickly from room to room, putting together initial impressions, getting a feel for the place. There were a woman's touches everywhere – the plants, the handsewn cushion covers, the blush of pink in the colourwashed walls, the amply stocked spice rack with the Indian recipe books in the kitchen. Upstairs, there were two bedrooms. One, at the back, was obviously a spare room, small, tidy, slightly clinical. The other, a bigger room at the front of the house, was where the woman evidently did most of her living. There were two big bookshelves, crammed with well-thumbed paperbacks, and there was a small desk, with a portable typewriter and an Anglepoise lamp and a wire tray. The tray was full of typescript. Curled on top of the typescript was a small marmalade kitten, sound asleep.

Ingle stood in the middle of the room, certain it could tell him what he wanted to know, wondering quite where to start. Downstairs, he could hear Kee applying what little he'd learned about rummage jobs to the living room. For his sake, he hoped the woman didn't make a surprise reappearance.

Ingle stepped across to the dressing table. In the lower of the two drawers, under an assortment of Marks and Spencer lingerie, he found a passport and a bunch of keys. He took the passport out. It was West German. The woman's name was Eva Hippke. She was twenty-eight years old. She'd been born in Ludwigshafen. She'd entered her occupation as "*Lehrer*". The small black and white photo alongside showed a round, plain face with a fringe of black hair and a slightly dead look in the eyes. Ingle thumbed quickly through. There were a number of German stamps in the passport, and a six-month visa for the States. She'd been to Malaga a couple of times, and there were three entry stamps for Dublin. He made a note of the Dublin dates, and the girl's name, and slipped the passport into his pocket. Whatever else happened, she'd now have trouble leaving the country.

He crossed to the bedside. There were a couple of photos on the shelf above the bed. They were both framed. One showed an oldish couple, sitting at a café table. There was a tram in the background and it was sunny. The other was a head and shoulders shot, a man of about twenty-five. He was very dark, almost Latin. His hair was slicked back. He was on a beach. It looked as if he'd just been swimming. His smile had an edge to it, a knowing look, a secret shared with the person behind the camera. Crumpet, thought Ingle, replacing the photo and thinking again of the passport stamps. A week or two on the Costa del Sol. A fortnight of brisk work-outs in some hotel bedroom or other. Then back to this studious life of hers, books about Kultur and Philosophie, visits to Marks and Spencer, the odd curry in the evenings.

He turned from the bed and crossed the room to the desk. On the wall over the desk was a calendar. He leafed back to January, finding a red circle around the 23rd. He looked at it, frowning. The GPO intercept had been logged on the 24th. On the 23rd, therefore, the letter had probably been posted. He examined the rest of the month. There was nothing. He went through February. February was empty. In March, though, the marks returned, small neat ticks beside the 22nd and the 24th. The 26th, for some reason, had earned itself a small red seagull and an exclamation mark. He paused for a moment. Then he looked down at the desk.

The desk had three drawers all locked. He went back to the dressing table, remembering the keys. The smallest key fitted. In the middle drawer, he found a collection of old cheque-books with a rubber band around them. He extracted the top cheque-book. The last cheque had been written only three days ago, 2nd April. According to the stub, it had been made out to a travel agent. The sum involved was £65. He leafed back, curious, looking for 26th March. He found the date at once, on the previous cheque stub. The cheque, for £450, had been made out to Cruisaway Ltd. He checked the date on the calendar again, then made a note of the name of the company. There were no other cheques missing.

He was about to replace the cheque-book in the drawer when he noticed the name on the unused cheques. It wasn't

Hippke at all. It was Weiss. He frowned. He looked at the other cheque-books. They were all in the name of Hippke. He hesitated a moment, then pocketed the Weiss cheque-book, going quickly through the other two drawers. Neither gave him any more surprises, just supplies of paper clips, cartridges of ink, and a battered old stapler with "University Property" on the bottom.

Ingle locked the drawers and looked at the kitten. The kitten was awake now, stretching out, licking the end of one paw, looking up at him from time to time, the invitation to a game. He lifted it carefully out of the tray and dropped it on the bed. He returned to the desk. The top sheet of typescript was warm from the heat of the kitten's body. He glanced at it. It was in German. He began to shuffle quickly through the tray. More typescript, each page sequentially numbered, perfectly typed. He was about to abandon the search, nearly at the bottom, when he found what he'd come for. It was a photocopy from one of the new reduction machines. It showed an inside page from a newspaper. Half the page was devoted to a single article. The article was headlined "Unlucky Break". Beside it was a grainy photograph of a woman on a horse.

Ingle read the article carefully, letting the facts settle one by one. Buddy Little. Thirty-eight years old. Working diver. Jude Little. Thirty-four years old. Wife. Terrible accident. Neck broken. Body paralysed. Life ruined. Hunt for a cure. Talk of an operation. Need for a great deal of money. Ingle gazed at the article. Diver, he thought. Capt. Harrison, he thought. *QEII*, he thought.

He bent quickly to the typewriter, inserted a sheet of paper, and typed through the entire keyboard. The intercept letter had probably been typed on the same machine. Later, he might need evidence. This would do.

He was still typing when Kee appeared at the door. He was carrying a small pile of magazines. He was smiling. Ingle glanced up at him.

"Yeah?" he said briefly.

Kee tossed one of the magazines onto the desk beside the typewriter. It was a copy of *Playgirl*. "Take a look in there," he said, "must be something about the American diet."

Ingle didn't even smile. "Get the phone directory," he said, still typing, "and the Yellow Pages."

Kee looked at him a moment, retrieved the magazine, and went downstairs again. When he came back, he was carrying the phone directory. "Can't find the Yellow Pages," he said.

Ingle nodded, tearing the sheet of paper out of the typewriter and folding it into his pocket. The kitten jumped off the bed and made for one of Kee's laces.

"The name's Little," Ingle said, "try that first."

Kee began to thumb through the directory. "First name?"

"B. For Buddy."

"You serious?"

"I think so."

Kee bent to the columns of names and addresses. Then shook his head. "Only three Littles. None with a 'B'."

"Any in the New Forest?"

"No. Two in Southampton. One in Eastleigh."

"OK." Ingle glanced at the article again. Jude's maiden name wasn't mentioned, but her riding stables were. "Fernleigh Stables," he said. Kee began to rifle through the pages again. The kitten had teased out one of his laces. He found the number.

"Ringwood 375664," he said.

The two men went downstairs, the kitten chasing their shadows along the hall. Ingle picked up the phone and dialled the number. While he was waiting for an answer, he nodded again at the directory.

"Find the coastguard," he said. "There'll be a twenty-four hour number." The Ringwood number answered. Ingle asked for Buddy Little. A man's voice came back. Buddy was out for the night, he said. Be back sometime tomorrow. Ingle hesitated a moment. Then he bent to the phone again. "Where's he gone?" he said.

The voice laughed. "Haven't a clue."

Ingle frowned. "Think," he said, "it's important."

There was a silence. Then the voice again, harder, more suspicious.

"Who are you then?"

"Police."

"Police?" A pause. "Is he OK?"

"That's what we're trying to find out."

"Oh . . ." The voice hesitated, then came back again, compliant, eager to help. "He mentioned Warsash. You might try there."

Ingle nodded, asking for a spelling, writing the name down on the pad by the phone. Then he resumed the conversation.

"Stay where you are," he said, "don't go out. We may need you."

"Sure."

"Mr . . .?"

"Reynolds."

Ingle hung up, making a note of the name, then looked briefly at Kee. Kee had already written down the coastguard number. Ingle rang it, introducing himself at once. Special Branch, he said. Metropolitan Division. Area Three. The coastguard grunted, and Ingle asked him about the QE2. Did he happen to know whether she was in port?

"Negative," the coastguard said.

"Where is she?"

"Florida."

"How do you know?"

"My mother-in-law's on board."

"Fine."

Ingle put the phone down again. The kitten was outside, running up and down the hall. Kee was squatting on the runner, making noises at it. Ingle picked up the phone directory for the last time. The QE2 was off the plot. Basing a Florida operation from here was inconceivable. He flicked through the directory. Under "C" he found what he was looking for. Cruisaway Ltd. His eyes followed the line of print, looking for the name that would clinch it. He began to smile. Kee glanced in through the door. The kitten was having another wash. "Where next?" he said.

Ingle shut the directory. "Warsash," he said. "Wherever the fuck that is."

Thompson lay in the wet grass overlooking the road, one

hand on Miller's arm. Against his better judgement, he was beginning to make some sense of the older man's thinking. Thankfully, after Dublin, they weren't going in blind. Contrary to appearances, there really did appear to be a plan.

From Cahersiveen, after the briefing, they'd motored south, towards Waterville. *En route*, no warning, Miller had ordered him off the main road, down a rutted track, towards a derelict row of cottages, overlooking the sea. The second car, Camps and Venner, had followed. Then, in private this time, Miller had taken them briskly through the evening's entertainments.

Their first call was to be a remote cottage, out on the coast, near Rosnaveel. There, they would recruit a shy but active thirty-two-year-old called Niall Quinn, a fringe supporter of the movement, currently in the doghouse for failing to deliver on a post office job. The name and the information had come from a friendly source in the Irish police, the Garda. This source, the man they called the Badger, had supplied Miller with a number of pages of raw material about the current status of the movement in south-west Kerry. From a list of names, Miller had selected Quinn.

Quinn, he said, had a car of his own. The car, an ancient Renault, they'd commandeer at gunpoint. The car was well known in the area. Everyone knew that Quinn owned it. When they drove inland, therefore, up through Waterville and into the mountains, no one would suspect that the Renault was remotely threatening. Miller had paused here, waiting for the obvious question. Camps had voiced it, squatting on a pile of masonry, out of the wind, his face invisible in the darkness.

"What about Quinn?" he said. "What do we do with him?"

Miller had smiled, a gesture of congratulation, explaining that Quinn would be driving their lead car, the one that Scullen was expecting, the one the old man in the undertaker's would doubtless have confirmed. Quinn would be at the wheel, his co-operation assured by a kilo of Semtex and a radio detonator under the seat. Ignore our instructions, Miller would tell him, and you're a dead man.

And so it had been. They'd driven down to Quinn's

cottage, and covered the rear exits and knocked at the door, and stood in the drizzle while his sheepdog sniffed them each in turn. When he'd finally opened up, they'd stepped politely inside, and explained the plot, and torn out his telephone, and handed him the keys to the Capri.

Ten minutes later, in a loose convoy, Quinn in the lead, they'd driven up through Waterville, a dark, wet night, and taken the road inland to Lissnatinnig Bridge. Thompson, coaxing a steady 35 mph from Quinn's Renault, keeping the Capri's tail-lights in sight, had been impressed — yes — but surprised too. He'd never known Miller ask for help before. Acquiring the Kerry intelligence had been a masterstroke.

"Difficult?" he'd murmured, the road unwinding steadily upwards, no sign yet of the expected ambush.

Miller, knowing exactly what lay behind the question, had shaken his head. "No," he'd said. "More pride than anything else."

"Whose pride?"

"Mine."

They'd been on the Lissnatinnig road for eighteen minutes when Scullen sprung the trap. The Capri had slowed for a series of tight bends, the mountains falling sheer to the roadside, the car hemmed in by the geography of the place. Two hundred yards back, Thompson had seen the first explosion, probably a planted charge, the rocky flank of the mountain jumping out of the darkness for a split second, illuminated by the blast. The Capri had been blown sideways, across the road, its nearside wing folding as it hit the rock. There'd been a lot of smoke, and the first lick of flame from the bonnet of the Capri, and Thompson had pulled the Renault into the side of the road, dousing the lights, and crouching behind the wheel, waiting for Miller. The older man had done nothing for at least half a minute, just watched the rifle fire pouring down from the mountain, stitching the Capri with holes, waiting for the one man who always wanted to administer the *coup de grâce*, the Volunteers' volunteer. Finally he appeared, a tall lank figure in a bala-clava and a camouflage smock. He had an automatic in one hand. He ran to the car. He paused beside the driver's door, peering in, and then Miller blew him to pieces, pressing the button on the transmitter, watching the roof of the Capri disappearing into the darkness, hearing the endless after-tinkle of glass, falling from the rocks, back onto the road.

Thompson grinned, out of the car now, scrambling up the side of the mountain, following Miller. On the other side of the road, he could clearly see Camps and Venner, two shapes in the darkness, making off to the left, targeting one of the other fire positions. Miller's orders at the second briefing had been quite specific. No prisoners, he'd said. Only bodies left in the wet, victims of yet another of Kerry's interminable Republican feuds.

Now, half an hour later, Miller was getting impatient. Since the explosion, nothing had happened. No one else had appeared in the road. The Capri was still down there, and the remains of the two bodies. Off to the left, a hundred yards away, Camps and Venner were listening out on the radio. Of the other gunmen – at least half a dozen judging by the muzzle flashes – there was no sign.

Miller stirred again, glancing back at Thompson. Their eyes were used to the darkness now. The rain had stopped and there was a thin, intermittent moonlight through a broken layer of cloud. Miller gestured up the mountain, ordering Thompson into a flanking attack, the wide high sweep that would take them in the rear.

"Get as close as you can," he said. "One if they're there. Two if they're not."

Thompson confirmed the order, patting the tiny belt-slung radio wired to the throat mike. The radio had a system that enabled the sender to transmit Morse code. On occasions, like now, it was simpler than speech and a good deal safer. He cradled his Armalite and disappeared into the darkness.

Miller waited for perhaps ten minutes. It started to rain again. Then he began to advance, flat on his belly, the big Browning out in front of him, his elbows and forearms levering his body over the patches of level ground. When the level ground ended, and he was out on the mountainside again, he picked his way forward at the half-crouch, making sure of each footfall, testing it for the loose rock and scree that could tumble away into the darkness and give him away. Once, he thought he saw a movement ahead in the darkness, and he froze, his body pressed against the wet rock. A hundred feet below him, at a new angle, he could see the wreckage of the white Capri. From here there was a perfect field of fire. He might be only yards away from their position.

He waited for five long minutes, knowing that you could always outwait the opposition, knowing that men had died because of their impatience, knowing that what he wanted was an operation so flawless, a kill so clean, that the Nineteenth could take back the ground they'd lost. But nothing happened, no more movement, and when he heard the single tone in his ear, Thompson's message, he knew why. They'd gone.

The big Cockney appeared at his elbow a minute or so later. With him, at the business end of the Armalite, was someone else. Miller peered at his face in the darkness. He was wearing a knitted black skull cap, pulled low. He had the wispy beginnings of a beard and a moustache. He looked about sixteen. Miller glanced at Thompson.

"Done his ankle in," Thompson explained. "Mates left him behind."

Miller nodded, understanding. He turned back to the youth.

"Where did they go?" he said.

The youth shook his head, saying nothing. He looked terrified. Thompson glanced at Miller, speculative, and Miller asked the question again, very patient, very sympathetic. The youth studied his feet. Miller looked at Thompson and nodded. Thompson lifted the butt of the Armalite and smacked it, very hard, against the side of the youth's face. The boy gasped with pain and collapsed in a heap amongst the rocks. Thompson lifted him up with one hand and was about to do it again when Miller intervened.

"Hang on," he said, "I think he wants to tell us something."

The boy looked up at the two of them. There were tears in his eyes. He was holding his ear. He didn't say a word.

"Well?" Miller enquired.

The boy looked away, into the darkness.

"They've gone," he said, a dense Kerry accent.

"I know they've gone," Miller said, "I want to know where."

The boy glanced at him, foxy, evasive. Miller could see him thinking, trying to work out what tiny parcel of information these men would accept, what present he could offer, what was acceptable in this new world of explosions, and slaughter, and sudden spasms of violence.

"Up there," he said, nodding inland, towards the heart of the mountains.

"Where?" Miller smiled at him. "Exactly?"

"I don't know."

"How many of them?"

The youth paused, and Thompson spread his legs, very slowly, easing the knees outwards, until the youth was straddling a metre and a half of ground. The youth looked round at him, more nervous than ever. Thompson simply watched him, giving nothing away.

"Well?" Miller said. "Six? Ten? Couple of dozen? Three?"

The youth began to say something, then thought better of it. Miller sighed, regretful, and Thompson took half a step backwards, then kicked the boy hard, driving his instep high into his pelvic arch. The boy screamed and collapsed and Miller was down beside him, his hand over the boy's mouth, his voice suddenly harsh, the game over.

"How many?" he said.

The boy was gasping for air. After a while, he swallowed hard.

"Eight," he said.

"Is Scullen with them?"

The boy nodded, looking up, terrified now.

"Yes," he said.

"And will they go back to the house? The farmhouse?"

The boy nodded, and sobbed, and nodded again, anything to stop the pain.

"Yes," he said. "Yes."

"Scullen's place?"

"Yes."

"Glannadin?"

"*Yes.*"

Miller looked at him for a second longer, then stood up in the darkness. They'd have to yomp the rest of the way, he knew it. They'd have to carry the weapons, and the radios, and the rest of the gear, and take the house before sunrise. He glanced at Thompson. Thompson was standing over the crippled youth, his Armalite in his hand. Miller eyed the youth a moment, then nodded. Thompson put the muzzle of the gun against the base of the boy's skull and pulled the trigger. The boy's body jerked upwards, and then he was still. Thompson eased his boots away from the boy's body. His boots were wet. Miller, bent to his radio, glanced up. If his calculations were correct, they had four miles to cover. Half a mile away, across the valley, Camps and Venner were awaiting orders. They'd have to do something about the cars. They might need them in a hurry afterwards. He looked at his watch and frowned. Five minutes to midnight, he thought. Six hours before dawn.

Buddy Little eased the yacht off the pontoon, tickling in the revs on the throttle quadrant, coaxing a low burble from the inboard Penta diesel. He was wearing a dark plaid blanket over his shoulders, hiding his wet suit and dive vest. With the two big bottles on his back, he looked – and felt – like Quasimodo.

Eva stepped carefully back along the deck, holding the rail. She'd coiled the forward mooring warp and hung it on the pulpit at the bow. In a quarter of an hour or so, with luck, she'd need it again, when she tried to berth the yacht, back at the marina, singlehanded. That would be the real challenge for her new-found seamanship. That would be the moment when she'd know whether hours of careful practice had paid off.

Now, shivering with cold inside her anorak, she joined Buddy in the stern. They'd left the shelter of the marina now, and were nosing out into the harbour, heading straight for *Invincible*. For Buddy, fully suited up, all movement was now difficult on board the yacht and so he would stay at the helm until they came about in the middle of the harbour, directly abeam the aircraft carrier. Then, according to the plan, he'd release the helm to Eva, shrugging off the blanket, and dropping backwards into the water. Surfacing briefly, on the blindside of the yacht, the engine in neutral, she'd hand him the two charges and wait for him to submerge and disappear before engaging gear and heading slowly down the harbour before a wide turn to starboard brought the yacht back again, in towards the marina.

That, at least, had been the theory. Now, afloat at last, everything ready, Buddy realized that it wouldn't work. He looked at her in the darkness, cutting the engine back, still outside the buoyed channel, a quarter of a mile from the carrier, letting the yacht come to a virtual halt in the water.

"Listen," he said, "this is crazy."

"What's crazy?"

Buddy peered across the harbour, at the dockyard, not answering her question. "Get the glasses," he said.

Eva looked at him a moment, then went below. She returned, seconds later, with a pair of battered binoculars. Buddy had used them for years, out on the rigs, studying the bird life. After Jude, they were his most prized possession. He lifted the glasses and trained them on the big carrier. Areas of the flight deck were still bathed in light. He could see teams of mechanics working on the Sea Harriers. Further aft, two men were strapping down the rotors of the big Sea King helicopters. He swung the binoculars upwards, following the rise of the command island, up to the bridge. Inside the bridge, the lighting was subdued, a low pale green luminance, but even so, he could count at least five heads, officers talking, men gazing out into the darkness, keeping watch. Take the yacht out into the middle of the harbour, nav lights on, and any one of them might lift their own glasses, take a curious look, fiddle with the focus, wonder what on earth a man in a diving suit was doing aboard a perfectly ordinary yacht, middle of the night, start of a war.

Buddy shook his head. A lift in the yacht half-way across the harbour was a false economy. It raised the odds on detection umpteenfold and would leave him nowhere to hide if they sent down divers of their own. The only mystery, the only thought in his empty skull, was why on earth he hadn't thought of it before.

He handed the glasses back to Eva. Then he engaged the engine again, and began to swing the boat around. She stared at him.

"What are you doing?" she said. "Where are we going?"

"Back."

"Why?"

"Because it won't work."

She looked at him for a moment. Then she disappeared below. When she returned she was holding the small black pistol. He could see it quite clearly in her hand. He held the tiller between his knees, and eased the straps on his shoulders. The big oxygen cylinders were heavy. He was getting backache. Eva was still looking at him.

"Turn around," she said.

Buddy ignored her, issuing an order of his own.

"Go forward," he said. "We'll berth again."

"Turn around."

Buddy laughed. "You've got a choice," he said. "My way or yours. My way will work. Yours won't. Your call."

He yawned and Eva looked briefly confused. The gun wavered. The marina was looming up, the beginnings of a sea breeze stirring the halyards against the metal masts.

"You'll still do it?" she said.

"Yes." He stood up, easing back the throttle again, trying to judge the distance to the pontoon, letting the way fall off. "Just do what you're fucking told."

Ten minutes later, safely back on the pontoon, Eva stood beside him in the stern.

"I'm sorry," she began, "I didn't realize."

Buddy shrugged. Shrugging, with the weight on his shoulders, hurt. "Turn off the lights," he said.

She disappeared again, dousing the cabin and navigation lights while he ran through the calculations in his head. Swimming there as well as back would bite into his time on target. With luck, he'd have fifteen minutes under the carrier. If anything went wrong, if he was slower than expected, less fit than he'd hoped, then his strictly operational time would shrink even further. He spat in his face mask, leaning over the side to wash it and put it on, over the thick neoprene hood, adjusting the strap at the back, getting the seal tight around his face. Then he bit on the regulator, and took his first lungful of oxygen, adjusting the flow rate on the cylinders, cutting back a little, giving himself a slender extra margin in case he needed it.

He looked at Eva a moment, then nodded at the charges, cocooned inside the plastic shopping bags, in the well of the cockpit. He had a slight headache. Working on the explosives, he thought, or perhaps the Pils. Eva bent for the charges, picked them up. Buddy was adjusting his weight belt. Eva put the charges on the bench seat. Then she smiled at him, and held out a hand, a farewell, a gesture of good luck, comrades in arms. Buddy looked at her hand for a long time, an oval of face behind the toughened glass, then he hinged slowly backwards, over the side, and disappeared. When he surfaced again, briefly, it was to reach up for the charges, one after the other, their weight suddenly displaced by the water. He hung beside the yacht for a moment, working the rubber mouthpiece between his teeth, getting it comfortable. Then, with scarcely a ripple to prove it, he was gone.

Ingle and Kee stayed at Warsash for the rest of the evening.

They found the premises of Cruiseaway, a suite of rooms above a greengrocer in a parade of shops near the water. They rang the bell and knocked at the door but there was no reply. They enquired at the Indian restaurant next door, and at the pub across the road, but no one could help. They even rang the number from a pay phone on the bar, but a pre-recorded voice advised them to leave a message or try again during business hours. Business hours were nine to five. Kee looked at Ingle, awaiting further orders. Ingle obliged.

"Pint," he said, looking down the bar, "something half-decent."

They drank at a small table next to a fishtank in a corner of the lounge. Kee bought some crisps, two different flavours, and Ingle tried them both on the torpid shapes inside.

Cheese and onion was a disaster. Roast chicken produced a flicker of interest in one of the smaller fish, but it didn't come back for second helpings.

A couple of hours later, last orders long gone, Ingle enquired about accommodation. The girl at the bar directed him to a motel about two miles away. They were open twenty-four hours a day, she said, and there was a pool. Ingle eyed her for a moment, weighing his chances, but she told him she hated swimming and had a big husband. Ingle smiled.

"Marinas," he said, "yachts."

"Yeah?"

"Where are they?"

"Everywhere. Up and down the river." She shrugged. "Everywhere."

Ingle nodded. "Firm called Cruisaway," he said. "Heard of them?"

She frowned at him, wiping the last of the glasses. "Never," she said, "can't be local."

At the motel, Ingle booked two single rooms and bought four miniatures of Scotch from a dour night porter. He and Kee split the Scotch, taking it neat in toothglasses from Kee's bathroom. Kee switched the television on, and they both watched, sitting in armchairs, sprawled in front of the set, knackered. Ingle had woken in Belfast, spent the afternoon in London, done an early evening B-and-E job in Southampton, and now he was here, in some remote motel bedroom, wondering what little sense he might coax from his day. Whatever else the German girl was doing, she wasn't blowing up the *QEII*, he was sure of that. Yet there had to be some other explanation, some other thread to connect it all, the letter to Dublin, the article, the diver and his poor bloody wife, the cheque account in the phoney name, the chartered yacht.

He gazed at the television, savouring another mouthful of Scotch. The programme they'd been half watching, *Nero Wolfe*, had come to an end. The credits had rolled through. Now they were looking at shots of a harbour. There were warships and men in uniform. There were convoys of lorries thundering past guards at a gate. There was music on the sound track, urgent, and a deep male voice talking about the countdown to war. The images rolled on, some kind of promotion, a trailer for a special programme they'd be showing the following morning, the Fleet putting to sea, a genuine moment of history, the real thing.

Ingle gazed at the sleek grey shapes of the waiting warships, the shots of the matelots streaming aboard, the piles of stores on the dockside, the big close-up of the white ensign, snapping in the breeze. The promotion came to an end. *Task Force South*, the voice said. *Tomorrow morning. Half past' ten*. The screen went briefly blank. Then there were more commercials. Soapflakes. Not patriotism.

Ingle stirred, aware of Kee watching him. The boy was tired. He needed to go to bed. Ingle reached for the second miniature and broke the seal.

"Sounds great," he said, nodding at the screen, "better than bloody football."

TWENTY-FIVE

Connolly had never seen a Kalashnikov before. It was big, a serious rifle with a curved thirty-shot magazine, and an old leather strap. It had a sight you adjusted up and down at the back, and a pin on the muzzle that you centred in the circle of the back sight. The wood of the stock and the butt was dark and well-seasoned, and tucking the gun into his shoulder, his cheek against the stock, he wondered how many other men had used it, where the thing had come from, whether it had ever killed anyone, and what the feeling would be like, the bang, the kick, the smell. Guns were like sex, he thought. Once you'd done it for the first time, pulled the trigger, they ceased to be a mystery.

The Kalashnikov had come into the farmhouse with Scullen, the hidden object in the long canvas carrier. The male nurse, John, had claimed it, opening the carrier, pulling the gun out, checking the mechanism through, loading the magazine from a wooden box full of bullets he produced from a cupboard under the stairs. He seemed familiar with the gun. He'd obviously used it before. And now, past midnight, the lights off, he had it propped on the window sill in the kitchen, a view of the road up from the coast, the box of bullets beside him, two spare magazines already loaded.

Twice, Connolly had asked him what was going on, what he expected to happen, but both times he'd mumbled that he didn't really know. Mr Scullen, he said, expected trouble. That was why he'd brought the weapons, the Kalashnikov and Connolly's automatic. He'd heard that the big guys – Scullen and the men on the coast – were expecting an attack, a raid, but these were serious issues, handled at the very top of the Brigade, and it didn't pay to be too nosy. Connolly had pondered this piece of half-news, wondering whether the men had got it right, whether Scullen really was under threat, or whether he'd simply confused Connolly's message to Mairead – and her impending arrival – with some other visitation. The latter thought made him uneasy. The last thing he wanted was John welcoming Mairead with half a magazine from the big gun on the kitchen window sill. Better, perhaps, to stay close. To watch the man. To save him from an ugly mistake.

Earlier in the evening, with Jude, he'd heard the gunfire in the hills, two loud explosions and half a minute or so of rapid small arms fire, but since then there'd been nothing. Just the wind outside in the trees, and the soft brush of rain on the windows. Now, relaxed again, knowing it was probably too late for Mairead, he left the kitchen and returned to Jude's room.

She was lying in bed by the window. Her eyes were wide open, but she didn't appear to be breathing. Connolly hesitated by the doorway. He was certain now that she was dying. Looking at her, she might even be dead. It was a curious thought, not simple, not even sad, just a fact, an extension of what he'd seen of her body, the remorseless consequence of the hole in her flank, of the noise she made when she tried to breathe, of the terrible debilitation of her paralysis. He looked at her a moment longer, and then began to step out of the room. Closing the door behind him, wondering whether he ought not to say a prayer, wondering if he knew any, he heard her voice. He opened the door again. She was looking at him. Her face was paler than ever, chalky white in the fitful moonlight. She blinked. She managed the beginnings of a smile. She tried to nod towards the window.

"Prop me up," she whispered, "I want to see."

He knelt beside her, putting his head against her cheek. She was very cold, the fever quite gone.

"See what?" he asked softly.

She tried to explain but couldn't. Her eyes went to the window. Connolly looked at her for a moment, then sat on the bed, slipping his hands behind her shoulders, pulling her body up towards him. She was very light. She seemed to have lost weight in the last day or so. She fell forward against him, her head on his shoulder, her breathing audible, a rasping noise in the back of her throat. The smell was back, too, overpowering.

Connolly plumped the pillows against the bedhead, building a pile of them to support her. Then he laid her gently back against them, a sitting position, giving her a clear field of view from the window. She looked out into the darkness. Her eyes were very black. She moistened her lips. She had something else to say. Connolly bent close. Her breath was warm on his ear.

"Have . . . you . . ." She closed her eyes, unable to finish the sentence.

He looked at her. "Phoned?"

She nodded, smiling, grateful. He shook his head. "No," he said. "But I will."

She closed her eyes again. She was still smiling. "Neat," she said softly, "real neat."

Buddy swam steadily north-east, underwater, at a depth of seven feet. He maintained the depth as accurately as he could, checking the single needle gauge on his wrist, not wanting to go any deeper, to bite into his precious oxygen reserve. At seven feet, in theory, he was easy meat for passing vessels but the harbour had been empty of shipping when he submerged, and if anything big turned up he'd hear the screws long before they became a real problem.

He swam on, 73 degrees on his compass. The water was colder than he'd expected, taking longer to warm up in the layer between his body and the thick neoprene wet suit, and the visibility was non-existent. At night, of course, that was all he could expect, but when he used the big waterproof torch he'd attached to his weightbelt, he could see the tiny particles of mud and other matter hanging in suspension, clouding the water ahead.

After ten minutes or so, he paused, checking the flow rate on the circuit valve. The rebreather was working fine, and the oxygen tasted OK, but even so there was something in him, some buried nerve, that mistrusted the whole system. Most of his diving had been surface supply, a big fat armoured hose right there to his helmet, a bloke on the other end who knew what he was doing, all kinds of checks and balances in the system, all kinds of clever strokes the guys up top could pull if he got into trouble.

This, though, was very different. Instead of a clean supply of gases, he was breathing – at least in part – the output of his own lungs, his own exhaust. Sure, there was stuff in the circuit to deal with that, and Harry's gear was superb. But if anything went wrong – if he'd misjudged the flow rate, or exceeded the depth, or the Baralyme gave out before it should – then he was stuffed. And if any of those things happened, he knew very well that there'd be no warning, no voice in his ear from the surface, no chance to put things right. You'd simply go funny where it most mattered, in your head, and your body would pack up, and your weights would drag you down, and that would be the end of it.

That, they said, was what had happened to Buster Crabb, this same harbour, years back. The man had hit trouble with his rebreather. He'd been poking around with a tape measure under the arse of some Russian battleship, and the set had gone wrong, and he'd surfaced to try and sort it out, right there, broad daylight, yards from the watching Commie sailors. Whatever he'd done hadn't fixed it, and months later they'd found his body down the coast somewhere. Fish had eaten the bits outside the suit. The rest, they said, was remarkably well preserved.

Buddy finned onwards, carrying the charges, one in each hand, trying to push the thought to the back of his mind, wondering whether bits of water could be haunted. Buddy played with the thought a moment, watching the blackness swirl past his mask, wondering what kind of bottle it took for a man to do this for a living, in peace or in war, confronting the longest odds in the book, natural or man-made. If the tide didn't get you, he thought, or the depth or the gear or some other rogue factor, then there were a bunch of guys on the surface just waiting for you to make a mistake.

He shuddered at the thought, trying to scale down the size of his present difficulties, trying to minimize the hazards, trying to pretend it was, after all, a piece of piss. He looked at his watch. He'd been swimming now for eighteen minutes. With luck he should be two-thirds of the way there.

Miller and Thompson came on the farmhouse by accident, a wrong turning in the dark, a mistake that put them barely two hundred metres from their target.

They crouched behind an outcrop of rock, peering down. The house was painted white. There were pines across the road. There was a low wall at the front, and a long oblong of turf at the back before the mountain fell away again, towards the valley floor. The house was in darkness. The walls looked thick. The windows were small. Miller could hear running water.

Thompson tapped him on the shoulder. He looked round. The younger man nodded down, towards the house.

"Is that it?"

"Yes."

"What do we do?"

Miller said nothing for a moment. The last time he'd spoken to Camps and Venner, they'd been on the mountain-side, below the road, advancing on a parallel line. They'd made no contact of any kind. They had to be pretty wet. They could use some action. Miller switched on the radio and muttered their call sign into his throat mike. A voice came back at once, Venner's, the radio distorting the rich Cornish vowels. Miller asked him where he was. Venner said he could see the house, about six hundred metres away. The ground between them was bare and open. If the cloud thinned any more, and there was moonlight, it wouldn't be easy. Miller nodded in the darkness, agreeing.

"Stay where you are," he muttered, closing the trans-mission.

Miller turned to Thompson. "I'm going down," he said. "Cover me."

Thompson looked at him. So far, the evening had worked out nicely. They were three up, away from home, and there were still four hours of darkness left. Miller, he knew, was going for broke. This single operation was his personal answer to the blokes up north who'd been making it so hard for him, to the zombies over in Whitehall who flannelled their way from one disaster to another. What they were doing tonight was the bottom line. They were talking the kind of language the Provos understood. They were giving Charlie the kind of send-off he deserved.

Thompson eyed Miller a moment longer, then handed him the night glasses. Miller would recce the place, Thompson would listen out on the radio. If Miller wanted him down there, he'd tell him. Otherwise, he'd be back. Miller cocked his head a moment, listening, then disappeared into the darkness. Thompson eased the Armalite, and worked his way left, across the mountainside, looking for the best fire position. He found it in the cover of the pine trees. He lay full length on the damp ferns, spreading his legs behind him, tucking the butt of the gun into his shoulder. From here, he could see the long, exposed flank of the house. It was very dark now, the cloud thickening, a curtain of rain sweeping up the valley. He could hear it pattering on the branches overhead, feel the first cold drips on the back of his neck. He peered down, immediately below him, where he knew Miller must be. He could see nothing.

In the kitchen of the farmhouse, the man with the Kalashnikov cursed the rain. It drove hard against the window, obliterating what little he could see. Minutes earlier, he thought he'd spotted movement, high on the hillside. He had good night vision. He'd been in these mountains since childhood. He had a quick eye for the wild sheep that haunted the rocky slopes. Only this hadn't been a sheep. He was sure of it. Wrong colour. Wrong shape. Wrong everything.

He reached forward and opened the window. A flurry of rain blew sideways into the kitchen. Then it cleared, and there was a sudden lull between squalls, and he strained his eyes, peering out, looking for that tell-tale sign, something human, some small part of the landscape that moved, and gave the game away. For a full minute, nothing happened. He eased his legs from under him, adjusting the half squat he preferred for the longer-range stuff. Then he saw it again, much closer, a place he'd not expected, barely a hundred metres away. There was nothing as precise, as definite, as a face, or an arm, but he knew instinctively that it was human. And that it shouldn't be there.

He let the gun settle into his shoulder, and took the shallowest of breaths, the way they'd taught him up in Donegal. He eased the gun a fraction lower, anticipating the target's next move, closing on the farmhouse. Then he squeezed the trigger, the gentlest of pressures, a real artist. The Kalashnikov spat flame into the darkness. He'd set the fire control for single shot. He squeezed the trigger again, bracketing the target, punching out an imaginary square where he thought the shadow might be. After four shots, he stopped and withdrew the gun, and stepped back from the window. If there were others out there, now was the time he'd find out.

Thompson saw the first shot before he heard it, the muzzle flash from one of the lower windows. Three more followed. He inched the Armalite left, sighting it squarely on the window. He could see nothing, just the open window and an oblong of darkness beyond it. He paused a moment, his finger on the trigger. The temptation was to fire, but he knew that these guys were good, that they'd fire and move, that he should look elsewhere, not react too quickly, not simply respond, playing their game, confirming what they wanted to know, that the attack was real. Real guns. Real bullets.

He eased his position slightly, wondering about Miller, whether he was all right. Overhead, it had stopped raining. The clouds were thinner now, and he could see moonlight puddling the valley to the west. There were three windows on the ground floor of the farmhouse. The firing had come from the window on the left. He brought the Armalite right, across the centre window. The branches began to stir over his head, releasing a shower of drips, and suddenly the moonlight was upon them, spilling over the farmhouse. Thompson blinked. In the centre window, he could see a face. No question. The details were indistinct at two hundred yards, and he cursed the lack of a night sight, but the moonlight had told him, and he knew the moonlight was right.

Once in a million years, the opposition made a real

mistake, a blunder so elementary you found it hard to believe. And when it happened, if it ever happened, the worst possible move was to ignore it, or to mistrust it, thinking that life had somehow set you up. Thompson blinked, his eyes fixed on the window, the oval of face framed by the darkness. No. Life had not set him up. No way. Not tonight. Not with the Guvnor exposed and the man with the big gun eager to empty the rest of the magazine.

Thompson centred the foresight on the face in the window. He closed one eye. His finger curled inside the trigger guard. He squeezed very slowly, very gently. There was a bang. The face disappeared.

After twenty-three minutes in the water, Buddy had still not found the carrier. He looked at his watch, convinced that he hadn't made a mistake. He studied his compass, double checking the course. On both counts, he was spot on. He slowed in the water, long lazy strokes with the big fins to maintain depth, wondering what else might have gone wrong. Unless he was going mad, unless Harry had made some terrible blunder with the gases and he was already half-narcotic, he should by now be through the carrier and half-way across the dockyard. He shook his head and kicked out again. The charges were getting heavy. His legs ached. And he still wasn't there.

Less than a minute later, he saw it. For a moment, still swimming, he didn't understand what it was. Only when he was a foot or so away, and the rivets and the weed had separated from the surrounding murk, did he realize that he'd found the carrier. He transferred one of the baskets, freeing his right hand. He reached out, touching the rough surface of the steel hull and switched on the torch. The hull was painted a dull red. The marine growth was thicker than he'd anticipated. It wasn't as bad as some of the older rigs he'd worked on – a thick crust of barnacles and tubeworms and colonies of mussels – but there was a lot of soft fouling, green stuff, brown stuff, different kinds of kelp. He shone the torch downwards a moment, seeing the wall of riveted plates extending, limitless, into the murk. Then he switched off the torch and began to swim slowly south, towards the stern. He was there in less than half a minute, recognizing the change in profile as the hull tucked in around the propeller shafts. Somewhere off to the right, deep in the darkness, was the huge blade of the rudder. Buddy congratulated himself, after all, on the course he'd swum. It had taken longer than he'd expected. He had little time to spare. But this, at least, was where he'd been headed. Clever fucker.

He trod water for a minute or so, loosening the wire ties that closed the mouths of the shopping bags. When he'd got one open, he consulted his depth gauge and headed down, careful to keep the charge inside the bag, following a line of rivets to the point where the plates began to curve inwards, forming the bottom of the ship's hull. At twenty-five feet, exactly right according to the stencilled markings he'd noted on the ship's stern, he stopped, swimming south again, looking for the glands where the propeller shafts protruded from the hull. He found them almost immediately. At a range of two feet, they were huge, a structure in their own right. He swam upwards, six feet, and then north again, looking for that point of weakness where the glands were faired into the hull. When he found it, he stopped in the water.

The magnetic clamps had a surface area about the size of a dinner plate. The shaped explosive charge was attached to the topside of the clamp by a thick plastic membrane. The membrane was penetrated by the detonator, a cylindrical object about the size of a Havana cigar.

Buddy studied the hull. To work properly, the magnetic clamp had to marry with bare metal. Buddy drew his diver's knife and began to scrape away at the patch of soft fouling, fronds of greenish kelp attached to the hull by a tough stalk. On the rigs, he'd have had proper tools, a needle gun or a pneumatic wire brush, but the knife was effective enough. The kelp came away in handfuls and soon he'd cleared enough to seat the clamp. Keeping the other bag over his arm, he took the clamp and the charge from the open bag and laid it carefully against the hull. As the clamp neared the bare metal, he felt the pull of the powerful magnets, and winced at the loud, hollow clang of metal on metal. He backed off a moment, inspecting the clamp. It looked obscene, a growth, a cancer. He reached out and tugged it. It was stuck fast.

Buddy glanced at his watch. Unless he was to surface on the way back, he had barely three minutes left. He loosened the other bag, and looked at it a moment. Then he reached inside and removed the detonator. Without it the charge was useless. He backed off from the hull. Six feet away, it was invisible. Then he let the second charge go, angling the torch downwards, watching it fall slowly into the murk. One day, Buddy thought, some matelot's going to try his luck over the side. Hook and line. Gash hour to waste on some sunny afternoon. And then? He shrugged, returning to the great red wall of the carrier's hull, reaching out for the detonator, arming it, ready for the morning. One charge should do, he thought. Two was pure greed.

He glanced at his watch again. He had a minute left. He took a final look at the clamp, and then switched off his torch, backing away for the second time, turning over onto his belly, free of the charges and the shopping bags, his night's work at an end. He finned slowly upward, checking his depth gauge, adjusting his heading to hit the right course, keeping his breathing regular, drawing the darkness around him, trying to empty his mind of everything but the rhythm of his legs, and the noise of the rebreather in his ears, and the cold kiss of the water as it sluiced slowly past.

Connolly lay on his belly on the cold flagstones in the darkened hall. The firing had stopped now, but he'd heard the last shot, the solid thwack of the incoming bullet, and he knew that it had lodged somewhere in Jude's room, a wall perhaps, or a piece of furniture. Whatever had happened, he knew he had to get in there. The woman was a sitting target, for God's sake. Literally.

He crawled along the hall, towards Jude's door. In the kitchen, he could hear the man with the Kalashnikov changing magazines. He seemed totally unmoved by this terrifying spasm of violence. He seemed to understand it all, this strange new geography, shapes on the hillside, muzzle flashes in the darkness, the cold bark of high powered rifles. He'd already told Connolly to find another window and use the automatic, but Connolly had declined the offer. His flirtation with firearms was over. Charlie had cured him of that.

Pushing Jude's door open, he checked for a moment before crawling in. The room was tiny. He levered himself up, hands and knees, an untidy half-crouch, alert for the slightest noise, the slightest movement. He looked at the bed. Jude was lying back, across the pillows. There was a small dark hole beneath her right ear. In the moonlight, the pillows behind her head were black with blood.

Connolly crawled to the edge of the bed and reached up. Jude's eyes were open and her mouth was budded around some sound or other, a gasp of surprise perhaps, or the beginnings of a question, but when he touched her face she was quite cold. There was no movement, no breath. The bits of her that had survived paralysis, the bits of her he'd got to know and like, had quite gone.

At the window, a small square pane was shattered where the bullet had torn through, and the wind from the west was chill. He looked at Jude again, pulling the sheet up, over her face, trying to keep his own body away from the window, not wanting another bullet, more glass, his own face, neatly drilled.

Jude shrouded, Connolly crawled back across the room, and into the hall. He knew now that he must get out. It was an overpowering feeling. He'd done what he could for Jude, sat with her, listened to her, learned about Buddy, the second marriage, the stables, what they'd planned together, the way they wanted their life to go. Sadly, in the time it takes to fall off a horse, it had all come to an end, and there'd been a very different kind of marriage, no less fond, no less intense, but hemmed in by the brutal truths of spinal injury. She'd agreed to go to Boston, she'd said, to please Buddy. It was what he wanted. It was the last big effort he felt he owed them both. But she'd never really believed that it would work. The only real cure, she'd said, was dying. Only then could they both – in their own ways – be released.

Connolly inched down the hall, hugging the shadows, back on his feet, making for the side door, knowing that this was the real message she wanted him to carry away, the real word in Buddy's ear, her parting gift. By the kitchen, he paused. John was back by the window, the Kalashnikov propped on a chair, gazing out, into the dark. There was moonlight in the kitchen and Connolly could see that he'd put on an old Sunday jacket against the cold. It was shiny at the elbows. The pockets were too big. Beside him, on the rush matting on the floor, was a plate and a glass of milk. On the plate was a pork pie, half eaten.

"What's happened?" the man said quietly, without turning round.

Connolly hesitated. "She's dead," he said at last.

"Oh." The man nodded. "You'll be off, then?"

"Yes."

"OK." The man tensed a moment, seeming to see something, then relaxed again.

Connolly stared at him, expecting some other comment, good luck perhaps, or fuck off. But the man said nothing, squatting on the rush matting, waiting patiently for whatever happened next. You're finished, Connolly thought, you're a dead man. Whoever's out there, whoever reached in and took Jude, will have you next. He smiled at the back of the man's head.

"Bye," he said, "Tiocfaidh Ar La."

Ingle awoke with a start, pitch darkness. He reached out and found the light switch, blinking in the sudden glare. Three of the miniatures were lined up on the bedside cabinet. Through the empty bottles, he could see the face of the digital clock. The clock said 2:41.

Ingle sat up in bed. The thing was quite clear to him now. It had taken more time, and more Scotch, than it should have done, but now he had it. Or most of it. He reached for the telephone, keyed an outside line, and dialled the number on the ATU Duty Desk. It was manned round the clock. Even Sundays.

A voice answered, a woman. Ingle introduced himself, using the special code, changed weekly.

"I need advice," he said.

"Yes, sir?"

"Someone in the diving world. Someone who knows a lot about explosives."

There was a pause. Then another voice, a man. "You've a choice," he said, "SBS or one of our own blokes."

Ingle frowned a moment. SBS was the Special Boat Squadron, the Royal Marine equivalent of the SAS. They spent a lot of time on and under warships, and they knew a great deal about explosives.

'SBS," he said.

"Thanks," the voice said drily.

Ingle grinned. "No offence," he said. "Your bloke needs his sleep."

"You're phoning *now*?"

"Yeah."

There was a brief pause. Ingle could hear pages being turned. Then the voice came back. Ingle reached for a pen.

"0202 747551," the voice said, "it's a Dorset number." There was a pause. "Good luck."

The phone went dead. Ingle emptied the last millimetre of Scotch in one of the bottles and dialled the Dorset number. To his surprise, the number answered on the second ring. Another man. Less sleepy than he should be.

"Yes?" he said briefly.

"My name's Ingle. I work for Special Branch. I'm sorry to phone you so late."

"That's OK." Slight pause. "What do you want?"

Ingle hesitated a moment, then said he had cause to believe an attack might be pending on one of the ships in the Task Force. He paused again.

"Would that be feasible?" he said at last.

The man came back at once, clipped, businesslike. "Yes," he said.

"What would you need?"

"Explosives. Expertise."

"How much expertise?"

"Fair bit."

Ingle nodded, still nursing the empty bottle, thinking of the man Buddy. "What about gear?" he said at last, changing the subject. "The right kit?"

"Wouldn't be a problem. Given the right contacts."

"Detonators?"

"Easy."

Ingle nodded again, gazing at the curtains. Hideous pattern. Turquoise zig-zags. Yuk. "What's the maximum setting?" he said slowly. "On a timer?"

There was a brief silence. For once, the man at the other end was having to think. Then he came back. There was real interest in his voice.

"You wouldn't need a timer," he said, "not if you were clever."

"No?"

"No. You'd use a remote signal. Simpler. Safer." He paused. "More fun, too."

Ingle frowned, not keeping up. "*Fun?*"

"Yeah." The other man laughed. "Have you ever seen the entrance to Portsmouth Harbour?"

Buddy knew he was in trouble when he heard the double splash behind him. The splashes were loud, real weight, real impact, and he knew at once what they meant. He'd been detected. They'd sent in divers of their own. And now they were going to find him.

He swam faster, losing a little depth, increasing his breathing rate, adjusting the flow valve to feed more of the precious oxygen to his tired muscles. The darkness pressed in around him, adding to this terrible sense of isolation. They must have heard me fixing the clamp, he thought. They must have picked up the scrape of the dagger. He was out of date on the systems they used, but he imagined they must now have some precise means of locating intruders, some hi-tech refinement on the crude old techniques of sonar pickets, and blokes on deck watching for bubbles. These are the eighties, he thought. They'll have field sensors, or magic eyes, or some kind of electronic moat ringing the ship at the touch of a button. They'll know exactly where I am. They'll know exactly what I've done. And if they don't kill me now, it'll be a state trial, and a footnote in the history books when they come to chronicle this silly fucking war. Buddy Little, patriot extraordinaire. The man who tried to sink half the Task Force.

He swam on, listening to his own heart beat, wondering whether it might be better to double back, and relocate the clamp, and extract the detonator, and surface by the carrier, and give himself up. In mitigation, he'd claim extenuating circumstances. He'd tell them the truth. He'd say he'd been under stress, engaged in a war of his own, hopeless odds, pitting the best marriage on earth against armies of medical scientists. All he'd ever wanted, he'd tell them, was his wife back. Have you ever met these bastards, he'd ask them, have you ever tried to reason with these guys in the white coats? Hopeless, all of them. Givers-in and takers-away. My wife. Her body. What right did any of them ever have? To tell him it was hopeless? That she'd never get better? What kind of medicine was that?

He swam on, pursued by demons, his own body beginning to weaken in the icy water, knowing that the moment of compromise was long gone, that he was committed to this deal of his, this deal he'd struck with the men across the water, the Queen's enemies, and that there was no turning back. The divers behind him might find the charge. Equally, they might not. Either way, when the Fleet left, he'd still be out there, with his flag in one hand, and his little control box in the other. Old times' sake, he thought, the phrase looming out of nowhere, the blackness in his own head. Old times' sake. My times. Jude's times. Our times. Not their times. Not the service. Not the blokes. Not the eight years he'd spent in uniform. No. Important, that. Jude. For her. Yeah.

Buddy hit the piling, not seeing it. The impact drove the rim of the mask into his face and tore the regulator from his mouth. He swallowed water. He felt himself beginning to sink. His fingers reached down for the weightbelt and released it. Freed, he kicked upwards, the first stirrings of tide pressing him onto the big concrete piling. He pushed at it, tearing his hands on the razor-sharp barnacles. He opened his mouth, feeling his lungs beginning to burst with the pressure inside, letting the oxygen bubble out. Then he broke surface, gasping for air.

He wiped the water from his face, tasting his own blood. Looming over him was the bow of a boat. He peered at it in the darkness, hearing the lap of the water against the hull. He reached out and touched it. It was a big boat, metal, with a heavy timber fender skirting the hull. He swam along it, up the harbour, very slowly, getting his breath back, looking for bearings. Then he had it. The boat was the Gosport ferry. He was off course, about a hundred metres, the tide probably, or his own mania. Either way he had to get back, up harbour, back to the marina. He reached for the release on the rebreather, and pulled it, feeling the weight of the big cylinders leaving his shoulders, Harry's gear tumbling down to the bottom of the harbour. Easier now, he thought. Might even make it.

Fifteen minutes later, exhausted, he found the yacht. He hung in the water beside it for a minute or two, his arm crooked round the ladder at the stern. Eva's face hung above him, pale, in the darkness. She'd been worried, she said. She'd been wondering what had happened. Buddy removed his flippers and his mask, passing them up. Then he slowly climbed the ladder, back onto the yacht.

Down below, the curtains drawn, Eva closed the door and poured hot water into a mug of coffee. There was a bottle of brandy, too, and a glass. Buddy lay full length on the bunk, soaking it through. His left hand was covered in blood, and Eva bent to it, staunching the flow with a tea towel, asking him how it had gone. Buddy simply nodded.

"OK," he said. "It went OK."

A little later, wrapped in blankets, warmed by the brandy, his wet suit folded into one of the forward lockers, he mentioned the other divers.

"Two of them," he said, "enough to stuff us."

He sniffed, swallowing another mouthful of brandy, his responsibilities at an end. Eva frowned. "What divers?" she asked.

Buddy explained about the two splashes. The guys in the water. The noises they must have picked up. The search they'd now be completing. Odds were they'd find the charge. Bound to. Eva laughed. "They're rubbish," she said, "your divers."

Buddy frowned, taking offence.

"No they're not," he said, "they're bloody good. Best in the world."

"I meant garbage. Waste." She smiled. "The stuff they chuck overboard."

She explained she'd been watching the carrier throughout, using the glasses he'd left. Half an hour or so after he'd gone, she'd seen two men with something heavy stagger to the edge of the flight deck. Whatever it was, they'd left it, returning with another. Then both objects had gone overboard. The splashes had been audible from the yacht. She remembered them quite clearly.

"Rubbish," she repeated, "*Abfälle*."

Buddy looked at her, wondering whether to believe her or not, admitting in his heart that it was probably true, but knowing – worst of all – that the feeling inside him was one of disappointment.

"Great," he said, reaching for the bottle again, "I thought they might have found the bloody thing."

Connolly followed the road, away from the cottage, away from the shooting, moving very slowly, a yard at a time, crouched low amongst the rocks. Every step he took, the mountainside became steeper, the footing more uncertain. Soon, he knew, he'd have to cross the road.

He glanced over his shoulder. The farmhouse was a hundred yards behind him now, big and solid in the moonlight. There'd been no more firing, no more fingers of flame from the darkness. Whoever it was, he thought, whoever had been out there, whoever had killed Jude, must have gone. They'd got what they'd come for. They'd tasted blood. And now they were away.

Cautiously, keeping as low as he could, Connolly climbed up to the road. The road was still wet from the rain. He paused a moment, then ran across, into the shadows on the other side. There were trees here, a stand of pines, and then the mountain climbed away again, up into the dark.

Connolly crouched beneath the trees, catching his breath. He'd no idea what lay at the end of the road. He knew only that he had to get away, to find a phone again, to find Buddy and deliver Jude's message. After that, the thing – his life, the future – was a total blank.

As he got to his feet, a sudden gust of wind, up from the valley, shook the rain from the branches overhead. The raindrops pattered around him. He shivered, moving again, up the mountain, still following the line of the road, one cautious foot in front of the other, silent on the thick carpet of pine needles.

He didn't hear the man behind him. Didn't see him, or even sense him. All he felt was a hand over his mouth, and something hard in the small of his back. He tried to struggle, to twist free, but the grip simply tightened. He fell full length, his face pressed against the damp earth, a knee in his back, something metallic nudging the skin behind his right ear. A hand reached down and pulled him over. He looked up. There was a face in the darkness, an oldish face, hair swept back. The man was wearing a leather jacket. He was holding a gun. The gun was pointing at Connolly's mouth. It was a big gun. It looked like the gun he'd used on Charlie, the gun he'd left in the house. He blinked, knowing that this was the end, that he was going to die, the way Charlie had died, the bullet tearing into his skull, dissolving his brain into a thin mist of blood and bone. He relaxed, lying back, closing his eyes. I've deserved this, he thought, I've had it coming. He held his breath, trying not to be frightened, knowing that he owed himself a little dignity, a little grace. Nothing happened. He opened his eyes. The gun was still there. The face, too, quite impassive.

"Where's Scullen?"

"I don't know."

The gun wavered a moment. The man began to frown. There was a silence.

"You're English," he said, "your name's Connolly."

Connolly nodded, blinking.

"Yes," he said blankly, "it is."

TWENTY-SIX

It was nearly dawn by the time Ingle found Buddy's cottage in the New Forest. He'd taken Kee along with him for company. Kee was asleep.

Ingle pulled the car to a halt beside a square of outbuildings to the left of the cottage. The buildings were painted white, breeze block with a dark tile roof. Stables, thought Ingle, remembering the article again. He nudged Kee. Kee opened one eye and grunted. He had a headache from the whisky. He needed more sleep. He was less than eager.

"We're here," Ingle said briefly.

The two men got out of the car. Ingle led the way to the front door. To the east, behind the cottage, the sky was lightening by the minute, a cold grey dawn beneath a ledge of cloud. Ingle glanced at his watch. It was 6.35.

He rang the front door bell, then knocked. He rang again, hunched against the cold in his long black raincoat. He hadn't washed or shaved, hadn't bothered. His hair fell lank around his shoulders. He still stank of whisky. There were noises inside, footsteps along the hall. A light came on. The door opened.

Ingle stepped inside without an invitation, pinning the man in the hall against the radiator.

"Who are you?" he said.

The man looked at him. He was wearing a red dressing-gown and not much else. His hair was thinning, and he wasn't tall, but he had big hands, and he was solidly built.

"Reynolds," he said, "Gus Reynolds. Who the fuck are you?" Ingle looked at him a moment. Kee was beside him, stifling a yawn. If it came to violence, it might take longer than he'd like. He reached inside the coat for his ID.

404

"My name's Ingle," he said, "Special Branch." He paused, softening his voice. "I phoned."

Gus blinked, outraged, half past six in the morning, private property, this tramp disturbing his sleep.

"What do you want?" he said.

"Do you know Buddy Little?"

"Yes. I told you. On the phone."

"Where is he?"

Gus looked at him, catching up fast. He'd led a blameless life but – like most divers – he'd never had much time for authority.

"Why?" he said.

Ingle glanced down the hall. Kee closed the front door.

"Anywhere we can talk?" he said. "Anywhere cosy?"

Gus hesitated a moment, then shrugged, pulling Jude's dressing-gown more tightly around him, knotting the belt. He led the way into the kitchen, and switched on the light.

"This going to take long?" he said. "You want tea?"

Ingle nodded, wondering if the offer stretched to toast. He hadn't eaten properly for twelve hours. He was starving. Gus plugged in the kettle.

"Why do you want to know about Buddy?" he said again.

Ingle shrugged. "General inquiries," he said. "Nothing serious."

Gus looked at him, one hand on the teapot. "This hour?" he said. "You've gotta be joking."

Ingle nodded at Kee. "We work flexitime," he said, "it's part of the contract."

There was a long silence. Gus dropped tea bags in the pot and sorted out some cups. Ingle looked round. There were three or four photos, up on the shelves. All of them featured the woman in the article. In colour, she looked quite tasty. Two of the shots showed another guy, shorter, close-cropped hair, open face, big smile. Ingle picked up one of the photos. It had been taken abroad somewhere. There were palm trees in the background and the back end of a camel. The man was wearing knee-length shorts, red and blue. He was powerfully built, wide chest, real shoulders. He had his arm round the woman. The woman was wearing a white bikini. From the look on their faces, they'd just spent half the day in bed.

Ingle turned to Gus. "This him?"

Gus glanced at the photo. "Yeah," he nodded, "Morocco. Honeymoon."

"Nice lady."

"His wife." Gus reached for the kettle. "The best."

"Had an accident, didn't she?"

"Yeah."

"Tragic."

"Yeah."

Gus poured boiling water into the teapot. Ingle watched him. "So where is he?" he said at last. "You still haven't told me."

Gus said nothing, stirring the pot. Then he turned round. "Buddy's my best mate," he said, looking Ingle in the eye. "I want to know what kind of trouble he's in."

Ingle shrugged. "If I knew," he said, "I'd tell you. Fact is, I don't know."

"But he might be in trouble?"

"Yeah," Ingle nodded, "he might."

"Serious trouble?"

"Yeah."

"Something he's done?"

"Something he's involved in." Ingle paused. "Might be involved in."

Gus nodded, thinking about it. Then he looked up. "But something important enough to bring you out here? This time in the morning?"

Ingle gazed at him. "Yeah," he said. "Obviously."

There was another silence. It was daylight now, outside the window. Looking out, Ingle could see a row of horse boxes, and a neat pile of bales beside a standpipe. The place looked empty.

"You mentioned Warsash . . ." he said slowly, "on the phone."

He looked round. The expression on Gus's face told him what he wanted to know. He smiled. Easy, he thought. Fucking easy. Gus poured the tea, uncomfortable, knowing he'd given Buddy away, some small betrayal.

"What's he doing there?" Ingle said.

Gus shook his head. "Dunno," he muttered.

Ingle looked at him a moment, knowing he wasn't going to get any further. He reached up for the photos, the shots of Buddy and his wife. He gave them to Kee. Gus didn't say a word. Ingle shepherded Kee towards the door, brushing past Gus at the sink.

"Nice idea," he said, "the tea."

Gus looked round and Ingle grinned at him, heading for the hall. Warsash, he thought. Time for breakfast.

Buddy slept for four hours, curled up under a pile of blankets on the triangle of mattress in the bow of the yacht. Eva awoke him at seven, with coffee. She'd been up all night, watching the big carrier across the harbour, the binoculars at her side in the freezing cockpit. She'd seen nothing that indicated any special alert, no activity around the stern, no divers in the water, and she was as sure as she could be that Buddy's visit had gone undetected.

"We're OK," she said, bending over him with the coffee. "You did just fine."

Buddy peered up at her. His sleep had been curiously dreamless, a heavy black void into which he'd disappeared without trace. He'd not thought about the swim across, the charges, the dull redness of the carrier's hull, looming over him in the darkness. He'd not thought about the clamp he'd abandoned, tumbling away beneath him, the scrape of the knife on the bare metal plates, the urgent paranoia of his swim back. He'd thought about nothing, and now – waking up – the episode seemed a thousand years away, a chapter from some fantasy novel. He took the coffee. It was hot and sweet.

"What time is it?"

"Seven."

"You should go soon. The tide turns at eight."

He propped himself up on one elbow, wiping a clear patch in the cabin window and peering out. The water level had dropped since midnight. It was low tide, the pilings on the marina green with weed. Eva looked at him a moment, then shook her head.

"We're staying," she said.

"We?"

"Yes. You and me. I've been thinking about it. It's better to do it from here."

Buddy laughed. "Why?" he said.

"Because . . ." she shrugged, "it's just better."

Buddy took another gulp of coffee and wiped his mouth. The transmitter was on the table, beside the chart. Harry had already tuned in to the frequency of the detonator. Under normal conditions, it would be OK up to a mile. He looked at Eva. "You don't trust me?" he said. "Is that it?"

She shrugged, and said nothing. Buddy reached for the transmitter. It was lighter than it looked, black, about the size of a paperback novel. It came with a length of rubber-coated cable.

"You want to do it from here?" he said.

She nodded. "Yes."

"There's a problem."

"What?"

"The charges are on the wrong side." He nodded out, across the harbour, towards the carrier. "I fixed it on the port side. When she sails, the port side will be furthest away from us. I need to be in Pompey. Over there. Across the water. Otherwise, the mass of the ship will block the signal." Eva looked at him, frowning. Buddy wondered whether she ever smiled, ever relaxed, enjoyed herself. Probably not, he thought. Poor cow. She looked at the transmitter. "I don't believe you," she said.

Buddy shrugged. "Fine," he said. "Then we'll do it your way." He paused. "Just make sure your friends know it was your decision, not mine. I want my wife back." He smiled at her, swinging his legs out from under the blanket. "OK?"

She looked at him for a moment longer, doubtful. Then she shrugged, extending her hand for the empty mug.

"OK," she said, "but I'll come with you. We'll do it your way. From over there." She paused. "Both of us."

408

•

After three hours, bright sunlight through the kitchen window, Connolly began to understand.

The man in the black leather jacket, Miller, the man with the gun, had taken him back towards the farmhouse. They'd paused for several minutes behind a rock. He'd asked who else was in the place, and Connolly had told him, one man, John, in the kitchen. Miller had nodded, and muttered something into the darkness, fingering the controls on a tiny radio on the belt of his jeans. Then there'd been more firing, two positions this time, and answering barks from the Kalashnikov. Looking down, Connolly had seen shadows beside the house, and heard glass breaking, and then a single, loud explosion. After that there'd been silence, no more firing, and then another message on the radio, definitive, terminal.

"House secure," the voice had said. "Out."

Now, eight in the morning, there were three of them in the kitchen, the other two outside somewhere, up in the trees. Connolly sat at the table, Miller opposite. Camps had been through the pantry and the fridge, and was cooking breakfast. What remained of John, the male nurse, had been dragged outside and left by a pile of chopped wood, shrouded under a blanket.

Miller stirred brown sugar into a second bowl of Camps' porridge. Connolly was telling him about Jude, where she'd come from, the state of the woman, her paralysis. She'd been some kind of hostage, he said, some kind of lever on the husband she'd left behind.

"Lever for what?" Miller asked, testing the temperature of the porridge.

Connolly shrugged. "I don't know," he said. "He was a diver."

Miller nodded, saying nothing, and Connolly told him about Jude's final few hours before she'd died, what she'd told him, the message he had to get to Buddy. Miller nodded again.

"We'll find a phone," he said, "you've got the number?"

"Yes."

"Good."

Miller dipped into the porridge again and Connolly

409

leaned back in the chair. He still had no idea how the man had known his name. He'd asked twice now, but each time the question had been ignored. The men clearly knew each other and Connolly assumed they were some kind of Brit hit squad, but beyond that, their identity was a mystery. The only thing he knew for certain was their target, Scullen. The house, as he'd thought, belonged to the man. Soon, said Miller, he'd be back. Connolly leaned forward in the chair, elbows on the table, determined to find out more, but Miller beat him to it, changing the subject.

"I've a message from Mairead," he said, not looking up.

Connolly stared at him. "You're serious? Mairead?"

"Yes. She says she misses you. She was a witness at an incident. We got involved." Miller glanced up, smiling. Then he bent to the bowl again, chasing the last of the porridge. "She sends her love," he said. "Nice girl." He looked up at Connolly again. Connolly blinked. He could feel the colour leaving his face.

"What incident's that?" he said. "Was she hurt?"

"No." Miller paused. "Bloke got shot," he said, "one of our blokes."

"Oh."

"She saw it happen." He paused again, pushing the bowl away. "That's why we went to see her."

"Ah . . ." Connolly nodded.

There was a silence. Miller was still smiling at him. Nice breakfast, the smile said, good scoff. Connolly looked at the table a moment, fingering the grain of the wood.

"Is that why you're here?" he said. "Because of the shooting?"

Miller shook his head. "No," he said.

"But you're looking for Scullen?"

"Yes."

"And what will you do with him? When you find him?"

Miller frowned a moment, a look of slight detachment, the kind of frown you'd bring to a crossword, or a game of Scrabble. The frown cleared.

"We'll kill him," he said.

Connolly nodded, believing him, wondering what else

Mairead had told them. They must have talked to her after he'd phoned. She must have trusted them. He looked up.

"So you've met Mairead," he said carefully.

"Yes."

"Talked to her."

"Yes."

"She say why I was down here?"

There was another long silence. Miller looked at him. Then he shook his head. "No," he said. "She didn't." He paused, then gestured around. "It's a free country. You've done nothing wrong." He paused again. "Have you?"

Connolly shook his head, saying nothing. Then he looked up. "How do I get back?" he said.

"Back where?"

"Belfast."

Miller shrugged. "We'll give you a lift," he smiled, "if that's what you want."

Connolly hesitated. In the last thirty-six hours, he'd seen three people die. One of them he'd killed himself. The other two had died with equal violence. These men had materialized from nowhere, English accents, and closed up the house with him inside it. At no point had anyone asked him what he'd been doing, where he'd come from, and now this man across the table was asking him whether he'd fancy a lift back to Belfast, back to Mairead, after they'd disposed of the man they'd come for, utterly benign, utterly matter of fact. It was surreal. He looked up again.

"I've got to make the phone call," he said. "Buddy."

Miller got up and put the empty bowl in the sink. "Sure," he said, "we've got some cars up the road. One of the blokes'll run you into town." He glanced back at Connolly, one hand reaching for the washing-up liquid. "That OK?"

Connolly gazed at him, thinking again of Mairead. "Yes," he said.

Ingle and Kee were back in Warsash by half past eight, the car parked across the road from the offices of Cruisaway. Ingle sat behind the wheel, the visor down against the strong morning sun. What little he could see of his face in the vanity mirror suggested he could use a wash and a shave.

Half an hour later, a woman appeared at the wheel of a small Toyota. She parked in the bay immediately below the Cruisaway offices, and got out. She was middle aged, with sensible shoes and a white cable stitched cardigan and a bag. Ingle could see a pair of knitting needles in the bag. The recession, he thought. No one hiring yachts these days.

The woman produced a bunch of keys and let herself into a small door beside the fruit and veg shop. Ingle gave her a minute or so to get settled in, then glanced across at Kee. Kee was asleep. He hesitated a moment, wondering whether to wake him up, then decided against it. He got out of the car and walked across the road to the office.

The office was little more than a single room, with a small loo and a kitchen tucked away down a corridor outside. Ingle knocked once and went in. The woman was plugging in a photocopier. The knitting needles were already on her typist's chair, and there was a tiny pile of mail on the desk. The woman turned round, startled. Ingle showed her his ID. She blinked at him.

"Yes?" she said blankly.

"It's about a customer of yours," he said, "a Miss Weiss."

"Yes?"

"You remember her?"

"Yes."

"She has a boat of yours?"

The woman nodded, walking across to a filing cabinet. From the top drawer, she produced a file. Inside the file was a photograph. She gave it to Ingle. "*Sundance*," she said, "nice little boat."

Ingle looked at the photograph. It showed a middle-aged woman standing in the cockpit of a white yacht. On the back of the yacht, over the stern, was a ladder of some sort. Ingle knew nothing about yachts.

"How big?" he said, waving the photograph. "What size?"

The woman consulted the file again, her finger in the text. "Twenty-seven foot," she said at last.

"Is that big?"

412

"No. Not really."

Ingle nodded. The photocopier began to hum. "Where is it," he said, "this boat?"

The woman looked blank. "I don't know," she said, "we rarely ask."

"Abroad?"

"Oh, no." She shook her head. "Somewhere local."

"Are you sure?"

"Yes." She nodded, checking again, making certain. "We ask for a Yachtmaster's certificate for the longer trips. Miss . . ." she frowned, trying to make sense of her own writing.

"Weiss."

"Weiss . . . she only had a Coastal Skipper . . ."

Ingle glanced at the photo again. "When did she go?" he said. "Do you happen to know?"

"Yes. They went yesterday."

"They?"

"She and her husband." She paused. "Nice couple. I popped down with a spare key to the engine hatch. Just in case."

Ingle looked at her for a moment, then reached in his pocket for the photos he'd taken from the cottage. He offered her the clearer of the two shots, Buddy and Jude, half-naked, on their honeymoon.

"Is that him?" he said.

The woman looked at the photograph. Ingle could tell from her frown that she disapproved. She looked up. She was blushing.

"Yes," she said.

Buddy sat in the cabin of the yacht, the door open, sweeping the harbour with his binoculars, to and fro, across the quickly flooding tide. According to the radio, the Task Force was due to sail about noon. Only the two capital ships would leave, *Invincible* and *Hermes*. *Fearless*, the amphibious assault ship, would now be delayed twenty-four hours for, as the reporter put it, "operational reasons".

Buddy leaned back against the edge of the table, enjoying

the sun on his face. The departure time, he knew, was more or less accurate. High tide was at 12.45, and the big ships would need as much water as possible to clear the harbour narrows. Already, on the radio and in the papers that Eva had bought from the marina store, the media had set the stage for the morning's pageant. Headlines were reviving the spirit of D-Day. Editorials were warning Galtieri of a terrible revenge. Even the Church was beginning to talk about "a just war". The Prime Minister's resolve, and the Navy's success in cobbling together the beginnings of a Task Force, had touched a deep nerve, and now – looking out across the harbour – Buddy could see the results of it all.

In the dockyard, and on board the ships, there was frantic activity, squads of sailors doubling back and forth, convoys of lorries still squealing to a halt on the quayside, mobile cranes unloading pallets of stores, officers in tiny groups, heads bent, chins cupped in hands, tussling with the million last-minute crises that an operation like this would produce. On the water, staying carefully clear of the buoyed channel, were a number of smaller boasts, hired out by the hour, crammed full of relatives, friends, camera crews, reporters.

Buddy settled briefly on one of them. It was a fishing boat, clinker built, with a registration number on the bow. There was a cuddy forward, with a skipper at the wheel, and aft, in the working space, amongst the big plastic baskets and hanging nets, there was a television crew. There was a cameraman, and another bloke beside him, and a reporter with a microphone was talking to a woman in the stern. The boat was too far away to make any real sense of the details, but the woman was young, and looked pretty, and as they drifted slowly past the great grey wall of *Invincible*, Buddy could imagine the line the TV people were taking: the woman's husband off to the South Atlantic, she and the kids left behind, the terrible prospect of combat beginning to loom. The woman would doubtless be bright-eyed and resolute and prepared for the worst, but for the first time in his life Buddy had begun to wonder about the sense of it all, this headlong plunge into war. All the old guff – the flags, the headlines, the national call to arms – was as potent as ever. But what no one seemed to question

414

was where it might lead, and whether a single life – in the end – was worth a handful of islands and two million sheep. The principle of the thing – freedom, sovereignty – was obviously at stake. And principles mattered. But did they matter *that* much? Were they worth the price of a man's life? His wife's widowhood? His kid's fatherless future? Buddy, lowering the glasses a moment, didn't know. Politicians made the decisions. Politicians sent these infant sailors off to war. And the only thing he knew about politicians was that they, when the bullets started to fly, were a million miles away. Lives were easier to spend, he thought, when they weren't your own.

Buddy shrugged, retreating deeper into the cabin, glad that he wasn't a politician, that he didn't have to take the decisions. Eva was at the tiny sink, washing up the remains of breakfast. They'd said very little for the last hour or so, ever since she'd announced that she'd accompany him over the water. He knew why she wanted to be there, and in a way he didn't blame her, but there was going to be a moment of truth, a moment when he had to press the hideous white button on the transmitter, and he'd infinitely have preferred to have done it alone. Grief, his father had once taught him, was a deeply private thing. You drew the curtains. And excluded the world. And simply got on with it. At the time, fourteen years old, he hadn't a clue what the man had meant. But now he knew that it was true.

Buddy picked up the paper again, a copy of *The Times*, and began to thumb through it. Distantly, he became aware of footsteps, outside, on the wooden pontoon. The footsteps got closer. He hinged upright on the bunk, and removed the transmitter, hiding it under one of the other papers. The rest of the gear was already stowed away. He looked at Eva. She'd stopped soaping the plastic dishes. She was staring through the curtained windows, up at the pontoon. Two sets of legs came into view. They stopped. He could hear voices. They were discussing the yacht.

Eva dried her hands quickly. Then she delved behind a cushion and produced the gun. Buddy stared at her. The legs were on the move again. A steadying hand stretched out, securing a hold on the cabin roof. The yacht rocked slightly. They were coming aboard.

"Come here," Buddy hissed.

Eva looked at him, the gun still in her hand.

"Come here," Buddy said again, very low, very urgent.

She stepped down the cabin towards him. He reached up for her and took the gun, stuffing it down the side of the bunk. Then he pulled her shirt open, hard. Two buttons came off. She was wearing a thin vest underneath, without a bra. He reached down and peeled it off her. She complied without a word, naked from the waist up, undoing the zip on her own jeans, letting the front hang open, straddling him, hands at his shirt, undoing it, moving her bum, her eyes fixed on the small square mirror on the forward bulkhead. A shadow fell over the open doorway. A voice, male, beautifully modulated, enquired whether anyone was in. Buddy, his eyes on Eva's breasts, smiled.

"Yeah?" he said.

A face appeared at the door. Eva closed her eyes. Buddy leaned to the right, looking round her body. The face was young, no more than twenty-five. It peered in, not quite believing what it saw, at once apologetic.

"I'm sorry."

Buddy shrugged, feeling Eva beginning to freeze on top of him, her body quite rigid.

"It's OK," Buddy said. "What do you want?"

"I was just wondering . . ."

"Yeah?"

"When you planned to pull out?"

Buddy frowned for a moment. Under the circumstances, it was a fair question.

"I don't know," he said, looking up at Eva. "It's up to my friend here." He paused. "How do you feel, darling? Had enough?"

Eva opened her eyes. She was furious. She refused to answer. She looked round. The face had gone. The legs were back on the pontoon, hurrying away. Outside, high over the harbour, Buddy could hear yet another helicopter, the heavy chatter of a Sea King, a late arrival, just in time. Eva covered

416

her breasts. Her breasts were nice, larger than Buddy might have expected. He smiled up at her.

"Is that it then," he said, "or shall we press on?"

She got off him and began to pull her clothes on. Buddy looked at her for a moment. Then he laughed, glad of this one small act of revenge.

"You know something," he said at last, "I think you'd have preferred to shoot him."

Ingle outlined the problem while they were still on the motorway, travelling east, towards Gosport. The secretary at Cruisaway had answered his questions about the harbour. He knew the layout of the place, how to get there, where the marina was, where they might find the yacht. He'd worked out, as well, what the problems would be if – after all – he'd got it right.

"There's one marina," he said, "on the Gosport side."

Kee glanced across at him. He'd bought a copy of the *Daily Mirror*. The report on the Spurs game, a 2–1 home defeat, hadn't pleased him.

"Yeah?" he said.

"Yeah." Ingle reached across and lifted the paper from his hands, tossing it over his shoulder, into the back, a single movement, 'So listen, fuckwit."

Kee yawned. "OK," he said.

Ingle signalled left, taking the Gosport exit off the motorway, outlining the plan. If the yacht was there, it would be tied up at the marina. The marina wasn't big. They could be through it and away in ten minutes. He paused.

"If the yacht's there," Ingle said, "we'll jump it."

Kee glanced at him. They both had hand guns, though Ingle was famous for his hatred of them. He detested loud bangs. Kee shrugged.

"OK," he said, "but what happens if they're not there? Or if we don't find this yacht?"

Ingle spotted a row of shops on the left-hand side of the road and signalled again. The car began to slow. He reached down, feeling for the parcel shelf. He produced the photos of Buddy and Jude. He gave one of them to Kee.

"It's the bloke we're after," he said, "in case you were wondering." He paused. "If it happens at all, it'll be a button job. The trick is . . ." He glanced at Kee again. Kee was studying the photo. He looked up. "Not to let them press the button?"

Ingle nodded. "You got it," he said.

The car stopped outside a camera shop. Kee was still looking at the photograph.

"This won't be easy," he said, "there'll be thousands of punters. Bound to be."

"You got it," Ingle said again. "We'll need binos. The gear."

"We haven't got binos. You're half blind, and all I've got is a tatty Polaroid."

Ingle nodded past him, at the shop. Kee looked at it. The shop was full of cameras. Kee frowned.

"How does that help us?" he said.

Ingle began to get out. "They'll have binoculars," he said, "all camera shops sell binos."

"They cost a fortune."

"I know. We'll use a credit card."

Kee looked at him a moment. The motel bill had been bad enough. Ninety quid. Excluding the Scotch.

"You've *got* a credit card?" he said at last.

Ingle shook his head. "No," he said. "But you have."

Buddy and Eva took the ferry across the harbour at half past ten. The ferry was crowded, mothers and young kids mostly. A lot of the kids had flags, and Union Jack paper hats. Buddy had seen them on sale at the kiosk beside the ferry terminal. "Give the boys a cheer," the chalked slogan on the blackboard had read, "stuff it up the Argies."

They climbed the stairs to the upper deck and looked down the harbour. Old Portsmouth, the pocket of land on the harbour mouth itself, was already black with people. They lined the railings overlooking the water, three or four deep, and the top of the Round Tower was already packed. There were one or two modest blocks of flats on the harbour-side, post-war buildings, flat roofs, stop-gaps for the blitz damage, and there were flags at the windows, and people out on the balconies, talking and pointing and sipping mugs of coffee. On a scaffold tower, beside one of the pubs, Buddy could see a big television camera, the kind they used for Royal Weddings, and Coronations, and the Opening of Parliament. Buddy looked at it, shaking his head. Another State occasion, he thought. But one with a difference.

The ferry berthed on the other side, and the passengers streamed off. Buddy and Eva walked up beside the railway station and got into a cab. Buddy named a pub. The cab drove off. Eva looked at him. "Where are we going?" she said.

Buddy eased the plastic bag between his feet. In it was the transmitter. "Dress circle," he said, "the best seats."

Ingle and Kee took three minutes to find the yacht.

Kee spotted it first, tied up at the outermost berth on one of the long wooden pontoons. It was smaller than the rest of the yachts, and a good deal less grand. The sails were furled, and there was no one visible on board. They walked slowly towards it, feeling the pontoon beneath their feet, easing up and down with the incoming tide. Ten yards away, Ingle put a hand on Kee's arm.

"Steady," he said.

Kee glanced at him. His hand was already inside his jacket, clamped around the butt of his gun. If half what Ingle had told him was true, these guys would be in earnest. It was very easy to get killed if you weren't ready. He looked at Ingle.

"How do you want to play it?" he said.

Ingle studied the yacht a moment. He nodded at the fifteen feet of empty pontoon beyond its stern. "You go first," he said, "go up the end there. Cover me when I go in."

Kee looked at him, then shrugged. He walked down to the end of the pontoon. He drew the gun. He settled into a half squat. Ingle walked towards him. He had his own gun out now, held loosely, his hand down beside his body. When he got to the yacht, he climbed quickly aboard, clambering down into the cockpit. Kee watched him carefully, edging closer, giving himself a better angle on the door. Ingle looked at the door, tried it. The door was locked. He took half a step backwards then kicked it in, two kicks, twisting his body to the right, out of the firing line, his back pressed against the cabin. Kee walked towards the yacht, peering inside, the gun held out in front of him, both hands, the way they taught you on the ranges at Hendon. He paused, and looked at Ingle. It was a small yacht to hide in.

"There's no one there," he said.

"Sure?"

"Yeah."

Ingle nodded, and stepped into the cabin, a single movement. Watching him, Kee was surprised at how quick he was, how agile. He clambered carefully aboard, his gun still out. Across the harbour, on the wind, he could hear a tannoy. Able Seaman Flynn. To report to the Purser's Office. Immediately. Kee stepped down into the cabin. Ingle had already found the mask and flippers stowed away in one of the cupboards under the bunk. He held up the mask. The mask was still wet inside.

"Shit," Kee said quietly, "you were right."

Buddy and Eva joined the crowds on Spice Island, a finger of land that curled around the eastern edge of the harbour mouth, part of Old Portsmouth. On one side, it was flanked by the harbour itself. On the other was the Camber, a tiny dock of its own, a harbour within a harbour, Portsmouth's oldest. Between the two areas of water lay an area of cobbled streets, narrow-fronted houses, a couple of boatyards, and the start of the elaborate system of fortifications that stretched away to the east, armouring the city against invasion from the sea. Way back, a couple of hundred years ago, Spice Island had been notorious. The guide books called it the wickedest square mile in Europe, packed with ale houses, brothels, and any other service the sailor might demand. Now, though, it had become genteel, a middle-class enclave in an otherwise rough city.

Buddy and Eva pushed through the crowds. The pubs

were already open and there were lads from downtown standing outside in groups, joshing together, elbows and grins, enjoying the sunshine and the lager. Buddy paused, looking round, the bag in his hand. In places, the atmosphere was carnival. There were street traders with trays full of Union Jacks, balloons on strings, tiny plastic whistles, lettered T-shirts. There was an ancient van parked up on the kerb, back doors open, selling hamburgers and hot dogs. But there were older men here too, men with memories, men who weren't smiling much. And with them, often, were young women, daughters perhaps, with kids in buggies. The women weren't smiling either, standing on their toes, trying to get a good view, gazing up the harbour to where the first of the big ships, the one with the helicopters and the jet fighters, the one they'd nearly sold to the Australians, was preparing to cast off.

Buddy felt a tug at his elbow. It was Eva. "Where do we go?" she said. "Where do we stand?"

Buddy looked at her. He'd given the answer a great deal of thought. He'd studied the tide times, measured the ships, paced every inch of this cluttered square mile. He took her arm, guiding her away from the water, back through the crowd, just another couple.

Ingle took the last ferry across the harbour before the service stopped to permit the passage of the big ships. He left Kee behind him, armed with a photo and a pair of binoculars. If you see the bloke, he'd told him, try and get close to him. And if you do get close enough, and he's doing what we think he's doing, shoot him.

Now, aboard the ferry, remembering his own instructions, he tried not to think of the million things that could go wrong. In theory, of course, he should have phoned. He should have contacted his boss, or his boss's boss, explained the whole thing, told him to get onto the Navy, or the Prime Minister, or the Queen, or whoever it took, and get the thing postponed. If there really was a device, and it was on a timer, then the charge would still go off. But at least it wouldn't do what he now knew was all too possible: put a huge stopper in this busy stretch of water, sealing it off for God knows how long, turning a careful piece of military stage management into the most public humiliation.

He closed his eyes a moment, hands on the rail, hearing the press helicopters overhead, imagining what the world would make of it. For a moment, running down to the ferry, he'd been tempted to make the call, finding a phone that worked, getting past the picket of secretaries, trying to convince the sceptics on the other end that he hadn't been drinking. It would, he knew, be one of the longer calls, with unimaginable political consequences if he'd got it wrong, and when the bloke in the ticket office had told him it was now or never, that the next ferry was an hour away, he'd been relieved. The decision had made itself. He was on his own.

The ferry nudged the pontoon on the other side. Ingle hurried off, pushing his way through the crowd. Outside the railway station, he took a cab. He'd no idea where Buddy Little might be, but he'd done what he always did, put himself in the other bloke's shoes, asked himself where he would stand, where he would press the button, and he'd come up with the obvious answer. The cab driver glanced over his shoulder at him.

"Where to, guv?" he said.

"The harbour mouth."

"Which bit?"

Ingle looked at the back of his head. "Fuck knows," he said, "don't get technical."

Buddy took Eva to Hot Walls, a stretch of fortification immediately to the east of the Round Tower. The walls were impressive, twenty feet high, with a broad promenade on the top, and a fine view of the harbour mouth. Built into the walls were bricklined casemates, once equipped with cannon, dominating the deep water channel. Beneath the walls, on the seaward side, was a beach, three hundred yards or so of pebbles, littered with timber and debris from passing ships.

Buddy and Eva stepped carefully onto the beach. The

beach was already packed, the rising tide pressing people back against the massive walls. Eva paused. "Here?" she said.

Buddy nodded. "Yeah." He smiled, gazing out. "We need to be at the front. Down by the water."

Ingle had climbed to the top of the Round Tower by the time HMS *Invincible* slipped her moorings and eased down harbour, towards the open sea. On the top of the Tower, every inch of space was occupied, every head turned towards the big grey carrier. Lining the flight deck, standing at ease, were hundreds of sailors, blue uniforms, white caps, white gaiters. Behind them, rotors folded like birds, were the big Sea King helicopters. Between the helicopters, midships, were half a dozen Sea Harriers, the new jump jets, the sunshine glinting off the perspex canopies.

Ingle watched for a second or two, aware of the silence around him, the hush, almost reverential, before he heard the thin wail of the bosun's pipe and the men were called to attention, and the officers on the bridge snapped their own salute, the traditional mark of respect when warships put to sea. The crowd around him began to cheer, one or two voices at first, then more, then a huge roar as the men on the bridge began to wave, acknowledging the crowd, the mums, the granddads, the watching millions on TV.

Ingle took a deep breath, pushing to the front of the crowd, looking back, looking for the face in the photograph, the face by the palm trees, the one man who could turn this rite of passage into catastrophe. There were hundreds of faces, pressed together, some in tears. He quartered the crowd, trying to do it logically, trying not to miss anyone, trying to be thorough, but knowing all the time that he could afford only the swiftest glance, the quickest trawl. Finding nobody, neither Buddy, nor the girl, he pushed back towards the steps, oblivious of the feet he trod on, or the comments he provoked. At the steps, he paused. From here, he could see a beach. The beach was packed. Behind the beach was a long wall, some kind of fortification. On top of the wall were more people, hundreds of them. He

423

glanced over his shoulder. *Invincible* was perhaps four minutes away. He lifted the glasses and began to sweep the beach, starting at the logical place, starting at the water's edge. What would I do, he kept saying to himself, where would I stand?

He saw them almost at once. He racked the focus. He steadied his hands. They were both there. No question. They were standing at the water's edge. She had her shoes and socks off, her jeans rolled up. The water was lapping over his shoes. He had a plastic bag in his hand. The bag was open. He was looking towards the harbour mouth. He was waiting for the ships. He was ready to do it.

Ingle hesitated another half-second, fixing their position, tracing the path he'd have to take, back to the hole in the wall where you got onto the beach, where the crowd was thickest. Then he dived for the stairs, scattering a family of four, muttering an apology, his right hand checking for his gun. The gun was still there. He hoped to God he wouldn't have to use it.

At the foot of the Tower he paused again, looking for the entrance to the beach. He saw it off to his right, across the flagstones. There were people everywhere. He could hear the roar of the crowd. He could hear the heavier rumble of machinery. *Invincible*'s engines, he thought. Time running out.

He sprinted across the flagstones, hitting the back of the crowd. A man turned towards him, seeing the expression on his face, stepping quickly aside. Another man, bigger, began to raise a fist. Ingle hit him first, dropping him with a single dig, muttering another apology. "Police," he said, as the bloke folded. He pushed on, towards the rectangle of blue that was the beach and the sea beyond. The concrete gave way and he dropped, feeling pebbles beneath his feet. The crowd was thickest here, roaring with anticipation, the carrier still not in sight, but visible any second, the crowd up on the Round Tower going crazy, a frieze of waving arms, flags, balloons, kids on shoulders. Ingle took a deep breath, remembering the line he had to follow, the line that would take him to the man with the plastic bag, carving through the crowd in front of him, knowing that already it was probably too late.

At the water's edge, Buddy felt gutted. He'd known it would be like this. He'd spent the weekend anticipating exactly this scene. He'd known it would be packed and emotional. He knew there'd be mums, and wives, and kids. He knew there'd be flags, and muttered prayers, and that big incoherent roar that means God Speed, God Bless You, Come Home Safe. But the reality – this, now – was far, far worse. He wanted to throw the transmitter away, to lift it head high, and whirl it around in the bag, and then let it go, miles out, away from him. He wanted nothing to do with it any more. He wanted out.

He looked round, desperate. Eva was watching him carefully. She was carrying the gun. He knew it. He didn't care a toss about the gun. She could shoot him for all he cared. But that still didn't solve the problem. He was here because he loved his wife. He was here because she was hurt. To make her better, he had to go through with it. To make her better, he had to apply a little violence of his own. With luck, no one would die. With luck, no one would even be injured. To that extent, he knew he'd squared the circle. But the rest of it: the crowd, the flags, his Queen, his country . . . He shook his head, thinking of Jude again. Means and ends, he thought. Means and fucking ends. He looked at Eva. He nodded. It'll be all right, the nod said. You've got me by the balls. We're nearly through.

He looked to the right, at the stretch of water between the Round Tower and the low line of HMS *Dolphin* on the Gosport side. Any second now, the carrier would appear. He'd planned it all out. He'd trigger the charge only when she was fully clear. That way, at the speed she was doing, no more than six knots, she'd settle in the channel just south of the harbour mouth. With luck, the rudder crippled, she'd swing broadside on. It would take days to drag her clear.

He closed his eyes a moment, then reached down into the bag. He pulled out the transmitter. The business end was connected to the main control box by a long rubber-coated cable. It had to be submerged to work. He waded a little deeper into the sea, and let it fall into the water. He still had the control box in his hand. He looked up. The bow of the carrier had appeared. Next came the flight deck. He swallowed hard. They were doing it for real. There were men, for God's sake, sailors, lining the flight deck. He looked down again, refusing to watch, not wanting to be part of it, trying to spare himself any more grief. He looked round for the girl, Eva, wondering if she absorbed any particle of this extraordinary scene, whether it raised her temperature a single degree.

He frowned. The girl had gone. She wasn't there any more. He looked to the left. All he could see were faces. He looked to the right. More faces. Then he saw her. She was talking to a tall guy, greasy hair, long black coat. He had a wide, flat face. He was sweating. He was trying to push the girl away. He wouldn't take his eyes off Buddy.

Buddy blinked, and glanced over his shoulder. The carrier was half out now, half visible. Fifteen seconds, he thought. Come on. Come on. He looked at the crowd again. Eva was still with the guy. He had something in his hand, something black. Buddy stared at it. It was a gun.

Buddy felt the fear rise in him. He turned away. He looked at the carrier. He didn't know what to do. He glanced over his shoulder. The guy in black had the gun up now, pointing it. At him. Eva lunged at him, pulling at his arm. The arm came down. Distracted, the guy chopped her, a short, vicious blow. Buddy heard her scream. He looked seaward again. The carrier was clear. He shut his eyes. His finger found the button. He heard the cheers of the crowd, rolling along the beach. He heard the ship's engines. He heard a child, quite clearly, call for his dad. And then he pressed the button.

Nothing happened.

426

TWENTY-SEVEN

Buddy ran along the beach, splashing through the shallows, keeping pace with the big grey carrier. He'd snatched a flag from some kid who'd been looking the other way. He'd got rid of the plastic bag with the radio transmitter, hurling it away, sending it in a long arc, out, over the sea. The crowd on the beach cheered him on, roars of approval, this sturdy little man with the Union Jack, galloping by, soaking wet beneath the knees, huge grin on his face, waving his flag like mad, just like the rest of them. Buddy half saw them, half didn't, this blur of bodies. He was looking out to sea. He was looking at the carrier. The carrier was intact. He was deliriously happy.

At the end of the beach, the crowd thinned. Here, the tide was lapping at the foot of the walls. Buddy ran through the icy water, and up the steps beside the stubby pier, pausing for a moment before ducking out, through the sally-port, back onto the street. Behind him, the beach was a mass of colour, reds, whites, blues, the cheers still rolling out across the water, heads turning back now, towards the harbour mouth, waiting for the second of the two ships, HMS *Hermes*, the old lady of the Task Force. *Invincible* was already picking up speed, away in the mist, the grey water boiling at her stern, leaving behind the flotilla of tugs and launches that had shepherded her through the harbour narrows. Buddy watched her go, the blue line of sailors on the flight deck at ease again, her voyage south finally under way. He muttered a prayer, wished her God Speed, glancing back along the beach again, looking for the girl, the bloke in the black coat, finding neither.

Out in the street, it was quieter. Buddy headed east, skirting the Square Tower, moving quickly, a steady jog, staying close to the waterfront. Up on his right, on the grassy slopes of Long Curtain, the crowds were thick again, the same faces, the same flags, the same anxious sense of pride, of not quite knowing where this giddy adventure might end. Buddy glanced over his shoulder. The road behind him was empty.

At the end of Long Curtain, the last of the elaborate nineteenth-century fortifications, there was a funfair, a couple of acres of Ferris wheels, and space rides, and roller coasters. On the seaward side, there was a wooden jetty, terminus for the cross-Solent pleasure trips, and the crowd were pressed against the railings, watching *Hermes* nosing out of the harbour, another lump in the national throat. Buddy pushed quickly through, the flag still in his hand. For him, the spectacle, the pageant, had ended. He'd pushed his button. He'd paid his respects. And now he needed a telephone.

He found a box a couple of minutes later, beside a public lavatory, set back from the seafront. He pushed inside and lifted the receiver. The phone worked. He fumbled for change, finding a fifty-pence piece. He inserted the coin, dialling his own number, turning round, watching the road behind him. This was something new, real paranoia, and he wasn't sure he liked it.

The number answered. He bent to the phone, recognizing Gus's voice. Gus sounded anxious.

"Buddy?"

"Yeah?"

"What the fuck's going on? There's been a bloke here from—"

Buddy cut him short, watching the road again, seeing a police car cruising slowly by, a hundred yards away.

"Listen," he said, "you've got to meet me. Soon as possible."

There was a brief silence. Then Gus came back again. His voice had changed. The anxiety had gone. They might have been back on the rigs. Nasty little problem. Something to get his teeth into.

"Right," he said, "tell me where."

"Pompey. There's a pub called the Castle. It's in Somerstown. You know Somerstown?"

"Yeah."

"OK." He paused. The police car had gone. "Soon as possible, mate. Oh . . ." he paused again, "and bring some money."

"How much money?"

"Lots."

He put the phone down and pushed out of the box. *Hermes*, the second carrier, was out in the deep water channel now, the flight deck packed with helicopters. The crowd was surging along the promenade, trying to keep pace, and half a mile out to sea, Buddy glimpsed the arse end of *Invincible* disappearing into the murk. Buddy watched her for a moment, glad, and then turned on his heel and began to walk quickly away, across the Common, towards the pub. As he did, he saw a television crew roll by, in a beige Volvo estate. The cameraman was standing on the front passenger seat, the upper half of his body through the open sunshine roof. The camera on his shoulder was pointing seawards, panning across the crowd on the promenade, the grey ghost of the carrier vanishing into the mist beyond. Buddy smiled at the irony of it, the cameraman's eagerness. He could hear him telling the driver to slow down, to flatten the bumps in the road, to help him get the pictures the world was waiting for. Wrong story, he thought, remembering the big guy in black, the length of his hair, the expression on his face. He watched the Volvo a moment longer, then set off again, inland.

Ingle found the squad car back in the street, away from the crowd. He ran towards it, the water still squelching in his trainers. The two officers looked up at him, suspicious, as he got to the car, leaning against it, hands outstretched against the roof, panting. He could hear the crowds behind him, down on the beach, up on the fortifications. The diver, the man in the water, had fled. Ingle had tried to follow him, stepping out from the crowd, into the shallows, same trick, but the girl had got in the way again, stopping him, throwing her hands around him, making it impossible for him to move. In the end he'd had to hit her again, a short vicious jab, lots of weight, and she'd gone down like a stone, moaning softly. Several men in the crowd had seen him do it, and he knew he had to get out before one of them summoned the bottle to lump him. And so he'd pushed back towards the street, checking on the ships as he went, the two carriers, safe.

Now, the younger of the two officers inspected his Special Branch ID card through the passenger window. Ingle tapped his watch. He needed the radio. He needed to close the city. Before the diver surfaced somewhere else. The door opened. The officer got out, reaching for his cap. Ingle looked at him. The thing was a game, and he was tiring fast. "Pass a message?" he said.

The officer nodded, back towards the car, the force radio tucked under the dashboard. "Sure," he said, "help yourself."

Connolly sat in the lounge bar of the Skelligs Hotel, drinking tea. He'd phoned Buddy's number as soon as they'd arrived. He'd got through after the usual tussle with the local operator, and he'd spoken to some friend of Buddy's. He'd said his name was Gus. He said he'd been staying the weekend. And he said Buddy would be back soon. Connolly had thought about leaving Jude's message for Gus to pass on, but in the end he'd decided against it, giving Gus the number of the hotel, and asking him to tell Buddy to ring. He'd wait, he said. He'd wait for Buddy to make the call. It was very important. He should get through as soon as he could.

Now, on his second cup of tea, he picked up the conversation with Thompson. They'd talked on the way down from the farmhouse. They'd walked the four miles back to the cars, rounding a bend in the road and coming suddenly upon the wreck of the Capri. Thompson had paused by the roadside, inspecting it with professional satisfaction, peering into the burned-out shell of the car. Inside, there was a body slumped over the steering wheel. The legs were missing, and the head had gone too, and what remained of the flesh had been charred by the explosion and the fire. Beside the car was another body, and Thompson had stood over it for a moment, stirring it with his foot. The man was lying on his face in the road. There was a gun in his hand, an automatic of some kind. Connolly had looked at his hand, seeing the line of letters tattooed across his knuckles. L-O-V-E Connolly had blinked, hesitating a moment in the weak spring sunshine, recognizing the hand. McParland, he'd thought, Scullen's bodyguard.

There'd been two other cars parked a little distance down the road, an ancient Renault, and a newer Vauxhall. Thompson had produced the keys to the Vauxhall, and they'd driven down to the coast, Connolly sitting up front, watching Thompson tuning the radio in the dashboard, dialling up a particular frequency, establishing contact with the man they'd left behind, in the farmhouse.

"Still there, Guvnor," he'd said, "no sign of interference."

In Waterville, they'd stopped at the first hotel, a grey sombre building beside a lake on the outskirts of the town. After Connolly had phoned Buddy's number and talked to Gus, he'd lifted the receiver again, meaning to call Mairead, but when he'd got through to the operator, and given her the first digits of the Belfast code, a hand had descended on the cradle and cut him off. The hand had belonged to Thompson. He'd offered no explanation, just a slightly apologetic smile and a suggestion that they share a pot of tea. Thompson had ordered, settling into a table by the window, talking idly about the prospects for the First Division Championship, and Connolly had listened to him, saying nothing, gazing out at the reeds, thinking of the body in the burned-out car. The bloke behind the wheel hadn't got a head. His body simply ended at the neck. And here they were, sipping tea, discussing football.

By one o'clock, they'd been waiting in the hotel for an hour and a half. Thompson looked at his watch. He'd stopped speculating about West Ham, and was half-way through the *Irish Times*. Connolly leaned forward.

"Listen,' he said, "leave me here if you want. I'll find my own way back."

Thompson glanced up. "Back where?"

"Belfast."

He looked at Connolly for a moment, amused for some reason, then he bent to the paper again. "Yeah?" he said.

Gus arrived at the pub in time for a late lunch. Buddy bought him a bottle of light ale with the top off, two pork pies, and a packet of crisps. He took them back to the table. He didn't sit down. Gus looked up at him. He'd cut himself shaving, and there were thin wisps of cotton wool still matted in the scab.

"What's the matter?" he said.

"We're off."

"Where?"

Buddy pocketed the food and made for the door. Gus caught up with him, outside, in the street. "What's going on?" he said again.

Buddy looked up and down the street. There were kids playing football outside a betting shop, and an old woman in a housecoat shovelling dog shit into the gutter. Otherwise the street was empty. Buddy nodded at Gus's car. It was parked across the road. "Let's go," he said.

Gus crossed the road behind him, doing up his coat. Buddy stood on the pavement, waiting for Gus to unlock the doors. Gus looked at him across the car. He was angry now, and Buddy could see it in his face. Gus could be difficult when he chose to, and now was obviously the time.

"Do you want the message or not?" he said.

Buddy frowned, still waiting for him to open the door.

"What message?"

"About Jude."

"What about Jude?"

Gus looked at him for a moment. "I've got a number in Ireland," he said. "The bloke wants you to phone."

They went back to the pub. There was a pay phone in the corridor outside the lavatories. Gus gave Buddy the phone number in Waterville. The bloke, he said, had phoned late morning. His name was Connolly. He wanted to talk to Buddy about his wife. He'd said it was urgent. Buddy lifted the phone and got through to the operator. He gave

432

her the number and put two pounds in the box. Waiting in the darkened corridor, the air smelling of disinfectant, he realized his hands were trembling. He got through to the hotel. He gave the receptionist Connolly's name. There was a brief silence. Buddy wondered how long two pounds would last. He looked behind him for Gus in case he needed more change. Gus had gone. He bent to the phone again. Connolly, he thought. Bound to be Irish. Name like that. Someone picked up the phone at the other end. An educated voice, soft, definitely English.

"Buddy?"

"Yeah."

"My name's Connolly." The voice paused. "You need to get here."

"Where?"

"Ireland. Place called Waterville." He paused. "It's in Kerry. On the coast."

Buddy nodded, writing down the details, hoping he'd be able to read his own scrawl. He returned to the phone. "Where's Jude?" He said. "Where's my wife?"

There was a brief silence. A ticking on the line. Then the English voice came back again. "She's up the road," he said, "it's not far."

"You've *seen* her?"

"Yes."

"Is she all right?"

Buddy shut his eyes. The carrier; he thought. The plastic bag. The voice came back again.

"You should come over. Today."

"*Today?*"

"Yes."

"How do I do that?"

"I don't know." There was another pause. "When you get to Waterville, find the Skelligs Hotel. I'll stay here. I'll expect you tonight."

Buddy began to scribble the name of the hotel. The line went dead. He looked at the receiver. Gus had appeared again, from the lavatory. He'd obviously been for a leak. Buddy looked at him. He nodded at the telephone.

"How is she?" he said.

Buddy shrugged. "No idea," he said, "I've gotta go to Ireland. To find out."

They left the pub again. They sat in the car together, Buddy gave Gus the pork pies and the crisps and the bottle of light ale. Gus lined them up on the dashboard, not opening any of them. Then he leaned back in the seat, making himself comfortable.

"OK," he said, "so tell me. What's been going on?"

Buddy glanced at him. A couple of minutes hard thinking about getting to Ireland had produced only one solution. He'd have to fly. Not scheduled. Not through any of the commercial airports. But some other way that would take them by surprise. They'd be watching the ferries, the airlines. They'd found him on the beach. They'd find him there. Bound to. He glanced across at Gus. Gus was looking out of the window. He was getting angry again.

"I asked you a question," he said.

"Yeah. I know."

"So what's it about?"

Buddy hesitated a moment. "Drive and I'll tell you," he said.

Gus looked at him. "Yeah?"

"Yeah. Promise."

Gus shrugged and reached for the keys. "OK," he said. "Where to?"

"Chichester."

They drove north, through a maze of streets until they hit a main road. Then they followed the signs for the coastal motorway. By the Ferryport, where the motorway entered the city, there was a roundabout. Two of the five exits were partially blocked by squad cars. Buddy had got as far as Pascale and the offer of the operation. He looked at the roundabout. Then he touched Gus lightly on the arm.

"Take the third exit," he said quietly.

"That goes down through the city again."

"I know. Just do it."

Gus glanced across at him, then shrugged. He swung onto the roundabout, and Buddy kept his head low as they swept round. Accelerating south, back into the city, Buddy told him to find a side road, any side road. Gus did what he was told, turning into a bleak estate of council flats. They stopped in a cul-de-sac. Gus turned the car round. Then Buddy got out. Gus looked up at him.

"What now?" he said.

"Open the boot."

Gus shook his head, disbelief. Then he got out and opened the boot. The boot was empty. Buddy got in. "Stop on the motorway once we're out of the city," he said. "Preferably where there's no traffic."

He curled himself into a ball and Gus shut the boot. Buddy heard the slam of the driver's door and the cough of the engine as Gus turned the ignition key. There was a smell of exhaust, and then they were moving again, slowly at first, and then faster, back onto the dual carriageway. Buddy felt the roundabout come and go, then the car moving at speed, Gus shifting down into overdrive, the tyres drumming on the road, the darkness almost total, a familiar sense of isolation, less than twelve hours old. After a minute or so, the car began to slow again. Then Buddy felt a change of road surface as it pulled over onto the hard shoulder, and stopped. He heard Gus get out. He listened to his footsteps on the road. The exhaust smell was back, and he was glad of the fresh air when Gus opened the boot again.

"OK?" Gus said.

Buddy looked at him. "Fine," he said, getting out and shaking the stiffness from his limbs. "Where were we?"

Back in the car, Buddy told Gus about Dublin, the offer from the Irish charity, the trip across with Jude, the drive to the middle of nowhere, his wife bumping away in the back of an ambulance, God knows where, at the point of a gun. Gus followed the story without comment, munching his way through the pork pies, shaking the crumbs of pastry from his lap when they settled briefly on the stretch of dual carriageway heading east, towards Chichester. When Buddy had finished, he glanced across at him. He'd made it sound like a game of forfeits.

"So what did you have to do?" Gus said. "To get her back again?"

Buddy hesitated, regretting that he hadn't managed to string the story out longer. Just beyond Chichester, at Goodwood, there was an airfield. There were charter companies there, people who'd fly you places for the right price. He'd used it before, getting down to Falmouth in a hurry, a repair job on a tanker that had run aground on a shoal and damaged its rudder. Only on that occasion someone else had picked up the tab. He looked across at Gus. In half an hour or so he'd have to ask him for a sizeable cheque. He owed him at least a little of the truth.

"They had a job," he said, "they wanted me to do it."

Gus frowned, wondering where the Special Branch fitted in, beginning at last to understand Buddy's reticence. "Underwater?" he said.

Buddy nodded. "Yeah."

"Big job?"

"Yeah."

"Difficult?"

"Very."

"Dodgy?"

"Yeah."

There was a pause. Question and answer. Gus frowned again, no closer to the truth. "You gonna tell me," he said, "what it is?"

"Was."

"You've done it?"

"Yeah."

"Go OK?"

Buddy said nothing. Then he smiled. "No," he said softly, "I fucked it up."

They got to Goodwood at two fifteen. The airfield lay inside a motor racing circuit, a wide ribbon of concrete that twisted and looped through the flat Sussex countryside. They drove in through a tunnel, under the racetrack, parking beside a low line of Portacabins. Gus wound down the window. Buddy could hear the howl of high performance engines, away to the left, near the pits area. Ahead of them were a couple of hangars and a wooden control tower. There were small private aircraft everywhere, parked in neat lines. The windsock beside the grass runway was limp. The place looked dead. Gus finished the last of the light ale and stowed the bottle under the dashboard. "What now?" he said.

Buddy reached for the door. "We hire a plane," he said.

They walked slowly along the line of Portacabins. Each one housed a business, either charter or a flying school. Three were closed, yet more victims of the recession, but a door at the end opened to Buddy's knock. He stepped inside. A big man sat behind a desk. He was wearing blue overalls. He had curly, close-cropped hair. His hands were huge, toying with a newly sharpened pencil. There were line drawings on the desk, a pile of them. Even upside down, Buddy could recognize the familiar lines of a Spitfire. The man looked up at him, a direct appraising stare, not unfriendly.

"Yes?" he said.

"I need to charter a plane."

"When?"

"Now."

"Where to?"

"Southern Ireland."

"Whereabouts in Southern Ireland?"

"Waterville."

"Where's that?"

"South-west. Kerry."

The man smiled, and looked at his watch. He picked up a phone. He had a brief conversation. The details sounded mechanical. He put the phone down and reached for a map, and a calculator. He did some measurements, rule of thumb, using the pencil on the map. He wrote down a column of figures. He added the figures up. Then he smiled for the second time.

"£490," he said. "Plus an overnight for yours truly."

Buddy looked at him for a long moment. "Are you serious?" he said. "You'll do it?"

"Sure."

"Now?"

"Yes." He paused. "Money up front, of course."

Buddy nodded, looking out of the window. Gus was outside, standing on the grass, his hands in his pockets, still eating the crisps. Buddy grinned.

"OK," he said, "done."

Ingle stood on the beach, two in the afternoon, waiting for the tide to go out. He had a very clear image in his mind of the moment the diver had thrown the thing away. It was black, plastic probably. It had a long cable with something on the end of it. It looked like a radio of some kind, and he'd let it fall into a white plastic bag, and wound the bag tight at the top, and whirled it around a couple of times, and let it go. Ingle had watched it rise and fall, marking the splash, lining up the spreading circle of white bubbles with marks on the Round Tower, away to his right. Looking at it now, the tide already half way out, he reckoned it was no more than a metre or so from the water's edge. Ten minutes, he thought. Fifteen at the most.

Ingle dug his hands deep into his pockets, looking for something to eat. The beach was nearly empty now, the crowds gone. There'd be no more warships today, no more flags, no more excitement. The big carriers were already out in the Channel somewhere. Soon, tomorrow maybe, or the next day, there'd be more farewells. They were talking about the *QEII*, and the *Canberra*. They'd be sending the big fleet tankers, and the new Type 21 destroyers, and anything else they could get their hands on. For a country that had trouble keeping the trains on time, or delivering a letter the next day, it was an impressive performance. All the more reason, he supposed, why someone had taken so much trouble to try to wreck it all.

Ingle found a packet of Polos and slipped one into his mouth. Kee, he knew, had sealed off the yacht across the harbour. He'd managed to patch himself through on the local force radio. He'd asked for forensic and a proper scenes of crime search. Odds on, they'd find traces of explosive, and probably a pile of gear as well. The job had obviously been a bit special. It would have needed careful planning, professional skills. Thus the diver. Quite how they'd recruited him, he didn't yet know. The article was part of it, had to be, the poor bastard on his uppers, his wife in a mess, an open door for the boys from Belfast. Over the radio, he'd issued a description – height, build, colour of hair, age, the usual details. Under normal circumstances, he knew they'd be lucky to find him. But Portsmouth was built on an island, only three roads out of the city, and if the man was silly enough to move at once, then they might – conceivably – get a result.

Ingle frowned, staring at the water. A passing ferry had sent a line of waves up the beach. As the water surged back, he'd glimpsed a small, black object, about the size of a decent box of cigars. It was covered again now, but he'd fixed the location in his mind's eye and he glanced at his watch, toying with getting his feet wet again, then changing his mind as the last of the Polo dissolved, and his fingers dug into his pocket for the rest of the tube. Lunch, he thought wistfully, retreating up the beach and finding a patch of dry pebbles.

Buddy took off from Goodwood at half past two, climbing steeply over the housing estates and market gardens that separated the airfield from the city of Chichester. The pilot, who'd finally introduced himself as Rick, had settled on a twin-engined plane, a six-seater Seneca. The plane added another £250 to the price, but it had the speed and range to make the west coast of Ireland by nightfall, and Gus hadn't grumbled at the extra cost. On the contrary, he'd written the cheque on the spot, and given Buddy another four hundred quid cash for "expenses". What the latter was supposed to include, Buddy hadn't enquired, but Gus had already asked enough questions to know that his mate was in deep trouble, and when they said goodbye, beside the aircraft, he'd put his arm round him.

"Ring," he'd said, "for fuck's sake.'

Buddy had nodded, telling him to stay at the cottage as long as he liked, but Gus had simply smiled, saying nothing, watching him climb into the plane, alongside the pilot, pulling the door shut behind him. The last Buddy had seen of him, as they turned onto the runway after the engine run-ups and the power checks, was an arm raised in salute. He knows I'm not coming back, Buddy thought as the plane lifted off. He knows I'm away for a while.

Now, level at three thousand feet, the airspeed indicator

showing a steady 145 knots, the pilot swung out over the Isle of Wight. Buddy, with the course already plotted on the map on his knee, queried the detour, and the pilot glanced across at him, a briefly reassuring hand on his arm.

"Task Force," a voice said in his earphones, "something to tell the kids."

Buddy looked at him for a moment, nodding his assent, then peered forward through the Perspex, the sun in his eyes. The long curve of Sandown Bay was already sliding under the nose of the plane. They crossed the south-east corner of the island, running down over Ventnor, the pier, the soft rise of Niton Down, and then the nose dipped and the plane began to lose height as they left the island behind them, off to the right, the sheer cliffs that ran out to the Needles clearly visible.

The pilot dipped a wing and eased the plane into a banking turn, and Buddy gazed out, down to the left, seeing nothing at first, not quite sure how high they were, how low, then suddenly the turn tightened a little, the plane standing on one wing, and there she was, *Invincible*, the weekend's waking nightmare, bigger than he'd anticipated, closer, moving at speed now, the Sea Harriers echeloned down her flight deck, the Sea Kings nesting in their carefully painted white circles, the water foaming back from her bows, the big spreading "V" of her wake, her private furrow in this otherwise empty ocean.

The pilot went round for a second time, looking for *Hermes*, but finding nothing, and then they were back again, a little higher, flying a farewell circuit around the new carrier. Buddy was transfixed by the sight, remembering the rough touch of her hull, the big ochre wall he'd found in the dark, the obscene little pimple he'd attached, safe now, unless they played games with the sonar frequencies and touched the thing off by accident. He twisted in his seat, keeping the carrier in sight, wanting a final glimpse, a final picture for the years to come. The plane levelled off, and picked up the heading chinagraphed on the map on Buddy's knee, but Buddy was still looking back, still had the ship in sight. Already, a mile distant, she looked like a toy in the ocean.

There was a crackle in his earphones, and the pilot came through again.

"Make your day?" he said.

Buddy nodded.

"Yeah," he said, smiling.

They droned west, over Dorset. They hit the Bristol Channel near Ilfracombe, the plump green cliffs of North Devon folding into the sea. Then the land had gone, and there was nothing but this huge expanse of sea, and Buddy knew that he'd be safe. He'd no idea where the man on the beach had come from, who he represented, what kind of powers he had. But he knew that every event had a consequence, that nothing was for free, and that his own crazy flirtation with law and order had come to an abrupt end. They were out to get him. That was their job. They were probably very good at it. And he didn't blame them in the slightest.

He sat back in the co-pilot's seat, the sun warm on his face, his senses dulled by the steady beat of the engines. A minute or so later, to the amusement of the pilot, he was asleep.

Davidson heard about the Portsmouth incident at half past five. He took the call at his desk in the Cabinet Office. There was a small television set in the corner, installed against his better judgement, and he was watching the lead story on the news. The pictures from the south coast were excellent. The Prime Minister, he knew, would be pleased. The crowds, in particular, had exceeded expectations. The selfless pursuit of a democratic principle did, after all, have a human face.

Davidson lifted the phone. The afternoon, so far, had been a good deal less bloody than he'd anticipated. He gazed at the screen, recognizing the Director-General's voice. The D-G, a model of self-control, talked for two minutes. Davidson listened carefully, watching the big carriers disappear into the mist. The D-G came to an end. Davidson lifted a pencil and made a note on the pad at his elbow. The man, as ever, was right. In the world of Intelligence, his experience was unequalled.

"I agree," Davidson said drily, "publicity wouldn't help.'

Buddy awoke four thousand feet above Kenmare, a small market town at the head of the Kenmare River. The sun was low now, out to the west, where the mountains of Kerry rolled down to the sea. The mountains cast huge shadows. The light was soft, pooling in the long valleys. Buddy gazed down. He'd never seen anything so beautiful.

They flew down the river, gradually losing height. The river began to widen, the water a deep blue, shading to indigo in the shadows. Ahead, where the river broadened into an estuary, he could see the last long fingers of land pushing out into the Atlantic. He glanced down at the map on his knee. To the south, across the water, lay County Cork, more mountains, tiny islands off shore, sudden outcrops of rock, bitten by the wind and the long swells rolling in from the ocean.

The pilot reached forward and throttled back, pulling the plane into a long, slow banking turn. They were out beyond the last promontory now, and looking back, Buddy could see a series of bays, crescents of white sand, pastures of sudden green, low stone walls casting long shadows in the last of the sun. Directly below them, as the turn began to tighten, Buddy found himself looking down at the end of the last promontory, a tumble of rock, cliffs falling sheer into the sea, tiny pockets of tussock and lichen, seagulls everywhere. His finger found the promontory on the map, and he glanced at the pilot, seeking confirmation. The pilot glanced down quickly, thumbing the button on the control column that accessed the intercom. "Lambs Head," he confirmed. 'We're nearly there."

Buddy nodded, gazing out of the window again, watching the waves breaking on the sheer black rock, the explosions of spray and spume, the water boiling at the foot of the cliffs. This is it, he thought, the furthest west you can go, the very edge of Europe. Beyond here, out west, an immeasurable distance, lay America, the New World, Jude's world, the world she'd so often talked about. Buddy closed his eyes a moment, thinking about it, the endless rollers, the nothingness beyond.

The plane straightened again, and the land dropped away, a huge bay, another perfect beach, bigger this time, then a mountain, shouldering down to a carpet of fields, and beyond the mountain, a town. He consulted the map again, knowing the answer before his finger found the end of the chinagraphed line.

"Waterville," the voice said in his earphones, "on the nose."

They landed ten minutes later, a rough country strip eight miles to the north. The pilot taxied to a small hangar by a dirt road, whitewashed breeze block and rusting corrugated iron. He pulled the plane around to the west, into the prevailing wind, and shut off the engines, one after the other. His fingers raced along the banks of switches on the panels overhead, going through the closedown checks. Buddy eased the earphones off and replaced them on the hook beside his knee. His head still drummed with the noise of the engines. He fumbled for the door. The air smelled fresh. He could taste the sea. He got out and stood on the wing. There was a faint sigh of wind off the ocean. Two hundred yards away, smoke curled from a row of coastguard cottages. He jumped off the wing and stamped the stiffness from his legs. He gazed around. He couldn't believe it. The peace. The silence. No one had been here for a thousand years. He'd stumbled into paradise.

They phoned for a cab to get into Waterville, making the call from one of the cottages. The cab, an ancient Toyota, arrived within minutes, from where Buddy didn't know. He sat in the back with the pilot watching the landscape roll past, the sea off to the right, the mountains ahead. Twenty minutes later, they arrived at the Skelligs Hotel. Buddy paid the driver, and walked into reception.

The hotel lobby was empty. He went to the desk. A girl appeared. He smiled at her. The evening had become quite unreal. He asked for Connolly. She nodded, recognizing the name at once. She lifted a phone. The pilot found a registration form and began to fill it in. A door opened. A man appeared. He was wearing jeans and a baggy sweater. He had glasses. He was looking weary. Buddy knew at once it was Connolly.

They went through to the bar, a big shadowed room, picture windows, a view of a lake, ghostly in the last of the light. Connolly led him to a table in the corner. There was a glass of Guinness, half empty. Connolly asked him what he wanted to drink. He shook his head.

"Where is she?" he said.

Connolly looked at him for a moment, then suggested they sat down. Buddy shook his head. There was a silence. Connolly sat down, reaching for the glass. Buddy closed his eyes, counted to three. Then he, too, sat down. "She's dead," he said quietly.

Connolly looked at him again. Then nodded. "Yes," he said, "she is."

TWENTY-EIGHT

Miller got the news on the satellite link from Bessbrook, the box of tricks that compressed into a single suitcase. Venner had set it up outside the kitchen window. The message, *en clair*, had been relayed from the SAS at Hereford. An SBS source had picked up rumours of a Provo attempt on one of the Task Force ships, *Invincible* or *Hermes*. The details were far from clear, and now the blinds were coming down in Whitehall, a total black-out.

Miller studied the message, remembering what Connolly had told him about the dead woman's husband. Buddy, he'd said. An ex-diver. Some kind of hostage deal. Some kind of lever on the man. He shuddered, sitting down at the kitchen table. If the rumours were true, then it was devastating. A hit like that – totally unexpected, brand new angle – was exactly what the Nineteenth was supposed to be about. And if the thing went back to Scullen, if he'd used the diver, Buddy, then it was even worse.

Miller shook his head, thinking of Mairead. The SBS message had mentioned a Special Branch involvement. Bloke called Ingle. Mairead had mentioned Ingle, too. Connolly's friend, she'd said. The man he had to phone up, to meet. Miller fingered Venner's piece of paper. If there had been an operation, and if it had Scullen's name on it, and if Special Branch had got there first . . .

He paused, looking down at his own hands. Somewhere, he knew, there was always a deal. He had the cards to play. He had Connolly. He had the dead woman. In an hour or so, he'd have her husband, Buddy, the diver. Somehow, there was a way out of it all. Justice done. Reputations preserved. The battle rejoined. He folded the SBS message and glanced at his watch. Mentally, he'd given Scullen twelve more hours. After that, if he didn't appear, they'd have to go home.

Scullen arrived at Buncrana an hour after sunset.

He'd driven north in response to a message from the Chief, a new driver at the wheel, a local boy. McParland's death had shocked him. He'd begun to depend on the man. They'd never talked much. He knew nothing of his family or his background. But that had never mattered because McParland had always been there, ever watchful, with his poise and his balance and those quick, deft movements of his hands. He radiated a sense of invincibility. He seemed immune from accidents or mistakes, life's nastier surprises. He'd made Scullen feel totally safe. And now he was dead, lured into a trap of Scullen's own making, falling victim to the man from Nineteenth whom he had – in the end – so badly underestimated.

The new driver eased the Mercedes into Buncrana, following Scullen's directions to the timberyard. The Chief's car, a big solid Ford with armour-plating, was already parked across the road, his own man still at the wheel. Scullen's driver parked the Mercedes beside it. Scullen got out, nodding a greeting to the Chief's bodyguard. The man barely acknowledged him. He had a sour, watchful expression. Scullen turned on his heel. His stock amongst the Chief's men was low, and he knew it. He buttoned his coat against the chill night air, and walked across the forecourt, towards the tiny step-in entrance in the big folding doors. The place smelled of sawdust. He switched on a light, making for the stairs. Above him, in his own office, he could hear the low murmur of voices. He hesitated, wondering who else might have driven over. The Chief's message had been blunt. "Eight o'clock," he'd said. "Be there."

Scullen climbed the stairs and opened the door to the office. The air inside was thick with cigarette smoke. He paused in the doorway, frowning. Smoking in the office was strictly off-limits. Everyone knew it. Even the Chief. Scullen looked around. The Chief was sitting on a chair by the filing cabinet. Two of the drawers were open and there was a pile of papers on the floor beside him. Scullen blinked. There was another figure in the room, sitting behind his desk. He was wearing an old combat jacket over a check shirt. His hair was cut short, *en brosse*, and he needed a shave. Scullen stared at him.

"O'Mahoney," he said quietly.

The man behind the desk looked up. There was a pile of crushed cigarette butts in the saucer at his elbow. He, too, was deep in a litter of documents.

Scullen closed the door behind him and unbuttoned his coat. Neither man had heard him on the stairs. They looked briefly uncomfortable. There was an exchange of glances. Then the Chief got up.

"You're early," he said.

Scullen didn't look at his watch.

"No," he said, "it's eight o'clock."

There was a brief silence. Scullen looked pointedly at his desk. O'Mahoney didn't move. The Chief fetched another chair from the far corner of the office. Scullen recognized it, an old bentwood chair the lads used for teabreaks downstairs. The Chief put it carefully in front of the desk.

"Please," he said, "sit down."

Scullen looked at the chair. There were smears of Swarfega on the back. He shook his head.

"No, thank you," he said.

The Chief looked at him for a moment, recognizing that Scullen was going to be difficult. For a moment, Scullen saw something familiar in his face, the ghost of a smile from the old days, then the line of the mouth hardened again, and his voice became brisker. "We've hired a machine," he said. "We thought we'd not want to miss it."

"Miss what?"

"The job you've been promising. The big one."

The Chief nodded at the floor behind Scullen. Scullen glanced round. There was a television set on the floor. Beside it was a small flat box, metal, with controls on the front. Cables connected it to the television. Another cable plugged it into a power socket on the wall.

"It's a video recorder," the Chief said. "You may have seen them."

447

Scullen nodded. His technicians in Dundalk had been gutting them for months, removing the electronic timers, wiring them into the new generation of delayed action bombs.

"I know," he said.

"We thought we'd like to keep the pictures," the Chief smiled, "for the scrap book."

He glanced across at O'Mahoney. O'Mahoney picked up a remote control unit, fingering a button and aiming it at the set. A light flashed as the videotape engaged. There was a whirring noise. Then the roar of a crowd and the blare of a ship's siren. Scullen gazed down at the set as a picture bloomed and steadied on the big 24" screen. They've gone to a lot of trouble, he thought. They're making the most of it.

A ship appeared, a big aircraft carrier. It looked enormous. There were men at attention along the deck. There were helicopters. Jet fighters. And thousands of people with Union Jacks lining the harbour walls as the big ships glided past. Scullen knew already that the Fleet had left intact. He knew that the operation had failed. But this was the first time he'd seen the raw evidence, the sheer size of the event, the spectacle it made, the sense of history in the making. Watching it, hearing the crowd, and the awed tones of the commentator, he knew that he'd been right to trust the diplomat, to believe him, to lay his counters on this single square, to hope that the girl and his new recruit would deliver what he'd always known was possible. The fact that they hadn't, the fact that the two ships were now somewhere in the South-West Approaches, outward bound, was a matter of some regret, but operations failed more often than they succeeded. Failure was a fact of life in the movement, always had been. It was something you accepted. Failure made success all the sweeter. No. What was important about these pictures, this operation, was the concept. The concept, he now knew, had been exactly right, the boldest stroke, a piece of vintage Scullen. He watched the broadcast a moment longer, the older of the two carriers sliding out through the harbour narrows, then turned back into the room, knowing in his heart that the dialogue was over, that there was no longer any room for discussions about concepts. The thing had failed. He'd built it up for them, given them the appetite for something truly special, and there it was, yet another Brit triumph, a media victory snatched from the jaws of military humiliation.

O'Mahoney fingered the remote control box again. The picture flickered and died. There was a silence. Scullen was looking at the Chief. He heard the scrape of a match, O'Mahoney reaching for yet another cigarette, taunting him, his own office, his own rules.

'Well?' the Chief said. "Hardly Mullaghmore, was it?"

Scullen shook his head, remembering the morning they'd killed Mountbatten, four kilos of Semtex and a remote detonation that had actually worked.

"No," he said, "it wasn't."

"So why? Tell me why? What happened?"

Scullen looked at him. "I don't know," he said, "I've yet to find out."

The Chief nodded and said nothing for a moment. Then he bent to the video player and retrieved the cassette. He held it in his hand, then tossed it to O'Mahoney. O'Mahoney fumbled it. It crashed to the floor. There was another silence.

"We believed you," the Chief said at last. "We had people on stand-by. It was a bit of a disappointment."

"No," Scullen shook his head, "it didn't work. That's all. It's not a disaster. It's not even a disappointment. It was worth a crack. You'd not deny that, I hope?"

He raised an eyebrow, the schoolmaster again, the dry tones of the Leitrim classroom he'd dominated for more than a decade. O'Mahoney whistled softly and shook his head, a gesture of disbelief, of derision, and Scullen knew at once how the conversation would have gone between them, up here in this office, waiting for him to arrive. He's shot, O'Mahoney would have said. He's yesterday's man. The day before yesterday's man. A relic. You should transfer him to the Bord Failte. The guy belongs in a museum. Operationally, he's a liability. He sets you up and lets you down and if you survive the mainland for more than a month or two, it's a fucking miracle. Scullen was still looking at the Chief. He had no intention of making it easier for him. Not now. Not then. Not ever.

"Well?" Scullen said. "What have you come here to tell me?"

The Chief held his gaze for a moment or two, then indicated the door. "Let's talk downstairs," he said, "eh, Padraig?"

Scullen shook his head. "No. Say what you have to say," he smiled thinly. "Now."

The Chief looked at him a moment longer, his face hardening again. Then he shrugged. "There's been a lot of debate—" he began.

"You mean trouble."

"I mean—"

O'Mahoney looked up. "He means trouble," he said. "Big fucking trouble. Because of you."

He stared at the Chief. "Tell him, for Chrissake. Tell him what you told me. Tell him what everyone knows. The mainland's a shambles. No one cares any more. You put it all on the line, and he lets you down. And then all this . . ." He nodded at the television and kicked the cassette. Scullen heard it skidding across the lino, hitting the skirting board with a crash. 'Biggest non-event since fucking Sunningdale. What's going on, for God's sake? Who's in charge? Who did the job? Who fucked it up? Guy Fawkes?" O'Mahoney shook his head. "Jesus," he said, "sweet Jesus."

There was a long silence. The Chief, embarrassed, fingered the neck of his sweater. Scullen didn't take his eyes off him. The Chief glanced up. "Problems," he said quietly, "as you can see."

Scullen began to button his coat. He knew now where the meeting would end, the decision that had already been taken. It was self-evident. It was sitting behind his desk, reaching for yet another cigarette. The Chief was looking at him again, and Scullen wondered how hard the man had fought for him, how long he'd been able to buffer him from the rest of the movement. Scullen extended a hand. The Chief took it, quicker than was strictly necessary.

"You'd be better off in Kerry," he said. 'That new place of yours. It comes to all of us in time."

"It does?"

Scullen eyed him for a moment, unforgiving, then turned on his heel and left.

Outside, in the street, his car was still there but the driver had disappeared. There was a long white envelope on his seat. The envelope had Scullen's name on it. He opened it. Inside was a cheque for thirty thousand pounds, drawn on the Bank of Ireland. Scullen recognized the account. It was the account used exclusively by the England Department, for operational expenses. The cheques were drawn up and signed by the Quartermaster, countersigned by the Officer Commanding. It had been that way for the last two years. Scullen knew, because his had been the counter-signature. Now, he peered at the cheque. The first signature was still the Quartermaster's. The second signature belonged to O'Mahoney.

Thompson and Connolly drove Buddy into the mountains. Buddy sat in the back of the car, saying nothing. When they got to the S-bend in the road where the Capri had been, the burned-out car had disappeared. Connolly looked out, curious, as they motored slowly past, but he didn't ask Thompson what had happened, and Thompson didn't volunteer the information. Police, Connolly thought vaguely. Or the Irish Army. Or some tinker up from the coast with his eye on the scrap, and a stomach for headless bodies.

They arrived at the farmhouse half an hour later. Thompson turned the car round and killed the engine. Getting out, standing in the windy darkness, Connolly looked up the mountain, trying to guess where Miller had posted his men.

They went inside, Buddy between them. Miller was in the kitchen. There was a half-finished bowl of soup at his elbow and a steaming mug of tea. He was bent over a foolscap pad, writing. There was a mustard-coloured file beside the pad, bulging with papers. Stencilled on the outside was the single word. Reaper.

Miller glanced up, hearing the footsteps in the hall. Thompson appeared first, standing aside. "Buddy," he said.

Miller smiled and extended a hand. Buddy shook it. "Who are you?" he said.

Connolly leaned forward a moment in the doorway, interested in the answer. Maybe it was best to be blunt. Maybe that was the language these men understood. Miller glanced down at the report, turning it over, face down on the table.

"Colonel Miller," he said, looking up again, "Nineteenth Intelligence, British Army."

"What are you doing here?"

"Looking for a man called Scullen."

"Who?"

"Scullen."

There was a silence. Buddy was looking at him. His face was quite impassive. "Is he Irish? This Scullen?"

"Yes."

"Do you have a picture?"

Miller faltered a moment, aware that control of the conversation had passed away from him. "Yes," he said at last.

"You want to show me?"

Miller looked at him for a moment longer. Then his hand strayed to the file. He opened it. He found the photo and passed it across. Buddy studied it, recognizing the long, pale face, remembering the meeting in the cottage, the man's hands, the briefing he'd offered on the two big ships. The cat, he thought. The cat knew him. He looked up.

"Where's my wife?" he said.

Miller hesitated a moment, still curious about the photo. "She's in the next room," he said.

"Where's that?"

There was a silence. Buddy looked at Miller, unflinching. Then Miller glanced at Thompson and nodded. Thompson touched Buddy lightly on the elbow.

"This way, sir," he said.

Thompson left the room. Buddy followed. He still had the photo in his hand. Connolly glanced at Miller. Miller shook his head, a barely perceptible movement. Outside, Connolly could hear Thompson opening the door to Jude's bedroom. Then he was back again, stepping into the kitchen. He looked across at Miller. "Leave him to it?"

Miller nodded. "Christ, yes," he said.

Buddy shut the door behind him. The room smelled of disinfectant. He put the photo carefully down on a chair and took three short steps to the bedside. The room was still in darkness. He didn't switch on the light. The bed was high against the window. The window was open at the top, and he could hear the wind in the trees. Clouds raced across a full moon. The light from the moon came and went, spilling onto the bed.

Buddy looked down. A body was shrouded by a single sheet. Buddy reached out and drew the hem of the sheet down, a single movement. Jude looked up at him. Her eyes were open. Her hair splayed out over the pillow, blacker than ever in the moonlight. There was a small hole on the left of her face. Buddy looked at her for a long time. Then he bent to the pillow and kissed her forehead. The flesh was cold and slightly waxy. There was an odd smell. He reached up and ran his fingers through her hair. Her hair felt strangely fresh, as if someone had recently shampooed it. He bent to her again, his big hands cupping her face. He kissed her on the lips. He drew the sheet up. She was very dead.

The door opened behind him, and Buddy stepped away from the bed. It was Connolly, the boy he'd met at the hotel, the English voice on the phone. He stood by the door. Light spilled in from the hall. Buddy looked at him for a moment.

"Shut the door," he said.

Connolly shut the door. Buddy was still looking at him.

"Were you here," he said, "when she died?"

"Yes."

"What happened?"

"She was shot."

"I know." He paused. "Were you here before that? Days? Weeks?"

"Days. Several days. Yes."

"How was she?"

"Very sick."

"In pain?"

"No. She had no pain. She knew she was dying. She said she was glad . . ."

Connolly broke off, not wanting to go too far, to make it worse for the man. He peered at his face in the half-darkness.

"She asked me to tell you something . . ." he began.

"What?"

"She said she loved you. She said she wanted you to know that."

Connolly saw the head tilt, an acknowledgement, some small consolation.

"And?"

"She said she wanted you to bury her."

"Where?"

"This side, she said. Not America."

"Here?"

"She didn't say."

Buddy nodded, another tilt of his head, a tiny movement. There was a long silence. Connolly wondered whether it was time for him to go. Buddy reached for the photograph.

"So where do you fit?" he said. "In all this?"

Connolly gave the question some thought. He could see the pine trees, out on the mountainside. He realized how cold it was, here, in this room.

"I don't know," he said at last.

Back in the kitchen, Buddy settled into a chair at the big table. Miller offered him tea. He shook his head. Then he laid the photograph before him, squaring it inch-perfect on the table. He looked up. Miller was watching him carefully, remembering Venner's message, the news from the SBS boys. He'd spent the last hour fitting it all together. Whether he'd got it right or not, he didn't know. Though the next five minutes or so would tell him.

"So how was it," he said, "in Pompey?"

Buddy blinked. "OK," he said.

"You were there this morning?"

"Yes."

Miller nodded. "But I understand it didn't work . . ."

Buddy looked at him. He said nothing. Miller smiled. "Well?" he said. "Did it, or didn't it?"

Buddy shook his head. "No," he said at last, "it didn't."

454

"*Should* it have worked?"

"Yes."

"Not your fault it didn't?"

"No."

Miller nodded again. There was a long silence. "Abusing Her Majesty's property," he said. "Would that cover it?"

Buddy gazed at him. "It didn't work," he said. "I just told you."

"Not the point."

"No?"

"No. Conspiracy's just as bad. Worse sometimes."

"Oh."

Buddy looked wooden. He didn't seem to care. Miller got up and walked slowly to the window. He'd known for a day now that this was Scullen's place. They'd found books upstairs with his name in, a spidery hand, black ink, the careful *ex libris* signature of an academic or a priest. There was a high, narrow bed, iron framed, and sepia photographs. It fitted exactly with what he knew about the man, his sentimentality, his very Irish attachment to land, to history, to the ancient Gaelic values. This was the man's spiritual home. He'd be back. Miller had never doubted it. But he'd be back long after they'd been obliged to go, to retreat back to the north, before the Garda got their act together, and began asking the more obvious questions. What he needed now was a representative, a proxy, someone who'd complete what they'd come to do. He turned from the window and looked at Buddy, putting it at its bluntest. "I could take you back to the UK," he said. "It's just up the road. Six hours."

"You could," Buddy agreed.

"You'd go down for a while." Miller paused. "Quite a long while . . ."

"Yeah?"

"Yeah."

Buddy nodded. There was another silence. Miller walked back to his chair and sat down. Buddy eyed him. "Tell me," he said. "No bullshit."

"What?"

"Who killed my wife?"

455

Miller glanced down at the file. Thompson was studying a line of stonework half-way up the opposite wall. Connolly was staring at the photograph over Buddy's shoulder. Miller looked up. "Scullen," he said quietly, "Scullen killed your wife."

Buddy nodded but said nothing. Miller's eyes flicked up, to Thompson. Thompson crossed the kitchen, pulling out a drawer on the big pine dresser. Connolly recognized the plastic bag he'd brought south. He could tell by the way Thompson handled it that the gun was still inside. Thompson put it on the table. Miller reached for it. He took the gun out and checked the breech. Then he reached inside the bag again and found the box of shells. He put them both on the table between himself and Buddy. The butt of the gun, Connolly noted, was angled towards Buddy.

Miller glanced up, a question on his face, the shape of the deal quite explicit. Buddy was still looking at the gun. He didn't pick it up. He didn't touch it. Instead, he smiled. A small, wistful smile that started at the corners of his mouth and went no further. He looked up at Miller. He sounded tired.

"I won't need that," he said. "But thanks all the same."

Ingle flew back to Belfast next morning. He'd talked to Davidson on the telephone from a call box outside the West London air terminal. He'd dialled through as soon as he'd got the message, and had hung up, as instructed, and had waited in the call box for the phone to ring again. By the time he was back in contact with Davidson, there were three people waiting to use the phone. One of them, third in line, was large, and female, and very angry.

Davidson had been brisk. He'd offered Ingle his congratulations saying that Ingle should feel proud of himself. And he'd added – almost as an afterthought – that the inquiry would now be handled at a higher level. Ingle wasn't happy, and had queried the latter point, but Davidson had dismissed his questions with another pat on the head, and a rather wooden reminder that he'd signed the Official Secrets Act. Ingle, who recognized where the conversation was going, had pursued the point. Someone had tried to blow up a capital ship, he'd said. This was hardly a parking offence. There'd been a silence at this, and Ingle wondered briefly whether he'd gone too far, whether the man had lost patience and simply hung up, but then Davidson had come back again, his voice quite empty of warmth or congratulation.

"I understand you were running an informer," he said, "a man called Connolly."

"That's right."

"And I understand that Connolly is wanted. For alleged murder."

"Correct."

"Then I suggest you find him."

Ingle had gazed at the phone, the threat spelled out. Back to business, Davidson was saying, back to Belfast. He'd bent to the phone again, angry now, but this time Davidson really had gone. Leaving the phone box, Ingle had paused for a moment, fumbling in his pocket for the new packet of Polos. The woman at the back of the queue had gazed at him, hostile.

"What are you doing in there?" she said. "Running a business?"

Ingle had looked at her for a moment, pulling his coat around him. "Painting and decorating, love," he said, "whitewash a speciality."

Now, back in Belfast, he took the bus in from the airport and walked the half-mile to his office. He pushed in through the armoured doors, still dog-tired, and made for the lifts. As he did so, the girl behind the switchboard recognized his coat. "Sir," she called, "Mr Ingle . . ."

Ingle hesitated, and changed course. The girl beamed up at him and handed him a folded slip of paper, the standard message form. "This morning," she explained, "first thing."

Ingle looked at her a moment, a little dazed, then unfolded the piece of paper. The message was timed at 05.36. It had come through Bessbrook. "13.30" it read, "34 Clonkilty Road, Andersonstown. A little present. For services rendered." Ingle paused, reading the message for the second time. The address was familiar. He ran through it again, trying to part the curtains on what was left of his memory. Then he got it. Connolly's bird. The woman in the white coat. He glanced at his watch. It was ten past eleven.

Connolly and Miller left Kerry at dawn, Thompson driving the Vauxhall. They dropped Buddy at the hotel in Waterville, stopping for an early coffee, and the last Connolly saw of him was the back of his head, buried in the local directory, looking for the number of a hire car company. He needed a van, and a spade, and a good map. The rest, mercifully, he left to Connolly's imagination.

They drove north-east, up from Kerry, up through Mallow, Cashel, Portlaoise, up round Dublin towards Belfast, one corner of Ireland to the other. Connolly sat in the back, his legs stretched out along the seat, his back against the door, thinking of Mairead. Miller had been onto her again. He'd said so. She'd passed a message through. She was dying to see him. It was an odd phrase. He'd never heard her use it before. But there it was. Better than nothing. Better, certainly, than the limbo he'd left behind him.

He gazed out at the flatlands north of Dublin. In less than an hour, they'd be over the border. By lunchtime, with any luck, he'd be back in Andersonstown, back in that steamy, damp little kitchen, back with Mairead. He settled himself deeper into the corner of the car. She must have forgiven him. Or she must have forgotten. Either way, it was going to be OK.

Buddy buried Jude at noon.

He hired a van from a man who ran a hardware store in Waterville. The shopkeeper lent him a spade, and sold him a map, spreading it on the counter and showing him where to find the Lambs Head. When he asked about the spade, a matter-of-fact enquiry, Buddy said he was planting his potatoes. The shopkeeper looked at him, smiling, and Buddy knew at once that he'd got the wrong season for potatoes, and that it didn't matter in the slightest. These people were like the weather. Soft.

He drove back, away from the coast, towards the mountains. He parked the van outside the farmhouse and went inside. The house was empty now, the men from the north gone. Miller had told him that the place belonged to Scullen, but he didn't know for sure, and just now he didn't care. There'd be plenty of time for Scullen later. Time would be the least of his problems.

Back inside the house, he went into Jude's room. It was the first time he'd seen her in daylight. It made little difference. The real Jude, the Jude he'd known, had long gone. Not yesterday, or the day before, or whenever it was that the bullet had torn through the window and into her skull. But months ago before Christmas, when she'd saddled Duke for the last time, and ridden off into the icy morning. Since then, it had never been the same, and even if Pascale had worked a miracle, he knew it never would. She'd been right all the time. She should have died. It would have been better.

He took the folded eiderdown from the bed and carried it out to the van. He laid it carefully on the metal floor. Then he went back into the house, and opened all the doors, and stepped back into her room, smelling the smell again, the sweet stench of rotting flesh. He collapsed her body over his shoulder, and stood up, his arms around her legs, making for the door. One of her buttocks was wet to the touch and he could feel the hollow of a deep wound through the thin cotton nightdress. He thought at first that it might be another bullet, but when he laid her carefully in the back of the van, on top of the eiderdown, he saw the stains on the nightdress, great circles of the stuff, and he knew it was an ulcer. Scullen, he thought to himself again, closing the doors of the van. Scullen not caring. Not looking after her. Ignoring the warning he'd issued, all those weeks ago, the promise he'd made. If she comes to any harm, he'd said, then I'll kill you. He climbed into the van, remembering the man again, his careful ways, his voice, knowing that life was a contract, and that Scullen's was due for termination.

He drove away from the farmhouse, back down the road, taking it easy on the bends, not wanting to disturb her. It was a fine day again, a bright eager sun in a nearly cloudless sky, the kind of day he and Jude would have made their own, and as the road dropped steadily down towards the coast, and he saw the first blue daubs of ocean in the distance, he began to talk to her, telling her about it, what a rich day it was, how lucky they were, how lucky they'd been finding this peace of theirs, then and – in some curious way – now.

At the coast, he turned left, up a long pass, the road tucked into the flank of the mountain, the air cooling as they climbed. At the top of the pass there was a statue of the Virgin Mary, and some flowers in a jam jar, and then the road dropped down again, spectacular views, the huge beach that Buddy had seen from the aeroplane, and in the distance that long finger of rock and tussock he'd circled on the map, the Lambs Head. He liked the sound of the place, the shape of the phrase. Peace, he thought again.

The road dropped to sea level again. At a tiny village – a pub, a handful of bungalows, a general store, a church – he turned right, and the road narrowed between banks of fuchsia, and he could hear water over the clatter of the engine, the lick of the waves on the rocks below, the springs bubbling out of the hillside above. He drove west, way, way out, as far as the road would go, and when it came to an end, no more than a track, the boulders no longer passable, he stopped, and parked, and fetched the spade from the back, and climbed up the rocks onto the tussock, looking for the spot he knew would be there, the spot where he'd finally lay her to rest. He found it almost at once, fifty feet above the track, a hollow amongst the rocks, sheltered from three sides, gloriously warm, utterly windless. The view to the west, colonnaded by rocks, was breathtaking, three thousand miles of nothing. He began to dig, cutting through the springy turf, shovelling it aside, praying that he didn't hit rock too soon, that there really was room for Jude in this little crypt of theirs.

He dug for an hour, naked above the waist, down through the black earth, judging it by eye, and when he was shoulder deep in the hole, and his muscles were on fire with the incessant twisting and heaving, he climbed slowly out, and stood in the sunshine for a full minute, his back to the sea, thinking of nothing. Then he went back down to the van, and opened the doors, easing Jude out, the fireman's lift again, scrambling up through the rocks, the pressure on his thighs, leaving the track below him, willing his body to make this last big effort before he could put her down for the night, the baby he'd never had. He made it, laying her body on the pile of earth, getting his breath back, wondering whether she really would fit.

She did. Perfectly. He laid her on her back, and covered her face with his shirt. Then he slipped off his watch and glanced at it, making a mental note, 11.57, wanting their time together to stop exactly here, on this day, under this sky, blessed by this sunshine. He folded her hands over her belly, and laid the watch on top. They'd never had any kids, never wanted any. What they'd created instead was this little pocket of warmth, into which he knew he could forever plunge his hands. Come what may, she'd never leave him, and he knew it, getting out of the grave, smelling the rich smell of the turned earth, shovelling in the first spadefuls, burying her.

Miller and Connolly got to Mairead's at two in the afternoon. They'd dropped Thompson at Bessbrook on the way up. He'd nodded goodbye to Connolly in the back, and gone off without a word. He'd looked, if anything, amused.

Now, parked outside the little council house, Miller glanced across at Connolly. On his face, was the unvoiced invitation. Go in first, he was saying. Go in now. Say your hallos. I'll be in later. Connolly smiled at him, genuine gratitude. He'd no idea what business the man had with Mairead, but there was a gentleness, a tact about him. He liked the man. He trusted him.

Connolly got out of the car and walked to the front door. He rang the bell. He rang again. He heard footsteps along the hall. The door opened. It was Mairead.

Connolly blinked in the sunshine. He felt tears again, that same hot sorrow he'd dumped on her months back. He reached out for her, tried to kiss her, following her into the hall, smelling the damp, doggy smell of the house, hearing

461

the radio on in the kitchen, the old familiar music. He stopped. Something was wrong. Mairead was looking at him. He might have been a stranger. He might have forced his way into the house. She was shaking her head.

"I'm back," he said hopelessly.

He reached for her again, pursuing her up the hall, calling her name, stumbling into the kitchen. Bronagh was sitting on the kitchen table tugging at a stick of liquorice. The child looked at him, inquisitive, huge eyes, her mouth smudged with black. Connolly grinned at her, pulled her favourite monkey face, bent to kiss her, then heard Mairead again, snatching the child away, turning her back to him.

"No," she pleaded, "no, no."

Connolly looked up, surprised. There was someone else in the room. He could sense it. Someone big. He looked round slowly, behind the door, recognizing the long coat, the flat, wide face, the coal-black eyes. He reached for the table, thinking suddenly of Leeson, of Charlie, all reason gone. Bronagh started to cry. Mairead pushed from the room, holding the child very tight.

"Shit," Connolly said quietly. "Shit. Shit. Shit."

He heard the kitchen door slam. He heard Mairead's footsteps, running up the hall. He heard the front door open. Then there was silence. Ingle began to button his coat.

"You're under arrest," he said, "for killing Charlie McGrew."

Connolly looked at him. He was suddenly very tired. "She told you?"

Ingle nodded. "Yeah," he said thoughtfully, "she did."

Buddy settled in Kerry.

He found work as a night porter in a new hotel up the Kenmare River, and he took a six-month lease on a near-derelict bungalow on a windy bluff outside the village of Caherdaniel. He spent weeks reseating the window frames, repairing the worst of the leaks in the roof, drying the place out. He slept when it felt right, and spent long afternoons on the road out to the Lambs Head, finding new paths to the end of the promontory, making friends with the sheep, leaving fresh flowers on Jude's grave. He led a modest, austere life, keeping himself to himself. He neither sought, nor missed, company. To his own surprise, he quite liked it.

Of Scullen, there was no sign. He never saw the man, never heard the name mentioned. If he was anywhere, he thought, he'd be back in the farmhouse in the mountains. Sooner or later, he'd have to come out. Then, and only then, would there be a decision to take.

The Falklands War came and went. Of the detail, Buddy knew very little, only that *Invincible* survived the attentions of the Argentinian Air Force, and returned in one piece to Portsmouth Harbour. Of that, he was very glad.

One night, at the hotel, he phoned Harry. It was two in the morning. He got the old man out of bed. He sounded groggy. Buddy told him who it was. He said he was living in Ireland. He thanked him again for the gear. He apologized for not being in a position to return it. The old man grunted.

"What happened?" he said. "Job go well?"

"No."

"You didn't do it?"

"Yeah. But the stuff didn't work."

"My stuff?"

"Yeah."

"Oh dear . . ."

Buddy could hear the chuckle in the old man's voice. He was still curious, even now. Why hadn't the transmitter worked? Why hadn't the charge gone off? There was a silence on the line. Then the old man came back.

"Bit of a con, wasn't it?" he said. "That Le Havre job?"

"Yeah?"

"Yeah. I checked up. Oil tankers, my arse. There were no fucking oil tankers. You never went near the place."

"So?"

"So who cares? I don't. Except I saw that chart of yours. Portsmouth Harbour. South Railway Jetty . . .' He paused. "*Where* are you living?"

"Ireland."

"Yeah. Good fucking riddance.'

Buddy hesitated. It wasn't the answer he wanted, but it was an answer just the same. He frowned, determined to be quite sure.

"You buggered the detonators?" he queried.

"Of course I did."

"You knew what I was up to?"

"Yeah. More or less." There was a long silence. Then Buddy heard the old man laughing again. "Fucking women . . ." he said, putting the phone down.

August, height of the season, Buddy met the young guys who ran the diving school over at Derrynane Harbour. They came into the hotel one night, late, looking for a client. Buddy found the girl they wanted, and afterwards they bought him a drink. They talked diving for several hours, impressed with Buddy's experience. Later that month, they asked him to fill in for one of the other instructors who'd got ear trouble. Buddy agreed, and spent four afternoons out on the water, air diving from a Zodiac dinghy.

The arrangement prospered. In September, he dived with them again, ten days this time, partly as an instructor, partly as another pair of hands on the lobster trawls. They dived commercially, supplying the hotels and restaurants up and down the coast. Lobster, in the shell, was selling for £4 a pound. It was good money, and Buddy began to wonder about chucking in his other job.

Then, late September, came the knock at his door. He had no phone. Messages from the school, when they were that important, were run by the girl who looked after the business side. She had a small Renault van and a faint Australian accent. She liked Buddy a lot. She stood in the windy sunshine, grinning.

They had a new client, an oldish guy who'd recently retired and wanted to go out fishing. He had no interest in diving but he had a pair of rods and an empty deep freeze and was happy to pay fifty quid for the hire of a boat and someone to take him out in it. As well as the Zodiac, the school kept an eighteen-foot dory, glass-fibre, with an Evin-rude outboard. The other two instructors had gone back to college in Cork, but Buddy had often used the dory as a safety boat and knew it well. Would he oblige the old fella and take him fishing? Buddy said he would. The outing was fixed for the following week.

On the morning of the fishing trip, Buddy got up later than usual. High tide was mid-afternoon. He'd agreed with the girl to be down at the boat for eleven o'clock. Weather permitting, they'd have five hours afloat before darkness and the full weight of the ebb tide turned against them.

Buddy rode down to the harbour on the ancient bike he'd acquired from the local postman. The day was breezy, with more wind and the possibility of rain forecast for the late afternoon. In the bay, there was already a chop on the water, and further out, beyond the end of the Lambs Head, there was a sizeable sea running. Parking his bike by the caravan that served as the diving school's offices and clubhouse, Buddy began to wonder whether fishing was such a great idea after all.

The client had already arrived. Buddy could see him down on the beach, talking to the girl at the water's edge. The girl had retrieved the dory from its moorings, and stowed the man's rods and tackle. Buddy walked down the beach towards them. He'd brought a pair of heavy seaboots and a couple of thick sweaters against the weather. He had some handlines of his own, too, in an old canvas bag, with hooks and feathers for the mackerel that were still shoaling in the bay. The girl saw him coming, and waved. He waved back. The client didn't move, his back to Buddy, his hands deep in the pockets of what looked like a brand new oilskin. Buddy joined him at the water's edge. The man was still staring out to sea.

"Dodgy weather," Buddy said. "Still fancy it?"

The man turned round. He was smiling. He extended a hand.

"Certainly," he said.

Buddy stared at the man. Nothing had changed. The same long face. The same careful parting. The same pale eyes. Scullen. The girl looked quickly between them, sensing the atmosphere, not altogether sure of herself.

"You guys know each other?"

Buddy nodded. "Yeah" he said.

"Hey—" the girl grinned, breaking the ice, pulling the

dory towards her, steadying it against the constant nudge of the waves, "great." There was a silence. Then Scullen glanced at the boat.

"I'm ready," he said, "if you are."

They butted out through the waves, Buddy in the stern with the outboard, Scullen up front, crouched in the bow, holding the painter to brace himself against the buffeting. Spray came flying backwards, and Buddy watched it flattening the man's hair, dripping off his bony face. He was smiling again, a deeply private smile, and Buddy knew that it was no coincidence, the booking, the request for the boat and a skipper. The whole thing was carefully contrived, and Scullen – as ever – was in control.

Buddy eased back on the throttle and glanced over his shoulder. Already they were nearly a mile out, the first of the big ocean swells lifting the dory, the unseen hand beneath them. Off to the left, across the bay, lay the Lambs Head. The tides around the end were especially dangerous, one current colliding with another, creating overfalls and eddies, a death sentence for anyone in a small boat. Buddy looked at Scullen. The man had yet to turn round. He opened the throttle again and set course for the end of the Lambs Head.

They were there in less than ten minutes. Away from the lee of the promontory, out in the ocean, the wind was strong, gusting across the water. It was much colder, and the blues and greens of the bay had given way to a gunmetal grey, laced with white as the waves crested and broke, roaring down on the dory. It was a foolish place to be, and Buddy knew it. They had less than half a mile of searoom, and if the outboard failed, they'd be on the rocks. He throttled back again, holding the dory bow first into the waves.

Scullen, at last, turned round. Water glistened on his face. Across the waist of the dory was a plank seat. Buddy nodded at it, an invitation to talk, and Scullen clambered carefully towards him, holding both sides of the dory, trying to brace his body against the surge of the waves. He got to the seat and straddled it. Buddy throttled back even more, shouting above the roar of the ocean.

"You knew I was here?" he said.

Scullen nodded. "Yes."

"You really want to go fishing?"

"No."

Buddy looked at him a moment, not quite knowing what to do next, what to say to this cold-faced zealot who'd walked into his life, who'd invited him to blow up half the Task Force, who'd killed his wife and now – once again – had seized the initiative. Buddy glanced down at the canvas bag at his feet. There was a knife in the bag. The blade was at least six inches long. If he chose to, he could get it over and done with now, half a minute's abrupt violence, the man overboard afterwards, the most unfortunate of accidents. He looked up again. "I could kill you now," he said. "Perhaps I should."

Scullen didn't appear to be listening. His hand had reached inside his oilskin. Buddy watched him carefully, half expecting a gun of some sort, but he produced an envelope instead. It was blue, with an airmail sticker. He passed it across to Buddy. "Read it," he said. "Please."

Buddy looked at him a moment, then slipped the letter from the envelope and flattened the single page against his knee. The sun had gone in now and it was even colder. He glanced at the letter, recognizing the address at once. Pascale's place. The clinic in Boston. He frowned, his eye racing on through the letter, oblivious for a moment to the wind and the waves. The letter was brief. It acknowledged receipt of "Dr Kennedy's" report. It confirmed that Jude's condition had deteriorated. Under these new circumstances, the offer of the operation had been withdrawn. The letter closed with an expression of polite regret. Buddy looked up.

"Who's Dr Kennedy?"

"A specialist. From Dublin."

"He saw Jude?"

"Here. In Kerry."

"And what did he say?"

"He said she was very sick."

Buddy nodded, suddenly angry. "I know that," he said, "that was your fault. When she came over, she was fine. You were supposed to take care of her. You didn't. That's why she died."

Scullen looked at him for a moment, then shook his head. "Dr Kennedy is a psychiatrist," he said. "Your wife was mentally sick. She'd lost the will to live. She told me so herself." He paused. "She wanted to die. She asked me to help her."

Buddy stared at him, trying to imagine the scene between them, not wanting to believe it. "She asked you to help her die?" he said.

Scullen nodded. "Twice."

"But you wouldn't?"

"No."

"Why not?"

"Because I'm a Catholic, Mr Little. We Catholics respect life." He paused, ducking a wave that broke over the side of the dory. "I'm simply here to tell you what happened. It's important that you know. That's why I came."

Buddy looked at him, then laughed. "But you're a terrorist," he said. 'You kill people for a living. It's your job. It's meat and drink to you."

Scullen shook his head. "I'm a soldier," he said softly. "There's a difference."

Buddy gazed at him for a long time, half repelled, half fascinated by this strange man who dealt in lives and deaths, who appeared to have no regrets, no shreds of doubt. There were a million questions in his head, and they all began and ended with Jude, and he was still trying to sort out the one that really mattered when the wave hit. It wasn't an especially big wave, but he'd let the dory drift off a little, enough to let the foaming crest steal beneath the bow, and hoist the dory up, the weight in the back, up near the vertical. Buddy reached out for Scullen, trying to steady him, the conversation far from over, but it was too late. The man fell bodily onto him, arms and legs and a wild cracking of skulls. Buddy found himself on the ribbed floor of the dory. He could taste blood. He could smell petrol. He grabbed wildly for the throttle. The engine had stopped.

The wave foamed past. The dory righted itself, drifting broadside on now, an easy target for the next wave. Buddy was on his knees in the stern, pulling frantically at the outboard. Then he saw the feed pipe to the fuel can. It had severed at the engine end, the connector smashed. Fuel was slopping everywhere. Buddy looked up. The rocks of the Lambs Head were barely four hundred metres away. He swallowed hard. No lifeboat, he thought. No helicopter. Just little me. And little him.

He reached down. Scullen was lying in the bottom of the dory. Buddy turned him over. His mouth was gashed and he'd lost a tooth or two but he was still conscious. His eyes were wide and his lips were moving. He looked like a wild animal, and when Buddy hauled him into a sitting position, he could feel the fear in the man, all control gone, his whole body trembling, blood bubbling wordlessly around his mouth.

Buddy glanced up again. He could hear the thunder of the surf on the rocks, tons of water exploding, huge gouts of spume. They were still beam-on to the waves. The wind and the tide would do the rest. In a couple of minutes, it would all be over.

He looked down at Scullen. His eyes were closed now. Buddy tightened his grip on the front of his oilskin and shook him hard. Scullen began to moan, a soft, almost imperceptible noise that came from way down. Buddy looked at him a moment longer, then slapped him hard across the face. The ring on his third finger scored a line across Scullen's cheek. The wound began to bleed. Buddy slapped him again. Concentrate, for Christ's sake, he thought. Listen to me. He pointed to the rocks. He put his mouth to Scullen's ear.

"In a minute," he yelled, "we'll jump."

Scullen's eyes opened. He looked up, hearing him, following the pointing finger, understanding, shaking his head.

"No."

"Why not?"

Scullen said nothing. His mouth was still pouring blood. "There's no point," he whispered at last, "I can't swim."

Buddy gazed at him, then he started to laugh, and Scullen looked at him for a moment, uncomprehending, then his eyes closed again, and the dory began to roll, sideways on to another huge wave, and Buddy tried half-heartedly to brace his body over Scullen's, but the boat had gone too far, and they both tipped out, the wave surging past them. Buddy reached up, trying to grab the lines looped around the side of the dory, but it was already beyond him, borne on towards the rocks by the next wave, carrying the sound of his laughter with it.

They found the bodies at last light. Scullen was sprawled on the beach, abandoned by the receding tide. Buddy was trapped in a gully amongst the rocks, way out, towards the end of the Lambs Head. The farmer who found him, looking for sheep, marvelled at the way the sea had left him, on his hands and knees, his head up, as if he'd found a path, or heard a summons.

EPILOGUE

Autumn, 1982

Late October, plans for the new mainland campaign well under way, the two men met once again in the tiny cramped office with the view of Lough Swilly. The Chief had motored over from Belfast. O'Mahoney was living in a flat down the road. O'Mahoney made the tea. The Chief poured.

The Chief sat down in front of the desk. O'Mahoney helped himself to sugar. The last evidence of Scullen he'd only found the previous day, two sheets of paper in an out of date London phone book. The handwriting on the paper had been Scullen's. He'd recognized it from the countless lists the man had once sent him, during the early days, his first tours of duty on the mainland.

Now, he pushed the notes across the desk. The Chief picked them up and read them without interest. He hadn't thought about the Qualitech job for months. It was part of an episode he'd consigned to the shredder. Scullen had gone. Scullen was history. The away teams must find new paths forward. He glanced up. "So?" he said.

O'Mahoney sipped his tea. He'd been thinking hard about Qualitech for most of the night. He'd woken up at two in the morning. He couldn't get the idea out of his head. He looked at the Chief. "The Brits planted the bomb, right?"

The Chief nodded. "Right."

"On a twenty-eight day timer. Yes?"

"Yes."

"Giving themselves plenty of leeway. Agreed?"

"Agreed."

"So . . ." He picked up the Chief's copy of *The Times*. The Chief had brought it over from Belfast. There was a front-page report on the first day of the Tory Party Conference.

"Why don't we pull the same stunt but think even longer term? Fifty days? A hundred? Find a place we'll know she'll be. Look at her diary? Make a date?"

He opened the paper. On page two there was a photograph of the Prime Minister. She was standing on the steps of her seaside hotel. She was smiling. O'Mahoney tore the photo from the paper, very carefully, and laid it on the desk. Then he looked up at the Chief.

"Well?" he said. "Don't they have these conferences every year?"